HEARTS

A PITTSBURGH ANTHOLOGY

OF STEEL

CHERI MARIE | LEIGH TAYLOR | DESIREE LAFAWN | ALEXIS R. CRAIG

REXI LAKE | CHASHIREE M. | SK MARIE | ABIGAIL LEE JUSTICE

VICTORIA MONROE | BRANDY DORSCH | JEN TALTY | MA STONE

TRACY KINCAID | SIDONIA ROSE | AVA DANIELLE | NICOLE ZOLTACK

JAIME RUSSELL | JM SCHALM | COURTNEY LYNN ROSE

JULIE MISHLER | CJ ALLISON

MW00911593

Cover Design: Tiffany Black, T.E. Black Designs

Formatting: Leigh Taylor

Dedicated to all the women who have
been used,
felt lost,
stumbled,
made mistakes,
hit rock bottom
suffered abuse mentally and/or physically.
And for those same women who didn't stay down long, got up, dusted them-
selves off and came back fighting harder each and every day.
But also to those of you that have yet to find your strength, know you have
it within you to rise above your circumstances. Fight not only for yourself
but for those who are not yet strong enough and be their example.

This one is for YOU.

CONTENTS

SNAPSHOTS & LYRICS

CHERI MARIE

PROLOGUE

I stare out the bay window in the front of our house as tears pour down my cheeks.

"Riann . . ." his voice is low, almost a whisper. He caresses my shoulder, but I shake him off.

"Don't touch me," I choke out through the tears.

"Riann, I know you're hurting right now, but this is what is best for the both of us."

His words turn my sadness to anger as I spin around, stabbing my finger into his hard chest.

"Don't Axel, don't pretend like you're doing this for me. You're doing this for you and *only* you. I've always believed you'd make it because you're an amazing musician, but I never thought when it happened that it would be the end of us."

"I don't know how long I'll be on the road touring and doing special appearances. It isn't fair to expect you to wait for me."

"But I would have waited. I would have waited for you, Axel, because I love you. Because that's what you do when someone you love has dreams that are coming true. You stand by them."

"I . . ." he stutters through his words, but it doesn't matter anyway. The damage is done, and anything he has to say now is irrelevant.

"Just leave." I push him towards the door. "Go, Axel, leave. I wish you all the best in your career, and I hope all your dreams come true." I keep ushering him toward the door. He picks up his bags, sadness and regret etched in his features. I open the door and wave him out. Axel takes a step out the door and turns to me.

"Riann, I'm—"

I slam the door in his face.

Pacing the living room, my emotions are somewhere between wanting to break down or break someone's face. A picture catches my attention on the mantle and I pick it up. It's of me and Axel at his first big gig after we graduated college. He opened up for a major eighties rock band.

Watching him on stage that night, it was like he had been there all his life. So comfortable, so free. I knew, at that moment, music was what he was meant to do. That's also the night he told me he loved me, that I was his queen and we'd rise together. I scoff at the memory.

"Liar!" I scream, throwing the picture frame against the wall and I watch as the frame breaks and the glass shatters into a million pieces onto the floor.

You know what's worse than mourning a loved one who's passed that you know you'll never see again? Mourning someone who willingly left you and could return at any moment to turn your world upside down.

The last few months have been rough, seeing Axel's face all over the television and hearing his voice on the radio. Good for him for living his dream though, I suppose. Is it possible to be happy for someone yet hate them at the same time? My alarm clock blares and I knock everything to the floor trying to shut it off.

"Damnit!" I mumble to myself as I climb out of bed.

Walking into the kitchen, I start the pot of coffee then head for the shower. Today is the day I take back control of my life. I've felt so out of sorts trying to get used to a new routine. But, that all ends today. With a towel wrapped around me, I stand in front of my closet, mentally doing inventory of pretty much everything I own. I need a power outfit. Something that says I'm worth the risk of giving a loan because there isn't anything I can't handle.

Except your boyfriend of four years suddenly deciding that you weren't important enough to keep around while he lived out his dreams. I roll my eyes at myself and mentally choke that little self-doubt bitch. The idea of owning my own studio has been something I've dreamt about since discovering my love of photography. There's something about being able to catch a special memory in a photograph that will never change, even if the people in them do. Not only that, there is a level of beauty that can be captured in a single photograph that might be overlooked by the naked eye. While browsing my selections again, a dress I bought before Axel and I broke up catches my eye.

It's completely out of my element but perfect for today. Grabbing the dress from the hanger, I pair it with a black cardigan and a pair of black kitten heels. I grab a hair tie from my dresser and pull my hair back into a tight, neatly wound bun. After a little makeup and a once over in the mirror, I grab my coffee and am out the door.

Pulling up in front of the bank, I say a silent prayer to myself that everything works out in my favor. I take another pull of my coffee and then head inside. There's a line of people waiting to talk with a banker, so I sign in and take a seat. Slowly, the line starts to dwindle as each person is called back. The longer I sit here, the more my anxiety goes through the roof, and I doubt this entire idea. Just as I'm on the verge of a full blown panic attack, a middle-aged woman calls my name.

"That's me."

"Come on back, Ms. Carter."

Standing, I follow her back to her office and take a seat in one of the chairs.

"It's great to meet you, Ms Carter, my name is Elouise. What can I do for you today?"

I take a deep breath and speak confidently. "I'm here to get a business loan."

"Great! What kind of business are you planning to open?"

"A photography studio. I'm a photographer."

"Oh, that's great! I love photography. So, let me just get you to fill out this form, and I will see what we can do for you."

"Okay."

Elouise hands me the form and a pen to get started. My hand trembles slightly as I fill it out. I need this, and I don't know what I'm going to do if they say they can't help me. Finishing up, I sign at the bottom and hand the paper back to Elouise.

"Thank you. I'm just going to put all your information into the computer, then I'm going to speak to my loan manager and see what we can do."

"Sounds great."

I sit with my hands in my lap, impatiently waiting and with each tap of a key, I think I'm about to lose it. Finally, she finishes and excuses herself as she leaves the office. I close my eyes, continuing to pray to whatever God necessary to make this happen for me. After about twenty minutes, she returns.

"Well, Ms. Carter, I have good news and bad news. The bad news is, unfortunately, we cannot approve you for the ten thousand you requested."

My heart sinks.

"But we can give you five thousand. Is there any way that will work for you?"

I think about it for a moment, not wanting to sound too eager before I agree.

"Yes, that will be fine. Thank you."

"Okay great! Just sign the bottom of these two forms, and we will get your loan account set up and cut you a check for the amount."

"Thank you so much!"

"You're welcome."

I read over the forms carefully before signing. Elouise goes over them with me, explaining the interest and when my payments are due. Thirty minutes later, I'm free and have the first two months rent money for my studio in hand.

As soon as I slide into my car, I immediately dial Carrie.

"Hey Ri, how'd it go?"

"I got the loan!"

"Really? That's fantastic!"

"It wasn't as much as I had originally asked for, but it's enough to get started!"

"That's great, Riann, I'm so happy for you."

"Thank you. I'm on my way to meet with the owner of the building to pay the first two months rent! Want to meet me at the studio in thirty minutes?"

"Yes! I can't wait to see inside!"

"Okay, see you soon."

2

It's only been two weeks since I put the down payment on the studio and it has been a whirlwind of crazy ever since. If it weren't for my best friend Carrie, I would probably still be getting things together for my grand opening. Carrie and I have been best friends since high school, she's more than a friend, she's like my sister. We've been through so much, and she has been my rock for the past few months since Axel left.

Since getting the keys to the studio, we've been painting and getting things set up just how I want them before we open. I even have shoots booked from our grand opening until two months out with clients from families to models. Most of the requests came from friends and family, while others came through my page on social media where I've shared my love for photography. I finish rolling the last coat of paint onto the walls when Carrie returns with food

"Oh, thank God, I'm starving."

"You finished?"

"Yep, I'm just hoping the walls will be dry in time for the grand opening in two days."

"They will be. Everything will be great! I think we should go out and celebrate!"

"Girl, I am exhausted."

"Come on Ri, you haven't had a night out in forever, and we have something to celebrate. I mean look around here, you did this! You finally have your own studio, and you did it on your own."

I sigh. "Fine. You're right. We should celebrate. Let's eat, then I'll go home to shower and get ready."

"Yay!" she says excitedly.

***

Three hours later, I'm fed, showered, and dressed to kill in a pair of skinny jeans, a low cut top, and heels I'm about to break my damn neck in. Carrie knocks on the door then lets herself in.

"Riann, are you ready?" she calls out as I turn the corner.

"You don't have to yell, I'm right here."

"Well, hot damn, look at you, sexy mama."

"Thanks."

"So, are you ready?"

"Ready as I'm going to be."

I grab my ID and phone, slipping them into my back pocket as we head out to the door to Carrie's car. I slide into the passenger's seat, and Carrie takes off towards downtown Pittsburgh. Apparently, there is some new club that opened tonight, and it's supposed to be the new hotspot. A short time later, she pulls up to the curb and the valet opens our doors to help us out.

Carrie hands over her keys to him as we walk toward the door. She knows *everyone,* so of course, we skip the line to get inside. The interior of the club is beautiful. Black lights and dim white lighting illuminate the room. The dance floor is full of people as the DJ plays a mix of rap, reggaeton, and house music. Carrie grabs my hand and pulls me along behind her as she pushes through the crowd to the bar.

"What can I get you, ladies?"

"Two long islands, please."

"Coming right up."

The DJ changes the track, and I suddenly feel sick when Axel's voice comes through the speakers. I try to fight it, but my mind goes back to the first time Axel played this song for me. We were out in a field somewhere in the country outside the city, lying under the stars. His dark hair was just a little longer than usual, and he had a look in his eyes that he only gets when he's playing music. This was our song. The song he wrote for me. Fuck, I didn't need this tonight.

"Shit," Carrie mumbles under her breath, pulling me back from memory lane

She peeks at me out of the corner of her eye to my reaction. "You okay?"

"Yep. When he brings that drink back, make sure to order another round. I'm going to need it if they keep playing his music."

The bartender comes back with our drinks, and Carrie immediately orders another round. I make light work of sucking down my first drink before he even returns with the second. A deep voice clears next to me, catching my attention. I glance over at him, and he smiles.

"Hey. Come here often?"

I look at him side-eyed. "Since they just opened tonight, I'd say no."

"Ah, yea, sorry. That probably wasn't my best pick up line."

"Yea, I think not," I laugh.

"What's your name, beautiful?"

"Riann, you?"

"Javier. It's nice to meet you, Riann."

He smiles and, for a moment, I'm mesmerized. He has a dazzling smile and deep dimples that make me feel a little weak. There's a tap on my shoulder as Carrie grabs my attention again.

"Here's your drink. Cheers!"

"Cheers!"

I down my second drink and place the glass on the bar.

Carrie leans in toward my ear. "Who's your new friend?"

"Oh, this is Javier. Javier, this is my best friend Carrie."

"Nice to meet you, Carrie."

"Nice to meet you, too."

"Would you mind if I steal your friend away for a dance?"

"Absolutely not. Have fun." Carrie shoos me off as Javier takes my hand and leads me onto the dance floor.

He spins me around then pulls me close against him as we sway back and forth to the music.

"Can I ask you something without sounding like a complete asshole?"

"Well, that's debatable but go ahead and give it a shot."

"Have you ever seen someone across a room and you just had an instant physical attraction to them?"

"Yes, actually, I have."

"Well, that's how I felt when I saw you walk into the bar with your friend. I immediately pictured having my hands all over your body."

I swallow hard. It's been four months since I've been intimate with anyone aside from my friend with batteries, and just having this man in close proximity has my hormones in an uproar.

"I'm sorry, I didn't mean to be so forward."

"It's fine. It's just that my boyfriend left me a couple months ago, so it's been a while since . . . ya know . . ."

"I see. Well, all you have to do is say the word, and I will worship your body in any way you want me to."

Pulling my phone from my pocket, I hand it to Javier. "Put your number in here for me."

"Yes, ma'am."

He types in his number and hands the phone back to me. "Thank you for the dance, Riann."

"You too, Javier."

Making my way back to Carrie, I shoot Javier a text.

Riann: No strings attached, right?

Javier: None. Just a night, or a few, of fun and that's it.

Riann: Okay. Give me an hour, I'll text you my address.

3

*M*y phone rings, startling me awake and I scramble to make it shut up as my head pounds from one hell of a hangover. I slide my finger across the screen without looking at who's calling.

"Riann! Get your ass up. Today is the last day before your grand opening, we have shit to do!"

"What time is it?"

"Seven."

"Fuck that. I'm going back to sleep, try again at ten."

I hang up before she can protest and toss my phone on the nightstand. I glance over to the other side of my bed, where Javier is still fast asleep in all his naked gloriousness. The pounding in my head is awful, but the ache between my thighs is delicious.

I close my eyes as I remember the night of unadulterated sex. I can still feel his hands over my body, and it reignites my need. When I open my eyes, I glance over at him again and find him staring at me with sexy, sleepy eyes.

"Good morning."

"Good morning to you too, beautiful," he says, flashing me that dazzling smile again. "How are you feeling?"

"My head is pounding, but otherwise pretty good."

"Oh, man, let me grab you something for your headache. Where do you keep your medications?"

"There's aspirin in the cabinet next to the fridge in the kitchen."

"Okay, be right back."

He quickly jumps up and walks out to the kitchen, allowing me to enjoy the view of his naked body. A few minutes later, he returns with two aspirin and a glass of water.

"Here, take these."

He places the two white pills in my hand, and I take the glass of water with the other. Tossing them in my mouth, I take a sip of water to wash them down before finishing off the glass.

"You good?" he asks.

"No . . ." I admit, biting my lip. "There's an ache somewhere else now."

"Ah, well, I'm sure we can take care of that, too," he says, as he leans in and places kisses down my neck.

I lay back on the bed as Javier rips away the blanket covering me and works his way down my body. Reaching the apex of my thighs, he dips his head between my legs, and I moan as his skillful tongue finds my clit. I moan again as he grazes the sensitive bud with his teeth. He takes his time, pleasuring me with his tongue and magic fingers, bringing me to the brink of another orgasm. My legs begin to tremble as my orgasm rolls over my body, making my toes curl and my fists clench the sheets.

"You good?"

"Fantastic."

"Glad that I could assist you," he says with a wink. "Well, I better get going. I have to get to work. If you ever need some assistance again, just give me a call."

"I will. Thank you."

I watch him as he dresses, every sexy muscle flexes and I almost want to beg him to stay. But, I do have work to do. He finishes dressing and kisses me on the cheek before heading out the door.

I pull myself from my bed and head straight for the shower to wash up so I can meet Carrie at the studio. Stepping out of the shower, my phone rings off the hook. I wrap a towel around me and rush into the bedroom to answer.

"Riann, what are you doing? I've been trying to call you for the last twenty minutes."

"I just got out of the shower. I'm getting dressed, and then I'm coming to meet you at the studio."

"Well, get a move on it, woman, we have a lot to do before tomorrow."

"Yes, I know. I'm sorry. I just really needed a morning to relax."

"I can understand that, but now it's game time! We have decorating and setting up to do!"

"Okay, be there soon."

I quickly dress, load up all my camera equipment, and head to the studio. Carrie is already waiting when I pull up to the curb. Putting the car in park, I hop out and open the back of my SUV.

"Let's get this unloaded and set up, then we can go shop."

Carrie claps excitedly, "Shopping is my favorite part."

Carrie grabs half the equipment, and we carry it all into the studio. Pulling everything from the bags, we set it up in the back area where the photos will be taken. After it's all put together, we lock up and head out to go shopping.

First stop is the print shop. I ordered enlarged prints of some of my photography to put on the walls in the lobby. They came out beautifully, and I can't wait to pick up frames so I can hang them up.

Leaving the print shop, we head to HomeGoods for picture frames, seats for the lobby, and other things for the studio. Walking through the aisles looking for things to decorate my studio, reality starts to really set it. This is really happening, and it's all mine. I can't help but start to tear up

"Hey . . . you okay?"

"Yea, I'm fine. It's just all really starting to set in. After how shitty the last few months have been, I needed this to happen for me and it did."

"Oh, honey." Carrie grabs me and pulls me into a tight hug. "You deserve this, and I am so incredibly happy for you."

"Thank you for everything; helping with getting the studio ready and dealing with my moping after Axel left."

"That's what best friends are for," she says, hugging me again. "Now, let's finish shopping and get back to the studio. I'm excited to start decorating."

After three hours in HomeGoods, and more stuff than should fit in my SUV, we head back to the studio to get down to business. Carrie takes charge of putting the lobby together while I organize the back studio.

I lean the table that will be used to photograph babies against the wall, stack the baskets and blankets in the corner, and load all the other props into the trunk that I brought from home.

Once I finish up, I make my way back out to the lobby when I'm brought to tears again. The lobby looks beautiful. Black suede chairs line the wall in front of the windows and the small suede sofas are placed on the walls to the left and right. Carrie framed all the photos and hung them like a checkerboard on the wall.

It all turned out so beautifully that I can't help but let the tears flow. Carrie reaches into her bag and grabs a tissue, handing it to me as she reaches into her bag again and pulls out a bottle of champagne. Popping the cork, she pours us both some into two plastic champagne flutes, handing me one.

She raises her glass, "To new beginnings and you rocking the photography biz!"

"Cheers!" I tap my glass to hers before downing the glass of bubbly liquid. "Let's go home and get some sleep! We have a busy day tomorrow."

"Let's! Have a good night, Riann."

"You too, Carrie and thank you again."

"Of course."

She gives me a quick peck on the cheek before heading out to her car as I lock up and slide into my truck to head home. I can't help but smile. This is it. My new journey of being a professional photographer begins tomorrow . . .

4

A YEAR LATER

*A*fter Axel left, I fought between two emotions; hating him and wishing he'd realize he fucked up and come running back to me. I watched as his career took off and soared into oblivion. He became one of the fastest rising stars of all time; his name and face were literally everywhere.

It was everything he ever wanted, and I was happy for him. My reality check was coming, though. Sitting at home with a few friends, watching the ball drop on New Year's Eve in Times Square, I watched as the countdown ended and the camera focused on Axel James kissing a blonde supermodel.

Watching it all play out on the screen hurt, God, it fucking hurt. But at that moment, I realized he had moved on and so should I. From that day forward, I'd poured myself into my dream of becoming a photographer, and that's what brought me to where I am now.

"Okay, Javi, show me your lady killer pose."

Javi laughs and rolls his eyes, "Ri, what the hell is a lady killer pose?"

"You know the one, abs all out and a big smile showing off those pearly whites and those dimples. Good lord."

"Stop it, you're making me blush."

"Yea, right."

I shake my head at him. He knows how beautiful he is, I mean, he has to be one of the top male models in the industry now. After our multiple sexual rendezvous, Javi came to me and asked me to work on his portfolio for modeling.

Since then, we've worked together many times, and he refuses to use any other photographer. I'm grateful to him, though. He's the reason I was able to up my photography skills and start photographing celebrities for major magazines and multiple modeling agencies. Though he'll tell you he didn't do anything, it was my eye and amazing talent for capturing the true beauty in people that landed me the job.

"Lunch is here," my assistant, Carrie, announces as she enters the studio with pizza and bottles of water.

"Pizza, Ri, really?"

I roll my eyes at Javi, teasing, "One piece won't kill you, pretty boy. Come eat."

"Maybe not, but what kind of person only eats one slice of pizza?" he asks, a perfectly tweezed eyebrow raised at me in question.

"Touche. That's okay, just means more for me." I start to move the box out of his reach, but he snatches it back.

"I don't think so, woman. I never said I wasn't having any. I've worked my ass off for this shoot, I deserve some cheesy goodness."

The phone rings from the front desk, and Carrie excuses herself to answer it while Javi and I dig into the pizza. Pulling a slice from the box, I take a bite and moan in satisfaction. When I open my eyes, Javi is staring at me.

"What?"

"Don't do that."

"Do what?"

"Moan like that. Fuck. It was hot. I haven't heard you moan like that since—"

I quickly cut him off as Carrie comes back into the room.

"Riann? It's Hot 100, the new music magazine. They want to book you to photograph the musicians that will be in their first edition."

"Absolutely! Whenever they need me, I'm there."

She nods and disappears out of the studio. Once I'm sure she's out of earshot, I turn back to Javi.

"I told you not to ever bring that up here. I can't have people thinking I make a habit out of sleeping with my clients."

"Riann, we were a thing before I became your client."

"First of all, we were never 'a thing'. It was just good company and great sex. But it doesn't matter, people will make assumptions and tabloids will tear us apart, no matter what the real story is."

"Okay, fine. I won't bring it up again," he says, raising his hands in surrender.

Carrie comes back into the studio, glancing between the two of us. Walking back over to the table, she is oddly quiet as she takes a seat at the table and grabs a slice of pizza from the box.

"Everything okay?" I ask, praying she didn't overhear our conversation.

"Yea, everything's great. Hot 100 is booked for February 20th."

"Great!"

She goes silent again as she looks at her plate, picking at her pizza. I can tell there's something she isn't telling me; we've worked together and been friends for way too long for me not to.

"Spill it, Carrie."

"Spill what?"

"Whatever it is you aren't saying. Just say it."

"Hot 100 Magazine is HUGE, probably your biggest job ever. Are you sure you're ready for that?"

I just stare at her, confused. This is my first time being the photographer for a full magazine, but Carrie has never doubted my skills before. She's deflecting and I want to know why. There's a sudden twinge in the pit of my stomach, and I have a feeling I know exactly why she's acting this way.

"Carrie?"

"Yes?" she answers, refusing to make eye contact.

"Did Top 100 give you a list of the musicians I'd be photographing?"

"Of course. Luke Bryan, Drake, Maroon 5, Tyga, Halsey . . ." she pauses and glances up at me.

"Anyone else?"

She sighs, "Ax-Axel James." Her voice is so low it's almost a whisper. I clearly heard her but I needed her to repeat herself. She looks up at me with sad eyes, "Axel James. It was actually him who asked for them to use you."

5

"*Y*ou okay?" Carrie asks when Javi leaves after finishing up his shoot. "I can call them back and tell them to find someone else."

Carrie is not only my assistant but one of my best friends. She knows everything about Axel and was one of the few people that helped me hold it together after he left.

"No, it's okay. I'm okay."

"Good. But just in case, I will be there with you. So if he pisses you off or upsets you, I will be happy to throat punch him in your defense."

"Noted." I laugh at her, and she throws her arms around me.

"By the way, why didn't you ever tell me about Javi?"

My breath catches in my throat, and I take a step back out of her arms.

"What are you talking about?" I try to play it cool.

"Seriously, Ri? I'm not blind. The pent up sexual tension between the two of you is off the charts."

I side-eye her. "Please don't say anything to anyone about it. I just don't want people thinking I make a habit out of sleeping with my clients."

"You totally should, they're fucking beautiful."

"Carrie!"

"Sorry," she says, but the smirk on her face tells me she really isn't sorry. "I promise not to say anything about you rolling around with your secret Latin lover."

"He isn't my 'lover,' it happened once . . ."

Carrie gives me a 'yea right, I wasn't born yesterday' look.

"Okay, maybe four . . . five . . . ten times. But it happened before he became a client. As soon as he asked me to help him build his portfolio, I cut it off."

She shakes her head at me in disbelief as she finishes packing up her things to leave the office. "I'll see you tomorrow?"

"Yep, 7 am."

"Ugh," she whines. "I forgot tomorrow is an early day."

"Yep! So get out of here and get some rest."

She salutes me as she grabs her bags and turns towards the door.

"Hey, Carrie?"

"Yea, Ri?"

"Don't forget my coffee!"

Carrie huffs and rolls her eyes at me. "Yes, your majesty," she says, bowing before disappearing out the door.

I laugh and shake my head at her dramatics. She's so ridiculous sometimes, but I don't know what I would do without her. I turn and walk back into the studio to finishing getting my equipment together for tomorrow when I hear the bell on the front door.

"What did you forget this time?" I call out as I walk towards the front desk.

A deep, familiar voice stops me in my tracks as I turn the corner into the front lobby.

"You," he says with a shrug. I stand there speechless as I let my eyes peruse over his body. His dark hair is cut short in a crew cut fade, his piercing green eyes eyeing me speculatively, waiting for a reaction I suppose. He's dressed in a white button up, the sleeves rolled up to his elbows showing off the colorful ink that now covers his forearms with distressed jeans and a pair of expensive dress shoes. He looks every bit the same guy I fell in love with in college but a total stranger at the same time. I do my best to keep my composure and reign in my emotions before I speak.

"Axel," my voice is a little more breathless than I'd like. "What are you doing here?"

To Be Continued . . .

ABOUT THE AUTHOR

Author of *Hearts Aligned* (Self-published 2016), a military romance, Cheri Marie lives for a good read with an alpha hero and strong, stubborn heroine. After many years of starting books and never finishing, she took to Word in April 2015 determined to write and finish her first novel. Nights that turned into mornings and a whole lot of unruly characters she finished Hearts Aligned. Currently, she is in the works of publishing multiple other novels set to release throughout 2017/2018. Residing in sunny Southwest Florida, she lives with family, five dogs, a cat, a tank full of fish, and a bearded dragon named Toad.

Connect with Cheri

 facebook.com/AuthorCheriMarie

twitter.com/authrcherimarie

 instagram.com/authorcherimarie

THE
FORGE

LEIGH TAYLOR

1

PENELOPE

I cover my eyes to block the sun's glint off of the perfectly polished steel letters attached to the facade of a newly renovated warehouse space.

The Forge.

What was I actually doing here?

I was already regretting my decision to spend the three dollars on bus fare to get here when I saw a very scantily clad woman wander out of the front door.

It wasn't a quick trip to get my apartment in Squirrel Hill all the way to the Strip District and I couldn't help but wonder if this would be a waste of my time. As I was lingering around deciding if I actually wanted to audition for this job, I saw another girl go inside with a pair of stripper heels hanging from her fingertips.

Stripper heels,

Clear.

Plastic.

Sky high.

Stripper heels.

God, if my former ballet company saw me right now, they'd have a field day. I know there would be plenty of laughter and I can almost hear all of the "how the mighty have fallen" comments.

Last year, at this time, I was perfectly positioned to become a principal dancer with one of New York's premiere ballet companies. My career trajectory was blossoming after all my years of hard work.

I had the "too handsome for his own good" Wall Street boyfriend, who I was just knew was going to propose at Christmas. I lived in a beautiful penthouse with a view of the park; and thanks to my family, I wanted for nothing.

I'm the first to admit, I was a spoiled Park Avenue princess but I was also a ballerina and a damn good one.

My entire life had been ballet. Every relationship, every decision tied back to my career goals in some way.

My every moment from the time I woke until the time I went to sleep was ballet...until it wasn't.

Now I was trying to pick up the pieces, in Pittsburgh of all places.

A new city.

A new me.

A new job?

Maybe that won't be checked off just yet after all.

I hitch my bag higher on my shoulder and cross the street. Even if it looks like a dead end, because I am not a stripper, I should at least let Mr. Hunt know I'm not interested.

It's polite and professional.

And my best friend and new roommate, Maddie, pulled some industry strings to even get me the audition. The audition is with one of the owners so I need to make a good impression for her sake, even if their stage is showcasing twerks rather than pirouettes.

Maddie is also a former Manhattanito. We grew up in the same social circle and attended the same private schools. Maddie decided to spread her wings and get away from the Empire City for college.

Now, she is a well known bartender in the Steel City; her side job while she works on her doctorate degree at one of the top universities in the country. Her parents are very proud of the schooling, but not so much of the bartending.

When I needed to escape the nightmare New York had become, Maddie told me to get myself on a plane and welcomed me with open arms. She gave me a shoulder to cry on, followed by a night out to get my mojo back and she got me an in at the most talked about new night club in town.

Maddie has made such a big deal about The Forge.

It's opening has been very top secret.

Some people are saying it's a strip club, which I'm beginning to believe is correct.

Maddie's assured me it is actually going to be a very classy *private* social club.

The owners are two Texans, with deep roots in old family oil money; and if old money in Texas is anything like old money in NYC, this place should be top notch and oozing with snob appeal. But I'm not getting those vibes as stripper heels pushes back through the front door.

She looks me up and down as she stops on the sidewalk. Her stare makes me want to squirm but I hold my head up. The first rule of surviving the ballet world is to never let anyone realize how body conscious you are.

It's an unspoken that everyone has body issues, and some dancers even become unhealthy trying to control their physique, but you never let your fears show.

"Good luck. He's a real prick. Didn't even let me finish my routine." She huffs and spins away; her stripper heels now dangling with a little less gusto.

The door comes open again and a behemoth of a man ducks his head out, an earpiece like security typically wears visible.

"Miss Kline, are you coming in? Mr. Hunt is waiting for you."

I nod dumbly at the well dressed man.

Is he security?

I guess you'd need that at a club with nearly naked women and handsy clientele.

"This way please." He says as he touches his ear and says something too low for me to make out.

We make our way into a small, but beautiful, lobby and then he holds open a door for me. I step across the threshold and am inside the club space. It looks similar to any typical club but there are lot of small areas to sit in addition to a fancy bar and a small dance floor.

There's also a stage; a stage I had hoped to dance across.

"Penelope Kline, of the Upper East Side Klines. Twenty six. Top of your graduating class but no college coursework to follow. Only ballet. Only ever ballet. The most impressive dance resume I've ever seen, if I'm being honest, and I do pride myself on honesty. Why are you here in my club sweetness?"

My eyes are drawn back across the room and my gaze slides over the man with the gravelly voice standing against the bar.

He just may be the most attractive man I've ever seen.

He has rich blonde hair that is styled in one of those messy "I spent twenty minutes making it look like I just rolled out bed" looks.

His burgundy colored henley is stretched across muscular shoulders and allow the outline of his biceps to be shown off.

His legs are clad in perfectly fit jeans and I can tell from here that he has cowboy boots on his feet. Not the kind of boots I would expect though. They aren't dusty and worn in but expensive looking leather that are polished to a high shine.

The boots look as expensive as the pristine cowboy hat laying upside down on the bar top.

I allow my mind to wander to the strangeness of his hat being on its crown to distract myself from staring at him. He clears his throat loudly, drawing my attention back.

"Mr. Hunt?" I croak out, embarrassed by the crack of my voice.

This man is something dangerous to my body.

I feel like I'm on fire and I haven't even gotten close enough to see if his eyes are just reflecting the lights hanging from the rafters or if they are flecked with gold like I think they may be.

I barely even notice when my bag slides off my shoulder and hits the floor with a soft thump.

"Who else were you expecting, darlin?" He replies with a slow drawl and a smirk.

Fuck.

Me.

When did a Texas accent get so sexy?

"I. Um. How do you know all that about me?"

God, I sound like an idiot.

I suck in a deep breathe and try to find my center.

"I vet every single person before they walk in for an interview. This is an exclusive venture and I need to be sure my employees have a level of discretion. I still want to know why a prima ballerina is in front of me, but I also want to know why you seem so surprised by me."

"I was told you were some kind of oil tycoon. I wasn't expecting someone so young. You took me off guard. I actually just wanted to come in and apologize."

"For what, Penelope?" He pushes off of the bar and comes toward me, eating up the space between us with long, powerful strides.

Why do I have to be getting tingles in all the right places when he says my name?

I can't be attracted to a guy who owns a strip club, even if he is the kind of man who also owns any room he's in.

"Well, I appreciate your time and your interest in seeing me perform but I believe we're on different pages. I'm interesting in dancing, but not getting naked." I bite my lip as he closes in on my personal space.

I should protest or take a step back but I'm mesmerized by this man.

"Who said anything about dancing naked?"

"Oh? Well. I just. I saw the last two girls who walked out of here. One of them even had platform plastic shoes for God's sake. How are you not hiring exotic dancers?"

"Didn't you see them walk out of the door?" He asks with a lifted brow.

Could he stop being sexy for one minute and let me think?

I finally nod slowly.

"They weren't right for this position. I'm hiring entertainers. I'm hiring talent. I'm hiring people who can sell sensuality. The Forge is a playground for people with very specific tastes and those tastes don't typically include a pole."

"So it's not a strip club like everyone is saying?"

"It's not a strip club."

"I can do ballet? With my clothes on?"

"I wouldn't mind seeing you dance with your clothes off but that would have to be my own private show. I'm not the best when it comes to sharing."

He smiles when he hears the soft gasp escape my lips.

"You, my sweet Penelope, can own that stage every night in whatever outfit you want. You're already hired. I'm not letting you walk out of that door. I do want to see you dance though."

I know my eyes are wide and I shake my head slightly.

"Just like that?" I squeak. "And this isn't some weird sex club?"

"Weird sex club?" He chuckles. "No. Not a strip club or a sex club. The Forge is a private, members only experience for those who need a sensual outlet. Kinks, you might say. At The Forge, you can escape reality in a safe and controlled environment and explore your inner most desires."

The entire time he's speaking, he's moving closer and closer until his lips are pressed to my ear.

"Kinks?"

His nose nuzzles into my hair and I feel him take a sniff of my scent.

"Kinks. Sexual desires, fantasies that don't align with accepted society. Everyday life can be very bland. Clients will come here to taste all the flavors the world has to offer."

My head should be spinning. I should be spinning my body away from this man and running away.

I cannot work at a sex club.

But instead I say glued to my spot and let out a whimper when his body pulls away from me.

"Mr. Hunt..." I say shakily as I look up into his eyes.

He has several inches on me and makes me feel small and feminine in a way that no man ever has.

"Mason. You will call me Mason. I like Sir as well, if you're into that."

I feel my mouth open and close but no words come out.

I'd be lying if the way his eyes dilate as they watch my mouth isn't exciting the hell out of me.

My hands have a mind on their own and I reach out and place my palm against his chest.

His smile makes me feel brave.

"I don't understand why you need a ballerina at a sex club?"

"Sweet girl. Stop calling my new home a sex club. This isn't a dungeon or somewhere to hide away. It's just an experience for people who need a little more. And I need a ballerina because your art is gorgeous. Think about it, Penelope. The connection you have to your body. The flow of your movements."

I shiver as his finger runs along my arm and up the side of my neck. I can feel his breath on my skin.

"When you dance for you, just for you, is it not exhilarating? Freeing? On some level, I'd say it actually turns you on. Your body feels alive. You are a ballerina but you are a sexual being. It exudes from everything you do whether you realize it's happening or not. My clients will experience all those emotions through watching you move."

I nod, despite myself.

Am I seriously agreeing that ballet belongs in a sex club?

"Why "The Forge"? It's not just to keep everyone guessing is it?"

"It is a clever play on something so engrained in Pittsburgh." He smiles and I can't look away from his handsome face. Its also a metaphor for what we want to do here. Most people spend their lives hiding all those dirty desires they have. They feel shame for wanting to either dominate or submit. They are embarrassed that violence turns them on, whether it be a simple spanking or full bondage scenes. Society makes us feel like anything that deviates from vanilla sex is wrong."

I shiver as I take in his words, not only because his fingers are trailing over my skin but because of the emotion he's stirring inside of me.

"A club like this is an outlet to reshape the world view for people with kinks. We'll encourage and guide our patrons to explore all of those deep desires in a safe and controlled way. This space acts as a forge, molding and fortifying their sexual lives. The Forge will allow a person to embrace kink and to make themselves into who they were always meant to be."

"So it's not just about sex?"

"Sex is typically involved. But it's much more about relationships. It's about trust. Give and take. There's a great deal of emotional bonding involved in this too. Some folks don't even have sex in their scenes. It's all based on what you and your partner need and want."

I nod dumbly, trying to process all of his words.

"Maybe now you'll quit calling it a sex club." He chuckles and the sound resonates through my entire body.

A zing in all the right places.

I feel myself tense as he moves his lips closer to mine. He presses a sweet kiss to the side of my mouth.

I'm torn between my fight or flight instincts.

This man is exhilarating and making me feel alive in a way I never could have anticipated.

But he's a total stranger. I shouldn't want his lips against mine.

"Right now, I can tell you're holding yourself back sweet girl. I want you to never hold back with me. Never hold back with your art. This isn't high stakes, cut throat ballet. This is you, on your stage. Now will you make my fantasy come true and dance for me?"

2

MASON

♥

*H*ave you ever seen something and felt a craving to possess it?

To own it and keep it all to yourself?

I've had that feeling often in my life.

Sometimes, it's as simple as seeing a chocolate dessert being served to another diner in a restaurant and immediately ordering one for myself.

Other times, it's seeing the newest model at a car show and arranging for one to roll off of the production line and into my driveway.

I have a dozen sports cars stored in a garage in Houston to prove that particular impulse.

I've gotten ahold of every material item I've ever wanted.

One of the perks of being a millionaire before my first birthday.

I'm on track to make my first billion before my thirtieth.

None of that felt like it mattered the second I saw my sweet girl's headshot in the dance portfolio she submitted to The Forge.

Never in my life have I wanted anything or anyone as much I want Penelope Kline.

I want her trust.

I want her submission.

I want her heart.

That last part scared the shit out of me at first.

Women have always been a means to an end for me. A one night experience. A room in a club. A mission to taste all thirty one flavors.

Kinks make relationships...difficult.

Being rich makes commitment even harder.

I've spent most of my life learning to read people; figuring out their motives by their eye movements, or the twitch of their lips. I am constantly evaluating who is in my life to cling on and gain whatever high they can and who will still be by my side when the party is over.

That's what has me in Pittsburgh in the first place.

Only one person has ever had my back.

Xavier Bishop is my childhood best friend.

We both are cut from the same cloth and that cloth happens to be soaked in oil. Our families are both members of the original Texas oil dynasties.

I followed him quickly when he suggested opening a fetish club in the downtown Pittsburgh building he won during a poker game in Miami.

It was a low risk opportunity to try out an idea we'd been floating around for years so we partnered together, each taking ownership of half of the building.

It's just another business venture for X but for me it's a chance to further explore the dark thoughts that swirl around in my brain.

And now it's become an opportunity to change my life.

I look down at Penelope.

I can feel the slight tremor of her fingertips as her hand continues to rest on my chest. I see the way her breathing has increased as I run my thumb back and forth over the soft spot behind her ear.

I also feel the slight shift of her weight as she leans her cheek against my palm.

Her raven black hair is as beautiful and glossy as it is in photographs. I know it'll hit past her shoulders when I tell her to take her hair out of the classic ballerina bun she typically wears.

Her ice blue eyes were startling when I first saw her. They are such a stark contrast next to her dark hair and porcelain skin.

But looking into her eyes today?

I know she's mine and I will do whatever it takes to make her understand that she belongs not only on my stage, but by side. Forever.

I know by her reactions to my body that she feels this spark between us as well.

She wants more.

My sweet girl is just terrified to let go.

"Penelope?" I ask in a low voice to garner her attention.

I smile as her eyes flick to my lips before meeting mine.

"Dance for me, sweet Penelope? You're the only thing that's been on my mind since the moment I saw your face."

Her pretty pink lips open and close but she doesn't make any sound.

She finally nods and I know she's going to be brave enough to explore the simmering passion we both feel.

"I. Um. I need to. Is there somewhere I can change?" She stammers and it's the most adorable thing I've ever heard.

Her eyes cut away from mine and a blush spreads across her cheeks.

"I didn't want to deal with the stares on the bus if I wore a leotard." Penelope offers softly.

"Come with me. We don't have the dressing rooms finished. I want to customize them to each performer's desires. However, we do have our private rooms completed."

I gather her bag from the floor and carry it in one hand as my other arm wraps around her slim waist. My hand rests perfectly in the small of her lower back. I guide her towards a hallway tucked away behind the bar area.

Penelope may be unsure of what's happening but the way her body allows me to lead her, I know she and I will be a perfect fit.

I push open the first door on the left, knowing it's the tamest and the least likely to make my sweet girl question the moment. The room looks like a standard bedroom with a massive four poster bed. It's done up in shades of silver and white with black leather accents.

The only thing that feels out of place from an ordinary dwelling is the wall of glass.

It's a two way mirror that has what will be a spectacular view of the main dance floor.

This room is for couples who want to dip their toes into the fetish pool. You have the sense of being watched, of being taken in public, with all the safety of actually being tucked away from the rest of the patrons.

"It's so pretty. I thought there would be whips and chains. Or maybe of those big X shaped things you see in the movies."

"A St Andrew's Cross?" I laugh as she shrugs. "All in due time, my sweet girl. We don't have to rush."

I gently place her bag on the bed and begin the unpack it for her. I carefully lay out her dance clothing and smooth any wrinkles out.

I grin at the red ballet shoes I pull out. I gingerly set them to the side of her dance gear.

Penelope needs to begin to understand that belonging to me has perks. She will never long for anything.

In exchange for her body and her heart, I will cater to her every whim.

Most people don't understand the power balance of true submission.

I want her body to be for my pleasure but I need Penelope to willingly hand her body over to me.

I want to guide her to feeling like the sexual goddess she is.

I am also responsible for her care and well being.

Submission is a beautiful exchange when done correctly. It's not ugly or violent as so many believe.

When I turn back to her, she chewing on that plump lower lip of hers.

"Stop that or I'll have to make you occupy your lips with another activity."

Penelope gasps at my bold words.

Her eyes widen as I place my hands on her hips and pull her body flush with mine.

She's so tiny. Tall but so slender. I have a primal desire to keep her protected.

"Look at me. Tell me what you're thinking."

"I. I was wondering, well. Is this part of your kink? Whatever your fetish is? Do you like women's clothing?"

I laugh as I place a kiss to her forehead.

"I like your clothing because it belongs to you Penelope and that is all. You belong to me now and that means that I am your caregiver. I protect you. I anticipate your needs before you even realize what you need. Do you understand?"

"I don't understand Mason." She nearly whispers as I cup her jaw.

"You'll learn. I'm a very patient teacher. Now get dressed and meet me back at the stage."

"Okay."

"Yes."

"Yes?"

"I want submission, sweet Penelope. Always yes and no. We don't do okays or maybes. You are either to trust my lead and follow without question or know that you can tell me that you simply are not comfortable with an activity."

She licks her lips and nods.

I can see her thoughts beginning to fall into place.

"Get ready and meet me in the front."

"Yes...sir."

Penelope's voice is like honey, dripping sweetness and acting as a balm to my soul.

I groan and pull her even closer, widening my stance to tuck her legs between mine, knowing she can feel my erection against her hip.

"Be a good girl and don't make me wait." I growl before releasing her and leaving the room.

It's either distance myself or throw her down and take what's mine before she's ready to give herself over to me.

I settle into an oversized lounge chair I pulled over to the middle of the viewing area earlier.

I can't hold back from palming my cock over my jeans. This girl has me hard as a rock.

I close my eyes and lean my head back. My hand slides back and forth in a rhythmic motion as I imagine what it will feel like to have my sweet girl's lithe body riding my cock.

I open my eyes when I hear a soft squeak.

Penelope is standing beside me, eyes wide and trained on my crotch.

She is absolutely stunning in an all black outfit.

Her bottoms look like barely more than full coverage panties rather than shorts and a cropped camisole ends just below her small but pert breasts. A simple, nearly sheer, mesh dress covers the two pieces.

The dress ends just above her knees but slits run up the fronts of both of her thighs, all the way to the bottom edge of her dance shorts.

"Fuck me." I groan, still touching myself.

I lean forward and see she has those red shoes on her feet.

"Come here?"

"Are you asking or telling?" Penelope asks as she continues to stare down at my hand.

I stop my movement and wait for her to look at me in the eyes.

"This time I'm asking. I expect to earn your trust. I won't just take."

Her chest rises and falls with her heavy breathing and for a moment she just stares at me.

Suddenly it's as if something inside of her snaps and she's on my lap, her long legs wrapping on either side of my waist.

She leans in and gives me a sweet, tentative kiss on my lips.

It's a shy kiss, but not awkward.

A kiss of promises, of new beginnings.

I wrap my arms around her, pulling her body into mine and grinding my hard on against her pussy. I can feel her heat through her thin costume.

"Mason..." She whimpers.

"What do you need my sweet?"

"I don't do this, you know? I'm not this kind of girl. You just do something to me and I can't help myself. I know this is wrong but I want you." She rushes out.

She quickly covers her face with her hands, clearly embarrassed by her admission, but she makes no move to leave my lap.

"Penelope, I know what a magnificent being you are. I feel this too. This isn't something you find everyday."

She slowly lowers her hands.

"You feel it too?" She says with such hope.

"What do you think?" I laugh as I thrust my hips up, and Penelope giggles as she bounces on my lap.

Her laughter quickly turns into a soft moan and I know she's ready to let just a little more go.

"What do you want right now, my sweet?"

"I. I um. I'd like to..." She stutters a bit and bites her lip.

"Do you want to cum my sweet girl?"

She nods frantically and rocks her hips against me.

"Tell me Penelope. Tell me what you need."

"Touch me. Please."

"And?"

She stares at me for just a beat.

"And make me cum. Please Mason. Please, sir."

"Your pleasure is all mine Penelope. My sweet sweet girl."

I settle one hand at the small of her back to help support her weight as my free hand slides over the front of her shorts.

I pull at the fabric, watching it slide between the soft lips of her pussy.

"Penelope, are you already wet for me?" I ask as she whimpers.

She nods as she watches my hand move between our body.

"Words, sweet."

"Yes." She manages to breathe out as I slip one finger under her bottoms.

My fingertip draws a line from her clit all the way to her taint and back again. Her pussy is drenched from just our short grinding session.

I'll have her ass one day but today is about building trust and teaching pleasure.

I pull my finger back and inspect the glistening moisture.

"Do you taste as sweet as you look?" I ask as I lick my finger to taste her juices.

Penelope moans as she watches my movements and squirms on my lap.

"Mason...please."

"You want my finger back?" I arch a brow at her, barely holding myself back but knowing I need to lay a proper foundation with my girl.

"Please. Please touch me. I feel like I'm on fire."

"Hold your shorts to the side."

She scrambles on my lap to lift the hem of her dress completely out of the way and bunches the spandex of her shorts for me, exposing her pink, bare pussy to me.

I stroke my fingers back and forth, slowly, over her clit.

I know it's teasing but I can see that she's already ready to fall apart and I want to extend the moment as much as I can.

She closes her eyes and her head tilts back she moans.

Her hips rock into my hand.

This is going to be too quick today but damn I want her orgasm.

I want her to scream my name.

I tease her opening with one finger, ensuring she's perfectly lubricated before slipping inside.

"You're so tight, Penelope. I'll have to get your sweet little pussy stretched to take my cock." I growl as I add a second finger.

"Oh my god..."

Her hips rock faster, taking her own pleasure as she rides my hand.

She's finally letting go and following her physical desires.

I curl my fingers and stroke back and forth until I find the sweet spot I'm feeling for.

When I look up and see the flush on her face, I can't deny her pleasure even if I want this to last.

I swipe my thumb over her clit as I rub her g-spot.

Penelope's hips begin to buck wildly and she loses any rhythm she had as her orgasm begins.

I savor the feel of her milking my fingers as she cries out my name.

Watching her come undone is the most spectacular sight.

She leans forward, her hands pressed to my shoulders for support, as she tries to catch her breath.

I slowly work my fingers for a few more strokes to wring every bit of her orgasm before pulling them out.

I smile at the popping sound as her pussy releases my hand.

Penelope watches me with wide eyes as I suck my fingers into my mouth, savoring her flavor.

She's like the wold's finest ice cream sundae.

The richest vanilla bean ice cream on the planet with a drizzle of hot chocolate made of the best cocoa available and all with a cherry on top. Classic but decadent none the less.

She's the flavor I've been waiting for.

"Wow." She finally says as she catches her breath.

"Wow is right, my sweet."

I see that blush spread across her cheeks again.

"Um." She begins to squirm on my lap. "Now what do we do?"

"Now you dance for me, my sweet. And then I'll have a proper taste of my newest fantasy."

3

PENELOPE

"You have a one track mind, Mason."

He just shrugs one shoulder as he continues to casually run his fingertips up and down my spine.

I'm still in awe of how he made my body feel just a few moments ago. I haven't even managed to move from his lap yet.

I've never had a man bring me to the edge so quickly, with such intensity.

I'm questioning if I really even knew what an orgasm felt like.

Somehow Mason knows exactly how to work my body over. He knows exactly what I need even when I don't.

But Mason is also everything I should be avoiding.

Handsome.

Rich.

He's got that devil may-care attitude.

It doesn't matter that I feel a real connection to him.

He'll use me and toss me aside when he's bored.

Or worse, when a new woman catches his eye.

"Why are you frowning?" Mason asks seriously as he tips my face towards his using a finger under my chin.

"I. I shouldn't be doing this."

"This?"

"Us." I sigh.

"Explain." He commands with a grumpy look on his beautiful face.

I suck in a deep breath. I've never been great at sharing my emotions. It's always been easier to bottle everything up while I nodded and smiled for everyone else's sake.

"I'd just be repeating all of my mistakes. I left New York for a fresh slate, not to be the dumb girl again."

"I thought you left New York because of your injury?" Mason asks softly as he strokes my cheek.

Despite myself, I lean into him.

"I did but I also didn't."

Mason just watches me, waiting.

"My injury was a set back. I got hurt in the middle of a show, which is never ideal. Everyone knows it. You can't keep it under wraps. But I got treatment quickly. I had the best doctor. I did my physical therapy. My position should have been safe. I'm a good dancer and I'm still young."

I pause to catch my breath.

Mason's hand slides over my hip, rubbing the location of my surgery scar.

No doubt he googled me when he got my portfolio.

But he still doesn't understand why I'm actually here; why I'm considering trading my dreams for a stage in a sex club.

"When I went with my medical clearance to the director, I was told my position was no longer was available. There had been a need to fill in the gap and I would be expected to wait until audition season and earn my place again." I say smoothly,

This part of the story is painful, but not the deepest cut.

I close my eyes and I feel Mason pull me even closer to his body.

"The dancer who replaced me is named Cassandra. I believed it when I was told she needed to step in and keep the company balanced in my absence. It hurt but I was confident I would be back in practices as soon as the formal auditions were finished.

"I went back to training with a private choreographer and I started putting my life back together. It was just a temporary issue until I went by my ex's apartment one evening, without calling first. I caught him in bed with Cassandra and everything spiraled out of control from there.

"He called me a spoiled brat. He told me just used me to get close to my father and try to lure my family to move to his investment firm. He told me that I disgusted him since my surgery, that I clearly didn't care about my ideal weight range anymore."

I feel Mason's hands grip my waist and I can hear how heavily he's breathing.

I don't need to open my eyes to know that he's angry.

"I thought we were on track to get married. I knew it wasn't a love match but I felt like we were suited for one another. He didn't monopolize my time that I needed for ballet and I showed well on his arm for important events. It was enough. You must know how it is when you live with your family's worth being public. But he shattered me. He broke me more than any fall on stage ever could. My father found out that there had been bribes to get Cassandra moved up and they traced back to my ex's bank accounts.

"I had spent my entire life working toward principal dancer. I took every class. I made every practice. I have danced until my feet bleed through my slippers and continued to dance rather than stop and change my shoes. I couldn't lose a single precious moment. And he destroyed all of it. None of my dedication mattered as much as his money."

I feel Mason's lips brush along my jaw line and he cradles me in his arms.

"I packed the few things I had earned for myself, and I ran away. Maddie welcomed me with open arms. I want to dance. I need to dance. I don't want to be the rich ballerina. I don't want my parents to take care of me. I don't want to worry about the three pound range that creates my perfect lines. I just want to dance and be happy. And you, Mason, are the same man I'm running from. I'm just a pretty toy that you'll toss aside when you get tired of me."

Mason's grip becomes almost painfully tight.

"Open your eyes, Penelope. I am not fucking him. I will never be him. I will support any dream you have. I will stand on the side of the stage and cheer on every success that you earn. I will never treat you as anything other than the gift that you are. I haven't been living, sweet girl. I've been going through the motions until I met you today. You have changed me already."

"How do I know?" I whisper as tears begin to form in my eyes.

"Do you not feel this, Penelope?" He places my hand over his heart. "I'm already half way in love with you. I want your body and your heart but I need you to trust me. I need you to trust my intentions."

"And if I take the job and you change your mind about us?"

"Is that what you think of me?"

"I. I don't know."

Mason lifts me out of his lap and takes long strides over to the bar.

I feel the anger rolling off of him as he returns with a folder in his hand.

"I intended to give you partial ownership of the business instead of a paycheck. I thought it would feel better for you to own a quarter of The Forge, if we were involved. You'd get monthly profit share payouts, never a payroll check. You would be equal to me and neither myself or Xavier could take this away from you."

"Oh." I say dumbly.

"Oh." He mimics.

"Mason...I'm just scared."

"I have done nothing but cater to you since you stepped into this room. I have never looked away from your eyes. I have been one hundred percent honest with every word I've said to you. I'm afraid I won't be able to prove myself to you if you would ask that question of me."

He holds the folder out to me.

"I don't need to see you dance. The job is yours regardless. Xavier and I would be thrilled to have you on board. His contact information is also listed on your paperwork. Please let him know if you decide to accept the offer. He'll complete the contract with you. I've already signed it. You should go change so you can get home."

"Mason. Don't be like this."

"Be like what, Penelope? Pissed off that you would question my fucking character? That you think I want to keep you as my personal whore?"

"Mason." I gasp.

I feel my heart breaking as he turns away from me and walks towards the door.

How am I aching for a man I barely know? A man I just met?

My brain and my heart are battling. I want so badly to chase him but I also want to tuck my tail and never set foot in this place again.

Logic wins out as tears stream down my face and I clutch the folder as I go back to change into my street clothes.

I tuck the paperwork on top of my ballet shoes once I've packed my bag.

As I enter back into the main club, I hear a male voice and for just a moment, I'm hopeful Mason came back for me.

"Are you sure you won't be my bar manager? I'm telling you to name any price, any terms."

"There's not enough money in the world, Bishop." A female voice huffs.

Maddie.

She sees me over the dark headed man's shoulder and comes to wrap me in a hug.

"Mason called this morning and asked me to be on standby. He told me you'd need me to help celebrate but I don't think that's what we're doing."

I burst into tears as she says his name and let her lead me out of the club.

"You don't deserve it but rot in hell Xavier Bishop." She calls back as we exit into the lobby and away from this place.

All I want is to be tucked back into our apartment with a bottle of wine and a pint of ice cream.

My heart has never felt this broken.

I hold my breath as I stand ready on the stage with my body in fourth position.

My toes turned out, feet crossed one in front of the other. One arm outstretched as the other curves above my head.

"Please let him show up." I whisper to myself.

Just as my arm starts to cramp, I hear the swoosh of the heavy door.

I know it's Mason so I begin my routine.

There's no music.

Just me and my stage.

And Mason.

I broke down a few days ago and I called Xavier.

It'd been nearly a week and I finally was able to process all the feelings I have for Mason.

We may have only known each other for a few hours but my body knows him. My soul knows him.

And as much as it scares me, they both want to be owned by him.

Xavier asked me if I was as broken and brooding as Mason was and I knew I had to fix this.

I need to give Mason a chance.

He's not the man who burned me and our relationship won't be like anything I've ever experienced.

It may be too fast and it may sound crazy to people when we tell them how we fell for each other, but I have no doubts that I want him to own every inch of me, inside and out.

I arranged with Xavier to get Mason to the club and make his fantasy a reality.

I signed along the dotted lines to become the third stakeholder of The Forge.

I didn't invest any money but I will be the lead entertainer.

I smile as Mason appears before the stage but I don't stop dancing.

I love the way Mason's gaze eats me up as I perform a series of pirouettes.

The stage lights glint off of the crystals on my leotard.

I had this rush made when I decided to apologize to Mason. The body suit is sheer mesh that perfectly matches my skin tone with strategically placed crystals over all the areas that are for his eyes only.

I close eyes as I return to the retire position and I feel an arm wrap my waist before I can move into my next position.

"I'm sorry." I croak as Mason lifts me up and carries me off of the stage in a fireman hold.

"Mason!" I laugh as he eats up the space between the stage and the playrooms.

He still hasn't said a word to me.

He nearly kicks open the door of the white and silver playroom that I dressed in that first day and tosses me onto the bed.

"Who do you belong to Penelope?" Mason says, sounding like he's nearly out of of breath.

I settle onto my knees on the edge of the bed.

"You, Mason. I belong to you."

He sighs and I can see the relief wash over him.

"If you like that outfit, I suggest you take it off now." He gruffs as he begins to unbutton his shirt.

I scramble to remove my ballet shoes and my leotard.

As I finally stand back up, bare and ready, Mason captures me in his arms.

He kisses me deeply.

He's branding me.

I can feel his thick cock against my belly and I press closer to him, wanting all of him.

When he pulls back, I realize he has a small blue box in his hand.

"I thought Tiffany would be appropriate for my New Yorker." He says with a sly smile as he removes a gorgeous diamond encrusted key from the box.

He places the chain around my neck and clasps it for me.

My hand falls over the key.

It's easily a ten thousand dollar necklace. I've coveted this style a time or two in the store.

This isn't a simple gesture.

I look up into Mason's eyes and he must see the question on my face.

"Until you're ready for a wedding ring." He says confidently.

I nod. As insane as this is, I know I will be his wife one day.

"Tonight is about us, Penelope. No kinks. No extra noise. I just need to feel you underneath me." He says sweetly as he walks me back towards the bed.

My knees hit the edge and I fall into a seated position.

I press my hand to his cock before he can follow me.

"Let me taste you." I whimper as I wrap my fingers around his thick shaft.

"Penelope." He rasps as I lean forward.

I wrap my lips around the head of his cock and continue to pump the base with my hand.

I suck and am rewarded by Mason's deep throaty moan.

I slide him further into my mouth and begin working my lips up and down to match my hand's rhythm. His hand catches my jaw softly and he pulls his cock away from me.

I whimper and look up at him. His eyes are so full of passion.

"You're going to make me explode sweet girl. I want to cum in my sweet little pussy tonight."

"Yes Mason. Please cum inside me."

Before I can blink, Mason has me on my back on the bed, his lips moving down my body. I squirm as he worships my breasts. I've always been self conscious of my size but with Mason palming my breasts and lapping at my nipples, I have never felt sexier.

His big body shifts and I feel his lips trail down my abs and between my legs.

I lift and prop myself up on my elbows so I can watch as he kisses my inner thighs.

He sets his trail from my knee all the way up to my hip. He even kisses my scar and I smile at him when he looks up to see my reaction.

"Are you ready for me, sweet girl?"

"Yes Mason. Please."

He nuzzles into my pussy and runs his tongue over my clit. I toss my head back and moan at the sensation.

"Mmmm. So wet, my sweet." He praises as he licks me with a few long, slow motions.

"Please."

"Words, Penelope."

"Please fuck me, Mason Please make me cum."

I spread my legs wider as he settles himself between my legs. He meets my eyes as he strokes his cock.

"Do you want me to use a condom?"

"No. We're protected. And. And I trust you Mason." I say sincerely.

"Fuck. You're killing me Penelope."

He thrusts into me with little warning.

I moan at how full I feel.

Mason doesn't move.

He leans down and places a sweet kiss to my lips. I part my lips and his tongue invades my mouth. Both of us moaning around the kiss, as I wrap my legs around him with my feet locked at the small of his back.

"I know it's too soon but I love you Penelope. I don't want to live another day without you." He whispers as he nuzzles into the crook of my neck.

"I love you too, Mason. I don't care if it's too soon."

"Fuck. I love you so much sweet girl." Mason grunts as he begins to rock his hips against me.

It's primal and animalistic.

He ruts into me hard and deep and I squirm under him trying to increase the friction and see how close we can get our bodies.

"You feel so good Mason. Please give me more." I whine.

"You feel like heaven Penelope."

His hands grip my hips and he lifts my bottom off of the bed so that my weight rests on his thighs.

I thrash as the new angle creates even more pleasure.

"Oh my god."

"Mason, my sweet. Just call me Mason." He chuckles as he bottoms out and draws another moan from my lips.

"Mason." I chant over and over as I feel my orgasm approaching.

He reaches between us and flicks his fingers over my clit just as I start to tumble over the edge because he clearly does know my body better than I do.

My legs tremble and my toes actually curl as the waves of pleasure pour over my body.

I can feel Mason's cock twitch and I know he's close as well.

A few more pumps and he collapses on top on me as he shouts my name.

He catches his breath and lifts up onto his elbows to look at me.

His smile is everything I need.

"I'm never letting you go, Sweet Penelope. You're all mine now."

"There's no where I'd rather be." I say before giving him another kiss. "Now, let's get The Forge opened."

ABOUT THE AUTHOR

Leigh Taylor is a native Texan who now calls the Windy City home. Leigh loves all things romance related including novels and classic movies. Her love of reading and Texas inspired her to begin writing and share her characters with readers everywhere. When she isn't working or writing about cowboys, Leigh enjoys spending time exploring her city, playing with her rescue pups and relaxing with friends over a cup of tea or whiskey.

Connect with Leigh

f facebook.com/leightaylorbooks

🐦 twitter.com/ltaylorbooks

📷 instagram.com/leightaylorbooks

SAVING BOWEN

DESIREE LAFAWN

1

BOWEN

All I wanted to do was sit down in a quiet damn bar on a boring Friday night and drink a beer in relative piece, but it didn't look like that was in the cards for me. I'd picked Auggy's specifically for that purpose too. It had been a dive back before I joined the service as a pimple faced 19-year-old kid, and now eight years later it didn't seem like much had changed. Oh, I had filled out some, went to war, seen some shit and become emotionally compromised, and my complexion had cleared up too—but Auggy's still looked like the empty shit hole it always was, and that was what I liked.

Peace and fucking quiet. That was all I wanted—but the hell with my plans, right?

"Bowen, you picked a bad night to come in here and brood, kid." August - Auggy -Dickerson, the surly, gray bearded bar owner, was standing in the kitchen doorway, wiping his hands on the bottom of his—was once white—apron. "Shit's gonna hit the fan here in about fifteen minutes. It's bout night."

"I don't know what you mean, sir." I replied, even though I knew what he meant just fine, at least about my attitude. "I don't brood. And what's a bout?"

"I'm not your commanding officer, Bowen." Auggy came around

the front of the bar and stood next to the booth I had holed myself up in, his brows knit together in irritation. "Drop the sir. It's weird coming from you."

His cantankerous attitude hadn't changed in eight years either. I almost smiled, and if that part of me that had a sense of humor wouldn't have died back in the desert then I might have laughed. But I didn't laugh anymore. Not since I'd been home—no, even before that. Before I signed on I spent my life calling my old man's friend "Uncle Auggy," but in the service I learned that once an officer, always an officer, and I'd give him that respect even if he didn't want it.

"I can't do that, sir." I could go back to calling him Auggy, but that name just didn't seem to flow from my mouth as easy as *sir* did. Sir meant commanding officer. It meant familiar. I was having enough of a hard time fitting back in to civilian life, if he could let me have this small comfort, I would appreciate it.

"Eat shit, Bowen. Also, don't say I didn't warn you" His words trailed off as he turned and walked back into the kitchen without so much as a goodbye. That was Auggy though. He'd been a growly old fart for as long as I could remember. Even back before the cancer took Dad, and they told old service stories over the euchre table while Mom pretending not to be listening and bitched about the cigar smoke in the house. Back when I all I wanted to do was grow up and be a soldier like them. Back when I didn't know shit about shit.

When being young and naïve was a special kind of privilege.

Fingering the letter, I kept in my pocket I stared down at my mostly empty beer and contemplated getting another one versus just going home. I had written the *to whom it may concern* in a moment of weakness about four months ago. Two months after I returned to civilian life and couldn't figure out how to fit into it anymore. I didn't have the courage to do the thing I had written about, but I kept it in my pocket anyway. Not because I was all better, I still struggled with what the fuck I was supposed to be doing without orders. I guess I just kept it because somehow, inside, I still thought I might go through with it. That thing I had written on the creased and worn pages in my pocket. Whenever I had a low moment, and that was pretty fucking frequent, I reached into my pocket to see if it was still there. I knew it was weird, but the only one who knew about it was me, so I took whatever I needed to keep grounded. To keep living and figure out what I was supposed to be doing with the rest of my life.

Auggy wasn't kidding when he said shit would hit the fan. It was five minutes later though, not fifteen, when the glass doors to the bar blew open and what I could only describe as a *horde* of women poured in.

No shit, there must of have been fifty people—and all of them tried to fit through the door at once. The staff seemed to have been expecting them though, because the servers took up an aggressive position at the bar, pads and pens held out like weapons. The booths filled up around me faster than a blink and I had a moment of panic about the crowd before I remembered that I was a grown ass man and calmed the fuck down. I had issues, but I didn't need to freak out and run from an old friend's bar because of them.

Escape would be difficult though, even the aisles in between tables were crammed with bodies. I'd have to be water to be able to slip through that *Jenga* mess. Closing my eyes, I leaned my head back against the cushioned booth behind me and took a deep, fortifying breath.

New orders to self. Sit in the crowded bar, have another drink, do not freak out. I could do it if those were my orders. I could handle the crowd of people if that was my mission. I would always carry out my mission. See, that was the difficult thing about civilian life. I didn't have a mission, a purpose to fulfill. Apparently, all that was expected of me was that I eat, sleep and pay my taxes—pretty damn pointless. Maybe someone else would have considered it a weakness that I talked to myself that way. But those other people didn't have a pre-written goodbye note in their pocket, so they could fuck right off.

It wasn't that crowds bothered me, more like attention bothered me. I didn't want to be noticed; I liked my alone time. I liked the quiet. The bar was very crowded now, and the noise was reaching migraine inducing levels. Feeling the panic setting in, I kept my eyes closed and focused on one sense at a time. The vinyl of the booth cushion was squeaky and soft under my thighs and behind the small of my back. I pushed my body down a little further to imprint the feeling into my mind and pressed my feet into the floor under the small square table. Those were the things I could feel. I needed to ignore the things I could hear because there were so many sounds competing for attention, I couldn't separate them if I wanted to keep the anxiety at bay. Things I could smell—the scent of beer, of fried food and grease—and something else. Something crisp and floral, a perfume? It was close, right next to me actually.

Curious, I opened my eyes to see a wide smile and startling green eyes set in an oval face surrounded by a mass of dark hair pulled into a thick braid down one side. My surprise was magnified when the vixen in question opened her mouth, and with a voice too sweet to be saying the words asked,

"Do you want a blow job?"

"From you?" I asked in surprise. She wasn't even trying to be quiet about it, just said the words like she was making polite conversation about the weather. *Nice day today, do you know what time it is? Would you like a blow job?* Jeezus she was a bold one.

"No offense ma'am, you seem like a real nice girl but I'm gonna have to take a pass." I liked a good BJ just like any other person with a penis but this was just weird. And I certainly wouldn't behave like that in Auggy's place. He was the next thing to a father figure for crying out loud, I wouldn't disrespect his bar by getting a blowie in the booth, no matter how angelic the person in question looked.

Her delighted laughter fell on my ears like a warm rain. A rain that kept falling, because she kept laughing. Laughing until tears leaked out of the corners of her eyes and her breath wheezed out into hiccups. She collapsed into the seat across the booth from me and that was when I saw the error. As she sat down, she placed on the table the two items she had been carrying in her hands so she was free to wipe the tears away from her eyes—still laughing. I recognized the little glass cups with tiers of beige and brown topped with little ruffles of whipped cream.

Shots.

She had asked me if I wanted a blow job shot, and dammit if I hadn't walked right into the joke.

"Auggy sent me over here to give you a hard time," she gasped, then cleared her throat and gained control over her giggles. "But God, that was funny. Your face. You should have seen your face."

"It's still a no, because I don't do shots, but let me ask you a question. What would you have done if I would have said yes, thinking you meant something else?"

She didn't miss a beat when she said "I would have given you the shot. I said what I meant, I'm not responsible for your misinterpretation of my words." The raising of a single perfectly arched brow followed the last bit—challenging me to disagree with her statement. She was full of sass, this one.

I couldn't even see through the mass of people to the bar, but I assumed Auggy was back there laughing his ass off at interrupting my *brooding*. What an asshole. I wasn't a recluse, I just didn't *people* much. His pranks were ineffective, although delivered most attractively.

"Let me start over, my name is Marie." She extended hand over the table in expectation, nails green, deeper than her eyes, with flecks of glitter in the polish.

2

MARIE

I'm normally not so aggressive, honest, but when I saw him sitting in that corner by himself, head resting back on the booth I had to know. I had to know why someone would look so lonely in a bar full of people on a Friday night. We had just come off a hard win, and I jammed for the first time and I was high on life. I would never approach a stranger and say what I said, but I still felt the need to ask Auggy about him anyway.

"That kid is moody as hell," Auggy had said when I asked him who the man in the corner was. He didn't look like a kid to me. He looked like a man grown enough to fill out that dark gray henley he was wearing just fine. "I've known him since he was born, that boy, and he's going through some things right now. Might be better if you don't bother him."

The disappointment took me by surprise. He was a stranger and I was just curious. So why was I so bummed out when Auggy warned me off? He was attractive, sure, but good-looking guys were a dime a dozen to me. I liked interesting men, men who grabbed my attention and kept it.

"Or," Auggy said, as if he had just changed his mind, "maybe you should bother him. Maybe he needs to be bothered to get out of his funk. Go over there and pester him Marie, if you can get him to crack a smile, I'll buy you a beer. Hell, if you can get that boy to laugh, I'll add two hundred dollars to my team sponsorship."

Holy shit—the Homestead Wheelers were a skater run roller derby league. We were a recreation league without a Women's Flat Track Derby Association accreditation. Pittsburgh already had a team like that, and we were more of a surrounding area tag along team. We still operated like every other league out there though. That meant we did all the work ourselves, and we survived on league dues and outside sponsorships. That sponsorship money helped pay for our advertising costs and our rink rentals and it was hard to come by. Tell someone you skated roller derby and they thought you were the coolest person in the world. Request sponsorships and suddenly there were a thousand things more important. Auggy already let us use his bar for our bout after parties. Ever since Chiodo's closed up on the hill it was the closest place where we could get together and celebrate as a group. It also brought him in money but it was good to have a home bar to advertise on our fliers when we had a bout. A team without an after-party home was sadness. In roller derby, the after party was just as important as the bout. It's where the fans and skaters from both teams can come and unwind after leaving their aggressions on the track. Derby is a difficult sport, and it is definitely important to chill and let your endorphins calm down.

If Auggy was willing to throw another two hundred bones our way just for making some guy laugh, then I would try my best. I was MPV Jammer tonight. I was on top of the world. I was on fire.

I still can't believe I offered him a blow job.

The look on his face was worth it though. His eyes widened in surprise and I could tell that they were gray like his shirt, but with flecks of gold and green in them. His dark eyebrows leapt from his forehead and the look of shock on his face when he saw the actual shots in front of me was priceless. I got him good. I hadn't made him laugh, but I had made him open his eyes and look at me. I could tell by his look and his manner he was military. If the way he was so polite and called me ma'am didn't tip me off, the haircut did. He must be pretty recently a civilian if he was still sporting the high and tight. The look wasn't foreign to me, I was a military brat myself. I guess I just knew what to look for more than others did. If he was recent military, there could have been any number of things on his mind that were weighing him down like stones. There was no way a girl in a bar on a Friday night would lighten the load at all.

I knew that. I did. But there was something about that polite, stoic man who just wanted to be left alone that made me want to stay with him longer. Talk to him longer. Learn whatever I could about him. I was interested. He was interesting. I didn't make him laugh, but by the end of the evening I had forgotten my arrangement with Auggy anyway. I had forgotten about my team, our win, and my triumphant jamming. I got lost in those gray-green eyes—and I was so interested in the man they belonged to that I brought him home with me.

I had never just randomly brought a man home with me. I had gone home with men I had been dating before, but I had never picked up a stranger in a bar and brought him home. He hadn't even been hitting on me. Quite the opposite, I threw myself at him and pretty much demanded that he come home with me. He did, with no kind of argument or affirmation, and by the time I got him home to my apartment, I was losing a little of my bravado.

I had to take a shower, I had skated a bout and even though I wasn't a haggard sweaty mess by any means, I still needed to wash the funk of the night off of my body. I asked Bowen if he wanted a beer while I took a shower.

"I think that would be just fine ma'am."

Ma'am. Seriously? It was cute in the bar, but I brought him home with me for what I assumed was some consensual fun. Although since I had never done such a thing before I assumed he would be more...I don't know, eager. I left him sitting on the sofa with his beer, and by the time I was done washing and towel drying my hair I was pretty sure what I had originally thought would happen would not be. He had followed me home because I asked him to, but it didn't seem like there was any real interest there. Maybe he was just complacent because of the beer, but a feeling of shame washed over me when I thought maybe he had no interest in me. I would not be a pity fuck because he couldn't think of anything else to do when the bar closed.

Embarrassed of myself I put on a soft pair of pajamas and let my still damp hair hang down my back. I kept it in a braid because it was so wild and thick, but at night I left it down. I would let him stay on the couch tonight, but I would not push anything romantic. We didn't owe each other anything.

He was sitting on the couch in the same spot I had left him, the now empty beer bottle on sitting neatly on a coaster on the coffee table in front of him. His elbows were resting on his knees and he had his face in his hands. *Oh God*, I thought to myself, *he doesn't even want to be here. Could this be any more awkward?*

I sank down quietly on the couch next to him and taking a deep breath tried to diffuse the awkwardness of the situation. "You know I'm not usually so, um, forward. I feel like I dragged you here and I am sorry about that." The nervous laugh slipped out and I wiped my suddenly damp palms on my cotton PJ pants. Shit, this was weird. He wasn't even moving, didn't even act like he heard me at all. Maybe I was messing with fire here but I had to say something, let him off the hook somehow.

"Look, I'm sorry I was so intense. I don't want you to do anything you don't want to do. I'm actually a nice, quiet girl normally. Ok, well I am at least nice," I amended. I'm surprised my pants didn't ignite at the lie about being quiet. What the hell was that like? I wouldn't know because I never shut up. "I'll bring you a pillow and some blankets." I told Bowen, who still hadn't moved from his statue position on the couch. "The couch is comfortable I promise. I sleep out here all the time." I was babbling now, embarrassment making me unable to close my lips, the words kept tumbling out. "I'm just going to go to sleep now before I say something else stupid. I don't think I can dig out of this hole. Goodnight Bowen, I had fun tonight."

Turning to walk away, okay run away, I was stopped by a hand on my wrist. He had some fast hands when he wanted, didn't he? I was shocked to find Bowen looking at me, his gray eyes stormy with some unnamed emotion completely at odds with his silence. I hadn't even thought he was listening to me, and now, my eyes meeting his, I forgot what I had even been talking about.

"Marie," Bowen said, his voice low and smooth as his thumb traced lightly over the pulse point in my wrist. "You brought me here for a reason, I thought. Did you change your mind?" Who was this man? That was not a voice you used on someone in plain cotton pj's, that was a voice you used in the movies, when the male main character is about to rip a lady's panties off with his teeth. It was a voice that made my nipples tighten and press painfully against my thin cotton top. A shiver ran up my arm causing me to tremble. Bowen was still holding my wrist, he had to have felt it.

"Well Marie," he prodded. "Did you? Change your mind?"

My mind was empty, his voice had swept away all previous thoughts. I knew one thing though, the man in front of me was definitely showing the same interest I had been showing for most of the evening. No matter what I had been thinking previously, the Bowen who had his hand on my wrist was definitely, inarguably, interested in me. So, had I changed my mind? Even though minutes ago I was giving him the ok to just sleep on my couch? Hell no, my mind still wanted him naked and touching me, more so now he seemed on board with the idea too.

"No," I whispered softly. Suddenly shy for what was probably the first time in my entire life. "No, I haven't changed my mind." With a quick tug of his arm I was off my feet and in his lap, knees pressing into the cushions on either side of him. His mouth covered mine, hot and hungry, and I forgot that we had just met tonight for the first time. His hands roamed, touched, caressed—memorizing the shape of me.

We had sex three times. Once on the couch and again in my bed, the second time a little less intense than the first. The third I was almost asleep, curled up on my side with my head on his chest and my breasts pressed against him. I had thought he was almost asleep, until I felt his hand graze my butt—once, twice, then move lower.

Moments later we added number three to the list before we both passed out from exhaustion.

J'm a light sleeper, always have been, but even if I wasn't, I still would have woken when Bowen had his nightmare. Not that he moved so much or made any noise, but I had been sleeping with my head on his chest, and I could feel the rapid beating of his heart under my cheek, and the rise and fall of his chest as the ragged breaths left his body. PTSD. Nightmares. It affected a lot of soldiers. More so than were documented, I learned that from my dad. It was nothing to be ashamed of, but I knew he probably wouldn't want me to fawn over him, asking "are you ok?" No, he wasn't ok at all, but me calling attention to something so personal would not help either so I kept my eyes closed and stayed snuggled against him, pretending to sleep right through it, silently sending mental waves of comfort from me to him.

It didn't work, but I still feigned sleep as he slowly slid out from under me, trying not to wake me as he slipped from my bed. I didn't move even though I heard the rustling of his clothes as he got dressed. I didn't open my eyes or even breathe until I heard the quiet snick of the apartment door closing as he left. I don't know what I expected exactly, I'd brought him home for a one-night stand—there were no strings or attachments. We didn't even have each other's phone numbers or last names. I guess I just didn't expect how lonely it would be when he left after last night, or how cold the side of the bed he had been sleeping on would be. I didn't expect him to leave some of his melancholy with me, but there it was, settling over my body like a weighted blanket. I let the pull of it lull me back to a fitful sleep.

3

BOWEN

I hated writing reports. I was good at following orders, making ambulance runs and doing medical shit. I was not good at talking to people, socializing, or writing reports. Today I drew the short straw and Marcus got cleaning duty. We had just got back from a run and dropped our patient off at the emergency room and because Marcus has to make everything a stupid game, we played rock paper scissors to decide who did what. I didn't give a shit about the game, but I didn't want to do reports either. Stupid me picking rock. Stupid Marcus for picking paper.

In my mind, If I chucked a rock at a piece of paper it would for sure put a hole in it, so how I lost is beyond me but whatever. Here I was, sitting in front of the computer in our office at the hospital, and I hadn't written word one of my report because I kept thinking of Marie and her crisp apple smell. Her wild hair, wet and curling across the pillow, and her perfect breasts as they bounced in my face when I had her pogoing in my lap on her couch.

Jesus, I scrubbed my hands over my face to try to shake the thoughts from my mind. *Get it together Bowen.* No dice. She had been in the foremost part of my mind ever since I crept out of her apartment like a thief. I felt guilty about sneaking out, but I shouldn't have even been there to begin with. I didn't know if I would be around tomorrow or the next day. I didn't have my own life right. I had no business forming attachments with anyone when I didn't even have an attachment with myself. I didn't fit into my own mind; I didn't deserve to fit in to someone else's life.

But Marie was so soft. And she smelled so damn good. She also a surprisingly sexy scallop and lace tattoo on the outside of her thigh. I never thought much about tattoos, people either had them or they didn't, but when I peeled her sweet cotton pajamas down her thighs, it felt like I was unwrapping a naughty Christmas present. My dick stirred just thinking about it.

"So, this is new." Instant boner deflation. Marcus scared the hell out of me because I hadn't heard him come in to the office, nor did I hear him plop his large 6-foot 4 frame on the smallish couch we had in the corner. I must have had my head pretty far up my own ass not to hear that behemoth come in. *Jesus, Bowen.*

"What's new?" I asked in confusion. I don't even know how long he had been sitting there, but I knew that if he was there then the ambulance was clean, and that wasn't a five second job. Especially since our last transport had a shallow head wound - probable concussion. He'd been playing basketball at the city park and taken a ball to the head. It wasn't the ball that knocked him out though, it was the subsequent being knocked off balance and kissing the pavement that had done it. The guy would be all right, it was a superficial wound. But those shallow head wounds were bleeders, and that guy was no exception. If Marcus had been on cleaning duty after that, and still made it up to lounge on the couch before I noticed him, I must have been out of it.

"What's new is you sitting there talking to yourself and not making with the typee typee. Normally you are a machine about your duties. Today you are just sitting there like a turd, mumbling to yourself." Marcus thought he was funny. Sometimes he was, but I wasn't feeling it today.

"What are you talking about, man?" I was so tired. I didn't even have the energy for a verbal sparring with Marcus, which was usually one of the few bright spots I had in my day. Eat, sleep, work repeat. Marcus working to crack a smile from me was usually my thin sliver of enjoyment I allowed myself. Maybe Auggy was right. Maybe I was a broody S.O.B.

"Bowen, you haven't written a damn word of that report. You aren't even looking at the computer, man. I wasn't even trying to be quiet, but I ghosted past you without you even noticing. Also, who's Marie?"

Oh. Oh no. So, I was talking out loud to myself now too?

"She's nobody." I was quick to explain her away, but I was a liar. She wasn't nobody. She was someone I broke my rules for. Someone I let my guard down around, if even for just a couple of hours. She was someone I didn't deserve.

"Mhm yeah, you said the words but your face doesn't agree, brother. I'll leave it alone for now, but listen, I have a favor to ask. What are you doing next Friday?"

"Next Friday?" I repeated the question like a dumbass. I wasn't doing shit next Friday. If I was still around, I would probably be sitting in my apartment. I didn't have shift so maybe I would go to Auggy's, but after the last bit of excitement maybe I would stay away from Auggy's for a bit. I didn't need the old man worrying about me any more than he did.

"Yeah, next Friday." Marcus looked excited for a moment. "I usually work with another guy, but he took a second job and doesn't get the time off anymore. They need two people at each bout with Emergency Medical training or the girls can't skate, so I need to find a replacement, or the teams can't play."

I didn't know what he was talking about. Needing EMT's, or the girls couldn't skate! Wait a minute, skate?

"Marcus did you say bout?" I remembered that term, Marie had talked about it, I think. I missed a lot of the words she was saying because I was distracted by her bright green eyes and the tail of her braid as it fell into her cleavage when she turned her head too fast.

"Yeah, roller derby, man. Have you heard of it? The Homestead Wheelers skate one Friday a month. They have double bouts this month because of a reschedule, so even though they just played last week—they are playing again this Friday. I need to get another EMT in there with me, or they can't play. It would be a big letdown for the girls, as well as all the fans."

The way he said the words, *the girls*, made it sound like he was real familiar with one or more of them, and if I was better at conversing I might have thought to ask him about it. Maybe give him a hard time like he was giving me. But that wasn't the way I operated, so I left it alone. I didn't know much about roller derby, and I had never asked Marie what sport she had been playing, but I remember her saying the word bout, and I remember seeing the Homestead Wheelers logos plastered all over the shirts and bags of everyone coming in to Auggy's that night. It had to be the same thing.

"Isn't roller derby that shit from the seventies with throwing people over railings wrestler style and projectiles and shit?" No shit they would need EMT's on staff if that was the kind of game that was going down.

Marcus' laugh boomed through the small office. It caught me by surprise so I didn't have time to suppress the smile that his laugh brought out of me. "No man, they don't do that shit anymore. I mean, it's still pretty wild and depending on the team there can still be some flashy outfits, but these girls are athletes. Believe me, this is a sport and it's hard and there are real injuries. League law states we need to be there, I need a wingman for bout night, you in?"

Two thirds of me wanted to say no. One hand crept in to my pocket to touch the wrinkled square of folded up paper I kept there, reminding myself that I do not have the liberty of making future plans, of having people rely on me to not be a complete fuckup when I wasn't for sure I could do that. But there was one third of me that remembered the smell of apples and that soft skin. That part of me really wants to maybe see her again, if even just to watch her play a game without her really knowing I was there. Marcus must have taken my hesitation for a no because he threw in another bone to get me to agree.

"I'll do this report if you say you'll go. Come on man, it's just a couple of hours and it's a really good time. I promise."

Score. I was probably going to say yes anyway but I would take this from him and not feel bad about it at all.

"Deal."

4

MARIE

♥

*T*here was nothing better than the feeling of flying, and that's how I felt with my new wheels. Like I was flying. It was our warm up time on the track before the bout started and I was breaking in those 93's and getting used to the slickness they provided on the normally grabby floor. Yeah, the 93's were good.

"Everybody turn to the right!" Right transition, smooth as silk and I was skating backwards on the track, facing the other direction. "Again!" Cerberus, our team captain shouted, and I transitioned again, facing forward, in sync with the other girls on the track. Another twenty minutes of drills and it was time to line up for gear check.

Full gear all the time - that was the golden rule. Safety was always a top priority. There were so many ways to get injured in roller derby, and we took every precaution to avoid them. That was why there were gear checks and why we had two EMT's on staff for every bout. No emergency medical personnel—no skating. It sucked, but it was a stipulation of our insurance.

We normally had two of the same guys, Marcus and Blaine, but from what I understood from the coaching committee, Blaine couldn't commit to the times anymore and had to pull out. Marcus had found someone else to sit in, but I didn't know who it was. I would have liked to have checked but before I knew it, the referee was standing in front of me, checking my helmet and pads. She made me smile to show my mouth guard.

"Hey Rizz," I mumbled around my thick plastic mouth guard. "Good to see you. How's the new job?" Ref–er-Rizzo was her derby name. It was a play on her real name, just like many people's were. She was an impartial ref, so she didn't belong to any home league, but I had skated enough bouts with her we were familiar with each other.

"Hey, back at you girl!" she said as she tugged on the straps holding my helmet in place, checking to see that there were only two fingers of space between the straps and my chin. "You know, it's a change, but hey—it beats the unemployment line." Her brown eyes flashed with mirth as she gave my helmet a pat to signify I was good and sent me on my way.

Two minutes to game time. The refs were finishing gear check and our announcer was getting ready to call us in. I felt an elbow lightly tap my ribs. "Ow Connie, what the hell?" If she wanted my attention all she had to do was speak, but Connie always had a flair for the dramatic.

"Holy shit Marie, did you see the new EMT Marcus brought with him?" Connie hissed in my ear. She was tugging on my arm trying to bring me down to her level, which was pretty far down considering I was 5'9" and she was maybe 5'5".

"No, I haven't had time. I'm just glad we found a replacement for Blaine at the last minute." It was sketchy for a few days, not knowing if we would cancel the bout at the last minute. Normally we would have a few weeks to find a replacement, but since we had back-to-back bouts this month we had to hustle. *Thank you, Marcus.*

"Oh my God Marie you have to look, but don't turn around real fast, look on the sly."

How in the hell was I going to look on the sly?

"Isn't that the guy from Auggy's last week? The guy who went home with you? Isn't that Bowen?" Connie's words were a string that whip cracked my head around. I couldn't have been sly if I wanted to.

Bowen. He was here and sitting next to Marcus no less. I hadn't seen him since he snuck out of my apartment at five in the morning while I pretended to sleep. I had thought I would never see him again, but oh man did I think about him plenty. Thank goodness he wasn't looking in my direction, he was looking at the announcer who had stood up and was clearing his throat getting ready to speak.

Marcus saw me though, and he grinned and gave me a wave. Usually I would have smiled and waved back, Marcus was a good guy and involved with the league. He helped us out a lot. I was too chicken shit to be caught looking by Bowen though, so I gave him the cold shoulder and quickly turned back around.

Sorry Marcus.

"Well?" Connie insisted when I snapped my head back around. "That's him isn't it? That's the guy you had so much fun with he left his hand mark on your butt cheek, right?" Connie clapped her wrist guards together excitedly, "Oh this is great. I'm telling everyone."

"Dammit Connie," I whispered. "Don't you dare!" But I didn't have time to tell her to shut it, because Begs the announcer was calling us to the track. The time for nerves was over, at least until halftime. I crouched down into my derby stance and glided onto the track behind my teammates, my sisters. Now was not the time to pay attention to who was on the sidelines. Now was time to play.

5

BOWEN

♥

I saw her before the announcer even said her name. She was taller than the rest of the girls, and she had on a pair of lime green sparkling hot pants with black fishnet tights underneath. Rainbow striped knee socks completed the lower part of the outfit, and her team jersey had the number 612 on the back, right under the letters MRE. *MRE, Marie*, I thought to myself.

Well, that was a damn clever play on words.

If I wouldn't have made the connection with her height and with the familiar thick braid slung over her shoulder, all I had to do was see that scallop and lace tattoo peeking out from under the leg of her shorts, underneath the mesh of her tights and I knew. There was my girl, right there.

She's not your girl.

Yeah, I could tell myself that all I wanted. It didn't take away from the fact she had been mine, for a couple of hours at least. I watched her skate, watched her lift her arm and yell out the "Whoop" as the announcer said her name. MRE. Military for meal ready to eat. Well she was fucking tasty looking, and I wouldn't mind taking a bite out of her that sexy tattoo peeking out of her shorts, reminding me of what I had held in my hands just a week earlier.

80

"You staring at Marie?" I had forgotten that Marcus was even sitting next to me, that was how far gone I was. "She's a cool chick but I doubt you'd get very far with her. She can be kind of... excitable." *Excitable* must have been Marcus's version of *she talks a lot*. I smiled at the memory of her bright green eyes and constant chatter in the bar. Yeah, she did talk a lot, but that wasn't such a bad thing.

"What are you smiling about? I don't think I've ever seen you smile before in the entire six months we have worked together. Holy shit, stop it, it's creepy. You'll never get a girl like Marie with that creepy face." Marcus was messing with me, I knew it, but I couldn't help but smile wider in response. It seemed that even though I didn't care about much at all, I could still feel roused to piss in the proverbial circle.

"We met last Friday." I don't know why I even mentioned it. I didn't need for anyone to know, but just something about him insinuating that there might be something about her I wouldn't like rubbed me the wrong way. I was broken. There was nothing wrong with her, she was perfect, and fuck him for thinking any other way.

"You met last Friday? But they had a bout last Friday. They went to the after party afterwards and . . ." Marcus abruptly closed his mouth mid-sentence and then opened it again. He grinned wide and then laughed. "You mean YOU are Bruiser?"

"Marcus, I don't know what the hell you are talking about. But I'm telling you right now, I went home with her Friday night. End of story." I didn't know why he was laughing, but if it was at Marie's expense, I was going to accidentally on purpose punch him in the face.

"Bowen. Man. You don't have to tell me you had sex with her, you left a calling card on her for everyone to see." Marcus was still laughing and I was still confusion. I didn't leave a calling card, what was he talking about?

"You must have been gripping her thighs hard to leave bruises where your fingers were. You left five marks on each leg—they showed right under her shorts at practice. They were still there on Tuesday when the girls had scrimmage. Bowen, they've been giving her shit about it for the whole week." Marcus was still trying to get himself under control and he was clutching his stomach like it hurt. He was so tall that even bent over laughing he was still taller than I was sitting down. *Giant asshole*, I thought to myself.

"She wouldn't give any details either, which is funny considering she never usually shuts up." Marcus continued, still enjoying his own private joke.

"Marcus, how do you know all this?" He certainly seemed like he was in the thick of things, gossiping like a hen out of the henhouse.

"Me and some of the girls, we talk sometimes." He waggled his eyebrows up and down. A woman would have probably thought it was cute, to me it was just gross.

Yeah, *talk*. I bet he did. I knew enough about Marcus to know what his meaning of *talk* was. Marcus got around. I wanted to pick his brain a little more about Marie, but I didn't have time to because the whistle blew on the first jam and the bout began.

Forget what I thought I knew about roller derby. It was nothing like what I could remember seeing on tv when I was a little kid. These girls flew. It was hard to keep track of everyone while they were all gathered in a tight pack, maybe that was why they wore such flashy shorts and socks, so people could pick them out on the track. I didn't know, but I kept my eyes on Marie. She was easily a head and shoulders taller than anyone else on the track. That probably worked to her advantage if she was one of the girls blocking, or making a barrier. But she had the helmet cover with the star on it, and Marcus explained to me that the skater who wore the star was a jammer, their job was to slip past all the other skaters to score points. It was hard to slip in between people when you towered over them. So, she didn't.

She went through them.

I watched in awe as she used her hip to jackknife through the wall of players and sent girls scattering like bowling pins. "Holy shit, that is brutal." I exclaimed, not even realizing I had spoken out loud.

"Yeah, but legal," Marcus countered. "You can't use your arms, but you can use your chest, hips and butt to move people however you want to. Sure, she would have the advantage if she was smaller and faster, but no one can stand in her way if she just peels them off the track like that. The trick is to be faster than the other jammer. That's the hard part."

The other team had an equal number of skaters on the track and they all occupied the same track space. There were four blockers from each team. The blockers from one team were supposed to keep the opposing team's jammer from breaking through the pack. That was how points were scored. The first jammer to break through the pack, and pass every opposing skater was the lead jammer. They were the only people who could "call off the jam" and part of the game was trying to get "lead jammer" status. Even if the opposing jammer made it through the pack, the lead jammer could call off the jam before they could circle back to score any points. It sounded complicated when Marcus was explaining it, but as I watched, I understood.

Marie had blasted through the pack, but the opposing team's jammer was right behind her. I gripped the edges of my seat, silently urging Marie to go faster, get ahead of her. Marie passed the further-most blocker in the pack and the ref blew a whistle, raising one hand in the air he skated next to Marie on the inside of the track, other arm leveled at her.

"That means she's lead jammer." Marcus murmured next to me. EMT's were supposed to be like non-skating officials - impartial. We didn't dare cheer out loud for Homestead, but we wanted them to win. The opposing team's jammer was fast though, and she might not have had lead jammer status but she was quick, and she was on Marie's ass. I leaned forward in my seat, willing Marie to just go a little faster, pull ahead until the jammer with the name *Jammerwocky* on the back of her jersey closed the last few inches and hip checked her. This girl was a lot smaller than Marie, so her hip check hit her in the lower leg and knocked her right off balance. Marie went down but instead of sprawling out on the ground she hit her knees and made an ex against her hips with her arms. She did this twice and the ref blew a huge whistle. The jam was over.

"Exciting stuff huh?" Marcus grinned as I nodded. It certainly was. This was some high energy sports and I had no idea we had a team like this in town. That there were any teams like this around. Homestead didn't score any points, but they kept the opposing team from scoring any points either, and the crowd went ballistic. And even me, a guy so screwed up in the head I couldn't tell on any given day if I had feelings at all, couldn't help but get caught up in it.

By the time the whistle blew for halftime, the Wheelers were up by six points and my hands were cramped from clenching my hands into fists over watching those girls skate. They were nuts. There was no other way to say it. It was a hard thing to put into words, but I have never seen a group of females be so brutally graceful in all of my life. I couldn't look away. But the halftime whistle meant everyone took a break, and since we hadn't been called upon to check any down skaters, I figured I'd better get up and stretch my legs because I was probably just going to be sitting for the next half too.

A clap on my shoulder stopped me before I could walk out of the EMS box and I turned to see Marcus smiling like he had a secret. Truthfully, I'd been so busy watching the bout I forgot he was even there, or what I was even supposed to be doing.

"So, think you can help me out with more bouts in the future?" Marcus wiggled his eyebrows knowingly. "It's pretty fun, right? Can I count on you for the rest of the season, Bowen?"

I couldn't say meeting one girl and watching one roller derby bout gave me enough purpose to completely forget what a whacked-out head case I was. I could tell Marcus wanted me to give him that, but I couldn't. We'd worked together for a few months and I knew he wondered about the times I got quiet. Or how I never made plans more than a couple days in advance; hell, I didn't make plans at all. I knew he wondered about the square of folded paper I absently played with when I didn't have anything else to do with my hands.

He had questions all right, but I didn't have answers. But after thirty minutes of watching those girls work their asses off, the roar of the screaming fans echoing in my ears, I had to admit, I was intrigued. At least enough to see what the season held. At least long enough to learn more.

I smiled, and Marcus grinned wider. Shaking off his hand I

scanned the crowd and took my first steps out of the box. "Who are you looking for?"

He didn't have to ask; he knew damn well who I was looking for. I was looking for the girl with the thick braid over one shoulder. The one who stood a head taller than the others and had the slightest peek of scallop and lace tattoo showing form the leg of her sparkly shorts. I bet she'd be talking a mile a minute when I found her, and I wondered if her bright green eyes would turn up at the corners when she saw me. I hoped they would. And the moment I had the thought, I realized it was the first time in a long time I'd hoped for any damn thing.

And then I realized something else.

I hadn't put my hand in my pocket all night. Was the note still in there? Did I even bring it with me today? I stepped out of the box and strolled trackside with Marcus's laughter still ringing in my ears.

Fuck that note. At least for now, I had other things on my mind.

ABOUT THE AUTHOR

Desiree writes contemporary and paranormal romance in Northwest Ohio with her husband, two children, and two rowdy cats. She is a craft addicted, roller skating amateur foodie who loves anime, wine and snacks. Mostly snacks.

Connect with Desiree

facebook.com/DesireeLafawnAuthor

twitter.com/DesireeLafawn

instagram.com/desireelafawn

A SECOND CHANCE FOR LOVE

ALEXIS R. CRAIG

1

_____

"Hey, do you fool around?" A gruff voice asked as I walked to my station getting ready for my first day of work at the steel mill.

"I don't fool around. I play for keeps and I don't think you can handle it." I said back to the man, with as much steadiness as I could muster.

"Lady, you don't know what I can handle." He came back with what he must have thought was a good retort.

"And you, sir, don't know what I can handle." This time my voice didn't waver. The man looked me up and down and shook his head as he spit off to the side. Before he could say anything else the whistle blew to let us know our shift was beginning.

Three months ago, I had no idea what I was going to do with myself. Here I am, a divorced mother of two and no work history to show. A year ago, my now ex-husband had decided that he no longer wanted to be bound by the ties of matrimony or fatherhood. He had left me and the boys and took off to who knows where. I managed, with the little savings I had, to make it this far but that money was just about gone, and I had no other choice but to find a job somewhere, anywhere... as long as it was here in Pittsburgh.

That's when I saw the ad for steel workers. The mill was hiring again, and I needed a job. I had no idea if I would be hired, there weren't many women workers in the factories and mills, and I know that women were not looked at in a good light when they took men's jobs. Nonetheless, I needed a job, so I answered the ad. I hadn't heard anything for a couple of months until last week. I got called in for an interview and to my surprise, I got the job. Today is my first day and it's already started off with a bang.

When I went in for my interview, Mr. Jacobs, the man that hired me, told me that I had to be tough and that it wouldn't be easy. He also told me that he understood my situation and he commended me for trying to make good for my boys. He too grew up with a single mother and he always tried to help when he could.

I wasn't shown much of anything before I started my shift; mostly where the break room and bathroom was but nothing to do with my actual job. I watched the men around me, trying to get an idea of what I was supposed to be doing. By the time lunch rolled around, I was already exhausted. I found a spot outside in the sun to have my sandwich that I had packed earlier that morning.

"Is this seat taken?" A male voice startled me out of my thoughts.

I just shook my head no and waved my hand to the free spot; watching the tall, burly man as he moved to the spot opposite me.

"Hi ya, I'm Danny. Danny Granage." He wiped his dirty hand on the front of his dirty work apron and then held it out to me. I looked at him a moment before I did the same.

"Kelly Wiseman." I shook his hand and returned to eating my sandwich.

"Nice to meet ya, Kelly Wiseman." He smiled; it was a nice, genuine smile that lit up his face.

"Like wise, Danny Granage." I smiled back at him and returned my attention to my lunch, not wanting to make small talk.

After a few minutes of awkward silence, Danny spoke once again.

"I see ya met Joe." I gave him a strange look, not knowing who Joe was.

"The nice gentleman asking ya so politely if ya fooled around this morning." He had a crooked smile. It made him look almost boyish. I tried to mentally guess his age; 35 maybe?

"Oh, him. He's a jerk." I said matter of factly.

"That he is. Just watch your back around here. These men can be rough and crude. They'll try to get ya to quit, ya know. They don't think this is a place for a woman."

"Let me guess, women should be home making babies and keeping house?" I was not amused.

He was nodding his head in agreement, his mouth too full of the sandwich he was eating to say anything.

"I don't really care what the men around here think. I'm here because I need a job and I plan on doing that job; if I only knew what I was supposed to actually be doing." I said with a worried tone; studying my peanut butter sandwich before I took the last bite.

Danny chewed his sandwich and took a big gulp of whatever was in his cup before he was able to say anything to me. I watched as he guzzled his drink, trying not to show my amusement of him.

"Sorry. I forgot that I was with a lady." He wiped his mouth with the back of his sleeve before he continued. "I'm not surprised that nobody showed ya what to do." He laughed.

"Well, I don't think it's too funny, Danny."

"No. Sorry, again. It's not funny. I wasn't laughing because it was funny. I was laughing because, well... I don't know. Because I'm not surprised they didn't show ya anything."

I looked at him like he had lost his mind. He wasn't making any sense.

"I've got to get back inside." I put my sandwich baggie and the apple I didn't eat back in my lunch bag and stood up to leave.

"Kelly?" Danny said this as a question.

I looked at him with suspicion before I answered him.

"Yes?"

"Hold up, I'll walk in with ya." He hurriedly gathered his things and stood up to walk with me.

"Why are you being so nice? I really don't fool around." I wanted to make sure he knew I was only here to get my job done.

"I'm not being nice."

I cocked one eyebrow at him.

"I mean, I'm not being nice because I want to fool around with ya."

Again, I just stared at him. He was embarrassed and I was amused.

"Kelly, Ms. Wiseman, I just want to walk back in with ya. I can show ya, quickly, what you're supposed to be doing. That way the guys won't have any reason to go on to ya. That's all." He seemed flustered at having to explain his actions.

"Okay." I turned once more towards the entrance to the mill and he followed.

2
_____

𝓜y first five weeks in the hot, dirty mills were hard. The guys there didn't want to help a woman. If it wasn't for Danny showing me from time to time what I was supposed to do, I probably wouldn't have a job today. Why he was helping me was beyond me. He's made it rough on himself by helping me. The other men called him pansy, pussy whipped, and other ugly names, all because he was helping a woman to learn a man's job.

I started off moving carts around from one place to another, to make sure the men had an empty one when needed. When they saw that I was getting the hang of that job, I was moved to another, and then another. I'm now doing a topman's job; cleaning the blast furnace tops and stove top platforms. Next week I they might have me being a clayman or a stove tender... who knows? What I do know is that I am tougher than I thought I was, and I am not going to back down. They can throw what they want at me. I have proven to myself that I can do this job, or any other job, and no man is going to tell me otherwise.

The shift whistle blew and I headed to the time clock. Looking for Danny across the sea of men mill workers, I see him on his way to the clock. I manage to move my way through to where he was waiting in line.

"Danny!" I waved my hand at him as I got closer.

"Hey ya, Kelly." He smiled that crooked smile that I've gotten so used to.

"It's Friday!" I said with a smile.

"That it is! And about damned time!" He took his time card from the rack on the left side of the work clock, punched it in the correct spot, and placed it in the rack on the right side of the clock. I did the same, and we both walked out of the factory doors.

"So, what's your plans for the weekend?" I asked, trying not to sound too curious.

"Ah, I don't know. Might catch a movie tomorrow, other than that, I have no plans. What's your plans, Kel?" He was maneuvering a path through the sea of people heading home.

"Well, I guess that depends on you." Did I just say that?

"Me?" He stopped at his car and was about to put his key in the lock when he gave me a confused look.

"Yes, you." I lightly poked my finger at his big chest, looking at him with more assertiveness than I felt.

Danny tilted his head slightly and gave me another crooked smile. That smile.

"I thought I would thank you for helping me this past month, with a homemade dinner." I hope I wasn't being too forward, or assumptive, by asking him to dinner.

"Dinner? Kel, ya don't have to do that. I was just trying to help and be a..." He trailed off.

"A, what, Danny?" Now, he had me curious.

"I don't know. I guess I thought ya needed a friend here, and, well, I wanted to be that friend." His face was turning a shade of red that was very attractive on him.

"Ah, Danny. You were right. I definitely needed help... and a friend." I smiled up at him and the look I saw in his eyes as he smiled back at me wasn't one I'd seen before, not from him.

"So," I managed to recover. "Are you going to let me cook you dinner?"

"Well, I guess that's up to you, Ms. Wiseman." He said in a low, almost husky voice.

"I asked you, didn't I?" His gaze had me intoxicated.

"I would be honored to be your guest." He gave a slight bow with one arm behind his back.

"Great. Tomorrow? Sixish?" I had to move a step back from him, I could feel the heat between us rising, and I didn't want to make a fool of myself.

"Sixish. Yes ma'am. Where should I be tomorrow at sixish?" He sort of laughed at this.

"Oh! You need my address!" I laughed with him.

"I do if you want me to come to dinner."

I quickly gave him my address, told him the best place to park so he wouldn't get side swiped, and headed to the other side of the parking lot to where my car was parked. I could feel Danny's gaze follow me until I got to my car. When I turned back to look at him, he waved and got into his car and turned on the ignition.

What are you doing, Kelly? I thought to myself. *What happened to no ties? What happened to no men?* I turned the key, put the car in drive, and told myself to shut up thinking.

The door was cracked on my apartment when I got home. I could hear the boys rough housing and Mrs. Markle telling them to quieten down. I pushed the door open and stood there in the doorway. There before me was Mrs. Markle with the television on, her cigarette between her red painted lips, the ash so far up that it was about to fall off, and the boys in the hallway wrestling over who knows what.

I cleared my throat loud enough for everyone to hear me over all the noise. Mrs. Markle looked up startled and the boys stopped their wrestling to see who had entered the apartment.

"Kelly, you're finally home. These boys of yours don't know how to listen at all!" She stood up and put her ashy cigarette out in the ashtray.

Mrs. Markle was around sixty years old and dressed as if she was thirty. Her tight knit pants and low cut tank showed more than it should. She always wore the brightest red lipstick and blue eyeshadow. Her hair was cut short and dyed the darkest of blacks. She got along well with the boys and she just lived across the hall. The best part was, she didn't charge me anything to watch the boys as long as I bought her two packs of cigarettes each payday.

"I'm sorry, Mrs. Markle, have they been bad?" I looked at Paul and Henry still on the floor, now sitting next to each other discussing something that seemed to be super important to them.

"Nah, your boys couldn't be bad if they tried." She waved her hand at me and turned the television off.

"Thank you, Mrs. Markle." I handed her the two packs of Kool's and followed her to the front door.

"See you on Monday, babe." Mrs. Markle padded her way out the door and across the hall to her own apartment. When she closed her door, I closed mine and went to the chair she had just vacated.

"Come here, boys." I had to talk to the boys and make sure they understood that they had to be on their best behavior tomorrow when Danny came over.

"Yes ma'am." Paul and Henry said in unison as they sat on the ottoman in front of me.

I couldn't believe they were growing up so fast. How could their father leave these two beautiful children? No goodbye, no see you later, just gone. How does a man live with himself knowing he isn't taking care of his own? No matter how many times I tried to understand, I just couldn't.

"You two look mighty handsome this evening." I reached out and pulled their t-shirts down and straightened their clothes.

"Thank you, momma." Henry, the youngest of my boys, didn't mind when I made over them. He was only six, but he was the one that knew when I needed hugs.

"Thanks, mom." Paul said as he tried to wriggle away from my tugging of his clothes. Paulie was almost nine, and he was a little more independent than Henry. He didn't like the fuss of motherly affections. How did he grow up so fast?

"Momma, why do you have to leave us with Mrs. Mawgle? She's smells funny." Henry had trouble saying some words, especially those that had the "k" sound, or those with an "r" sound.

"Mrs. Mar-kle, Henry. Slow down and try to say it right." I tried to help him as much as I could, but he didn't seem to catch on too well with his sounds.

"But why do you have to leave us with her?"

"Oh, love, momma has to work, so we can keep this apartment and have food to eat." How do you explain to a six year old why you have to leave him and go to work? They just don't understand.

"Yeah, dummy. If John hadn't left us, Mom wouldn't have to leave us with that old bat." Paulie thumped Henry on the forehead as he said this.

"Paulie! That's enough of that! I will not have you thumping your brother on the head! And, I will not have you refer to your father by his name!" When did he start talking like this?

"But, Mom."

"No but Mom me, young man. Apologize to your brother, now!" I said sternly.

"Sorry, I thumped you dummy."

"Paul Edward Wiseman." I looked him directly in the eye, letting him know that I would not tolerate this kind of behavior.

"Sorry, I thumped you, Henry." He said to his brother and then looked at me as if asking if he did it correctly that time.

"That's better. Now, I need to talk to the two of you about something."

I spent the next thirty minutes explaining that we would have company for dinner tomorrow, who the person was coming to dinner, why I was having a man come to dinner, and that no, this man was not going to be their new daddy. By the end of the conversation I was more exhausted than when I walked through the door that evening.

The boys took their baths while I made dinner. After dinner they brushed their teeth and we settled in to watch The Brady Bunch and then The Partridge Family. Poor Henry was already asleep before The Partridge Family went off, so I carried him to bed and tucked him in. Paulie was getting into bed as I kissed Henry on the forehead.

"Mom?" Paulie asked quietly.

"Yes, Paulie?" I walked over and sat on the edge of his bed, tucking the cover around him.

"I know how tired you are when you come home. I'm sorry that I'm not old enough to get a job, but I will one day and you won't have to work anymore." His words broke my heart. Tears immediately burned my eyes.

"Oh, Paulie, don't you worry about things like that. You just help take care of your brother for me, okay?" I combed his hair over out of his face with my hand.

"Yes, ma'am. I love you, mom." He turned onto his side and closed his eyes.

"I love you, Paulie." I took another glance at my boys and right then I knew that no matter who or what came at me, I was going to make it.

3

I got up early and got the boys ready so we could head down to the strip market to get some groceries for dinner tonight. We spent the morning walking along the market picking out the best ingredients for the beef stew I wanted to serve with the perogies, both potato and cabbage. I picked up some apples for a cooked sweet apple side to accompany it all.

I allowed the boys to pick out some candy for later, and then we headed back to our apartment. I sent the boys to clean their rooms and I set out rolling the dough for the perogies. The time went by faster than I expected. I looked over at the clock on the kitchen wall and it was already four o'clock. I still had to take a shower and get ready!

I set the six cans of Duquesne Pilsener beer in the ice box and two glasses in the freezer to get frosty, and then headed to the shower. I was starting to get a little anxious now that it was getting closer to dinner. Would he like what I made? Maybe he didn't like perogies. Nonsense, everyone likes perogies, but what if he didn't?

I quickly towel dried my hair and applied some makeup. I wrapped my robe around me and went across the hall to my bedroom. I had laid out my pink dress but now I was wondering if it was too much. After all, it was only a friendly dinner, right? I looked at the clock next to my bed and decided that I didn't have time to look for anything else, so I pulled on my pink dress, looked for my pearl earrings, couldn't find but one so I clipped on my opals. I rushed back to the bathroom and pulled a brush through my half dry hair, decided to pull it back in a loose ponytail and I was finished.

"Momma, there's a man here that says you're expecting him." Henry yelled from the living room. *Oh my, am I ready for this?*

"Momma!"

I rushed out of the bathroom and into the living room where my youngest was rudely yelling for me. There Henry stood, guarding the door like a sentry standing guard at the entrance of our castle. Then there was Danny, a rose in one hand and a bottle of wine in the other, standing in the doorway towering over my little soldier.

"Danny, hi. I'm sorry about not answering the door myself. Please, come in."

"Is it alright with you, sir, if I enter your abode?" He addressed this to Henry.

"My what?" Henry looked up at this giant man with a confused expression.

"Your abode, it's another name for your home. May I enter?" Danny had a serious look on his face but an amused tone in his voice.

"Oh. Yeah, sure. Come in, but wipe your feet." Henry turned away from the door and headed in to the living room.

"Of course." Danny wiped his feet with exaggeration to make sure that Henry had no reason to tell him again.

"Dinner will be on the table in just a few. Would you like a beer?" I was nervous but I hoped it didn't show.

"A beer would be great! But, what about..." He waved the bottle of wine that he was holding.

"I'll put it in the fridge to chill while I get the table ready. We can have it with dinner." I take the bottle of wine from him and head towards my tiny kitchen.

My boys were watching Danny's every move with sharp eyes. I sure hope Danny's not scared off easily.

"Whatcha watchin on the TV?" He addressed this to the two boys.

"Wrastlin. You like wrastlin?" This was asked in a very serious tone from Paulie.

"Yessir, I sure do. I think it's probably the best thing to watch on TV." Danny knew how to sound serious right back.

"Well, you can watch with us if ya want, I guess."

"Much obliged..." He didn't know my boy's names.

"Danny, this is Paulie, my oldest. And this is Henry."

"I'm not the oldest." Henry was so proud of that fact.

"Oh, well, that's because only one can be the oldest, unless you're twins." Danny replied to the young Henry.

"We're not twins, silly." Henry laughed, grabbed Danny's hand, and pulled Danny into the living room to watch the TV with them.

I turned my attention to placing the wine in the fridge to cool and then I began to set the table. Within fifteen minutes I had the table set with the dishes, the food in bowls and placed on the table as well. I called out to the boys and Danny to let them know that dinner was ready, and they came without hesitation.

For the next hour we chatted about which wrestler was the best and whether or not the Steelers had a chance at the Super Bowl this year. It seemed we talked about anything and everything but work, which was okay with me. I wanted to leave work at work when I came home. My boys didn't need to know the dirty details of me having to put up with snide remarks about me being a female in a man's world.

It was getting a little late and the boys were getting tired. I told them to tell Danny goodnight and to go brush their teeth. Of course, they hem-hawed around, as young boys do, but then they went off to brush their teeth and to put their jammies on.

Henry came out after changing and walked up to Danny. He had such a serious look on his face and Danny and I were worried that something was bothering him.

"Do you like my mommy?" Straight to the point!

Danny looked a little startled by the question coming from my youngest, but he recovered quickly. He moved to put his elbows on his knees and leaned forward so that he could be on Henry's level.

"Well, sir, I guess I do. Is that okay with you?" Danny was trying to be as serious as Henry had been.

"Ya won't make her cry, will ya?" Oh, my dear son. This brought tears to my eyes and I tried not to let him see them.

Clearing his throat, Danny glanced over at me before he spoke again.

"Henry, I wouldn't dream of doing anything to make your mama cry. I like her very much, and, with your's and Paulie's permission, I'd like to come by and visit again." Danny's eyes hadn't left mine as he said this to Henry.

"Mommy, can I give him my permission?"

"Do you want to give him your permission, Henry?" I tried to be just as serious.

"Yes, ma'am. I think he might be a pretty good fella."

"Well, then by all means, Henry. If you like him and want him to come back for a visit, then you may give him your permission." I smiled at my little man.

"Okay, then. You can come back, but if you ever make my mommy cry, I will have Paulie beat you up." He held his little hand out to Danny for a handshake. Danny took Henry's little hand in his giant one and shook it like he was shaking a grown man's hand.

"I wouldn't have it any other way, Henry."

"Goodnight, mommy. Goodnight, Danny." The little man turned and headed for the room he shared with his brother. Paulie was standing in the doorway as Henry walked past him.

"Yes, Paulie? Everything alright?" I asked my oldest.

"Goodnight, mom. Goodnight, Danny." He turned to go back into his bedroom but stopped and turned back to face us.

"Danny, I will beat you up." Paulie also was so serious.

"I wouldn't doubt that one bit, Paul." Danny looked at Paulie with sincere respect in his eyes.

Paulie turned and went to his room, shutting the door after him.

Danny looked over at me with a look that I hadn't seen before. His eyes were speaking volumes to mine. I could see that he wanted to say something, and it was something important.

"What is it, Danny?" I was becoming concerned that my boys had scared him with their talk.

"Kelly, I will never understand how a man could ever leave a woman as fine as you, and two boys as brave as yours."

"Well, Danny, that makes two of us." The sincerity in his voice had the tears resurfacing. This time they flooded over and ran down my cheeks.

Danny got up from his chair and moved over to the sofa and sat next to me. He placed his large arm around my shoulders and pulled me to him, stroking my hair as he told me it was all going to be okay.

"I meant it, ya know."

"Meant what, Danny?" I raised my tear stained face from his shoulder, realizing I had left a wet spot where my tears had fallen.

"What I said to Henry. I really would like to see more of you, and the boys."

"Really?"

"Yes, ma'am, really."

"I would like that." I smiled up at him.

He looked at me for a long minute before he lowered his head and kissed me lightly on the lips.

"I better go." He rose from his place on the sofa next to me and pulled me up with him.

"Do you have to?" I asked, knowing what his answer would be.

"Yes, Kelly. I really think I should. I want nothing more right now than to stay here and hold you all night, but I don't think that would look good for you."

He was right, of course, but I really didn't care what anyone thought anymore.

"Alright, Danny. I'll see you at work on Monday." I stepped in close to give him a hug around his waist. He wrapped his strong arms around me and gave me a little squeeze before he let me go and headed for the door.

"I'll see ya in my dreams tonight, Kelly." He opened the door and stepped out of my apartment, leaving me wishing I had asked him one more time to stay.

4

---

*P*ittsburgh is a bustling town. The steel mills are booming, and the town is growing. It even looks like our football team might make it to the Super Bowl this year! There's talk that some of the mills might have to lay some people off, but I don't see how that could be true. Our factory just hired another woman and four other men. I'm not going to worry about all that until I see a slow-down in work. Right now, I'm working tons of overtime and I don't see a slow-down in sight.

It's been two months since Danny came to my apartment for dinner. He's been back a few times to say hi to the boys and eat with us. It's nice having a male influence for the boys to look up to. It's also nice having Danny around just to talk to. After the boys go to bed, we'll sit on the sofa and watch television. He'll usually put his arm around me and sometimes we'll talk about work. Danny will always kiss me goodnight when he leaves.

I don't know why, but it seems like he's almost afraid to do more than just give me a goodbye kiss. Maybe he doesn't want more than what we already have. Could it be because we work together? He doesn't show public affection at work, and I don't blame him for that. The other men would have a field day with that if they knew. But, at the same time, I feel like he's trying to hide 'us.' I don't even know if there is an 'us.'

I turn my bedside lamp off and try to still my mind so I can get some sleep. Tomorrow, I'm going to ask Danny if he wants to go out for dinner. I'll have Mrs. Markle watch the boys so we can have a real date. I'm sure she won't mind, and I want to have a little bit of time with just Danny. I need to ask him to define 'us.'

The whistle goes off for lunch and I'm so ready to just sit down for a few minutes. I grab my lunch out of my locker and head outside to my usual spot. I unwrap my sandwich and look around for Danny. I didn't see him come in this morning and I haven't seen him around any of the work areas today. I look back towards the doors of the mill and still don't see him. I wonder if maybe he's sick. It's not like Danny to miss work.

Looking at my watch, I only have five minutes before the whistle goes off letting us know it's time to go back to work. I put my sandwich wrapper back into my lunch bag and head back to the factory. I rush into the bathroom to relieve myself and wash my hands, and then I quickly make my way to the time clock. I find Danny's card and notice that he didn't punch in at all today. The whistle blows and I punch my card. I place it in the correct slot and go back to work. It's going to be a long rest of the day wondering what could possibly be wrong with Danny.

The end of the day whistle just went off, I made my way to the time clock and then headed out the door to my car. I always park out to the far end of the lot because it's actually closer to the gates. It only takes a couple of minutes to reach my car, but today I took my time. I was worried about Danny, and why he didn't show up for work today.

"Hey! Kelly!" I could hear someone calling my name, but didn't see anyone looking my way, so I turned back towards my car.

"Kelly! Wait up!" It was Marcus calling me. He worked in the same area as Danny. I remember Danny mentioning that they were buddies.

"Hey, Marcus. Do you know why Danny didn't come to work today?" I had reached my car and was leaning up against it when he caught up with me.

"Didn't you hear?" He looked at me puzzled.

"Hear what, Marcus? Is something wrong with Danny?" Now I was standing straight up and the worry was overwhelming.

"No, not that I know of."

"Then, what, Marcus?"

"Oh, yeah. Danny was laid off this morning."

"What?" No, this can't be true.

"Sure was. He came in this morning and the boss man caught him before he clocked in. Took him to the side and then Danny got back in his car and left."

"Oh, my. Why? Why would they lay him off?" My mind was running a mile a minute. If they laid him off, I could be next.

"It wasn't just him, Kel. They also laid off Joe Thorndyke, Mike Wellman, and a couple of other guys." I just can't believe it. Why would they lay those men off, that have been here for years, and keep me?

"Thank you, Marcus. I appreciate you letting me know." I smile at him and unlock my car door.

"I would have told you earlier, Kelly, but I didn't get a chance to get over to you."

"I understand, Marcus. I have to go, thank you, again." Marcus tips his cap and turns to walk to the bus stop.

I have to find Danny. I have to talk to him. I'm sure he's devastated with being laid off. I get in my car and rush home. I want to see if Mrs. Markle will watch the boys just a little longer so I can go to Danny's and talk to him.

5

*P*arking my car, I get out, lock my doors, and head to my apartment building across the street. I manage the stairs to my floor and open the door to my apartment. I stepped in and shut the door behind me, not really paying attention to anything except my thoughts.

"Mommy!" Henry yelled when he noticed me shutting the door.

"Hen..." I look towards my youngest son playing in the living room with Paulie. Sitting on the sofa watching them was Danny.

"Danny?" He turned at the sound of my voice.

"Hi ya, Kel. I hope you don't mind that I stopped by. I let Mrs. Markel go so she could get a manicure." He rolled his eyes and smiled at me.

"Danny? Are you okay? Marcus told me what happened this morning."

"Oh, that. I'm fine." He waved it off like it didn't matter in the least.

"You're fine? You lost your job!" I walk over to him and sit on the sofa next to him.

"Kelly, it was just a job. I was eventually going to quit sooner or later, anyways."

"What? I don't understand, Danny." He had me so confused, I'm not sure that I was even hearing him correctly.

"I was going to talk to ya about it, but, well..." He ran his hands through his thick hair.

"Talk to me about what, Danny? I don't understand what's going on. Please, enlighten me." I was getting frustrated by the minute.

"My grandfather owns one of the busiest restaurants in town. I used to work there growing up, and I still pitch in when he needs someone in the evenings."

"Yes?" I was still lost.

"Well, my father wants nothing to do with the business. My grandfather is getting older and he can't handle the work anymore. He was talking about shutting the restaurant."

"And?"

"And, Kelly, I told him I would run it for him." He smiled so big, as if he was so proud of his decision.

"You're going to run a restaurant?" I didn't know whether to laugh or cry. I didn't even know he could cook!

"Not just any restaurant. The Center Square!"

"The Center Square is your grandfather's?" I was stunned. The Center Square just happens to be one of the top restaurants in the city!

"Yes, it was my grandfather's. It is now mine."

"Danny! I'm so happy for you. Are you sure you're up to running a busy restaurant, though?"

"I'm sure, Kel. I've run it a few times when my grandfather needed to go home to rest."

"Wow, and I have been so worried about you losing your job." I lean over and hug him.

"Sorry, I guess I should have talked to you about it first."

"Why on earth would you need to talk to me about it? It's a great opportunity, and you're apparently happy about it." I pull back from him and rest my hands in my lap.

"Well, I didn't get laid off, I came in and quit."

"But, Marcus said..."

"The bossman must have told him to save face, I don't know. I hope you're not upset with me." He looked nervous for some reason.

"Upset with you? Of course not, Danny. I'm glad that you weren't laid off."

Danny looks over at the boys and winked. They giggled and came over to stand beside Danny. Something was up and and I was starting to get a little nervous.

"Mommy, if you could have one wish..." Henry started.

"Any wish in the whole wide world." Paulie interrupted Henry.

"What would it be?" They both asked in unison.

"Well, hmmm... I'm not sure. What's going on, boys?"

"Think of something, Mom." Paulie was excited, he was fidgeting with his shirt tail.

"One thing. Anything?" I asked the boys, trying to play their little game.

"Anything." They said together.

"Well, I guess I would wish to be able to spend more time with you boys." And, that was my biggest wish.

The boys giggled and glance over at Danny.

"Danny, can you please tell me what's going on?" I could see that he knew something.

"Yes, Kelly, I think I can." He looks at the boys and stands up.

Taking a small box out of his pants pocket, Danny gets down on one knee and takes my left hand in his. All of a sudden, I realize what he's about to do and tears begin to burn my eyes.

"Kelly... Ms. Wiseman, I fell in love with you the day you walked into the mill, and into my life. I have grown to love your boys, and I have already asked their permission, but now I'm asking yours. Will you marry me, and make me the happiest man in Pittsburgh?" He takes a deep breath and lets it out slowly, as if he couldn't believe he got the words out.

"Danny Granage, I would be honored to be your wife..." I look at the boys, their eyes all lit up with excitement. "... as long as my sons are okay with it."

"We are! We are, mommy!" Henry jumps up and down.

"Paulie?"

"Yes, mom! Please marry him. He'd make a great day."

"Danny, are you ready to have a ready made family?" I was a little worried at his answer, but he did ask the boys first.

"I am so ready, Kelly, that I have asked them if I could be their daddy."

"Their daddy? As in?" Is he saying what I think he's saying?

"I want to adopt them as my own." He was smiling at me as the boys wrapped their arms around his neck.

"Oh, Danny." That's all I could get out.

"And, I would like to try and give them a baby sister. That is if you would like another child."

"I would love that! But, I don't know how I can carry a baby and work where I work. I just don't see that happening."

"Well, Kelly, that's another thing I wanted to talk to you about. What do you think about coming to work with me at the restaurant?"

"At the restaurant?" I really didn't know how to answer that.

"You can work at the mill for a couple of more months, just until Christmas is over, and then you can come and help at the restaurant. If you're fine with that."

"I'm totally fine with that, Danny. But, there's something I have to say to you."

"Okay?" He said this as a question, as if he was afraid of what I had to say.

"I love you, Danny Granage. With my whole heart, I love you." I leaned forward and placed a big kiss on his mouth, hugging him tight. The boys laughed and hugged us both.

"We're finally going to be a family. A real family." Paulie had a tear fall down his cheek.

"Yes, Paulie, we are!" We all had happy tears filling our eyes.

"Ya'll have made me the happiest man alive. I will have a beautiful wife and two strong, handsome sons. A man couldn't ask for more."

Not the end, but a new beginning

ABOUT THE AUTHOR

Alexis R. Craig lives in North Carolina, half way between the beach and the mountains. She writes all forms of romance – Contemporary, sweet, erotica, romantic suspense, new adult, etc. She's a hopeless romantic and believes that everyone deserves a little love.

Connect with Alexis

facebook.com/TheAlexisCraig

twitter.com/TheAlexisCraig

instagram.com/TheAlexisCraig

ETERNAL STEEL BEGINNINGS

REXI LAKE

Rexi Lake

1

*H*er body was on fire. Burning like she was encased by the sun. She moaned, a long low sound that echoed in the space around her. Space she couldn't see, could only feel. Complete and utter darkness enveloped her. Enveloped *them.*

"Please," she whimpered. She didn't know who she begged, but she trusted him. She knew he was there. And she knew they belonged in this place together.

"Not yet."

The dark voice, accompanied by a near growl, made her tremble.

Hot air rushed across one nipple before it was enveloped by the warm heat of his mouth. Sharp pinpricks of pain raced through her as his teeth closed over her sensitive flesh and left her breathless and reaching toward that pinnacle of pleasure.

La petite mort. The little death. She understood the comparison so much better than ever before. And she was desperate for it.

The pain lessened as his tongue swept across her aching breast. His fingers stroked over her hip, dancing along her side and leaving a trail of goosebumps behind.

She raised her hips from the bed, her legs spreading as she tried in vain to position herself beneath his body, to align them perfectly for the ultimate pleasure she sought.

"Greedy, aren't you?" His voice rumbled and she felt the vibrations of his words against her flesh.

"Fuck me, already," she whispered harshly. Demanding. She was rarely so direct. But she'd ached for too damn long.

"You aren't ready for me yet."

"I am. I swear." Her body twisted, seeking fulfillment as she begged for release from the bonds he'd wrapped around her pleasure. Somehow. She was riding that edge where she could easily tumble into a mind-shattering orgasm. But instead, he kept her balanced. Poised on the ledge as he drove her mindless with his fingers, his lips, his teasing.

Her body shook from the overload of sensations that sparked her nerves and tweaked her senses. The lightest of touches was almost painful with pleasure.

"You aren't," the voice insisted. "But you will be. Soon."

She moaned again. This time it was a needy, whimpering sound that voiced her disappointment in his answer. She was ready. She was beyond ready. She just needed him to *move*. To take her over that edge by pushing his cock into her and finally - *finally* - claiming her as his.

She pulled at her arms, intending to hold him close and shift herself where she wanted to be. But they were held fast in the softest strips of cloth. So soft, that until she'd tried to move, she hadn't noticed their presence.

He chuckled, sitting away from her and leaving her shivering as the cool air wrapped around her heated body.

"Patience," he cautioned.

She groaned, her fingers flexed into fists as she realized she was well and truly caught. She had no control. Nothing to give her leverage to let her claim what she desperately wanted. *Him.*

"I need," she said softly.

"I need as well," he answered.

"Take it. Take me." She insisted.

"When you're ready," he replied.

She was ready. She was beyond ready. She was aching and needy and her body was weeping for his claim.

"When?" she asked, desperate for an answer.

"Soon. Soon." The words were soft, hopeful.

Then his lips touched hers and words fled from her mind as he took her mouth in a slow, sensual kiss that stole her very breath and fed her his own. "You are my heartbeat," he murmured. "My eternity. And when you are ready, you will find me." His words whispered through her soul. His lips never left hers. But she heard him.

She cried out against his kiss, an ache blossoming from her chest and spreading through her limbs. Her heart stuttered. A beat skipped once. Twice.

*L*izzie's eyes flew open as the hazy light of dawn crept into her bedroom. Her sheets were soaked with sweat and her body trembled with unfulfilled desire. A desire she knew wouldn't be satisfied with her own hand. It never was. In fact, it only made things worse most of the time.

She squeezed her legs together and wrapped her arms around one of the pillows nearby, hugging it to her chest as she let the trembling wrack her, shaking the need from her body as she cried silent, painful tears.

For months she'd been having the same dream. She didn't know how she got into his bed, or who he was, or anything about him really. But she *knew* he was hers. She *knew* she was his. And the desperate begging increased each night. The aching inside her body had become overwhelming and overpowering. Every nerve sparked and shocked her, like she was filled with endless sparklers, all lit up and crackling beneath her skin. If she closed her eyes, sometimes she could still feel the heat of his breath against her skin.

But come dawn, each day, she was pulled from him. The first time, she'd thought she was having a heart attack. The pain in her chest had been excruciating and terrifying. The shortness of breath and the endless ache in every part of her body hadn't helped.

Her doctor had assured her that she had not experienced any heart attacks, strokes, heart murmurs, or anything else. She knew because she'd insisted on every possible test. By now, half the heart and pulmonary specialists within the UPMC system knew her by name.

She hadn't mentioned anything to her family though. She didn't want them to worry if there was nothing to worry about. Instead, as every test was negative, she had to wonder if perhaps her grandmother's stories and predictions were coming true. Fae-born, her grandmother claimed. The blood of those magickal creatures that were often portrayed as tiny fairies. Or perhaps she was simply going crazy. She really hoped it was the former. Sometimes she hoped it was the latter. If only because believing in creatures from fairytales and folklore seemed too surreal. After all, how could creatures like mermaids and demons and vampires hide in the modern world of technology? Wouldn't that be impossible?

But it wasn't. She knew that. She herself was sensitive to the feelings and emotions of people she came in contact with. She could read them by the haze of color that she saw surrounding their features. A glow, translucent and yet it could be blindingly bright or terrifyingly dark. Most people never saw the colors. They might feel the energy, but they didn't know it. Not like Lizzie did. Still, being a little sensitive to the energy of others didn't equate to being magickal. Not like Tinker Bell or Morgan le Fay, or even the mischievous Puck. Nor was she a magician, capable of pulling a rabbit from a hat. She simply knew who to trust and who to avoid.

Slowly, as the sun climbed higher in the sky and the rays filtered across her bed, the trembling ceased and her body temperature regulated back to normal. The ache didn't disappear though. For the past two weeks, it had grown and stayed with her, even throughout the day. Before, it had faded after an hour or two. Now, she lived with this feeling of emptiness in her heart. In her soul.

Soon, my eternity.

The words whispered deep inside her soul. The aching promise of him. The promise of *them*.

She groaned and forced herself to sit up. Slowly, with greater care than she'd had even two weeks before, she stood and made her way on trembling legs to the bathroom. A lukewarm shower would help. An explanation would be even better. Her grandmother had never said anything about dream lovers or heartache so physically painful.

As she stood beneath the spray and gently washed away the night's desires that had settled over her skin, she knew she had to visit the one person who could give her that explanation.

After her appointment, she'd run to Grandma Lizbet's. The woman was nearing ninety and still more spry and stubborn than anyone Lizzie had ever encountered. While long retired from the waitressing job she'd had as a younger woman, she still kept busy. Book clubs, card games, and the occasional psychic service. Grandma Lizbet's life was never dull and never slow. Lizzie hoped she could get a moment or two alone with the woman to talk without an audience.

A deep sigh escaped as she turned off the water and followed her routine to finish getting ready. It was still early enough that she could make a nice cup of coffee before she had to leave.

2

An hour later, she was sitting in traffic on Route 28 instead of driving at the posted forty-five miles per hour speed limit. It wasn't where she wanted to be at eight in the morning. But that was where she was. Still, ten miles from her exit, hoping she would make it to her nine o'clock meeting, and wishing for a second cup of coffee. She growled at the car in front of her. Not anticipating the backed up traffic, she'd left her apartment with, what she'd assumed, was plenty of time to reach her destination *and* grab another cup of coffee.

Wrong.

She'd be lucky to make it on time sans the coffee.

Thirty-five minutes later, two miles down the road, and a few unpleasant phrases muttered under her breath, she inched past the bright swirling lights of two cop cars, an ambulance, and a fire truck blocking half the lanes and surrounding four vehicles in various states of crushed and twisted metal. As the road opened up, she shot forward. Twenty-five minutes. She could make it with five minutes to spare if she didn't hit any more issues. She needed this appointment to go well.

Six minutes before nine she parked her car outside a large commercial property in Aspinwall. Taking a deep breath, she straightened her jacket and walked into the large, open entrance of a home that had been renovated into offices.

"Elizabeth?" An older woman was waiting beside a built-in reception desk.

"Yes." She held her hand out. "I'm Elizabeth Benton."

"Charlotte Noir. It's a pleasure to finally meet you." The woman smiled with a serenity that seemed to emanate from her. "Mr. Stein will be here in a moment, but he instructed me to show you around while we wait."

"Excellent. I must say, this reception is wonderfully set up." She glanced around at the area they stood in, brightened by the light filtering in through the large windows that took up the front wall.

"I think you'll be pleased by the setup. I know we had some issues with your specifications at the outset of this process, but the location here in Aspinwall is ideal. You have the Waterworks shops just a few miles down the road, plus a UPMC hospital. And the open area here can be renovated with a few walls removed to turn it into the space you want." As Charlotte spoke, outlining some pros for the location, she led Lizzie deeper into the building.

"Don't forget the dinosaur out front," Lizzie added, when the woman took a breath.

"I have to admit, that's one of my favorite parts of this property." A deep voice behind her had Lizzie turning swiftly to face the newcomer. He was tall, darkly handsome, and had an aura that screamed danger to her. Not at all what she'd expected of the realtor she'd hired. Although, he was wearing a suit and a matching, tailored jacket that said he was there for business.

"Mr. Stein?" she inquired.

"No. I'm Eric Lawson. The new owner of this property."

Piercing blue eyes crackled with interest at her. Lizzie caught her breath as she felt the intensity of his stare wash over her. Having lived with the ability to read people's auras all her life, she was used to immediately having a sense of a person. However, no one had ever caused her to react so powerfully - *so viscerally* - to their presence. No one except her dream lover. But that was an entirely different type of reaction.

"I'm sorry, sir. When did you acquire the place? We weren't made aware of any offers being on the table." Charlotte stepped forward, a frown on her features.

"Just this morning, as a matter of fact. I must say, I was a little startled to find the front doors open when I arrived, but given the speed of my purchase, I'm not surprised there was another interested buyer." He smoothly replied to the older woman whose presence had redirected his attention away from Lizzie.

Lizzie kept the smile on her face in place, even as she sighed inwardly at the loss of the building. "Congratulations. You've acquired a beautiful space." She turned to Charlotte. "The area is definitely what I'm looking for. Please tell Mr. Stein that if another location along Freeport Road opens, I'll be happy to look at it for my needs."

"I'm so sorry, Ms. Benton." The woman's frown hadn't disappeared. If anything, it had become more pronounced.

"You can only do what you can, Charlotte. The place is quite lovely and would have suited nicely for my gallery and workspaces, but I'm sure you'll find another space." Lizzie assured the woman.

"Are you an artist, Ms. Benton?" That smooth, deep voice interrupted again.

Lizzie shifted her gaze back to the man that was too interesting and too dark for her better interests. "I am, Mr. Lawson," she answered politely.

"What kind of art?" He pressed.

"Charcoal drawings and watercolors," she replied. It wasn't that she didn't want to discuss her art. In fact, she usually adored talking about her work and the time and effort and passion she poured into her pieces. But this man, this Eric Lawson, was off. There was something her senses were screaming at her. She couldn't place it. She couldn't identify it. But there was something. Dangerous? Maybe. She didn't feel threatened though, just thrown off balance. And that was unsettling. She didn't like feeling unsettled.

"As I set up the space, I'll be looking for artwork to display in both the waiting areas and back rooms. Perhaps I could view what you have available?" He arched a brow in question. The movement was as much a challenge as a demand. It was like he knew he threw her off kilter.

She could turn him down, but the place was two floors of beautiful offices and that could mean a big sale for her. Could she afford to say no when she was struggling to break away from the nine-to-five world and launch herself as an artist?

Reaching into her purse, she pulled one of her business cards from her wallet and handed it to him. The card was simple. Her name, her website, and a stunning black and white background that was a small section of a larger work of hers that featured the Pittsburgh skyline.

"You can view my available pieces here and purchase them. Contact information is on the site as well." She managed to hold back the strange shiver that ran through her when his fingers grazed hers as he took the card. Her nerves sparked briefly. Her breath caught in her throat as the light touch brought a flood of memories with it. Dream memories. *Him.*

"Thank you, Ms. Benton. I'll be sure to do that."

Lizzie nodded, not capable of speaking just then as she fought to bring her racing heart and erratic breathing under control without him taking notice. She turned to Charlotte and managed a tight smile. "Please, let me know if you find anything else." She didn't know how she uttered the words when she couldn't find the right commands to send to her lungs to draw breath. But she managed. Somehow. She needed Grandma Lizbet.

"Of course, Elizabeth." Charlotte returned the smile as Lizzie moved as swiftly as possible to the door. She had to skirt around Eric Lawson and the intense stare of his that burned her with fires that didn't exist and sent flames licking along her skin that brought every ache alive in her body.

She didn't look back as she started her car and turned back the way she'd come. Grandma Lizbet had better have some free time.

Lizzie couldn't handle waiting if her grandmother wasn't there. She didn't know if she could survive the rage of need that was spiraling deep inside her and making every breath a desperate attempt to draw cooling air inside her. She blasted the AC as she drove. Even in the early Spring, fifty degrees and with a light breeze, she was sweating from the internal fire that refused to be banked.

3

*E*ric couldn't believe he'd found her. After searching for four months, he'd returned to Pittsburgh, a place he'd always felt drawn to, in a last-ditch attempt to find her. His eternity. His dream lover. The mate he was meant to have.

He'd sunk to the floor the moment he'd seen the realtor's secretary out the door. He'd taken a gasping breath. A deep inhale that had brought with it the lightest scent of her and left him pressing a hand to his chest. Just above the spot where his heart had started beating again the moment he'd heard her heartbeat. The unused organ had sat in his chest for centuries. Waiting for the one heart that it would beat in rhythm to. Her blood sang to him in a way he'd never heard before. Her heartbeat was his. She was his eternity. Wrapped in a bright, sunlit package.

A grin spread across his face. He was a vampire, but the legends were wrong about a lot of the aspects of his species. At least, in part. He was only six hundred years old, so he'd never lived in the dark days when vampires had been cursed and left to walk the night, listening to the screams of agony from victims long dead. He also hadn't lived through the hiding times, when humans were prone to beheading and burning them simply for being a little different.

No.

He had been a willing gifter of his life's blood, as most of the members of his family had been going back several generations, and forward a few as well, thanks to his brother and sister and their families. Typically, being a gifter did not result in death and turning. However, when he'd been injured by the French in the Battle of Castillon, his wounds had been mortal. His friend and the one he gifted his blood to was one of the vampiric leaders in England at the time. Richard had refused to let him die without giving him a choice. Eric had chosen the life of a vampire over death and he'd never looked back.

Richard had found his eternity shortly after the war ended. He was long gone from the world, but his gift to Eric would never be forgotten. And nor would Richard.

Hiding among humans wasn't less difficult in the twenty-first century as it had been in centuries past, but it was difficult in different ways. For one, blood donors were abundant now. In fact, the research and subsequent medical knowledge of blood collection, storage, and transfusions was directly linked to vampires who had sought a way to collect and store blood for their own survival from willing gifters. That, coupled with the rise of a love of all things gothic and morbid, had allowed them to blend into the communities around them with a little more ease. But cameras everywhere meant they had to be more cautious about their surroundings. So long as they were careful to keep their extras - extra speed, extra strength, extra intelligence, extra long life - hidden, they were safe.

Eric had led so many lives and done so many things, he sometimes forgot his present. But for more than two hundred years, he'd returned to Pittsburgh and the surrounding areas many times. He'd always been drawn to the place, to the land where the three rivers met. He'd helped build Fort Pitt in the 1700s, then returned later when the first bridges were being constructed in the early 1800s. He'd returned less than a generation later and established relationships with Andrew Mellon and Thomas Carnegie during the time when the 'Burgh was thriving as a leader in the steel industry. Later, he's had some interesting times with Andy Warhol during the 1960s and '70s. Granted, that had been in New York, but as Warhol was originally from Pittsburgh, Eric counted it as a connection to the city. And now he was back again. He'd been surprised to find the house he'd lived in during his last Pittsburgh lifetime still standing and for sale. Purchasing it had been a spur of the moment decision. But in reality, the plan he'd had for his next 'life' fit well with the property that was now commercial, not a residential one. A few checks in the right hands and he knew he could convert the space into exactly what he needed.

But just then, he needed a different kind of plan. A plan that would help him woo and win the heart of the woman who'd just jump-started his heart and began his final life. Finding her in Pittsburgh explained why he'd always been drawn to the city. Her soul had probably called him well before it was born in her body. Souls could be like that. Existing in the space around the physical world without truly being a part of it.

He drew a deep breath as his body continued to adjust to the newness of his heart beating and the blood flowing again. And the necessity of air. Breathing wasn't something he'd done in centuries and his lungs were aching in his chest as the muscles expanded and contracted with every inhale and exhale. He'd anticipated that the change would be abrupt. But he'd not thought through the ache and discomfort of forcing his organs and muscles to work again after so long without needing them.

He felt old just then. Old and tired. Two things that weren't vampire-like. But were dinosaur-like. He chuckled to himself. That had been a surprise to see sitting on the corner of the property.

The dinosaur outside was a new addition since his last time in the city. He'd been in Pittsburgh when Andrew Carnegie had brought the first dinosaur bones into the city. That had been a day. And an adventure. The Carnegie brothers, Thomas and Andrew, had rarely seen eye to eye, although they did operate their businesses together in one capacity or another. But the dinosaur bones had been a fascination to everyone, himself and Thomas included. They'd spent hours looking at the bones. Eric had developed a fascination with them, and subsequently, the artwork that began surrounding them. Andrew's collection of works, coupled with Andrew Mellon's later endeavor to open the National Art Museum in Washington DC, had opened a new world of creativity to Eric. He owed his current profession to the two men, as well as Warhol, and others he'd met along the way.

Of course, none of those men would recognize him now. The former suit-wearing businessman and carefree hippie artist were gone. The servant turned soldier in the Hundred Years' War was long gone. He'd truly died on that battlefield and been reborn with a million new lives ahead of him. In their place was a rough looking, motorcycle riding, pierced and decorated tattoo artist.

*ith a groan, he heaved himself off the floor and left the building that needed some work before it would be what he needed. Grabbing his phone from the pocket of his coat, he dialed as he slid into the cab of the truck he used when he couldn't ride his bike. He'd had to dress up to go to the bank, but he needed to get out of the suit and tie and get down to business. Finding the card Elizabeth had handed to him, he had just started the engine when the ringing stopped and a voice came over the line.

"Eric? What's up?"

"I found her, John."

A loud thud sounded as Eric turned the truck onto the Highland Park Bridge. He'd not anticipated finding a place immediately, so he'd arranged for a room at the Omni William Penn Hotel. Heading back into the city, he'd decided to take the slightly more scenic route and drive by some of the places he had fond memories of from his previous times in the city.

"John?" he asked after a moment of silence.

"Yeah. I'm here. You caught me off guard."

"You? How do you think I feel?" Eric's shock had begun to wear off, but the ache in his chest was still prevalent and the repetitious beating of his heart reminded him of the very reason he could draw breath.

"Good point. What do you need?"

"I bought a shop location and I'm going to need about three months to get it set up. There's an annual expo every March. We missed this year's, but I'll put us into the lineup for next year. We'll need three more artists for the place. Can you put out some feelers in the community? I'd like to give some others a new start if possible." Establishing new lives was getting harder with all the security and technology in place, especially for the younger vampires. They didn't always have the funding or the connections to help them out. That's where Eric and John stepped in. The two of them had met before Eric had moved to the New World. Over the years, they'd crossed paths on occasion. When technology had begun expanding, John had found his way into the tech world at the ground level and had learned along the way the intricacies of programming, developing, and building software, hardware, and wares that weren't even released yet.

The two had worked together a few times before to help some other vampires change lives. So when technology became the newest way to hinder them, John had reached out and the two had built a network to connect vampires around the world to assist each other in the day to day, decade to decade, and even century to century challenges that they faced. This was Eric's first restart since then. He'd decided to help a few others along the way to fast track their restarts as well.

But best-laid plans had been put on hold when he'd suddenly been visited by the woman of his dreams. Literally. Their nightly time together had left him shattered. After six hundred years, he was finally getting his eternity. But it had taken four months to find her. One hundred and twenty-seven long, endless and aching nights of heated desire that couldn't be quenched.

"I'll put out feelers. There's a few I know might need the start, but I don't know their skills with what you'll need."

"At least one won't need the tattooing background because we'll need someone to handle the schedules and office stuff. And we could have someone do just piercing. That's an easier skill to teach. But if anyone wants to apprentice and has some drawing background, we could work with that too." Eric's mind whirled with the possibilities.

He looked around as he drove down Fifth Avenue. The street was a weird dichotomy of old homes that he'd visited in decades past, and twenty-first-century things, like stop lights. When cobblestone streets filled with horse-drawn carriages had once been the norm, now there were teens and adults hopping buses and listening to music on hand-held devices. The change was always startling. Especially after so many years away. But behind the new, the old manors still held their stately presence. Buildings that had watched the change from their steady foundations.

Shaking his head to clear the memories, he left the manors behind and pulled into the valet drive before the hotel. He grabbed his phone and switched it off the Bluetooth setting. "The plan is still the same. But I'll be settling here for my last life, so there will be more opportunities down the line for others as well."

"Congratulations, man," John said softly.

Eric heard the wistful note in his friend's voice. John had loved fiercely before being turned. His wife had too. She'd never remarried and had remained faithful until her final breath early in the sixteenth century. John held hope that she would be reborn to him in the future. "Thank you, my friend."

There was a long pause. Both men remembering their many long conversations that had often resulted in the what-ifs of the future.

"I'll see you in a few months," John finally said.

"I'll keep you updated," Eric promised. He hung up as he opened the door to his room. The first thing he needed to do was get out of the less than comfortable clothing he had on. While he'd worn suits often in his past lives, the more recent ones hadn't required them. Worn jeans and soft cotton t-shirts were much more comfortable.

4

*L*izzie walked up the steps to her grandmother's home. She'd spent the drive working to bring her speeding heart, her irregular breathing, and the painfully sharp desire under control. It hadn't really worked.

Before she reached the top step, the door opened and the woman she was named for stood smiling brightly at her.

"You met him." She said the words softly, but with such certainty that Lizzie couldn't help the wave of emotion that tumbled over her, dragging at her until she broke into a soft cry and launched herself into Grandma Lizbet's welcoming and soothing arms.

"I've been waiting all morning for you to arrive," Grandma Lizbet said as she stroked Lizzie's hair. "You've been waiting for months."

"How did you know?" Lizzie asked. She slowly straightened and allowed the older woman to lead her deeper into the house. She sat at the kitchen table while her grandmother poured two cups of tea and brought them over.

As she set one in front of Lizzie and took the seat opposite her, Grandma Lizbet began speaking.

"I've told you many stories over the years. Yes?"

Lizzie nodded.

"There's one that I haven't told you wholly." The older woman dropped a small cube of sugar into the teacup before her and stirred the liquid until it had dissolved. "When I was a young girl, my father told me about the fae that hid from the world with secret veils that concealed them from human eyes. He also told me of the other creatures that hid in plain sight and how truest love could free us from being stuck in our endless ways. I didn't understand then what he was really telling me. But over time, his words have become clearer to me. And over time, I discovered the truth about myself, and in turn, about you."

"What are you talking about Grandma?" Lizzie asked, frowning in confusion. Her great-grandfather had passed when Lizzie was a baby. Grandma Lizbet's stories had often included him because she'd learned many from her father as a child herself.

"Just listen," Lizbet replied, waving a hand through the air.

Lizzie sat back and wrapped her hands around the teacup, letting the warmth seep into her and bring a comforting blanket of her grandmother's love with it.

"I've told you the origin stories of the Imagi. The creative contest between the old gods and the resulting species of humans, shifters, fae, merfolk, vampires, and demons. I've told you about how many of these creatures are hiding among us, and how they came to do that. Do you remember those?"

Lizzie nodded. Listening to her grandmother's stories had often been a favorite way to spend an evening. The tales she wove were wondrous. Better than any fairytale or Disney film.

"When the vampiress gave her life for the Imagi to create the veils, the Fates decided to reward her. Instead of death, the young vampire became immortal. She became the fourth Parca - a Fate."

"But there were only three," Lizzie protested.

"There *were* only three. But although Jupiter's curse was lifted, the Fates decided that the vampires deserved someone who would have their own interests in mind. So they gifted the girl with their own brand of immortality. She, like the others, could dictate the fate of an individual. But there was a rule. She could only do so if the individual was a vampire. She would have no say over the other species."

Lizzie frowned into her cup. She supposed that made sense. But she didn't understand why she had to hear this story. Vampires and fae didn't interact. Not that she could recall.

"Her name was Carna. She was little known, but her recognition as a goddess that protected the heart and organs within a person was partially true. She was the keeper of a vampire's eternal life. But Carna was also wise. She stepped forward to offer her life not just to save the Imagi, but to save herself and her brethren from the endless torture of the souls screaming from the depths of Pluto's domain. When the Parcae, the Fates, accepted her sacrifice, Morta, the cutter of the life threads, gave her a choice. She could die and be reborn as a human, or she could have immortality and watch over those she'd saved.

"Carna chose immortality. But in doing so, she again sacrificed her own destiny - that of a love and family meant for her. Her second sacrifice was revealed only after she made her choice. Carna accepted the truth of her own loss, but she took that loss and the destiny she was meant to have, and she twisted it to give every vampire a chance at the life she would never live. A chance at love, family, and a true, *living* life."

Lizzie's breath caught as the meaning behind the words, the power in her grandmother's voice, filled the air.

"I told you your true mate would find you when you were ready. But, what I failed to tell you was the power behind that. You are not simply fae-born. You are the first non-human to be the eternal mate of a vampire. And with that meeting, you have opened the doors for Carna to protect and provide for the hearts of every being, regardless of species. You have elevated her from a minor goddess over vampires' mating humans and being given a human life alone, to a powerful-in-her-own-right goddess that could rival Venus and Cupid over affairs of the heart."

"I - what?" Lizzie's shock had her lost for words.

"You are a prophecy come to life, my dear. And with your true heart's mate, you have released Carna. There are so many who would never find their truest love without you first finding yours." Lizbet smiled softly, warmly. "Your grandfather was my dearest friend. But he was not my truest love. Had I met my truest love, I would have felt anew. Fae do not age as humans. We age slower, we live longer, but only if we meet our truest love do we capture the full use of our magick. You, my dear, are about to embark on a brand new journey in life as well as love."

"What?" Lizzie squeaked again. She took a gulp of the now luke-warm liquid in her cup, hoping that would shake loose the words that seemed to get stuck in her throat. "Grandma, this is insane. You know that, right? I simply met some guy who happens to remind me of the amazingly - er, um - the dreams I've been having. Coincidence."

Her grandmother raised a single brow and waited.

"It's crazy. Right? That's just a story. A good one, and really inter-esting. But it's still just a story." Lizzie protested, desperately now.

"Close your eyes, my dear."

Lizzie looked suspiciously at the older woman.

Lizbet nodded in encouragement. "Put down your cup and close your eyes," she said again.

Lizzie sighed, slumping back in her chair as she set the cup on the table. With one last look at her grandmother, she closed her eyes and waited.

"Take a deep breath."

She did.

"Now take another one, and as you release it, I want you to picture your favorite stuffed animal from when you were younger."

Immediately, the image of a ragged little kitten - grey with age and one ear missing - popped into Lizzie's mind. She took a deep breath and exhaled slowly, picturing the kitten she'd loved until it was falling apart.

"Now open your eyes." The instructions were tinged with a smugness.

Lizzie blinked open her eyes and jumped at the sight of the tiny stuffed kitten sitting beside her teacup.

"Your magick is already strong enough to call upon at will. And it will only continue to grow."

"But...but..." Lizzie's stuttering came to a halt as she looked from the stuffed animal to her grandmother and back again. "What do I do?" she asked quietly.

"You find your mate. He will be your anchor in the storm. And trust me, my dear, there will be some storms on the horizon soon. None of the old gods will be happy about this change. Although they may be long forgotten by most of the world, they are not gone. And you have just changed their status quo."

Lizzie's eyes widened. What was she going to do?

"Find your mate," her grandmother repeated. "You will need him, just as he needs you. Together, you will fight for all of our eternities."

ABOUT THE AUTHOR

Rexi Lake has been writing stories in her head for as long as she can remember. Her goal was always to write in the genre she loved - romance. She has always believed in the reality of true love, and that the world could use more happily ever afters.

She currently lives in southwest Pennsylvania. When she's not hard at work on her next book, she's busy being an accountant, learning guitar, making jewelry, and chauffeuring her socially active daughter to her various activities.

Watch for the rest of Eric and Lizzie's story, coming Spring 2020 and connect with Rexi

facebook.com/rexilake

twitter.com/rexilake

instagram.com/rexi_lake_author

THAT NIGHT IN STEEL CITY

CHASHIREE M.

1

LAZARO

I have been looking forward to this game all season. Not to mention, I never take the day off for myself, so this was a much needed 24hr vacation. My friends thought I was crazy to fly all the way to Pittsburgh from Chicago for the Steelers vs. Bears game. They don't understand though. Pittsburgh was where I spent my summers with my grandmother. The whole summer I had to hear about how much better their sports teams were than ours back in Chicago. I vowed that when I got older, I would always come to any game the two teams played against one another, so I could stick it in their faces when Chicago beat their ass. I have stuck to that ever since I could afford it.

I look down at my watch. This damn concession line is taking forever. I am going to miss the first kick. I look around me and notice that everyone in the line is seemingly as impatient as I am. Finally, after about ten minutes in the slowest line on the east coast, I am one person away. I move up as the woman in front of me places her order. When she is handed her popcorn, I notice the concession worker post a sign that says, 'popcorn sold out'.

"Are you freaking kidding me!" Comes out of my mouth before I can stop it. I am turning around to walk into the stadium after wasting ten minutes of my life I won't get back, when I hear the voice that will change my life.

"I'm so sorry." Stopped in my tracks by what can only be called a Melody of Angels. I am almost afraid to turn around. Afraid that when I gaze upon her, she will be doomed to ashes like Eurydice in Hades. I choose to tempt fate. I must see her face. I turn and holy fuck! She is beautiful. That is literally an understatement, but my mind can't conjure up anything else in its catatonic state.

"I didn't realize it would be the last one. I would have taken a smaller bag. I certainly don't mind sharing. We can just ask for a bag." I must look crazy right now. I am staring at her, no words leaving my mouth. I can only imagine what my face looks like. Does it convey the absolute heat that my lower half is feeling?

"Sir? Would you like me to get another bag?" I finally take a breath and all of my senses return, though heightened and aware that somehow, I have to keep her with me.

"I'm sorry. Yes. That would be lovely. Though if you don't mind, we could just share from the bucket you have."

"I suppose," she says with a bit of a blush and a giggle. "But for this little thing called assigned seating. Unfortunately, there is a person sitting next to me."

I can feel the tension in my hands as my body goes into fight mode. The idea that she is here with her boyfriend or husband has me seeing red. This angel is supposed to be mine. I think as I look at her hand. No ring. But nowadays that means nothing. Shit.

"Rather chatty guy too." she says.

I take a stab at the possibility that she isn't acquainted with him.

"Not a fan of strangers talking your ear off at sports games?"

"Not really." Yes! She is here alone.

"Well it just so happens, there is no one sitting beside me because I always buy out the seat next to me. Not a fan of strangers much either. What do you say, we change our stranger status and you join me?"

She looks down, face turning the cutest shade of pink. Her lip ends up in between her teeth and I'd be lying if I said I didn't want to do all sorts of things to her mouth and that lip. I need her to say yes to sitting with me. So that later I can convince her to say yes to everything else that will follow.

"I promise I don't bite and I will even shut up unless you want to hear me talk."

"Deal. Lead the way Mr........" Crap. We haven't even exchanged names.

"My name is Lazaro. Lazaro Ruiz. Pleasure to meet you Miss..." I take her hand and gesture to kiss it. But first, I wait to see if she will trust me with her name.

"Stefahnee Macarbee." Perfect name.

I escort her down to my second row seating. Chest pumped out when she shows me her evident sign of being impressed.

The rest of the game we spend watching intently, but also talking. I found out she is 25 years old. She too lives in Chicago. She won these tickets in a raffle for charity. She's a preschool teacher. Not married. No kids. Though she would love some. I told her all about me as well. I am 30 years old. Never married. No kids. I am the CEO of Steel Tek. A security firm that specializes in Cyber Security as well as technological security.

"Wow. What are the odds we would both end up here? On the same night." She calls it odds. I call it fate. For the last half of the game we are both intently watching, neither of us willing to miss this. With just one minute left on the clock, the Bears score a touchdown and like that we win the game. Stefahnee and I jump out of seat, screaming and yelling for the team we both love. The stadium erupts in excitement and disappointment and none of it can drown out the drumming of my own heart as it laments that once we leave this dome, we are going separate places. My mind repeats this over and over as we walk toward the exit. Almost as if she is having the same thought, she looks at me almost expectantly. Like I somehow hold the key to keeping this night going. Taking a chance, I grab her hand and ask her simply.

"Care to see where the night takes us?" She looks at our joined hands and up into my eyes and answers.

"I thought you'd never ask."

Thank God.

2

STEFAHNEE

*W*alking beside him, holding his hand, just simply feels...right. I peek over at him, wanting to once again gaze at his handsome striking profile, only to find that he is already looking at me. I turn back around, feeling the heat creep into my cheeks. I have always been shy around boys and men. In high school I walked around with my head down and in the books. Literally. I read everything. From textbooks to fiction. I started out with V.C. Andrews books. I mean Flowers in the Attic, who doesn't love that? I moved on to romance novels. I began reading things like Say Please, by C.M. Steele, Chocolate Kisses by KL Fast and MK Moore and my absolute favorite, Pixie Chica's Sealed With a Kiss. I lose myself in these stories of men who find their soulmates and within a second, make the women theirs. I always told myself it wasn't real. But walking down the street with him, I am happy to say I am not so sure.

"So, what are you in the mood for?" he asks me as we wait for the walk signal.

"Uhm, what are you in the mood for?" I give the question back to him. My stomach is in knots right now. I haven't been this nervous since my first day of college. I am a mess of jumbled nerves. I don't know how to do this. Almost as if he can read my mind, he lifts our joined hands and kisses mine.

"Relax baby. This is done. There is no going back now. The minute you turned around and offered to split your popcorn with me, it was settled. Now, what would you like to eat?"

Well hell. My hand begins to shake as I try to calm down my raging hormones. Not only has he sent my pussy into a tizzy, but he managed to calm me at the same time. His words sent some sort of signal through me, that instantly set my mind and body at ease.

"Wow. Ok. I don't...know what to say?"

"Right now, all I need is for you to tell me where you want to eat so I can feed you. Then, we will talk about the rest." He stops moving and turns me toward him. His hands are holding both of mines and I must admit, I have never felt so safe. He stares at me like he can see to the very part of me that needs this to be real. When his hands move up the side of my arms, and onto my face, I lean in to his hand, letting the feeling wash over me.

"Look at you. So sweet and beautiful. I don't know who to thank for bringing you to me, but fuck if I'm not the luckiest man alive." His left hand roams into my hair as his other slithers back to my hip. He pulls me further into him, his grip in both places getting firmer. "Do you feel that baby? You feel the melody floating between the two of us? That is destiny baby. Fate. I was meant to be right here, in this moment with you. I was meant to find you." he says the last part closer to my mouth. So close I can feel the heat on my face before he leans in and kisses me. The first contact is sweet and almost soft. I find myself wrapping my arms around his neck, trying to get as close as possible to him. Holding me closer to him, I hear the rumble from his throat, right before his tongue comes out to play. My mouth opens like he gave a 'Simon says' command.

We stand in the middle of the sidewalk, mouths fuse together, moaning and groaning. It must sound like a jungle of animals I can't help but think to myself, with an inside chuckle. Our mouths do a dance that our bodies recognize the rhythm to. Finally, after lord knows how long, we stop, gasping for air, trying to calm to need we have for each other. His forehead touches mine, "Shit Stef. That kiss...tell me you felt it."

"I did. I felt it Lazaro. I just...it's only been a couple of hours. How can we trust it?" I know what I am feeling. But how do I know it's not just simply lust overtaking my commonsense?

"Trust yourself baby. I know, I have never had feelings like this for anyone. Never met a woman I wanted to give my last name to and my baby. The minute I saw you, my chest began to burn. My heart kicked up, and head began chanting over and over how much you belong to me. How fast I needed to claim you, take you, make you mine unequivocally, no questions asked. I trust when my mind and heart are working together. Now the question is: Will you trust me and yourself? I swear I will never hurt you."

What is a girl supposed to say to a speech like that? I look in his eyes, and in them I see sincerity, heat, need, desire and something I am not ready to admit yet. He once again holds his hand out to me, waiting. I know once I place my hand in his, I am not only, agreeing to continue our night together, but I am also answering his question and validating I feel the same way. I bite my lip as I take a moment to make sure, I am ready for my life to change.

I try to imagine my life if I don't take his hand and I can't. I can't imagine one moment when I am not somehow within his orbit. Is that crazy? On the contrary. I *can* picture us living in a home filled with light and laughter, chasing little kids around while there is another one inside me. Oh God. My hand goes to my mouth as I gasp realizing my eyes are filling with tears at the vision. I want that. I want that life.

"Yes. Lazaro. I trust us." He takes a deep breath. "Thank fuck baby. Now, tell me what you want to eat."

"Pizza. I want pizza."

"Excellent choice."

This is definitely an excellent choice.

3

LAZARO

♥

hank fuck she didn't walk away from me. I know I am coming off strong and quick, but I feel the urgency in the fact that we have this one night and then we go back home. A home where we live in separate places. Lead separate lives. The beast inside of me is demanding I take her somewhere right now and get my ring on her finger and my son in her belly. I need to make her mine. Now.

We walk to Mercurio's Pizza. It is the only pizza I eat when I am in the Burgh. The owner and I go way back. We used to hang together all summer with the other guys when I was out here with my grandma. His little sister, decided to go to college in Illinois at the University of Illinois and after she graduated, she became my personal assistant.

"Zar the scar. How you doing man?" He asks as we bro hug. "Long time no see."

"Adolfo. You know I hate it when you call me that." I really do. "And I just saw you when you came to visit your sister." He backs up from me laughing.

"Who do we have here?" He licks his lips as he looks my woman up and down and the urge to punch his face in is prominent.

"Dolf, put your tongue back in and show some respect. This is my fiancée, Stefahnee. Stefahnee, this I am sorry to say, is one of my best friends, Adolfo. He owns this place." I ignore the shocked and confused look on her face at my use of the word fiancée. If I have it my way she will be within the next 48 hours.

"I had no idea. Congratulations brother."

"Thanks. Listen, we are starving."

"Oh yes. Of course. Follow me."

He leads us to his empty party room that is only in use when he has an event going on. I am thankful for the privacy. Once we are seated and give him our order, it is just the two of sitting across from one another.

"Tell me more about you Lazaro." she asks her face bright and flushed.

"What do you want to know baby?"

"Everything." Mmmmm. Her face became almost mischievous when she said that. She has no idea how much that turned me on.

"I am third generation Italian American. Grew up in Chicago. I have a younger sister named Gia. I run 10 miles a day. Workout 6 days a week. Never been married. No kids. Your turn." I want to know everything. But most of all, I want her to tell there is and have never been anyone special in her life until me.

"Well, not much to tell. I'm 25. I am a preschool teacher. I graduated with a bachelor's from Illinois State University in Advanced Human Development. It's been just my little brother, mom and I for years. No kids. Have not ever been in a relationship to be honest." Thank fuck. Knowing my cock is the only one she will ever know, the only mouth that will ever know how sweet her pussy is, is making me harder as fuck under this damn table.

We spend the rest of the night talking and laughing. It feels like we have known each other for our whole lives. We pay the check, say goodbye to Dolfo and walk outside. As soon as we step outside the door, she begins to shiver. The temperature has certainly changed since we got here. Nothing like Fall and winter in the Burgh.

Pulling her into my chest, I wrap my arms around her giving her as much of my heat as I can.

"Geesh. It wasn't this cold when we got here."

"It wasn't. But, it gives me an excuse to hold you."

"You don't need an excuse for that." She leans up on her toes and plants her mouth on mine. I know I should take it slow, but having her initiate it, revs something in me. I turn her toward the brick wall behind her. Lifting her by her ass as our mouths go at each other, tongues tangling, teeth knocking against each other, she wraps her legs around me and even in the cold I can feel the heat between her legs.

"Shit. You're so fucking warm. Are you wet for me baby? Is my pussy raining down for me?"

"Yes." She whispers, barely able to catch her breath before our mouths are fused together again.

"Fuck baby. I want to drop you right here on this ground and rut into you until I'm sure my son is inside you. Savage is how I want to take you Stefahnee." My jean covered cock is pumping against her denim covered pussy and I can still feel the type of connection we have.

"Lazaro. Yes. Please. It feels so good." Damn she lit up quick. So, fucking sexy. I need to get her to a bed and love her right. I move my mouth from hers, sucking in the oxygen like it's an oasis. Once we have calmed down I flag down a cab. I'm done waiting.

"Let's go baby. I can't wait any longer to find out how you taste."

And to figure out how to keep her.

4

STEFAHNEE

*T*oo bad the cab isn't more private. His hand on my thigh, moving up and down, I can feel my pussy throbbing as it drips in my panties. I find myself opening my legs a bit wider, trying to be not so obvious. But I need his hand to move up and ease the ache, like I need the latest Jessa Kane book.

"You keep opening your legs like that baby, I am going to make this cab driver stop and get out, so I can fuck you in the backseat. Now be good. We are almost there." he whispers in my ear sending shivers of sensual wanton need through me. I am so out of my depth that even my mouth is acting up.

"Why would we have to wait for him to get out of the cab?" My eyes get big as I realize the words that have left my mouth. Even as I can feel the embarrassment takeover, it doesn't stop my legs from opening wider as his hand gets higher.

"If he heard your moans of ecstasy, I would have to kill him. Your sounds are just for me, Stefahnee. No one else." My oh my. I need something to calm me down.

"What time is your flight tomorrow?" There. That's a safe subject.

"Mine is not until later. I am going to stop by and see two of my other buddies who still live here. We don't get to catch up much, so I booked a 3pm flight. What about you?"

"I am back bright and early. I got a special deal on Priceline. The only thing is, I didn't get to pick my flight time." Wishing that was different now.

"Well shit, baby. Let's make the most of tonight shall we."

The cab comes to a stop and after paying we are walking inside the hotel. The elevator ride is the worst. I know this would totally be a Fifty Shades elevator moment if it weren't for the elderly couple to the left of us. My lip is permanently planted in my mouth as I squeeze my legs together trying to cool the fire building between them. So, in tune to me already, he leans over and in the most growly voice possible he says, "I don't give a shit how old he is, if I can smell your need, so can he. Be patient, baby. That pussy is going to get what's coming to her." Holy fuck! This man is everything.

It's finally our floor and we stumble off drunk on the lust and unspent desire. Not in the door two seconds when he is on me. Pinned to the door, my chest heaving up and down, body demanding I give it what it craves, I do the only thing I know to. I jump on him, wrapping my legs around him as my mouth attack his. Long gone are the thoughts of doubt, the moments when I wonder if I can be *this* woman. Contemplating if I am even capable of letting go and just letting desire overrule me, because here and now, I have the answer to all of those. YES!

"Fuck baby. You have no idea how hard it makes me know you want me as much as I want you. I want to show you everything tonight. How slow and methodical I can be. Pleasing you. Teasing you. Loving you. Like you deserve. But shit, I am too far gone to slow down now. Tell me you understand. Tell me you're with me Stefah nee." No hesitation.

"I'm with you Lazaro. I don't care about slow. I just need you. Please. I have never felt like this. I want to feel all of it before it's over and too late." My heart whimpering for just a second at the knowledge that this might very well be for only one night. I know what we both say we want, but in the light of day, when we are back to our normal lives, will he still want me?

"Hey. Where did you go? Where did that beautiful little head run off too?"

"Doesn't matter. Bring me back." I don't even know who I am right now.

"With pleasure," he says as he pulls my Chicago t-shirt over my head. My bra is gone before I know it and then he's kissing down my neck, eventually pulling one then the other nipple into his mouth. My moan comes from deep within me and I don't recognize it. When his hand pulls the button on my jeans open, I am ready for him.

His fingers dip into my panties. A knuckle grazes my clit and I gasp. My own hand has never felt so amazing. So, everything. His lips find mine and I put everything I have into this kiss. With a growl, he lifts me and carries me over to the bed, my sandals falling off as he walks us. Tossing me on the bed, he pulls my jeans down over my legs and throws them across the room. My panties soon follow. I can tell that I'm blushing as his gaze washes over my naked body. He quickly takes his shirt off followed by his pants and shoes.

"Wow," I breathe. The outline of his cock in his dark boxer briefs has my mouth watering. Once the boxers are gone and there's nothing between us I start to shift to get closer to him, but he stops me. Gently he pulls my thighs apart and stares at my pussy.

"Damn baby all this pussy cream for me?" He asks as he runs his fingertips through my folds. Seriously, just this small touch has me about to come. Leaning closer, he inhales my scent. I should be ashamed but I'm not. Getting closer still, I jump when his tongue touches my clit. Good Lord I've never felt anything like this. I can't even describe it, but it feels so good. He alternates licks and bites nibbles and sucks until I come epically.

All over his gorgeous face.

"Fuck," I scream before crying out his name.

He stands over me slowly jerking his cock.

"Once I take you Steph, I own you. This isn't just tonight. Do you

157

understand?" I nod, but he grabs my chin to halt my movement. "Use your words," he demands.

"Yes. I understand," I somehow manage to say.

Between my thighs, he moves his cock through my wetness before sliding into me slowly. He takes my virginity in a slow and seductive way. Like he knew. Like he's taking care of me. The fleeting pain is gone so I wrap my legs around his waist and spur him on, my heels digging into his ass. Leaning up, I wrap my arms around his neck and pull him down to me. I can taste myself on his lips when we kiss, and it turns me on even more. It's almost as if my spurning changed his demeanor. He's fucking me savagely now. My screams and moans echoing off the walls. His own groans give me goosebumps. I come hard and I feel him do the same. For the first time, I realize he's bare inside me and my womb is unprotected. Why the fuck do I like that? I literally just met this man a few hours ago but I never want to let him go.

Isn't life crazy?

5

LAZARO

I have been awake for the past hour just staring at my beautiful woman as she sleeps. She looks so peaceful. Her hair spread out over her pillow, such a contrast against her pale angelic complexion. Eyelashes, lain upon her cheeks. The sheet is barely covering her nipples, peeking out at me, taunting me, begging me to take them in my mouth, bite them lick them. My cock twitches as it calls me a dumb ass for not waking her over and over throughout the night. Don't get me wrong, it's not that I didn't want to. Fuck that. I fucking crave to wake her up and rut my unmannerable cock inside her. But, finding out she was a virgin, changed everything about the plans I had for the night. Hurting her, was not an option.

I move to get out of bed and go to the restroom, when she stretches, and the sheet falls lower. Son of a bitch! Fuck it! My head lowers and before I can stop myself, my tongue is tracing lazy circles around her nipples. Taking my time to taste her, revel in the sweetness that is all her.

"Mmmmmm. Zaro." she says as she comes awake. I can't wait any longer. I move between her legs, kissing her awake the rest of the way.

She kisses me back with the same urgency and I am inside her in an instant.

"Lazaro." she moans my name as I move in and out of her, sucking her neck leaving my mark. "I'm here baby. Right here. With you." I know she is sore and I should go slow, but something about being inside of her makes me a mad man. She moves in sync with me as I move in and out of her wetness, pushing further in as I go.

"Shit you feel so good baby. This sore abused pussy is squeezing me so tight. You know, don't you? You know exactly what's happening. I'm inside you, bare, knocking up against the place that is going to house our children. You want me to stop?" I hope to hell she says no. Because I won't be able to either way.

"No. Don't stop. Lazaro. Don't ever stop. Give me your baby. Yes. Yes." Fuck I can't hold it any longer. "Come with me baby. NOW!" Pinching her clit, I yell out my release as she does the same. My seed making its way into her womb, binding us together forever.

"Oh my gosh. Good morning to you too." she says. Chuckling as she catches her breath. I laugh back at her. So fucking happy to have been given this blessing called Stefahnee. Eventually, we both come back and she lays her head on my chest.

"Can I ask you a question?" she asks me, swirling the hairs on my chest around. I like having her touching me in any capacity I can get it.

"You can ask me anything baby. What's up?"

"Have you ever believed in love at first sight?"

"That's an easy one. Not until I met you." She looks up at me, the warring of her feelings evident in her eyes. I can read the shock, disbelief and hope as clear as if she had written it on her forehead. "I'm serious. I used to laugh at people who said things like that. Shrugged it off as some, chick-lit fantasy crap. And then you turned around and offered me popcorn and made a believer out of me. I knew, immediately, without a shadow of a doubt, that I was in love with you and would do whatever it took to keep you forever."

"I-I don't know what to say. Wow! I thought it was just me. I thought it was only my heart going crazy, dreaming up the plans and laying down the future. How is this possible? I mean ...I know it's real, but......what are we going to do?" I can see the worry and I don't want that for her. I know we need to talk about this but, right now, she needs to sleep and so do I. We will get up early and talk over a nice hotel breakfast, before her flight. I am about to tell her just that when I hear the soft sound of her sleeping.

My mind won't quit racing about everything that needs to be done. My life changed on this trip and I am not going to run from it or deny it. On the contrary. I am going to embrace it. I know just where to start. I grab my phone and call my PA.

"Good evening Zaro. What do you need at this ungodly hour?" Smartass. As the kid sister of one of my best friends, she gets away with things others would not.

"Sorry to wake you Evangeline. I need you to get a listing of all houses for sale in LaGrange, Western Springs area. Four to five bedrooms, big backyard."

"A house. You want me to look for a house? For you? Am I being punked or did you all of a sudden grow a family overnight?" she asks chuckling. See I told you smartass.

"Don't worry about it brat. I want them in my email when I wake up. Goodnight." Knowing I am well on my way toward securing my families future, I take a deep breath and some of the tension leaves me. Kissing her forehead, I wrap my arms around her and slumber off. Holding my future as tight as I can.

6

STEFAHNEE

$\heartsuit$

I should be running out of this room. My flight is in two and a half hours. I need to get to the airport, but my heart won't let me leave. How am I supposed to pick up and go like I won't be leaving half of me behind? Running my fingers over his face, I try to commit everything about him to memory. The hard line of his jaw, his dirty blonde hair, that sinful mouth that kisses me like I am his everything...everywhere. I won't even get started on his body.

Damn adulting. I roll out of bed, gather my clothes and toiletries and after putting on my traveling clothes. I don't shower because I want the smell of him to stay on me throughout my travels. I sit at the desk and leave him a note.

Lazaro,
The past few hours have been the best of my life. I don't know where we go
from here, but I want to find out. 555-782-9330.
Love,
Stefahnee

Kissing his lips one more time, I lay the note on my pillow and walk out, barely holding back tears. Once I am in the cab, I finally let go and let the tears flow. Poor cab driver. Ass crack of dawn and he has a crying blubbering mess of a passenger in his back seat. He hands me a tissue and very cliché, I blow my nose in it thanking him for his kindness.

Less than two hours later I am sitting in my airline seat rubbing my fingers across my lips as I remember what it felt like when he bit it as his cock battered in and out of me. Remembering how much I gushed as he marked me on my neck. A mark still there this morning as I got dressed.

Good morning ladies and gentlemen. Welcome aboard United Airline flight 1265 nonstop from Pittsburgh to Chicago. Please make sure your belongings are stowed in the overhead compartment. Make sure your tray is in the upright position and your seatbelt is fastened. In just a few moments we will go over the emergency procedures and exits with you. Just seating the last remaining passengers. Thank you for your patience.

I wish I could just get off the plane.

rudging myself into my apartment door an hour and thirty two minutes later, I look around and it is glaringly obvious that something is missing. I pull my cell phone from my pocket, eager to turn it on and see if there is a message from him. I feel a bit foolish. Like a high schooler, going all gaga over the popular guy in school or something. Nevertheless, I eagerly urge my damn LG to hurry up and boot. When it finally does, I have only one missed call from my co-worker asking how I enjoyed the game. My heart sinks, a bit, realizing that I set myself up to with the anticipation.

I spend the rest of the day doing laundry, eating, and showering. When all is back as it should be, I check my phone again. Hey, can you blame me? Maybe I missed it or it didn't ring. You never know. But of course, nothing. I can't tell you how many times I have checked my phone over the past eight hours. Or simply stared at it willing it to ring. Oh well. I have work tomorrow and I need to get up. I slip into my gown and turn down my bed. After washing my face, removing the many tears I have shed since I have been home and haven't heard from him, I brush my teeth and walk into the bedroom. I am about to lay down when I hear a knock at the door.

Who the heck? It better not Mrs. Beal from next door asking me to help her find her cat again. That was the longest night of my life. I walk to the door and look through, but no one is there. Hmm. I look once again and am about to walk away when the voice of my dreams says, "I see your feet baby. Open the door."

Oh my gosh. He is here. I mean, how is he here? Who gives a hell? Opening the door, the gasp slips out of my mouth as the sight before me sets in. Down on his knees, in a blue button up and black slacks, is my future. My love.

"I almost lost my mind when I woke up to you being gone baby. I never want to feel that way again. Nothing in this life makes sense when I don't have you in arms. I know to others it may seem crazy, but to me, this is the only thing that has ever made sense. We have much to learn about one another and I am more than willing to do that, but with my ring on your finger. I love you baby. Stefahnee Macarbee, love of my life, will you marry me?"

Is it nuts that I don't need to think about the answer to that question? My first response is my only response.

"Yes. Yes, Lazaro. I will marry you. I love you too." I fall to my knees, and our mouths meet. I feel him put the ring on my finger, but my focus is on feeling complete being in his embrace, once again.

"I missed you so much baby." he says in between kisses.

"Then take me inside and show me."

He does. All night long.

EPILOGUE

LAZARO

♥

12 MONTHS LATER

"*B*abe. Can you put some sunscreen on me?" We are currently sitting on the beach in France enjoying our week long honeymoon, two months after the wedding. The night we got engaged was one of the happiest times in my life, only to be eclipsed by the news six weeks later that my boys did their job on the first time. So, we decided to wait until after the baby was born to get married. Well, more like I decided. I didn't want her planning a wedding stressing herself out. Seven and a half months later, our baby girl Zara was born. And four weeks after that we were married. Stef, didn't want to leave the baby quite yet to go on our honeymoon afterward and to be honest, neither did I.

"Of course, my love. Turn over." She turns over on her back and as I begin to apply the sunscreen, the desire I have for her, builds into this overwhelming need to be inside of her. It's a feeling that never fails. I feel it every second of every day.

"Why don't we go back to the villa and you can thank me proper-ly." I whisper in her ear.

"Mmmmm...thought you'd never ask." Little vixen gets up and as she makes her way to the villa she slowly starts shedding her clothes leaving her entirely nude by the time she makes it to the door.

Growling I storm after her. She knows how even the thought of someone seeing any part of her makes me a beast. She like the beast in me.

I take a second to look out at the horizon and thank God.

I never imagined my life could be this amazing. Who knew that night in steel city could turn into forever?

I am a lucky man. And I know it.

ABOUT THE AUTHOR

ChaShiree lives in the Windy City though she is trying to move as fast as she can. Lol. She loves connecting with readers and writing is one of her passions.

Connect with ChaShiree

 facebook.com/ChasShiree
twitter.com/AuthorChaShiree

TAKING CHANCES

SK MARIE

For J.S.
"Only you can calm my storms while creating others."

1

I had to be out of my mind. Driving down to meet a guy I'd been talking to online for only the last couple of months. *What am I thinking? Who in their right mind does this?*

My friends said this brash decision was the result of my broken heart, but I've argued the opposite every time they've mentioned my ex. They only knew our relationship from the outside, so they didn't understand that our relationship was dead long before Adam walked out on me. Yeah, I was broken up about it for a little while. And yes, maybe that happening played a small part in my decision to make plans to finally meet this guy in person. But it wasn't the sole reason for my going.

I needed to do something for myself.

"You only live once, right?" I said to the woman staring back at me in the rearview mirror.

Without fail, my phone began to ring right as I was giving my reflection a pep talk. Checking the caller ID flashing on my mounted screen, I chuckled when I saw my best friend's name and picture interchangeably blinking on the screen.

Laughing, I reached over and tapped the screen to answer her call. "I thought I told you to remove all the bugs you planted in my car."

"Huh?" came her puzzled reply.

"Never mind, Nicole. I was just giving myself a pep talk about my decision to get in my car this morning and make this drive," I quickly explained.

"Having second thoughts again?" she teased.

"NO!" I screamed at her picture on my phone.

"Relax, girl, I'm just teasing you. I know how your mind works. You made the decision to drive down there and have since gone over every reason why you should turn around to come home at least a hundred times already. But keep in mind—you're still driving to see him. That should tell you that you know what you're doing," she conceded.

She knows me so well, and that alone is comforting.

Nicole has been my best friend for as long as I can remember and she's always been my sounding board or voice of reason whenever I've thought I was making poor decisions. In all the years I've known her, she's only steered me wrong once.

"Thanks for that," I sighed with a smile. I released the breath I didn't realize I still had trapped in my lungs as I waited for her lecture about my trip. *Lord knows I've heard it enough times over the last couple days from so many other people.*

"Any time. So where are you now?" she asked.

Clicking back to the GPS map on my phone, I glanced from the road to the screen and back again before I answered her. "I'm about 35 minutes from his house according to the directions on my phone."

"Not long now, and you'll be in the arms of your oh-so-hot mystery man," Nicole teased. She'd named him that when I first told her about talking to him. I could almost picture her expression as she dramatically fanned herself the way she always did when she referred to him like that.

"His name is John, in case you conveniently forgot. Again," I reminded her. Though I couldn't help smiling at her dramatics.

"I know. 'Johnny Boy' is probably chomping at the bit to get into your bits."

"Oh my God, Nicole!" I squealed.

"What?"

"He's not like that," I argued. "Besides, that isn't why I'm going to see him." Everything I said fell on deaf ears. I knew she was rolling her eyes and shaking her head at me without her having to even say anything.

"Whatever, harlot."

I pretended to stew a moment, while she pretended to mean what she said. Not even five seconds later, our laughter echoed around the interior of my car.

"Seriously though, are you okay?" *Again, she knows me too well.*

I took a deep breath and told her the truth. "I'm honestly terrified. Talking to him online is one thing, but meeting him face to face is a whole different monster altogether. I mean, what if...." I started to doubt myself and, as usual, Nicole jumped right in to shut me up before I got too far into my own head.

"Zip it," Nicole's harsh tone echoed. She hated when I put myself down. "You've been talking to this guy for more than a few months, and he's obviously okay with your going to stay with him this weekend. If he had any reservations about meeting you, he'd have made up any excuse to get out of this weekend, right? Of course, I'm right. Now shut it and just keep driving; everything will be fine."

I knew she was right, but Adam's parting words had seared themselves in my memory. *"You'll never be enough for anyone."*

"I'm going to hang up, Nic. I'm getting off the turnpike and I need to pay attention to my turns so I actually make it to his place. I'll talk to you later," I said, signaling my exit off the pike.

"Give lover-boy lots of hugs and kisses," she teased before I heard the momentary silence preceding my music starting again.

She left me with a smile on my face, but the butterflies in my stomach started to have a fit the closer I got to Johnny's place. Navigating the final few directions, I turned into his complex and watched the house numbers carefully. As the numbers counted up, house-by-house, the butterflies in my stomach knotted themselves into a bundle of nerves telling me I was crazy for doing this.

When I passed a house two numbers off from his, I slowed down. Spotting his house, I turned into his driveway. There was no backing out now. As I shut off my engine and put my hand on the door, about to open it and step out of my car for the first time in three hours, the front door of the house opened and Johnny stepped out onto his porch.

Taking a deep, calming breath, I climbed out of my car.

"Hey there, beautiful," he called as he started down the steps towards me. "I'm glad you made it." When we reached one another a few steps later, Johnny wrapped me in a big hug and all my apprehension about this visit instantly melted away. Pulling back slightly, a soft kiss brushed my cheek before he released me. "How was the drive?"

"It was okay. With family over in Sewickley, I was familiar with the majority of the drive. I'm just glad to finally be here and out of my car," I joked.

Opening my car door, he reached into my backseat and grabbed the two small bags I'd stowed. "Let's get you inside, Thumper." He winked at me and motioned down to my shirt when he caught my raised eyebrow.

"Oh, yeah. I forgot I'd put this shirt on this morning when I was getting ready to leave," I replied, suddenly embarrassed by my childish shirt. "I'd meant to change it."

"I love it. And now, that is what you will forever be known as," he declared, motioning with his arm to follow him into his house.

Stepping over the threshold, I chuckled. "I can live with that."

2

---

*A*fter eating the delicious dinner Johnny had prepared, pasta with homemade Alfredo sauce, we sat around talking with the remainder of our glasses of wine. I'd insisted on helping him with the dishes from dinner, despite his objections. It didn't take us long before we fell into a natural rhythm and were soon finished with clean up. It was strange, I'd only been here for a few hours but I felt like we'd known each other forever. Everything with Johnny was so relaxed and natural; everything with my ex, Adam, was always so forced. I had to internally shake my head at myself; on the drive down, I'd sworn to myself that I would not compare Johnny to Adam, no matter what. And here I was, comparing the two men that couldn't have been more different from one another.

I don't know why I'd been so nervous to come down here. Nicole was right, there was no reason I should have thought that finally meeting Johnny in person was going to be a disaster, or that he would find some flaw with me.

I was so lost in my own thoughts that I hadn't even realized that my wine glass was empty, or that he'd taken it out of my hand until I felt a pillow hit me in the face.

"Hey!" I yelled, grabbing onto the pillow before he could hit me again.

"What? You were so zoned out that you didn't even realize I'd said your name like a hundred times."

"It wasn't a hundred times, not even close," I challenged.

"Okay, so maybe it was only twice, but still. Where'd you disappear to in that pretty little head of yours?"

I was hoping he wouldn't ask, but as my luck would have it, I wasn't so lucky. I'd promised myself not to think of Adam while I was here but I had been, and I'd been caught doing it too. "My mind wanders sometimes. I honestly don't even know what I was thinking about," I lied, unwilling to tell him the truth.

"If you say so," he said, finishing his wine. Picking up my glass from the coffee table, he walked into his kitchen, my eyes following his every move. I couldn't help but admire his ass as he walked away. "Quit staring at my ass," he shouted playfully over his shoulder.

"What? I–I wasn't," I sputtered.

The look he shot over his shoulder at me was enough to make me melt. I don't think anyone had ever looked at me the way he just did, and I was having a hard time getting my heartbeat to slow to a normal pace.

"If you say so," he teased as he walked back toward the couch to hand me a full glass of wine. His eyebrow was arched in a 'you-are-so-full-of-it' sort of way, almost begging me to keep denying the truth.

I sat silently, smirking at him as I sipped my wine. When I turned to place my glass on the side table, I was quickly greeted with another pillow to the face and Johnny laughing at me. Before I even had time to react, he jumped off the couch, pillow still in-hand and stuck his tongue out at me, tauntingly.

"Oh, it's on now," I replied, grabbing the pillow I'd stolen from him the first time he'd hit me. I jumped off the couch and we began playing a fun game of cat and mouse, neither one of us making the first move.

"What's the matter, little girl?" he taunted after a few minutes of our standoff.

"Afraid to make a move?" I shot back.

Before I could say anything else, he threw the pillow down and stalked towards me. My heart hammered in my chest as he stopped directly in front of me. His face was calm but I could see his pulse thundering behind his eyes. For a moment, I regretted my choice of words.

He reached out and easily pulled the pillow out of my grasp. With no barrier between us, he stepped forward until we were practically flush against one another. I didn't know what to say and I was afraid to move. Ever so slowly, Johnny raised his right hand until he brushed his fingertips against my cheek.

I couldn't speak if I tried and remembering to breathe was proving to be just as difficult.

"Thumper," he whispered as I willed my eyes to remain open.

Not trusting my voice, I simply raised my eyebrow at him. A silent challenge to make the move I accused him of being afraid to make.

"Never assume I'm afraid to make any move," his gravelly voice whispered. Before I could reply, he hit me with the pillow I hadn't noticed he'd pulled off the couch next to me. My mouth dropped open in shock. I watched as his straight-faced expression remained fixed for another half second before he busted out laughing and retreated to the other side of the coffee table once again.

I don't know what came over me, but before I knew it, I was charging after him, swinging away with my newly reacquired pillow. I caught him in the back of the head before he managed to turn around. Caught off guard, he tripped over his other attack pillow and fell awkwardly onto the couch.

Worried that he had gotten hurt, I dropped down next to him. "Oh my God, are you okay?" I breathed out quickly, suddenly feeling bad for my playful antics.

Pulling me down next to him, Johnny rolled over on top of me. Before I could make a sound, his lips were on mine and all thoughts fled from my mind.

His lips were softer than I'd imagined and the fire they ignited in my belly was more intense than anything I'd ever felt before. Instinctively, I melted into his kiss as he consumed me.

3

I relived that kiss the rest of the evening, wrapped up in sheets that smelled completely of him. I wouldn't have been able to get him out of my head even if I had tried.

After I closed myself in his room, which he had graciously offered for me to sleep, I was up for over an hour texting with Nicole. There was no way I could keep that kiss to myself. Knowing Nicole like I do, I could practically hear her giddy squeal through the phone when she got my initial message.

She made me admit that there was no way I'd have made the first move and that I hated the fact that I was scared. As much as I didn't want to admit it, she was right; there was nothing I should be scared of––but Adam's parting words still lingered in the back of my mind. Though just like she always does, she was able to get me out of my own head with just a few words. I guess that's what I love most about her. After we sent our mushy goodnight messages, I stayed awake for a little longer, trying to convince myself that the kiss wasn't a mistake.

After some time, I eventually drifted to sleep with thoughts of his lips on mine.

*W*hen I awoke the next morning, my mind was still on the searing kiss from the night before. After climbing out of bed, I decided to jump in the shower and get ready for the day. After my shower, I opened the bathroom door determined not to overthink things anymore this weekend. *Just live in the moment.*

"Sleep well?" came a welcomed voice as I stepped out of the bathroom.

"I did, thank you," I admitted with a smile. "Though you didn't have to give up your bed. I told you I would have gladly slept on the couch."

He gave me the same stern look he'd given me last night when I'd tried to turn down his offer to have me stay in his room while he crashed on his couch.

"Zip it, woman. No way would I let you sleep on my couch. It wouldn't have been right, so let's not go there again," he shot back, eyeing me sternly.

"I surrender," I muttered, hands in the air.

Shaking his head, he handed me a steaming cup of coffee. Taking a sip, I savored the taste while it worked its way through my veins to wake me up the rest of the way.

"I thought we could walk around downtown today," he suggested, leaning against the wall in the hallway across from me. He must have caught the flicker of disappointment on my face because he continued, "Or we can go to the zoo."

There was no hiding my excitement when he said that, and I didn't even try. Feigning nonchalance, I replied with, "Whatever you'd rather do."

He rolled his eyes and shook his head at me. "I should have known. The zoo it is," he muttered. I could tell he was trying hard to hide the smile tugging at his lips. Leaning over, I placed a gentle kiss on his cheek, garnering a wink from him. "You're worse than a little kid, I swear."

Sticking my tongue out at him, I practically skipped down the stairs toward the kitchen, careful not to spill my coffee, whistling the whole way. "I'll make breakfast," I called back over my shoulder.

"Deal," he yelled as he started after me. "What's for breakfast?"

As he turned the corner into the kitchen, he eyed me suspiciously while I peeled a banana. Grabbing an apple from the fruit basket on the counter, I held the banana out to him. "Breakfast is served. Let's go!" I squealed excitedly.

The look on his face was hilarious as he took the apple from my hand. "There is no way you're getting me to eat a banana in front of you."

"Suit yourself," I responded, putting half the banana into my mouth before biting off a chunk and chewing. I smiled and headed towards the front door, leaving him to pick his jaw up off the floor.

What has gotten into me? I thought to myself. *I guess my chat with Nicole last night did the trick and got me out of my head after all.*

"*Y*ou really are like a little kid," he said with a smile as he handed his credit card over to the woman working the gift shop at the zoo.

"I told you I'd buy my own stuffed animal," I reminded him.

"Like I would let you do that. What kind of man would I be if I didn't get you a souvenir to remember our date?" he asked rhetorically.

I couldn't help but roll my eyes at him as I hugged my impossibly large snow leopard stuffed animal. "You didn't need to get me the biggest one either."

"Everything with me is bigger," he muttered under his breath. Too bad for him, I heard him, and so did the cashier. I swear she blushed.

"T–thank you for visiting the Pittsburgh Zoo and PPG Aquarium. Enjoy the rest of your day," the embarrassed girl stuttered, avoiding all eye contact as she handed Johnny his credit card and receipt. He flashed her his panty-dropping smile and I swear, she'd have melted into the floor if she could have.

I rolled my eyes at him before following his lead out of the gift shop before exiting toward the parking lot. Once outside, I was slightly taken aback when he intertwined his fingers with mine as we walked to his car. Everything with him was so natural, and I couldn't help but smile.

"Thank you again for my snow leopard," I sincerely said again when we reach his car. He said nothing, just tilted his cheek towards me and tapped for a kiss. Of course, I happily obliged.

"You're very welcome," he said after he helped me into his car, handing me back my new furry friend. I waited as he walked around to the driver side and climbed in behind the wheel. Starting the car, he glanced over at me and asked, "Where would you like to go for a late lunch?"

"Really? You're asking the girl where to go to eat? Isn't that usually the last thing a guy wants to do?" I teased.

"Well, we can go to Primanti Brothers for one of their 'Almost Famous' sandwiches...."

"I don't think so. I'm not all about putting my whole plate of food on one sandwich," I announced, slightly disgusted. "I like my fries on the side, with tons of ketchup."

"Okay, so we're definitely not going there then. What about pizza?"

"I'm good with pizza," I agreed.

"Just don't ask for bleu cheese down here. The server will look at you like you have three heads," he reminded me.

"Well, good job destroying my favorite way to eat pizza," I pouted. "I guess I can suffer through a naked pizza."

He rolled his eyes at me once again before putting the car in gear. "Beto's Pizza is on the way back to my place and their pizza is pretty good."

"I trust you," I said. To be honest, I was surprised by how much I meant it.

After smiling at me, we were on our way. The fifteen-minute drive flew by as we talked non-stop about our favorite animals at the zoo.

"Mine is obviously the snow leopard," I pointed out, giving my new friend a tight squeeze.

He glanced from the road, to me, to the giant stuffed animal that barely fit on my lap, and back to the road again before commenting. "I couldn't tell. Your eyes practically jumped out of your head when you saw that in the gift shop. Though I will give you credit––you tried, and failed miserably, to play it off by picking out the smaller one."

He was laughing at me, but I didn't care. I just hugged my snow leopard tighter while scrunching my nose up at him. That only caused him to laugh harder.

"You're cute when you play mad, Thumper," he teased.

My childish side came out in full force as I stuck my tongue out at him, not for the first time today. I loved how easy things were with him.

When we pulled into the parking lot, Johnny had to force me to leave my new friend in the car, but he promised to lock the car to keep it safe. We walked hand-in-hand to the front door of the restaurant and Johnny held the door for me. Once again, I found myself nearly comparing him to Adam and I had to mentally slap myself.

After taking a seat at a table, the waitress took our order. We decided to order a large meat lover's pizza to share and a beer each. Once our server was out of earshot, I couldn't resist the urge to point out what he decided on for pizza toppings. "So, you like to eat meat, I see. Something you want to tell me?" I asked, trying not to burst into laughter.

The smirk on his face could almost pass as a scowl before he laughed at me. "There is a lot I want to tell you, but you'll have to pry it out of me. Can't give away all my secrets at once. How would I convince you to come back if I did?"

I couldn't help but stop momentarily, my beer halfway to my mouth. "I see," is all I can say to hide my shock.

"Yo, Johnny, that you?" a voice called across the restaurant. Instinctively, we both turned to see who called out. I couldn't help but notice the tattoos snaking their way up both arms of the man walking towards our table. "Hey, man, thought that was you. Haven't seen you in a while. How've you been?"

Johnny stood when the stranger reached our table. Their 'bro hug' was adorable, and you could tell they were good friends.

"I've been good. Been meaning to come see you but haven't had the time, or the cash to do so."

"We'll have to set something up," the stranger continued.

I couldn't help but be drawn to the colorful ink covering his arms. Glancing my direction, the stranger caught me staring.

"Johnny Boy, we're being rude. Who's your friend?"

"Sorry. Aaron, this is Katlyn. Kat, this is my buddy, Aaron," Johnny said by way of an introduction.

"Nice to meet you, Katlyn," Aaron said politely, extending his hand. "Didn't mean to interrupt."

"It's Kat. And no interruption," I replied. "Would you like to join us?" I offered kindly.

"No, no, I couldn't. I just came in to pick up a pie for the shop, but I'm a few minutes early," he explained.

"Shop?" I questioned in confusion.

"Yeah, I work at Human Canvas. It's a tattoo shop over on Banksville," he explained.

"Oh, nice. My friend, Nicole, and I were talking about getting some new ink once I got home. Sadly, neither of us knows what we want to get."

Pulling a business card out of his wallet, he quickly handed it to me. "Well, when you guys decide what you want, give me a call and we can set up an appointment."

I glance down at the card before carefully sliding it into my purse that was hanging on the back of the chair I'd been sitting in. "Thanks, I'll do that."

Just then, Aaron's name was called from behind us. The three of us turned towards the take-out counter where a pizza box was being lifted into the air. "Guess that's my cue to head out. The guys will probably be wondering where their food is. Catch you later, Johnny. It was nice to meet you, Kat."

"See you, Aaron."

"Nice to meet you too."

When Aaron exited, Johnny motioned for me to take my seat once again before taking his seat opposite me.

"Your friend seems nice," I observed after a minute.

"Yeah, he's a good guy. So, you're really looking to get a tattoo?"

I smiled. "Absolutely."

"You just don't strike me as the type of girl to have tattoos."

"I already have tattoos," I stated matter of fact.

"You never mentioned that before." He looked over at me and attempted to find my ink. "Where?" he asked in curiosity when he couldn't find any sign of my tattoos.

"You can't see them."

"So, where are they?" he asks, leaning in closer.

"Wouldn't you like to know?" I quipped, dropping my voice to almost a whisper.

"Damn right I would."

All conversation ceased as our meat lover's pizza was deposited on our table. We ate in comfortable silence, punctuated by generic conversation, but the look in Johnny's eyes told me he hadn't forgotten the hidden tattoo conversation.

Once we'd eaten our fill and driven back to his place after paying our bill, I flopped down onto the couch, stuffed. Johnny dropped down next to me and we sat in silence for a few minutes. For the first time since arriving, there was an awkward silence between us.

"Want a drink," he began.

"I think I'm going to go to bed," I said at the same time.

We both stood awkwardly and just looked at one another.

"Oh, okay," he said, seemingly disappointed.

Picking up the snow leopard stuffed animal off the couch, I started to make my way toward the bedroom. "Thank you again for today, Johnny."

"You're welcome, Thumper. I'm glad you had fun," he whispered softly, placing a feather light kiss on my cheek.

He stood there, waiting for me to make a move but all I could offer him was a small smile before I scurried around him and raced up the stairs. Closing myself in his room for the evening, I leaned against the door, mentally bashing myself for running away from him.

A few minutes later, I heard him on the stairs. Holding my breath, I listened carefully. Though I didn't have to listen long. Just then, a soft knock sounded at the door.

"Kat?" he called through the closed door.

Stepping away from the door, I took a deep breath to stay my nerves before opening it. Before I could even say anything, he pulled me to him and pressed his lips firmly to mine. Just like before, I was completely lost in his kiss. One hand in my hair and his other cupping my cheek, his lips took possession of mine, his tongue begging to tangle with mine. My hands gripped his shoulders and I leaned into his kiss.

Slowly walking me backward towards his bed, we fell on top of it, our lips still locked together. My hands instinctively pulled at his shirt as he did the same to mine. *I need to feel his skin against me.* Our lips only parted long enough for him to shed his shirt and quickly help me out of mine. Before I could react, his lips were on my skin and I could feel myself arching into his touch. His lips and fingers were searing my skin everywhere he touched me.

I was so lost in the feeling of his touch that I scared myself when I screamed at him to stop. Backing off quickly, Johnny had a look of confusion upon his face. Jumping off the bed, I clutched my shirt to my chest.

"J–Johnny, I can't," I heaved.

His chest was heaving as much as mine, but the look of fire in his eyes was dying with each inhale. He stood and reached for me but I shrank back away from his touch. Dropping his hand, the look of hurt etched upon his features was nearly enough to make me cry. Unable to make eye contact, he looked away in hopes I wouldn't see his hurt.

"I'm sorry," I whispered.

"I would never force you to do anything you didn't want to do and

I would never hurt you," he said quietly, still unwilling to look me in the eyes. "You don't need to be afraid to let me get close to you."

After picking his shirt up off the floor where he'd tossed it, he exited the room and closed the door behind him silently without another word.

All the emotions I'd been holding in for the last few months burst to the surface and streamed down my face in tracks of hundreds of wet tears. Exhausted from the emotions rolling through me, I climbed into his bed and cried myself to sleep.

4

———————

The next morning, I awoke to a silent house. I wasn't sure I could face Johnny after rejecting him last night, but I knew I'd have to sooner or later. Opening the bedroom door, I peeked my head out into the hallway. *Silence.*

"Johnny?" I called out. Hearing no reply, I took a deep breath and walked out of his bedroom. Making my way down the stairs slowly, I listened for any sound of him, but there was none. As I stepped into the kitchen I spotted a note lying on the kitchen island.

Thumper,

I got called into work for a few hours. I shouldn't be too long. Here's a key so that you're not stuck in the house all day.

I'll see you soon,
Johnny

My heart sank as I placed the note back on the countertop. I felt horrible about last night, and I needed to explain why I freaked out––but it would have to wait. Needing some advice, I made my way back upstairs and called Nicole. After explaining what had happened the previous night she read me the riot act. And she was one-hundred percent right in what she said. Adam had killed my trust when he told me I'd never be good enough for anyone, and I was letting that ruin any chance I had at having anything real with Johnny.

After the forty-five-minute phone call with Nicole, I felt better and made the decision to get out of the house. With my family nearby, I decided to call my cousin and we met up for a little retail therapy. *This is sure to get my mind off of things until I can talk to Johnny.*

*A*fter some much needed retail therapy to clear my mind, I returned to Johnny's house and let myself in with the key he'd left for me before he'd gone to work this morning. Shopping with my cousin today while Johnny had worked may not have been my smartest decision, but I didn't want to sit alone in his house all day––especially not after last night.

Checking my phone after getting inside and locking the door, I saw that he'd text saying he was on his way home and would be here soon. Rushing upstairs, I quickly jumped in the shower, hoping I would be finished before he got home.

After taking one of the quickest showers of my life, I wrapped myself in a towel and had just stepped into his bedroom to get dressed when I heard the front door close. My heart pounded nervously in my chest. It was beating so hard it felt like it was going to jump out of my chest. Knowing he was home had me frozen in fear, standing in only my towel.

"Kat?" he called out to me. I couldn't answer him. "Are you home?" *Home. That sounds so nice coming from him, and it almost feels right,* I thought to myself.

Just then, I heard the bottom stair creak, pulling me from my thoughts. I knew it was only a matter of moments before he'd be in his room. Yet, despite that knowledge, I still couldn't move.

As expected, Johnny stepped into the room a few seconds later with such purpose that it took my breath away. The look that crossed his face at the sight of me standing there in just a towel was enough to make my body tingle. Sadly, he didn't come to me. Instead, he stood there, just looking at me with lust building in his eyes.

Turning, I started to walk back towards the bathroom but his deep whisper stopped me in my tracks. "Don't move."

Unmoving, I stared straight at the window in front of me, an undeniable ache beginning to build between my legs. Slowly, he moved across the room and stood behind me. With a feather-light touch, he grazed my shoulder. A shiver of pure ecstasy moved down my spine as my body broke out in goosebumps. Firmly pressing himself against my back, both of his hands lightly moved across my chest before tugging the towel free. My breath caught in my chest and I closed my eyes as the towel fell to the floor. A soft moan escaped my lips as one of Johnny's hands cupped my bare breast while the other traced a pattern of swirls down to my hip. Gently, he kissed the nape of my neck. Unable to hold myself stable, I had to brace myself on the edge of the bed. It was all I could do not to collapse.

"Turn around and look at me," his thick voice commanded. Doing as instructed, I slowly turned to look into his eyes. "Do you want me?" he questioned.

"Yes," I whispered.

"Do you trust me?"

Closing my eyes, I took a deep breath. "Yes," I answered truthfully.

Without another word, his hands were on me once again, though my eyes remained closed, getting lost in his touch. Slowly, Johnny traced the contours of my neck and the curve of my collarbone. Lightly tracing the curve of my breasts, his fingers left trails of fire on my willing skin. With each newly conquered inch, the ache inside me grew.

With slow purpose, Johnny once again traced the swell of my breasts and back up to my shoulders. Dipping his head to my chest, he took one of my hard nipples in his mouth, smiling at my sharp intake of breath. Teasing my nipple with his tongue, Johnny massaged my other breast with one hand, while pulling my body closer to him with his other.

I arched against him, my body begging for more. He knew what I wanted, but he was determined to fan the flames of my desire just a little longer—he was going to make me voice my desires. Gently, his hands roved down my thighs causing the ache between my legs to become nearly unbearable. I craved his touch. While still teasing my nipple with his tongue, Johnny gently nudged my knees apart with his. I wanted to speak, to beg him to touch me, but no sound passed my lips. I was rendered completely speechless.

Oh God, I want him. Any fear that I'd felt last night instantly vanished. I could fully admit that I wanted him, and I wanted him now.

Stopping, Johnny took a few steps backward. My body tensed, and my eyes flew open as my entire body seemed to scream out in a panic. To my surprise, Johnny was smiling. "I like the ink. It's sexy."

Heat from an embarrassed blush spread across my chest and worked its way up to my neck and cheeks. Seeming to read my mind, he shook his head 'no' at me and then smiled. I couldn't help but return his smile.

His eyes still on my body, he slowly removed his work shirt and pants. My heart beat faster, my breaths short, as I watched him slide his boxers down his strong legs. The raw energy that emanated from his naked body made my lust burn hotter.

Johnny stood there for a moment, allowing my eyes to travel over him. The power of his arms. The strength of his legs. The muscles of his chest and stomach. I loved every inch of him. At that moment, I wanted nothing more than to reach out and touch him but I was frozen in place. My eyes traveled every inch of his body, a small smile tugging at the corner of my mouth as I stared longingly at his growing erection. He wasn't ashamed to let me look either. It was obvious that Johnny wanted me too.

Stepping towards me, I felt the heat inside me grow exponentially. Within seconds, his lips were on my breasts once again. Softly trailing a path up my thighs, I felt my knees growing weak. Slowly, he lowered himself to his knees and kissed a trail down my stomach. Bracing myself on the edge of the bed, I found myself unable to stand on my own any longer. Tenderly, Johnny traced the contours of my inner thighs as my pussy began to throb with need.

Johnny kissed trails along my skin, teasing me with whispered touches of his lips along the hot skin between my legs. I wanted him to taste me. To pleasure me. But I also wanted this exquisite, torturous teasing to last. Everything he was doing to me was making my world spin faster. I knew it wouldn't be long before I exploded in a bright display of colors.

"Lie down," he instructed, his voice thick with desire. My body already weak with desire, I did as I was told. Lying back on the bed, I felt him nudge my legs further apart. Grabbing my ass, he pulled me to the edge of the bed before grabbing my legs and gently placing them over his shoulders. By this point, I was wet, ready, and waiting. Unfortunately, the torture was going to continue.

Teasingly, he gently nipped everywhere except where I wanted him. In the haze of my mind, I began to wonder if this was as straining on him as it was for me. My body was wound so tightly with desire that I was trembling. As his mouth hovered over my wetness, my legs tightened. Flicking his tongue out, be barely touched me when I jumped, my body betraying me. I wanted desperately to move against his face as he tasted me, but he held me firmly in place, his teasing continuing. Just when I thought I couldn't stand his teasing any longer, Johnny covered my wet pussy with his mouth. I cried out in ecstasy. Moving his tongue with purpose, Johnny licked and sucked me as if it were the only thing that would keep him alive.

Arching my back on the bed, I moved against him, desperate for his touch. With every movement, his mouth became more aggressive. I couldn't get enough. What he was doing...the way it felt--God, the way I moved against him only intensified my pleasure. Suddenly, I felt him dig his fingers into the muscles of my ass and pull me closer to him.

Animalistic moans echoed from deep within him, matched only by my small screams of pleasure. I couldn't take it anymore. Knotting my fingers in his hair, I pulled him closer still. His tongue was driving me mad. I wanted to pull away from him so I could catch my breath, but I needed him to keep going. The heat burning inside of me was so great I knew his touch was the only thing keeping me from disappearing. Frantic now, I moved against him, pulling his head even deeper into me. When I arched against him again, Johnny's control finally snapped. He sucked my clit relentlessly until I began to shake. Harder and faster he sucked and licked me until I bucked against him uncontrollably, digging my fingers into his scalp as my orgasm washed over me.

My body shook frenziedly as Johnny held me against his face, slowly licking me until I fall still, completely exhausted. My breathing was fast and I was certain it mirrored his own. Climbing up off of his knees, he leaned over me on the bed and tenderly kissed each breast. Despite the earth-shattering orgasm I had just had, I still wanted more. And he knew it. I wanted to completely lose myself with him. Still positioned at the edge of the bed, Johnny placed himself between my legs and began to tease my still wet pussy with the head of his rock-hard cock. My breath caught in my chest with each teasing touch. Grinding my hips against him, I begged for more. Teasing himself at the same time he was teasing me seemed to be driving us both crazy.

Pulling away from me, I heard him rustling in the drawer of the nightstand. Moments later, I heard the familiar sound of a condom wrapper being torn open. Watching him slide the latex down his thick shaft turned me on even more.

After a few more seconds and teasing strokes, he thrust deep inside of me with a guttural moan. I screamed out in ecstasy before wrapping my legs around his hips tightly. Johnny grabbed me by the hips and held me tightly as he pounded himself inside me. Seemingly afraid he was hurting me, he slowed his strokes after a moment.

I began to shake my head from side to side as I tried to find my voice. "No," I moaned.

A devilish smile crossed his lips. "What do you want?" he asked.

He knew I was too shy to say it. "What do you want?" he asked again, more firmly than before.

"I want," I started, too embarrassed to finish my thought. He waited. Slowly, he pulled out and my panic began to set in. "I want you to fuck me. Hard," I blurted out.

That was what he wanted to hear. Without warning, he flipped me onto my stomach and thrust himself deep inside me once again. The wave of relief that flowed through me at the feeling of him inside of me was pure bliss. He felt amazing. Desperate to feel him every-where, I met each of his thrusts with a thrust of my own, urging him deeper. Arching against him, I was pleasantly surprised when he grabbed my hair and pulled my head back. Using his other hand, he grasped my breast firmly from behind and pulled me into him harder. It wasn't long before his animalistic nature took over as he fucked me hard and deep. He fucked me like he wanted to make me scream his name, and I did.

In that instant, something inside of me broke. For the first time in a long time, I felt free.

With each new thrust, I screamed his name and begged him to go harder. I couldn't get enough of him. Letting go of my hair, Johnny frantically grabbed my hips to pull me back into him harder with each forward thrust. My head was spinning and the burn in my belly was building to an explosive point. I was about to lose control. My moans and screams reached a crescendo as I felt my muscles begin to clench. Sensing my impending orgasm, Johnny moved faster against me. I could tell he was close. Deep down, I wanted him to fuck me all night like this, but we were both so close and I needed to feel his release. A few more hard thrusts later and my orgasm tore my body like the waves of a tsunami.

Feeling my wetness tighten around him soon proved to be too much to bear as he lost control. Shuddering through his release, Johnny collapsed against me and held me as he stayed nestled deep inside of me, both of us trying to catch our breath.

After a few moments still intimately connected, I felt him pull away from me slowly. I turned my head to watch him walk into the bathroom holding the towel I'd had wrapped around me when he'd first gotten home. A moment later, I heard the cupboard under the sink, where the bathroom garbage was stowed, open and close followed by the familiar sound of the faucet running for a few seconds before he stepped back into the room. Walking over to me, I closed my eyes when I felt the exquisite heat from the wet towel against my sensitive flesh as he carefully cleaned between my legs.

Once he had finished, he tossed the towel across the room towards his laundry basket and climbed onto the bed behind me. Pulling the thin sheet over us, he gathered me into his arms and held me close.

"Please don't leave tomorrow, Thumper. I don't want you to leave. Ever," he confessed.

I smiled but didn't answer him.

Nothing could ruin this moment, and I wanted to stay like this for as long as I could. Snuggling up closer to his chest, I was just about to close my eyes when the worst sound ever filtered out from my purse.

Adam's ringtone.

GOING
DOWN

ABIGAIL LEE JUSTICE

1

*A*sshole. I curse under my breath as I walk past the empty cubicles of "Pittsburgh Tribune," Pittsburgh most famous smut magazine. *Not just any asshole, but a fucking asshole.* That editorial was possibly the best in my entire career. Just as he wanted... but no, it still hadn't been good enough for *Mr. Asshole.*

Making the changes he wanted had taken almost eight hours. I glanced at the clock on the wall. *11:30 p.m. Thirty minutes until the magazine hit the presses.* I already had one of the worst days of my life and now I had worked a double without even stopping for a dinner break. *He must be curled up in his warm, comfy bed, or even worse probably with some expensive hooker. He has the good life, while I'm here busting my ass for him.*

As I approach the elevator, I'm still cursing him for how the day unfolded. And like magic, there he is. *What the fuck? He's still here? I wonder why he's still in the building.*

"Miss Lake," he says in his usual southern drawl.

"Mr. Peters," I reply in a not so nice curt way.

When the niceties are over, the bell for the elevator sounds. I watch as the door opens; he waves for me to proceed. *Just like a gentleman. Please give me a break. He hadn't been so nice this afternoon when he was ripping me a new asshole in front of the entire staff.* I press the button for the ground floor and move as far back in the corner as possible. Watching him saunter in made everything seem to vanish. Seeing him with his tie off and his shirt unbuttoned to the third button, has my heart racing in my chest. It's not easy to refocus but I must if I'm going to survive the elevator ride to the ground floor.

I watch the numbers light up as we descend, trying to block my gorgeous boss from my thoughts. Three flights down, THIRTEEN to go. *Damn this is going to be a long fucking ride.*

"So, any plans for the weekend?" *Now he wants to have small talk just to kill time? Well, I'll give him small talk if he wants it.*

He's squashed every weekend plan I've had for the past six months while working on his pet project. I shoot him a glare that says you had better believe I have plans even if I don't. It's none of his business if I have plans or not. So, I do the next best thing. I lie.

"Yes." With the biggest smile on my face, I tell him a big fat lie.

"With your boyfriend?" He gives me a look that says he can see straight through me. Just like *Superman* can see through *Lois Lane.* He has that same ability. He can see straight through my lie. What boyfriend? Oh, right. I have a made-up boyfriend so that Curtis in accounting would stop asking me out. Curtis is cute and all, but not my type. Rumors had been spread around the office for months that I'm very serious about my boyfriend.

I want someone that will take care of me like a princess. Not Curtis who still lives in his mother's basement. I don't think that guy could take care of a puppy let alone little ole me.

On the other hand, my fictional boyfriend wines and dines me every chance he gets. Flies me off every now and then just to have a romantic dinner. Wait that sounds too much like the guy from *Fifty Shades of Grey.* Yeah, that's the kind of man I want. Hell, he can even have his own red room of pain, with all the whips, floggers, canes, and toys. I can be just as kinky.

I haven't had a single date in the past six months because of Mr. Asshole standing next to me. My sex life is nonexistent, not even my battery-operated toy is providing relief. No time. And no, I don't call him BOB for short. My vibrator's name is Grant Peters or Grant—named him after Mr. Asshole—when I need a good orgasm, but even he hasn't been doing his magic on my girl parts.

"No." he chuckles and shakes his head. "Quite taciturn tonight, aren't you?"

"I'm tired and hungry that's all." I say in a denunciatory tone. "I'm not in a talking mood." I return my attention to the number above the doors. THIRTEEN, it goes dark, and the elevator comes to a screeching halt.

What the hell is going on? No, don't fucking tell me. The emergency lights come on; I press the button several times and wait for someone to answer my call. Nothing. After several rings, no one answers.

"You've got to be kidding me."

"This thing has been on the fritz for months. Don't worry. The emergency generator should kick on in a few minutes. This happened a few weeks back. No biggie."

"I hope so."

"Someone sounds desperate. What? Don't you like my company?"

I turn towards him. He has a smirk on his face that enhances his handsome features. Yep, he's gorgeous; any girls' panties would be wet just by looking at him. His dark wavy hair against his light skin gives him a more sophisticated look. His fit body inside the Armani suit adds a touch of class. But he's still an asshole to me. He gets his looks from his father, the late Mr. Grant Peters. I admit, when he took over the company after his father's death, I went a little googly-eyed like the rest of the female staff members. It was only a few months after he started as CEO when he began to treat me like shit. The crush I once had went away just like the crush I had on my high school sweetheart.

"I just want to go home." I answer.

Accepting my silence, he leaves me alone. I drop my purse on the floor, and kick off my heels before I start pacing. I need to get out of here before I have a fucking melt down.

"Shouldn't the generators have come on by now?" I say more to myself than him. Not caring if he answers me or not.

"You're right." He pulls his phone from his pocket and holds it to the ceiling. "No signal. You? "

I dig into my purse and pull out my cell, then stare down at a blank screen. *Fuck! I forgot my charger at home this morning.* "Shit dead battery."

I drop it back into my handbag and resume pacing.

"We can't do a damn thing except wait," he says in his deep baritone voice.

Wait for how long? "What if the power doesn't come back on? No one will be back here in the building until Monday!"

Wow, I can't believe how hot it's already getting. Sweat trickles down my back, making my top stick to my skin. To cool down, I remove my jacket and drop it on top of my purse. Just as my jacket falls, I watch as Mr. Asshole takes off his three thousand dollar Armani jacket. He gently folds his jacket inside out, the only proper way to protect a jacket like that, and lays it on top of mine. *No way is that baby going to hit the dirty floor of the elevator car.*

He rolls up the sleeves of his crisp steel colored dress shirt revealing his forearms. "Huh...I've never seen you without your heels on before."

I stop mid pace and turn to him. *For Christ sake, why won't he leave me alone? I don't want to have small talk with him. I just want to go home and spend a boring weekend to myself.*

"I make it a habit of keeping my shoes on during work time, Mr. Peters."

"Call me Grant, Ms. Lake."

Shit the asshole keeps staring at me.

"So?"

"Nothing. You're just not as tall as I thought."

"Great. Now my height is a problem for you. My work's not good enough either. I give up. You know what? I'm done! Nothing I do is ever good enough for you. I bust my ass day in and day out. I'm the first to arrive in the morning. Hell, I'm always the last one to leave. I take work home on the weekends just to catch up when I walk back in on Monday. No matter what I do, it's still not good enough for the boss. I bet that if I walked around the office half-clothed, my tits hanging out, with my ass barely covered, I'd get your attention quick enough. Shit. Now I'm not tall enough for you. Why don't you just fire me? Get it over with. Better yet, I'll make it easy for you. I—"

Before the word 'quit' can leave my lips, he silences me with a kiss. What the hell?" I push off his chest, and he steps back.

"What are you doing?" I ask in a panic.

"What I've wanted to do for the past year."

He pulls me against his big muscular chest and leans in once more, but I push at him once again. What does he mean 'for the past year'?

"I don't understand."

"Sweetheart, I have tried to fight my attraction to you by being as mean as possible. I'm sorry. "

Shit he is an asshole. "Oh, great just what I needed to find out. My gorgeous boss has been playing me for a fool. "

"Go ahead call me an asshole, as I'm sure you've called me that many times already."

"Oh, you bet I have. You're nothing but a petulant schoolboy. Pick on the girl you like until she goes off on you, is that it? Then you stomp on her some more by telling her you have feelings for her. You planned your attack on me today by getting me madder than a hornet. You've got some nerve."

"If you say so." He reaches for me again, and I do the same as before move even further from him. "Get off me." as I swat his hands away.

He stumbles back, surprised. I guess he's never been told no before. Not Mr. Asshole, he takes what he wants and throws away the rest.

"What do you think you're doing? You're my boss! Or did you forget that?"

"I'm sorry I can't fight this anymore." I watch as he moves towards me once again, pinning me against the wall with his body. I draw in a sharp breath as his erection prods my thigh.

Hearing his words of endearment has my mind spinning. Why all of a sudden today does he sound like a man and not my boss? Is he trying to seduce me?

"Fuck."

"I need you, Christy."

"After making my life a living hell for the past year you think a kiss and pressing your erection up against me is going to make it all better? I don't just hop in the sack with just anyone. I have standards too. "

"Bed? I won't last the rest of this elevator ride, let alone wait to get you in my bed. I need you now. Here in the elevator. Then I'll take you to bed like a proper gentleman. I have to have you. The beast inside me needs you. All you have to do is say the word "RED" and I will stop"

Without an invitation, he covers my lips with his and takes. I stand like a statue, thinking this can't be real. I must be dreaming. Today has been nothing but a big old dream. At any moment, I'll wake up. He pulls my hips against him and my mind goes blank. What dream?

All at once, his musky, manly scent envelopes me. Desires course through my body for the first time in a long time. With a moan, I slide my hands around his neck. I embrace the kiss. Suddenly, I'm overpowered by the need for him to rip my clothes off and fuck me here in the elevator as I've fantasized about so many times. His hands slide slowly up around my waist. His right hands settle in the curves. While he explores my ass with his other hand. He caresses my cheek with a moan.

"God, you feel so good. You're perfect." He murmurs in my ear. He nips at my bottom lip, teasing it with his tongue. *Where does he think this is going? God, he's a great kisser. I'm fucking doomed! All because the elevator was stuck on level THIRTEEN.*

The way he's kissing me drugs my senses. His hands are now on my breast, which alerts me to the fact that he's about to unbutton my blouse. He spins me around and pulls me against his erection. I can hear his harsh breathing against my ear. In a low tone, he seductively says all kinds of dirty things in my ear. *He's gone from being asshole to lover within minutes. I must have lost my mind. I know all I have to do is say the word "Red" and he will stop.*

I gasp as he exposes me. His hands cover my breasts he gently massages them. I'm lost just by his touch; I rock back and forth against his erection. Air hisses through his teeth as he pinches my nipples.

He whispers. "I could stay like this forever."

My knees are weak. I don't know how much longer I can stand on my own will. Just that fast he grabs at the hem of my skirt and tugs it over my hips. My nipples are hard from his touch. A moan escapes him as he caresses my thighs. *Good thing I wore my fancy panties today. It's not every day I wear a garter belt and stockings but something told me to dress up.*

He moves up cupping my pussy with a moan.

"So, fucking wet. God, I can't believe I waited this long. I could have been in heaven with your luscious body."

He slips his finger under my soaking panties and zeroes in on my clit.

"Fuck...oh fuck that feels so good. I gasp between every stroke on my clit. I don't know how much of this I can take. He's hit my spot dead on. "Right there. That's it doesn't stop. Please." It's all I can do from falling over; I brace my hands up against the wall. He speeds up with his blazing fingers, heating my entire body up. *Yeah it was hot before but I feel like I'm on fire.*

Moving down, closer to my entrance, he teases me with his middle finger. As he nips my earlobe. I can't control my body from shaking as I let a small whimper escape.

"I want to hear you scream at the top of your voice. Don't hold back, sweetheart. I've dreamt every night to hearing you scream my name. You won't hold back anymore. Let me hear you. "

I reach behind me, and slide my palm down to his very hard, erect shaft. He moans as I work him through his clothes. Just as he works my clit. I'm close to coming and he knows it. I move vigorously squeezing his shaft, as his hand tugs on my engorged clit.

I can't hold back a second longer. "Oh God, that feels amazing" As the words slip from my mouth I feel my body convulse from his touch.

"Let it go baby. I've got you. I want you to fly. Soar to a new place. A place where it's just you and me only. "

That's all it took, his words and touch on my clit. Finally, I feel the orgasm start to subside, he holds me against his body, as a second orgasm takes hold. Cooing in my ear he tells me how good I feel, and how much he wants me. I'm a little unsteady, as his firm hand holds onto me.

Before I even stop shaking, he turns me around to face him. His lips attract mine. His tongue does a fancy tango with mine. I take my right hand and run it through his thick, inky hair. He pulls me away, fumbling in his pocket. I work on the buttons of his shirt. Revealing a dragon tattoo on his entire chest.

Sharp talons circle his belly button. A red eye encases his left nipple. Underneath his fancy suit, he hides a beautiful piece of art. He has the perfect formed six –pack abs my fingers have ever touched. I gently trail my nail from the tip of his left nipple down to the top of his dress pants. He moans from my touch as he rips open a gold condom packet. To speed things up, I undo his belt, and unbutton his button, so that I can release his zipper.

His penis is hard and erect pushing up against his black boxers. I reach inside, delighted by what I find. I wrap my fingers tightly around his thick length. Now, *he* is perfect. I just want to devour him. No wonder he's so cocky. He has a lot to be proud of.

"Christy, don't," he warns me.

Impatience in his voice lets me know he's about to blow just from my touch. Exactly what he did to me, I continue to do to him. I stroke him a few more times. His eyes darken with desire and penetrate me as he pushes my hand away. He rolls the condom down his shaft. *Shit, he does want me.*

He grabs my ass, lifts me off the floor. My legs dangle just for a few seconds when I hear him say, "Wrap your legs around my waist." I do as I'm told. He slowly reaches my ponytail and pulls out the band holding my black hair up. The sheer pressure he uses sends a sting to my scalp. I forgot what it feels like to have a man take charge of my body. I feel like a princess. My mind. Submit, Submit, And Submit.

"So, beautiful, sweetheart."

Just when I think he's going to plunge inside of me, he licks my nipple, sending more pleasure through me. His hot mouth takes my nipple into his hot mouth and begins to bite down. The same sensation I felt when he removed my ponytail is now focused on my nipple.

"I've waited so long...now you are mine...forever?"

With a little tug, I feel my panties being ripped off. Gently he slides his cock up to my entrance. I'm already wet, so it doesn't take much for my vagina to suck in his cock. I cry out at the invasion. Not knowing what to do with my hands I link them around his neck and hold on.

"I knew you'd feel incredible. The way your body reacts to my touch. It's just fucking amazing." Both of us are now breathing hard. I feel him start to move, savoring every stroke. Until I feel him sink in all the way. He's so big I wasn't sure I could take him all.

I throw my head back, my breath coming in slow steady puffs as he moves his hips back and forth. Feeling every inch of him inside of me. Has me riding the orgasm wave again. *I don't ever remember sex feeling this good. Maybe it's been so long that I forgot how good it could feel.*

He may have been an asshole to me, but feeling this good has erased that from my brain. Both of our bodies are glistening with sweat.

"I've dreamt about this every night for the past year. Sinking my face between your breasts, sucking on your tits, and devouring your wet pussy with my mouth. All dreams. No more. This is for real."

Just hearing his words of endearment has me craving more. *I wonder if he says that to every woman he fucks in an elevator shaft.* Suddenly my desires to submit are shaken. Nevertheless, his words are just what I need to hear. He trails his tongue up my spine across my neck. Sending shivers up and down my spine.

"Sweetheart, you have tormented my days and night. I've thought of no one else but you. I couldn't even force myself to be with anyone but you."

Sighing with those last words, I know now that his words were true. Especially the part that about only wanting me and no one else.

"Oh, God..."

Just as I'm about to orgasm. He says. "Look at me, Christy." I force my eyes open, and for the first time I truly see his steel blue eyes. That look alone makes my pussy spasm. He moans and moves faster inside me.

"Tell me you want me too," he says with a sense of urgency.

"I want you." I didn't want him in the beginning but my brain had been clouded for so long. Now, I do. Especially when he is balls deep inside me making me feel so wonderful. Any girl would want to feel this way. I'm awakened for the first time in a long time. With each thrust, I feel my pent up sexual desires unfold.

My nails claw at his shoulders digging deeper with each thrust he delivers to my core. I cling to him just as a cat clings to a tree. Holding on for dear life. For each one of his grunts I answer back with a moan of delight.

"Say my name."

Shit I realize that all I've ever called him in my head was Mr. Asshole or Mr. Peters when we've been in the boardroom. With a sterner voice, I hear him say "Grant."

For months, I've secretly said his name, while in the privacy of my bedroom but saying it when he's touching me forces me to break even more. Without hesitation, his name escapes from the back of my throat and ricochets throughout the elevator. I scream his name over and over, for what seems like minutes is only a few seconds.

"Yes." Is all I heard him say as he groans, sinking his teeth into my shoulder. Marking me as his. Damn he's the sexiest man alive. I throw my head back as I begin to come. My body shakes and shudders with every thrust. Feeling him pound deep inside me. Just then, I feel warmth spread throughout my entire body. He screams out a few curses of his own, I know he's coming, too.

For a few minutes, which seems like days, I know what it feels like to be sated. I close my eyes and throw back my head exposing my neck to him. He plants a line of kisses up my neck reaching my chin, when I meet his lips, he kisses me, I know at that very moment I'm his. I draw into his clutches. He pulls out of me, and I instantly feel the warmth and fullness vanish. I clutch at him to feel the closeness again; suddenly I sense that the ride that I was just on has come to a halt. *Fuck, what have I just done? I crossed the line by submitting to the one man I call asshole.*

I do what any woman does when they realize that they fucked up. I grab for my clothes as fast as I can. As I pull on my skirt, I watch him with hawk eyes, not the doe eyes I had sported for him while making love. I make sure he doesn't come anywhere near me. He removes the condom and ties it off, checking for any leaks. He too makes hast of getting his clothes back on, he shoves the tied off condom into his pocket. Not a word is spoken between the two of us for a few minutes.

When we're both dressed, he moves towards me. Guilt written across my face forces me to turn away from him.

"Christy...don't."

The lights flicker on and the elevator resumes its decent. *Thank God.* Not wanting to look him in the eyes. I pick up my jacket and purse, slip on my heels. For the first time, tonight I notice the camera in the corner of the room. We are in opposite corners; I don't know what to do at this point. All I know is that I can't look at him. I try everything in my power not to look at him. Ignoring him, I busy myself, straightening up my hair. *I don't need to be seen with fuck me hair.*

"Christy, will you look at me?"

"Don't. Please I can't do this."

The moment the doors slide open, I make a hasty retreat. In the lobby, I encounter the night security guard. I mutter a curse under my breath.

"Ms. Lake, I didn't know anyone was still in the building."

Just when I have to deal with the security guard, Mr. Asshole strolls out of the elevator. He still makes me flush when I see him.

"We got stuck in the elevator."

"Wow Mr. Peters, I didn't know you were still here too. When the power went out, I went down to the generator room flip the switch. I'm sorry I must have missed the emergency call."

"No problem, Marty. On Monday, call for service on the backup generator. You never know when the powers going to go out again. "

"Sure thing, Mr. Peters."

It takes everything inside of me not to run from the building. But I know that if I do, Asshole will be on my tail faster then what I can run. So, I do the next best thing I wave goodbye to Marty acting liked nothing happened in the elevator. I've got my keys in my hand when I reach for the door leading to the garage. I hear his footsteps behind me.

"Christy. STOP!" I keep moving, putting one foot in front of another, trying not to become distracted by his voice. Maybe if I ignore him, he'll get the hint and leave me alone.

"I said stop, Christy." As he grabs my arm, I hit the button on my key fob for my car. My hand comes so close to grabbing the handle but suddenly he turns me around to face him. I can't look him in the eye. I stare at his chest remembering the dragon tattoo hiding under his shirt. His hands feel just like the talons of the dragon. His finger tightens around my wrist. There's no way I can break free, but worst of all I don't won't to free myself from him.

"Damn it. Tell me what's wrong. How can I make this better? Why are you running from me?"

Afraid to meet his gaze, I can tell by the tone in his voice he's not happy. I finally get the courage to look at his eyes; they are back to the same steel color when we were making love. He's back to being the lover and not the asshole.

"Damn it Christy why are you running?"

"I'm not running from you; I want to go home. We had our fun and now it's time to move on. "

"Is that what you think it was? Just fun. Baby you got me all wrong." Just when I think about pulling back from him, he takes the keys from my hand and clicks my locks back on. He pulls me in the opposite direction. The parking garage isn't that big. Only three cars are parked. Mine, his, and I guess the third car is Marty's. Before I can even protest. I hear him unlocking his car.

"Don't worry. I'll send someone to get your car." He has a determined look on his face. I've seen that look may times in the board room when he scolding me for this or that.

"I'm not going anywhere with you. Don't you get it? You're my boss. I work for you. You're rich and I'm just an everyday girl." Before I can get another word out. He grabs me and shoves me against his vintage, black Bentley. *Never In a million years would I have guessed his taste in cars would be so refined. I took him for a racy sports car type.*

I love the feel as he traps my body with his. Using his knees, he separates my thighs. That's when I know my body is a traitor. My breasts tingle from his touch.

"Do you think once would be enough for me? I told you, you are mine and I mean it. I've only just begun."

I moan as he traces my lips with his tongue. I feel his touch down to my pussy. I know this is wrong, but I want him so much. That's when I melt. The invisible barrier is broken. He doesn't waste any time reaching under my skirt, tugging my panties to the side. His fingers trace my pussy lips. I'm just as wet as I was in the elevator. It only takes seconds and he's found my weak spot once more. He pushes his fingers in deep, glides out. He's a man on a mission. And that mission is to take and conquer my soul.

"Do you feel that? How hot and wet you are for me, baby. I did this to you, Christy. You know you want me too." He growls in my ear. "Stop fighting the demons in your head."

All I want to do is feel. He's right. All I want him to do is to keep his fingers deep inside me and make me come. Just as he promised, I scream out his name, "Mr. Asshole."

ABOUT THE AUTHOR

Abigail Lee Justice writes emotional, erotic, romantic suspense that includes a BDSM theme. She creates strong characters who seem real but are flawed in some ways; some couples Happily Ever After will be a work in process. Some characters' problems are just too steamy to fix in one book.

Born and raised in Baltimore City by two wonderful, supportive, loving parents, as a child Abigail made up vivid tales in her head. Until one day, a friend told her instead of keeping her stories locked her head she needed to put them on paper and that's exactly what she did.

Abigail met her husband thirty years ago on a blind date (thanks Dan C.) while working a part time job to put herself through college. She fell madly in love with her Prince Charming and has been since the first day they met.

By day, Abigail practices medicine in a busy Cardiologist practice. By evening, she switches her white coat for more relaxed comfortable clothing. She has two wonderful adult sons and a very spoiled chocolate lab. In the wee hours of the night, she writes BDSM romances. In her spare time when not working or writing, Abigail enjoys reading, concocting vegetarian dishes, scuba diving, high adventure activities, living in the lifestyles she writes about, and doing lots and lots of research making sure her characters get it just right.

Connect with Abigail

[f] facebook.com/abigailleejustice

[twitter] twitter.com/abigailljustice

[instagram] instagram.com/author_abigail_lee_justice

BARGAINING FOR MORE

VICTORIA MONROE

1

XANDER

*I*t amuses me that everyone who is already involved in their work and preoccupied with tasks, find it necessary to overly engage when I walk through the halls. 'Good afternoon, Mr. Prescott,' 'You're looking well, Mr. Prescott,' 'Sir.' The greetings come in a variety of ways from elaborate ass kissings to simple nods, but despite the differences, there's always trepidation in the eye of the beholder, and that's exactly what I like. It gives me every advantage against my prey in this man-eat-man business world.

"It's been a good day, ladies and gentlemen. Let's get some deals sealed," I address the group as I take my place at the head of the gleaming cherry table located in the large boardroom dubbed the *war room*. It sits at the top of the steel and glass building that houses the company I've built from the ground up. The war room is where all of the meetings and negotiations are held for each and every merger and acquisition that happens at Foxx Enterprises.

"Marcus, where do we stand with the final negotiation on the Onyx acquisition?" This deal doesn't end with the same number of zeros as the deal with Stone Holdings, but that doesn't make it insignificant.

"It's excellent, sir. Legal is drafting the final clauses this morning, and we are on schedule for closing tomorrow."

"Has there been a confirmation on commencing liquidation?"

"As early as next week."

"Make that a definite, Marcus."

"Yes, sir."

I seethe as I look at the empty chair to my right. A meeting with Gregory Edward Stone, II is in forty minutes, and I need today's briefing immediately. "Where's Chandler?" I'm sure the gruff tone of my voice doesn't go unnoticed by the group. Kyle Chandler is literally my right hand. I trust him with everything. I've known Chandler since we were kids, and he knows more about me than anyone. To most people, I'm a closed book, so they invent the details they don't know. Everyone utters their lack of knowledge regarding Chandler's whereabouts, and it's the information he's providing that I really need this morning. The war room door opens abruptly and a very winded Chandler—who typically wears a poker face well—is clearly shaken.

"This meeting is over—we'll regroup tomorrow morning at seven," I address everyone in the war room and wait patiently impatient for each person to collect their things and depart.

"We have a problem, Foxx." Chandler still calls me by the nick-name I was given by my friends decades ago. I was the kid who thought of all of our shenanigans, only to find a way to get us out of some of the trouble—not all, but some. I was sly as a fox.

"I gathered. What problem?"

"Stone Holdings."

"Not what I want to hear—what's the problem?"

"Grayson Stone."

"Who is Grayson Stone? I've never heard that name, and we've been through everything—business and personal—on Gregory Stone, II and III."

"Apparently, this person is Stone, III's son—Stone, II's grandkid—and he's reviewing everything regarding the acquisition with his grandfather in light of his father's health issue."

I snap my briefcase closed and enter my office through the hidden door on the far wall of the war room.

"I. I. I don't know what to say, Xander." Kyle follows behind me, stuttering an attempt at an explanation. "I can't explain how this went undiscovered. We're finding out bits and pieces of information. Nothing is well known about Grayson, or G.E. Stone as he's referred to in most of the facts we've learned. This all came to light in the last couple of hours."

"What exactly are we dealing with here? Is this missing grandson anything more than a hiccup to this deal?"

"Magna Cum Laude from Duquesne University. Master of business administration, Master of Laws and Juris Doctor all from Harvard. Twelve years of combined practice in corporate and international law..."

"You're kidding me, right?" I gasp the words from a state somewhere between horrified and mystified that this proverbial *stone* went unturned. "Pittsburgh born and raised, and we don't know about him?"

"No." Kyle seems just as in awe as I am at this new development.

"Where has this Stone family progeny been hiding all this time?"

"A few places from what we know..." I growl at Chandler's answer with irritation, "...London, Paris, Istanbul. Look, Xander, we're all over this. At this point, all we know is G.E. Stone is a major player in corporate law for some of the most arduous international companies. He did serve as head legal counsel for two corporations in both the Asian and European markets, before moving to the private sector and onto independent consulting."

"This just leaves me speechless." Speechless isn't something I'm accustomed to—ever.

"Xander, until Greg Stone suffered a stroke and the elder Stone had to take the reins once again—neither of them—ever spoke of their son/grandson, G.E. Stone. There's nothing documented about him anywhere, in anything, from Stone Holdings. I haven't even seen a picture anywhere, and I've been in both Stones' offices and skiing at Stone, II's private chalet at Seven Springs Mountain Resort."

The view from the floor-to-ceiling windows from my office on the sixty-second floor of the UPMC Building frames an unusually clear day in Pittsburgh. The sky is blue and the rivers sparkle in the brilliant midday sunlight. The day reflects exactly what I felt this morning—brilliant. I thought today's scheduled meeting with Gregory Edward Stone, II, would surely be the final stop before everyone signed on the dotted line—ending this buyout and making me an even richer man, as I break apart Stone Holdings and sell it, one lucrative piece at a time. Now the game has changed. A soft tone precedes the announcement from Ethan, my administrative assistant, that Mr. Stone, II is waiting for me in the war room.

"Raise the atlas," I command. Kyle slides his finger across the rocker switch near the bookcases behind my desk, and the framed global atlas on my wall lifts as the lights in my office dim. Through a one-way mirror, I observe a very distraught Gregory Stone, II sitting ominously at the board table in the war room. The burdens of all of the parts of his life appear to be taking a toll on him.

"I don't need this aggravation at the eleventh hour, Kyle. The prodigal son rushing home to help Daddy." I look into the eyes of the man I knew since we were kids, and I see fear in them. I don't need that either. "Introducing a new player this late in the game isn't favorable. Dinner. Tonight. Set it up. I want to meet Grayson Stone personally, I need to know exactly who I'm dealing with and what kind of static this new development may cause, so I can eliminate it immediately."

"Are you sure that's a good idea?" Kyle questions. I can only glare at him in response. I pace the room and nod to the secret window overlooking the war room. Kyle takes the hint and quickly departs my office.

I switch on the sound and firmly plant my hands on the credenza against the wall under the mirror, watching Kyle interact with Stone. "Mr. Prescott would like a meeting with you and Grayson no later than dinner this evening."

I watch Kyle's face as he listens intently to the elder Stone. "Grayson can attend alone, I'll be with my son."

"Alright, Mr. Stone. Mr. Prescott will meet Grayson at eight o'clock at Altius. I'll forward the details to your office."

Stone sharply replies and excuses himself from the meeting.

"Thank you, goodbye," Chandler says to himself, as Stone has already left the room.

"Foxx, I don't know if this is a good idea." Kyle calls out into the empty room, knowing very well I'm watching and listening. I enter the war room through the hidden door, stopping just inside the door frame.

"I do, Chandler, if you want to win the game—you have to understand all of the players."

2

GRAYSON

*N*o matter where I turn my attention lately: business headlines, earning reports, local paparazzi exploitation channels, gossip within every circle of people I find myself in, even this phone call from my grandfather—one name is at the center of everything—Alexander Prescott. No matter how the topic involving Mr. Prescott varies, one thing is always the same—from the board-room to the bedroom—he's a ruthless son of a bitch. Every move he makes is calculated and controlled. He leads by intimidation and his tactic has served him well over the years. There's just one problem for him now. There's a new player in town and I'm not easily intimidated —not at all. Xander Prescott is about to meet his match.

"Yes, Granddad, I've received all of the information you've sent to me. I've also done some of my own research." I briefly look away from the monitor on my MacBook to the volumes of information provided by my grandfather's chief executive team at Stone Holdings. Stacks of files and boxes of information consume the rectangle table in my dining area. A soft buzz from the speaker fills the silence that's fallen between me and my grandfather, Gregory Edward Stone, II. I turn my attention back to his image on my screen. The lines on his face seem deeper. My grandfather typically masks his age with his aura of finesse and virility, but right now, he looks like a tired old man. "How's Dad today?" Granddad looks into his camera, and it feels as though he can see right through the screen into my eyes.

"He's... okay. The doctors expect that he'll make a complete recovery, but the timing of his recovery is entirely up to Greg, himself." My father, Gregory Edward Stone, III, is a tremendous businessman and the third generation of leadership of Stone Holdings, the business my great-grandfather started in the early 1930s. Like his father before him, my dad inherited the helm of our family's business. Stone Holdings is a tremendously successful holding company with lucrative assets. Until my dad suffered a stroke, everything was running perfectly. Now, the company that has become a family legacy is in jeopardy of falling to Prescott's cunning strategies as he preys on the company in the wake of my father's health crisis, and capitalizes on my grandfather's worry and grief for his son.

"Listen to me," my grandfather's warning tone reaches to the pit of my stomach causing an ache to settle there, "you must be careful. You cannot underestimate Prescott. He's as sly as a fox—he appears to know everything and gives away nothing—the man is a walking conundrum."

"I understand." A feeling of duty and an air of resilience wash over me. This is my time—my responsibility—my dad ensured that I had every opportunity to become whoever I wanted, and for a long time, who I wanted to be was anything but next in line for the family business. But all it takes is one event to change everything. One phone call—one unforeseen event—can trigger a change in perspective. That's exactly what happened to me. My third floor flat in Paris is now an expansive loft apartment in a posh urban development on Pittsburgh's north shore. I have spectacular views of the Allegheny River and of downtown. I haven't had time to make a friend yet, but I have one formidable adversary waiting for me. "I know exactly how I need to handle Xander Prescott. I need to prepare for the meeting this evening." Even though I'm doing exactly what I need to be doing, I feel a sense of guilt for not going to visit my father tonight. "Please tell Dad that I'll see him tomorrow."

"I'll tell him. Grayson, please remember what I said."

"I'll remember."

I drop my closed MacBook a little firmer than I intend on the accent table next to me. The sound startles me, and it's every indication I need to relax and get ready for this meeting. A hot shower and fresh suit should do the trick to help me relax.

3

XANDER

♥

*T*he city is beautifully illuminated, and without a doubt will look incredible on television tonight for the broadcast of the Pirates vs. the New York Mets. It's the first of a three-game series here at PNC Park, and if all goes well with my meeting tonight, I'll be able to relax and unwind at the ballpark tomorrow night for game two. Chandler is there tonight with his little boy. I graciously gave him the tickets to share the evening with his son at the ball park for free shirt Friday. The fountain at Point State Park is a quintessence of symbols for this incredible city and looks enchanting nestled at the confluence of the Allegheny and Monongahela Rivers—marking the source of the Ohio River. The fountain is beautiful all of the time, but at night it carries an aura of majesty as it powerfully dances casted in rainbows of color. The view of Pittsburgh from Altius is magnificent. Perched high on top of Mount Washington, this restaurant boasts a premier atmosphere, five-star cuisine and stunning panoramic views of the steel city.

I check my watch for what seems to be the hundredth time since I arrived at the restaurant at approximately seven forty-five p.m.—for the eight o'clock meeting. The maître d' successfully arranged for an entire corner of the restaurant to be privatized for this meeting, without compromising the pleasure of window dining. She has also stoically delivered two messages of apology regarding the late arrival of my guest. First, there were airport security issues which resulted in delays. Then there was an accident on inbound parkway west, at the Fort Pitt Tunnel, which caused another change to arrival. For the second time today, my patience is running thin because of Grayson Stone. The waiter sets a third bourbon in front of me without a question. He's already been instructed to bring the check after a third drink. Another glance at my wrist, marks nearly an entire hour of waiting. An hour of calculating every possible move from my opponent in this game, and every possible way I'll get retribution for this missed dinner meeting. I'm not a patient man, and my time is precious.

I hear the footsteps of the maître d' approaching once again, before she arrives to deliver another excuse, or my check, or both—I toss back the remainder of bourbon. It burns enough that I look down, to squint away the pain of the large swallow. When I pry my eyes open, I see the sexiest shoes at my right. I take in their porcelain-hued, patent-leather-pointed toes and stiletto heels, and transparent sides. I realize immediately this isn't the maître d' in her smart black heels. My eyes graze up smooth, shapely legs to where a snug navy-blue suit skirt covers them from the knees and over curvy hips—to where a white blouse is belted at a small waist—and met with a short, single-button jacket. As the full-bodied taste of bourbon eases from my palate, the rich aroma of vanilla mixed with something fruity inundates my senses. The woman reaches her hand toward me, uttering words that fall to silent when I look at her face. Pouty lips, creamy skin, and bright, sparkling-blue eyes leave me feeling drunk at the sight of her. I take her hand in mine—surprised by the strength I find there—but it doesn't keep me from noticing the softness and warmth of her skin.

"...and you're Alexander Prescott."

"What? Excuse me. I beg your pardon."

"I apologize for being late and understand completely if you'd prefer to reschedule, I'd be happy to accommodate you in any way I possibly can—tomorrow perhaps?"

Just when my synapses begin to fire correctly, she stuns me with offering to *accommodate me in any way she can...* Those words pull my brain right out of the moment and into thoughts of her in my bed.

"Mr. Prescott," the inquiry from the waiter brings me back to the moment, "would you still like your check, or should I put it off now that Miss Stone has arrived?"

Miss Stone.

"You can hold off on the check. Please," I rise from my chair, claiming my full height, and finally gaining control of the situation— although, I'm still holding her hand in mine. "Bring Miss Stone whatever she'd care to drink, and I'll like a glass of water." I release her hand and feel the cool air penetrate the warmth she left behind. I pull out her chair as she mentions water is fine for her as well.

"Mr. Prescott—"

"Xander." I correct her immediately. For some reason, I don't want her to be so formal with me.

"Alright then, Xander." She smiles slightly, and I swear her cheeks blush—it's too difficult to tell in this light. "Again, I want to offer my apologies for making you wait."

"No apologies necessary. You're here now, Miss Stone, and if it suits you, we can continue with the meeting."

"Yes, Xander, that suits me fine."

"It's interesting..." The way my name falls from her lips forces me to pause—I want to commit it to memory.

"What is interesting?" Grayson raises a curious eyebrow, and it's a complete turn on.

Get a grip, Foxx. You're acting like a schoolboy.

"It's interesting that you were delayed at the airport—your grandfather made it seem as though you were already in town."

"I was... I am. Most of my luggage was detained in customs, and I received the call that I could collect it. I had plenty of time to get the luggage and make it to our meeting with time to spare... or so I thought. After a long security check line, I was quickly reminded that Pittsburgh traffic has a time table all its own."

She grins and seems content despite the obstacles she faced today. "That it does, and if it rains—no one remembers how to drive." My sarcastic confirmation of Pittsburgh traffic elicits laughter from her... I've never heard a laugh quite like hers.

"Oh, I remember!" Her laughter fades into a full-on smile, and I'm enamored with every stunning detail, from her shiny white teeth, to the natural pink color of her full supple lips. Grayson Stone is exquisite.

"There was one good thing that came from my delays." She looks down bashfully, before raising her brilliant blue eyes back to mine. "It's something I'm not apologetic for..."

"Don't keep me in such suspense," I playfully quip.

"It was dark before I made it through the Fort Pitt Tunnel." She smiles brightly, and her eyes take on a dreamy stare. "The view of the city from the end of the tunnel is absolutely incredible all of the time, especially at night, and especially tonight... The city is completely lit up. PNC Park is packed, the lights are on... For the first time, in the days since I've been back, I finally felt like I was home."

I rest my elbows on the table, mirroring the body language Grayson assumed moments ago. "You're right, there's nothing like it." I drive Parkway North in and out of the city, so it's a rarity I come in that way. It doesn't matter how many times you exit that tunnel, the feeling is always the same."

"My city."

"My city."

We utter the same words, at the same time—and we hold each other's gaze. Conversation flows from high school, to university days, to corporate careers, and continues until the restaurant closes, forcing us to cash out—and we never discussed business... not once. Standing on Mount Washington, with the city we both love nestled stunningly below us, we make a loose plan to schedule a meeting

Monday or Tuesday to discuss the business deal that will make me a much richer man. While on the other hand, it's a deal that will also be the end of an era for Stone Holdings and the family who built it.

Chandler Cell

How'd it go with Stone?

Foxx?

What the hell, man?

Where are you?

WTF is going on?

Did this guy off you?

My texts clearly indicate Chandler is a frantic mess.

Call me.

My phone chimes immediately after I text him back. "Yeah," I answer unenthused.

"Foxx, where the hell have you been? I've been going crazy here. What happened with Stone? Is he a problem?"

"I don't think *HE* is a problem... at least not the kind of problem I expected *HE* could be."

"Why are you saying *HEEE* like that?"

"Kyle Chandler, you are my top advisor and most trusted friend. I consider everything you provide me as accurate information."

"Yeah, okay... Foxx, where's this going? What happened? Yeah, I give you everything—the best of me—I always have—we always have. What's with the cryptic messages?"

"You fucked up with G.E. Stone, Grayson Stone... you got it wrong?"

"How? Tell me."

"Grayson Stone is a stunningly gorgeous *woman*—SHE."

"A woman." There's silence except for Chandler fumbling through papers and clicking his keyboard.

"Stop looking. I've been through it all. There's nothing indicative of gender in anything. Grayson is very careful of any published accolades. She's very good at privatizing and limiting available information. The best I've ever seen, actually. Using G.E. in a long line of Gregory Edward Stones leads to a very inaccurate, but easily made assumption. Clever."

"Clever?"

"Don't you think? Hell, her strategy worked on you."

"Foxx, what happened at the meeting? The deal? Where do we stand?"

"We actually didn't discuss business."

"WHAT?"

"We're going to set something up Monday or Tuesday."

"Are you serious?"

"Yes. Look, Chandler. I need time to reevaluate everything we know about Grayson. I've learned some other things about her tonight. She's going to spend time with her father tomorrow, and I just need a break."

"You're taking a break, while she spends time with her father? This doesn't sound like you, Foxx. Why aren't you going for the jugular here—like you always do?"

"I don't have a heart of steel. Nothing would happen until next week anyway. Let Grayson state her case... why rush this now?"

"Alrighty then. You're the boss."

"You're right, I am the boss. So, how was the game? Did Jace have fun?"

"Yes! Jace started to fall asleep by the seventh inning stretch. I carried him across the Clemente Bridge and was home before the game was over. I caught the end on TV. We won 6—5."

"Are you in for tomorrow night?"

"Yeah, Meg has a girl's thing planned, but we have a sitter for Jace. I'll meet you at the gate."

"Sounds good. Later, man."

"Later."

4

GRAYSON

♥

I knock timidly as I enter the sterile hospital room. A man in green scrubs stands next to my dad's bed, asking him how he's feeling. I'm happy to hear Dad begin to answer him, and immediately saddened as he becomes hung up on the first letter of the word he's trying to say. After searching and trying, Dad kicks his leg in frustration, causing the bed table to roll away with a clatter. I step out into the hallway to collect myself and to give the caregiver time to finish his assessment. When the man exits the room, I introduce myself and ask for any new information. Once I provide the nurse the information required from me, he tells me that the stroke primarily affected Dad's language—he can communicate, it's just challenging because he will lose sight of certain words and not be able to retrieve his thoughts. And there will be good spells and bad spells with this condition. I was assured that with therapy and time, Dad will fully recover. Dad's hypertension is a primary focus—dietary changes and medication are critical to managing his blood pressure and preventing another occurrence of stroke—so are life-style changes...

"Hi, Daddy." I smile, and Dad's face lights up. He holds out his arm, and I fall onto him, hugging him with every ounce of strength I have. I quickly hug my granddad, before taking Dad's hand in mine and telling him to stay calm, reminding him that recovery is a process and will take time.

"I—I know."

"You're going to be fine, Dad. Just pace yourself." I sit on the chair on the opposite side of the bed from where Granddad sits.

"So, I'll speak for my son, how was the meeting with Alexander Prescott?" I'm not surprised that Granddad got right to business, but he shouldn't talk shop in front of Dad—he doesn't need this stress.

"It was fine. We're setting up a meeting for Monday or Tuesday to discuss his plan, and I'll present my strategy to dispel it."

"You didn't do that last night?"

"No, we actually never spoke of business at all."

"What'd you do, have a staring contest? I've never known Prescott to discuss anything but business." I can't help the giggle at Grand-dad's question—it's off color from his constant professionalism.

"We talked about a lot of things; I was surprised by him actually. He was quite different from so much of what I've heard about him. I mean, he's even more handsome in person than he is in pictures, but I never expected him to be so charming."

"Charming?" Dad questions perfectly clear and without hesitation. There's a secret delight in that for me... Dad has always been protective anytime there was boy blood in the water. I'm thirty-nine years old, and I'm still Daddy's little girl.

"Yeah..." I shrug my shoulders, "Xander is not only extremely handsome, he's also quite charming." There I said it. There's no denying it. "Let's just stop talking about this, I have it under control. Trust me."

I make rounds, offering kisses on the cheeks of the two men I admire most in this world. My granddad blushes and pats my cheek in return. I stand at the window, looking out at another clear day in the steel city. It feels really good to be back here.

"Get out of—" Dad pulls my attention when he begins to speak, "h... here."

"You want me to get out of here?" I tease.

"Yes. Go do someth... thing. I'm fine. I'm going h... ho... home tomorrow."

"You are? The nurse didn't tell me that." I'm happy to know Dad is going home so quickly.

"Yes," Granddad chimes in. "They said tomorrow or if not, first thing Monday. I've hired a private nurse to be there around the clock. Therapy will begin as soon as we get a green light to start."

"I'm so pleased." I smile brightly and offer Dad's hand a squeeze.

"Go, Grayson. H... have some fun."

*T*he walk across the Roberto Clemente Bridge to the park never gets old, and I've missed it. The energy from the fans already buzzes outside the park. SOLD OUT. Great, so much for catching game two.

"Grayson?"

I turn quickly to the direction of the whiskey smooth voice. I don't recognize the man who obviously recognizes me.

"Yes, I'm sorry, have we met—Xander?"

"Yeah." He smiles brilliantly as he approaches, and my feet carry me straight into his arms for a brief hug. The gesture is too informal considering our business situation, but we've never had a true business discussion, and the hug felt easy and welcome.

He's much taller than I realized now that I'm without my stiletto business heels. I look down, delighted to realize we're both wearing Chucks. Xander looks almost unrecognizable from the astute business man I met for dinner last night. He seems to have nailed the perfect outfit for a baseball game. What makes him stand out is the way his black v-neck t-shirt fits. It's snug across his broad shoulders and swollen biceps, and fits closely against his torso to where its front tucked into his belted, low-slung khaki cargo shorts—hanging low on his trim waist. A waist which was very firm to the touch when I hugged him. His chestnut hair which was perfectly styled last night, is mostly tucked under a black baseball hat. The style of wearing hats today doesn't really appeal to me. I think the wide flat bill is silly compared to the way boys rolled bills back when I was younger—they wore their hats backwards, or pulled down low—exactly the way Xander wears his now. The hat casts just enough of a shadow to hide the truth in his beautiful blue eyes. The same eyes that couldn't hide the surprise that it was a female he was meeting last night and not a male. Priceless.

5

XANDER

♥

I pocketed my cell after responding to Kyle's text that he couldn't make it tonight because Jace isn't feeling well, and he didn't want to leave him. Before I texted him well wishes and understanding, I noticed the girl in the cutoff denim shorts and tight Pirates t-shirt with the long blonde ponytail. It wasn't until I could give my undivided attention to her presence, that I realized something familiar about her. When she turned around, it was evident she wasn't just a girl... it was Grayson. Her hair was artfully pulled back and pinned up last night at dinner—I had no idea it was this long.

"Are you going to the game?"

"Nah, it's a sellout. I couldn't get a ticket, and I don't like buying them from scalpers."

"Well..." I reach into my pocket and pull out the tickets, "if you can tolerate sitting with me—here's a ticket that isn't getting used, unless you use it."

"Xander! I'll sit with you. Are you sure?"

"I asked, didn't I?" I mock frustration.

"Yes," she snatches the tickets from my hand and smiles—and I swear it lights up everyone around her, "you did!"

236

"Let's go!" I put my hand at the small of her back, encouraging her to lead the way.

"Yeah," she returns before shouting, "let's go, Bucs!"

Immigrant Song from Led Zeppelin rocks the park as we make our way to our seats. It's a perfect night in Pittsburgh. The city skyline touches skies kissed by the golden hour of the setting sun, and is framed spectacularly from inside the park. After hitting the concessions for nachos and two beers—I return to a smiling Grayson. "Thank you so much for this. It's been a long time since I've been to the ballpark. I didn't stand a chance at tickets with this sellout crowd."

"It's my pleasure!" She takes the nachos, placing them gently on the bare skin of her toned thighs, and my mouth goes instantly dry. She's so damned attractive. She doesn't come close to looking a single day in her thirties, and she's almost past them. With hardly any makeup on her face, she's such a refreshing change from other women our age. There's a youthfulness about her that I'm quickly becoming addicted to... I've never struggled with the fact I'm forty-four and have nothing in my life but my company, but I've never wanted more... before.

We sip our beers, taking in the sights and sounds that only a live ballpark experience can provide. "You know," Grayson begins, "the last time I was at a game was five years ago. I remember, it was a concert night."

"I love the concerts—some of them are great."

"Yeah, they are. I saw O.A.R. the last time I was here. I loved that band from their start. When they sang *Peace* with the backdrop of the Pittsburgh city lights and the starry night sky above, I remember thinking I didn't want to go back to Paris." Grayson smiles sheepishly at me. "It's not everyday you'll hear someone say they'd rather be in Pittsburgh over Paris." She shrugs her shoulders. I've noticed that reaction from her a few times, and it's completely endearing.

"You've been out of the country for so long, will leaving here be difficult when you go back?" I swallow, feeling immediately empty at the thought of seeing her go—even after such a short time.

"Well, I think it would be difficult... but I'm not going back."

"You're not?"

"No." She beams. "We'll cover that at our meeting. I'll be staying here and taking my seat at Stone Holdings." My poker face shifts into place creating a blank slate—it's clear she notices. "See what happens when you bring up work? Now you're all beside yourself," she teases with a laugh and leans into me with her shoulder. "Don't worry, Xander, this city can handle both of us." She looks at me with a tilt of her head and an arched brow.

"Yes, I suppose it can." Suddenly, I can't help but think about the potential for more moments like this with her. I feel a shift happening... a shift in my perspective.

Five innings of baseball have never gone so damned fast. Time just slips away when I'm with Grayson, everything seems so easy. With the opening notes of Pink Floyd's *Run Like Hell*, Grayson leaps from her seat, jumping up and down and laughing as carefree as a child. It's a sight I could never tire of seeing. Grayson pulls at something in me, and I feel just as carefree as she does. "Ladies and gentlemen, it's time for The Great Pittsburgh Pierogi Race—N'at! Brought to you by the folks at Mrs. T's Pierogis. Let's meet the runners: Jalapeño Hannah, Cheese Chester, Sauerkraut Saul, Oliver Onion, Bacon Burt, and Pizza Penny!"

Grayson grabs my arm—"Hannah's got it in the bag!" She rolls her sparkling-blue eyes to me and winks.

"No way—it's Oliver!" I put my hands on her shoulders and shift her in front of me, leaning down next to her face so we have the same perspective. The shallow spacing between the rows puts her body against the length of mine, and her long, blonde ponytail rests against my face—surrounding me with its fresh fruity aroma. We watch excited and giddy as the mascots race to the finish. Saul leads most of the race, but Oliver makes a go for the lead—and so does Hannah. It's nose and nose between Saul and Oliver with Hannah just behind—just before the finish line, Hannah pushes her handbag ahead and captures first place—leaving Oliver and Saul to second and third respectively.

"See?" Grayson turns to face me and shrugs, "I told you, she had it in the *bag*."

I playfully push her in front of her own seat, "Don't get too cocky, Miss Stone."

"Miss Stone? So formal, Mr. Prescott." Just like the first time I heard her address me last night, I don't like it. I continue to stand as she takes her seat, tossing her long ponytail to hang down her back.

"I told you—Xander."

"And outside of the boardroom, Grayson works for me." She offers me a smug glance. I'm rattled from being put into check two times, in a blink, by this enigmatic woman.

I lean down to her, almost nose to nose, and she freezes, holding my eyes with her own. "Grayson," I whisper.

"Yes," she whispers back. I watch her pupils dilate, revealing a secret she carries. She finds me attractive, too.

"Do you want another beer?" She rolls her eyes gently, pushing my face away with a hand to my forehead.

"Yes, I think I'll need it to help you through your pouting."

This woman is maddening, and I can't get enough of her.

The coming innings find us effortlessly holding hands with the crowd while singing *Take Me Out to the Ballgame* during the seventh inning stretch and raising the Jolly Roger as the Pirates win game two of the series. I can't remember a night that I had this much fun. I don't want it to end... Several seats around us are empty from people who have left to watch the fireworks from elsewhere.

"Ladies and gentlemen, The Pittsburgh Pirates now present the Zambelli firework display brought to you by Highmark. Let's begin." The lights in the park become dark as the crowd counts down from ten. The first few pops explode in the air, and the crowd reacts as several more whistles indicate a magical display to come. The music of Queen's *Don't Stop Me Now* is the soundtrack as the explosive booms light the sky above Pittsburgh. As fire rains onto the buildings, which seem to touch the fireworks, I feel the thunder of them in my chest. I look at Grayson, and she looks at me. I see flashes of colorful light on her face and the flickering reflections in her eyes—only I don't hear the sounds anymore—and I realize the booming in my chest is my pounding heart. I don't know if I moved, if she moved, maybe we moved together, but as the grand finale captures everyone's attention —I'm lost to everyone and everything as Grayson's lips meet mine.

6

GRAYSON

♥

*T*he bed feels soft. The hard body lying next to me is warm. The air feels cool against our uncovered bodies. As I lie tangled with Xander Prescott, on top of rumpled sheets, one eyelid flutters open to assess if it's still early in the morning. It's a dark and dreary day in the steel city. I came back here to help save my family's company from a buyout, but instead, I found myself enamored with the enemy, and now he's in my bed. I should be feeling all kinds of regret this morning. These early hours that I've been lying awake feeling him next to me, I should have been trying to find a way to get Xander out of my bed, my life and away from my company. Instead, I can't think past when I'll see him again, and I'm not ready for this moment to end. I haven't moved a muscle to keep from waking Xander, but I want to look at him. I carefully shift away from him, to give myself room to roll onto my other side to face him. Xander lifts his arm, which laid heavy in the bend of my waist. I roll over only to see wide-open, deep-blue eyes looking at me.

"I was wondering how long you were going to lie here as still as a statue." Xander's voice is gruff and raspy from the night. It's the sexiest sound I've heard.

"I just woke up," I lie, and he chuckles.

"I already know several things you do far better than lying." A sexy grin kisses his lips, and I ache for another taste of him. He places his finger over my lips as if he could read my thoughts. "You've been awake for a long time, Grayson. I knew the moment you woke—your breathing changed. I could feel your mind working. Before another minute passes, before I make love to your gorgeous body again, there's something we need to discuss. It can't wait."

We lie facing each other—completely bare.

"Okay."

"My entire perspective has changed. You changed it."

"What does that mean?" I ask him softly, wanting to hear him explain exactly where he is, and what his new perspective means for my family's company. But most importantly, I want to hear what it means for us.

"I no longer wish to take down Stone Holdings, but I don't want anyone else to either."

"You don't?"

"No."

"What do you want then—what are you bargaining for?"

"I'm bargaining for more—you—I want you, Grayson. What we've found together in the past couple of days means more to me than any business deal. I knew it last night, the moment I touched you."

"Xander," I sit up immediately, touching his face, "are you sure?"

"I've never been more certain of anything in my life." He sits up and slides himself back against the headboard. I do the same and tug the sheet over us.

"What happens now?" I don't doubt that Xander has a plan in place for moving forward.

"First, we're going to shower and get dressed, then we're going to Pamela's for breakfast. You worked up one hell of an appetite for me last night. Then we're going to see your grandfather and father and make them aware of my change in interest in their company. Then, we're going to Soergel Orchards for lunch and some fresh fruit. Then we'll swing by my place so I can pack a bag. Then we're coming back here and staying in bed until we have to leave for our offices tomorrow. Before the sun hits the fountain at Point State Park in the morning, I'll know the taste of every inch of your body. Every step you take away from me will be a beautifully sore reminder of what we have when we're together, and that's exactly where I plan to stay —together."

Xander did meet his match, but not in the way I expected. It turns out, we both met our match—our life match. I said it before, *all it takes is one event to change everything. One phone call—one unforeseen event—can trigger a change in perspective.* And that's exactly what happened to us.

The End.

ABOUT THE AUTHOR

Author Victoria Monroe—finding forever one romantic story at a time...

Connect with Victoria

 facebook.com/victoriamonroeauthor

 twitter.com/sTORIbooks

 instagram.com/sTORIbooks

CHASING
BREN

BRANDY DORSCH

PROLOGUE

MEGAN

The first time I saw him I knew that he was the one that I was going to marry. He was tall, dark and handsome. He intervened when my brother, Marcus shoved me and I twisted my ankle. It was gratifying to see my brother taken down by someone who didn't condone his bullying tactics. I was eight years old but I knew that it was love at first sight.

His name was Brenigan Michaels but all the kids called him Bren. He was new to the area and was a few years older than me. I was a second grader with a crush on a fifth grader but I was not the only one. He had a presence, as my grandma would say. He helped me off the ground that day and when he touched my hand, I felt electricity. You know the feeling of touching something metal and getting a shock? That is what it felt like.

He never really paid me a lot of attention after that moment, but my brother became his best friend, so he always seemed to be around. It was hard on me because I wanted to be important to him as he was to me, but the only thing that mattered to him was his music. I chased after Bren and he chased after his music. My name is Megan O'Connor and this is my story.

1

BREN

There was not much in this world that I love more than music. Since I was old enough to know what it was, I have been driven to produce my own. I started writing lyrics when I was in elementary school and started producing music when I was in junior high. By the time I hit high school, I had found a group that was just as passionate about music as myself. Marcus, Kennedy, Dominic, and I made up the band, Insurrection. We came up with the name when we were battling our parents over our desire to move to Los Angeles after graduation in order to play larger venues and make a name for ourselves. They weren't very supportive and we raged against their hold on us.

Graduation night we all packed up what we could fit into the van that we bought for gigs and we took off for the west coast. We made it to just outside of Pittsburgh before we ran out of gas money. We were at the point of calling our parents when we got a lucky break. Dom had wandered into this little dive bar to go to the bathroom and discovered that they were looking for a band to play a couple of nights a week. We went in and talked to the manager, and the next thing we knew we had a paying gig. It didn't pay a lot but the manager hooked us up with the garage behind the bar for to stay in. Pittsburgh embraced us in a way that our small town in Maine never had, and it became our home. We were on our way.

2

MEGAN

I stared at the acceptance letter in my hand and drew a shaky breath. My parents were going to lose their minds. Overprotective was an understatement when it came to them. When my brother Marcus left our hometown in order to chase his dream of being a musician, I thought they were both going to have heart attacks. Instead they decided to lock me down. I was monitored for everything. Where I went, who I went with, and when I was coming home. It has been a nightmare for the last three years but things were about to change. I just hope they understand my decisions better than they did when Marcus left.

I always knew that I wanted to go into the medical field and when I started applying to colleges, I knew where I went would depend on what kind of financial aid packages I received. I was looking at a letter that included a full ride to the University of Pittsburgh.

I had been accepted to several schools but this was the only school that offered me everything I needed and wanted. My parents wanted me to go to the state school but I had to get out of here and I needed more than I would ever find here.

"Sweetheart, did you get the mail?" I sighed as my mother walked into the living room and sat down on the couch across from me.

"Yeah. I put the bills and magazines on your desk." My mom was a nurse at the local urgent care and my dad was a consultant but I didn't really know what he did.

"Thanks, Megan. What is that?" She gestured to the letter in my hand and I knew that it was time to tell them what I was planning on doing when I graduated in a few short weeks.

"It is my final acceptance letter. I applied late and I wasn't sure if I would even get in so I didn't mention it." I rose from the loveseat and handed the letter to her. I watched as her lips turned down and she paled.

"No. You are not following your brother and moving to Pennsylvania. I don't know why my children are in such a rush to get away from me but I will not allow you to move out of state. You can go to school here and do the things that you want."

I sighed because I saw this coming from a mile away. My parents talked to Marcus about once a month. They didn't know that the band was performing all over the city and had been opening for huge bands at some of the local venues. Marcus told me that they had just finished writing the songs for their first album and would be in the studio recording it this summer. I was so happy for him...and Bren.

"Mom. It is a full ride. I would be an absolute fool to turn down the chance to go to school there. The medical school is one of the best in the entire nation and I would have an in because I went to school there. I want to be a doctor mom, and I need to take my chances where I can, to make it happen."

She looked at me and I could see the anger and pain in her eyes. I didn't want to disappoint my parents, but this hold they wanted to keep on me, was ridiculous. They interrogated me when I talked to Marcus, because they thought he would be a bad influence on me. He was following his dreams and that is what I wanted to do.

"Henry!" I winced as my mother yelled for my dad. I could feel the tightening in my chest as he came into the room and my mom told him about my acceptance letter, and that I wanted to move to Pittsburgh to go to school. My father was not a cruel man, but the truth is that he had a way of talking to you that was worse than a punch to the face. By the time my father got finished berating me, telling me that I was ungrateful for everything they did for me, I was in tears. I ran to my room, slid down the wall and listened as they continued talking about me.

"Roman. I don't want her going to that school. If she leaves you know that she will never come back. We have already lost one child, do we really want to lose another?"

"Karen, that child is not going anywhere. She is still infatuated with that Bren boy and wants to follow after him. She can go to school here and that is what she is going to do. I am not having any more of this leaving the state business."

I was going to have to start making my arrangements to leave. I had a feeling that the two of them would be making my life difficult for the next couple of months.

MARCUS

I threw my phone on the bed and stomped out of my bedroom. The band shared a house in the South Hills of Pittsburgh. It fit our needs perfectly and it fell in our laps through the manager at the bar we started in, when we found ourselves in Pennsylvania.

I marched past Bren who was sitting at the piano in our living room and grabbed a beer out of the fridge.

"What's up asshole?" I shot him a death glare.

"I just got off the phone with Megan." I swallowed the grin that I felt on my face as he missed the key he was aiming for. It was never a secret that Megan had a crush on Bren. I had a feeling that he would have gone for her if we hadn't been friends.

"Is she okay? Your parents good?" Bren didn't like my parents. They blamed the band and our move on him.

"She is fine but my parents are being dicks to her as usual. You know that Meg got into a bunch of schools, right?" Megan was one of the smartest people we knew. She had tested at genius level and had been taking college classes in high school.

I took a deep gulp of my beer before I continued, "She got into the University of Pittsburgh with a full ride. She got partial aid at all of the other schools that she got into. Since she is going to be premed, she needed to get all the assistance she could. When she told the 'rents that she was coming here for school, they went ballistic on her."

Bren turned on the bench and faced me. "What can we do to help her? I know your relationship is on the rocks with them. Will this make it worse?"

I snorted, "It can't get any worse. My father told me that I was dead to him since I was going to be a deadbeat musician. He doesn't know about the gigs, the album or anything. My mother doesn't want to hear about it either. Megan told me that they have put her on lockdown since we have been gone. They monitor everything she does. I never wanted that for her during high school. I want to help her, man."

Bren, Kennedy, Dom and I had been close since elementary school. Bren was always the most serious about his music but the rest of us always knew that it was our dream as well. Some of our parents were great about it but some weren't.

Bren sighed and I could see the anger on his face when he thought about what Megan had been dealing with back home in Maine.

"You know that Megan is always welcome here, Marcus. That is a no brainer. We have two other bedrooms and she fits in with us. She can come here after graduation and we will get her set up. I am sure she will be living on campus once school starts and she can come here on weekends if she wants. She is your family and will always have a place with us."

I knew he would say something like that and I was glad he had agreed. "I told her to come here. She is going to pack up her stuff after graduation and head down. Our parents aren't going to like it, but she turns eighteen next week so they can't really stop it. She graduates in a couple of weeks."

Bren stood and walked to me. He slapped me on the back as he grabbed a beer out of the fridge. "Come on, brother. Let's go move some of the equipment around so your little sister will have a room to sleep in."

I finished my beer and followed him up the stairs.

3

MEGAN

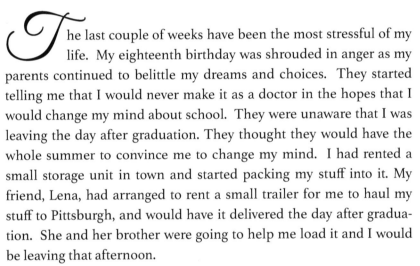

The last couple of weeks have been the most stressful of my life. My eighteenth birthday was shrouded in anger as my parents continued to belittle my dreams and choices. They started telling me that I would never make it as a doctor in the hopes that I would change my mind about school. They were unaware that I was leaving the day after graduation. They thought they would have the whole summer to convince me to change my mind. I had rented a small storage unit in town and started packing my stuff into it. My friend, Lena, had arranged to rent a small trailer for me to haul my stuff to Pittsburgh, and would have it delivered the day after graduation. She and her brother were going to help me load it and I would be leaving that afternoon.

When Marcus told me to come stay with the band, I was hesitant for half a second. I had love Bren Michaels since I was a child but he never gave me the slightest indication that he was interested and I didn't see that changing now. I knew that it was a child's infatuation and it was time to move on. This move would put me into an environment that would allow me to meet new people, and maybe I would find the man I have been waiting on.

"Megan, come on! We have to get to the school so you can have your final practice before graduation." I sighed as I finished applying my makeup, grabbed my cap and gown and rushed out of my bedroom. Tomorrow couldn't come quick enough.

BREN

She would be here in forty-eight hours. I gripped the microphone in my hand as I belted out the lyrics to the song

I wrote when I was sixteen.

I see the way you move in my world,
The stars align when you are near,
My heart beats with yours
and the love I have for you is forever.

You are the missing piece of my soul,
My mate for all time,
To the moon and back,
Our love will be true.

I knew from the moment that I helped her off the ground that Megan was the one that I was meant to be with. I was aware that would seem strange as young as we were, but something just clicked in my heart and I knew she was mine. I couldn't let her know that though. She was too young for me but now things were different. My soulmate was on her way to me and I was not going to waste another moment without her. She would know that I waited for her. Yes, I had dated but no one had ever owned my heart. That belonged to the only woman that made me shiver when she brushed against me. The woman that I would spend my life loving and making sure she knew how amazing she was.

We finished up the song and Trey our mixing engineer gave me the thumbs up that he had gotten the tracks he needed to finish up the song. We were beyond excited at how far we had come. We never intended to set up shop in Pittsburgh, but the truth is that once we got here, we were stunned at how diverse the music scene was. We lucked out when we wandered into that bar and met Benny. He was the manager there and hired us to play. He started introducing us to musicians that came in. It turned out that "dive bar" was actually a huge draw in the area. Huge musicians that came to play the arena's here, showed up to jam, play acoustic and hang out with the locals. We opened for several huge bands and several musicians that were from the area and made it big.

They all gave us positive reviews and helped us network with agents and producers. That led us to our first record deal with an indie label that has been producing huge names. We would have our album done by the end of the summer and would be starting a regional tour in the fall. Our dreams were coming true.

I gulped down a bottle of water sitting next to me on the stool and watched as the band headed out of the studio. Marcus had been in touch with Megan multiple times over the last few days. Today was her graduation day and her parents told her that Marcus wasn't allowed to come. My heart broke for her. She and Marcus have always been tight and I knew how hard the last three years have been on them. I hoped that she would be able to leave Maine with little fuss from her parents.

I headed out so I could catch up to the band and noticed that Dom and Kennedy were already heading out of the parking lot.

"They are heading to the store to pick up groceries. We are out of just about everything and they want to pick up some of Meg's favorites to make her feel at home. My parents have been horrible to her and embarrassed her at the senior awards ceremony the other night."

I growled at his words. She should not have to deal with the bull-shit they were doing to her. It was beyond ridiculous behavior for parents with a child as smart and talented as she was. "What did they do to her?"

"When she was called up and introduced for her acceptance to the University of Pittsburgh and they started listing the scholarships and grants that she won, our parents got up and walked out. They were loud and obnoxious about it and everyone is talking about it. She was mortified and ended up staying with Lena because she was afraid she would say something about her plans. She sent me the link to the live streaming of her graduation so I was going to head home so I could watch it. She is leaving tomorrow afternoon, stopping for the night and then she will be here the day after tomorrow."

I felt my cock harden at the thought of seeing Megan for the first time in years. I had seen pictures of her on social media but they have never done her justice. "Not a problem, man. We got the room set up. I know she wasn't bringing any furniture but we had the extra bed and stuff and I think it will work for her."

He nodded as he scrolled through his messages. "She is excited to be getting out of there. I can't imagine what she has been dealing with since we have been gone. I know she hasn't told me all of it because she doesn't want me to feel guilty, but I do anyway."

I cleared my throat as I thought about the words I was getting ready to say to my best friend. "Marcus." I waited till he looked up from his phone. "I have been in love with Megan for the better part of a decade and a half. If she is interested in me at all, I am going to make her mine."

I held my breath as I waited to see if I would need to duck a punch but I was surprised to see the smile spread across his face. "I have been waiting for you to say something about her. I have always known that you two had a thing for each other. I don't have a problem with that at all but you may find that Megan was unaware of your feelings for her. She thinks you never saw her at all and is prepared to find someone new when she moves here."

My fists turned white as I clenched them next to my thighs. "She is and always will be mine. I couldn't do anything until she was legal and away from your parents but I will make sure she knows what she is to me."

4

MEGAN

♥

They had almost ruined my graduation but I was not going to let that change my mind on my choices and decisions. I was leaving and there was nothing they could do about it. They hadn't realized that most of my stuff had been packed and moved out. That surprised me because I thought they would go through my room to further monitor what I was doing but the camera that I had installed in the corner of my room never caught them.

"Megan? Are you and Lena going out tonight?" I groaned as my mother yelled out to me from the living room. I knew if I responded in kind, she would fuss at me and I didn't want to listen to it.

I walked out toward the sound of voices and saw that my mom, dad and a few family members who had been at my graduation were eating cake and talking amongst themselves.

"Yes, Mom. Lena and I are going down to the italian place on the river for dinner, then we thought we would hit up the theater and see what is playing."

"Wonderful, honey. Make sure you tell Lena congratulations for us and say hi to her parents. What time will you be home tomorrow? I want to take you shopping for stuff for your dorm room at State."

I hated all of the lying that I had been doing but they weren't giving me a choice. I hoped in the future that we would be able to rebuild our relationship. "I should be home tomorrow afternoon. I am going to grab my stuff and head out. Love you, Mom."

I hugged my parents and my family turned and headed back to my room. I tossed the last few of my bags out the window to where Lena was waiting. "I will throw these in my truck and then come around to the front door, Megan. Anything else in there?"

"No. I have one bag and my purse. I will wait a few minutes and then head out to the door to meet you there."

I shut the door as she lugged my bags to her truck and made my final preparations. I did a factory reset on my phone and made sure everything was deleted. I knew that they would figure out where I went but I didn't have to make it easy on them. I left my phone in the dresser and turned on the new one that I purchased for the move. The only people with the number was Marcus and Lena. I knew they wouldn't give it to my parents. I took one last look around my childhood room and knew that I would never come back. I didn't even feel sad. I was excited to start college and begin my dream of becoming a doctor.

I headed toward the front door as the bell rang, "Bye Mom. Bye Dad!" I felt the tears in my eyes as they said bye. I opened the door to Lena and gave her a tremulous smile. "Let's go, babe! I am starving for some italian goodies!"

We jumped into her truck and headed to the restaurant. The plan was to eat, and then head back to Lena's so we could veg out with sappy romantic comedies. We would head over to the storage unit in the morning so we could load everything up and I could head out. I would stop about halfway and then finish up the next day. I was so excited to see everyone. Espucially Bren. Even though I had every intention of moving on, I couldn't help but wonder what it would be like to be his.

*L*ena and I had a blast watching movies and spending time together. We had just finished loading everything in the trailer and her brother had hooked it up to my car. I was not ready to say goodbye to my bestie, but I was ready to get on the road.

"Call me when you get to the hotel tonight and when you leave for Pittsburgh in the morning. I just want to know that you are safe and on the road."

I smiled at her as she tried to boss me around. "Of course I will call you, mom." I laughed at the blush that spread across her face.

"I worry. You know that. But this is different than you going down the street. What do you think Bren will say when he sees you?"

I sighed deeply as I thought of how to answer. "I don't know, Lena. I would like to say that he will take one look at me, realize that he has always loved me and we will live happily ever after. However, I think it will be like it always was. He will look at me, say hi, help me with my stuff and that will be the end of it. I don't really expect anything else."

Lena grinned at me mischievously. "I have a feeling that you never really knew what Bren felt for you because that man is like a fortress. He keeps his feelings buried deeply. I think he has always loved you but with the age difference and your parents, he had to wait. I think this will be a new beginning for both of you."

I smiled at her as I got into my car, "Anything is possible, Lena. I have to believe that."

5

MARCUS

*J*hit the red button on my phone as I hung up with Megan.
I sighed in relief, knowing that she would be at the house in less than twenty minutes. I turned to my best friend who was looking at me expectantly. "She should be here in a few minutes. I told her that mom had already called me. She wasn't surprised by that at all."

The guys were all sitting around the living room waiting to unload all of Megan's things. They were as excited about having her around as I was.

Dom shot a wicked grin toward Bren. "So are you finally going to take a chance and ask Megan out?"

I laughed out loud at the disgruntled look on his face. "Seriously, Bren, We all know about your crush. I am totally fine with it. Just ask her out already. Now is the time to lock her down or you may lose her forever"

He looked up at me, "Do you think I could lose her? I love her, Marcus. I have for years. I just couldn't take a chance when she was still in school and we were here."

I shrugged my shoulders in his direction. "Bren, she thought you weren't interested. She asked me to show her where to go to meet guys when she got here. I think if you want her, you need to show her that is what you want and go from there."

He stood up and stretched his arms above his head, "You are right and I think it is time to make sure she knows she is going to be mine."

MEGAN

"Lena, I don't know if I can put myself out there again. I have been chasing after Bren since I was eight years old. While I was after him, he was after the music that ran through his soul. He found his soulmate. It's his music. I don't know if he would even have room for me in his heart."

I listened to Lena as I followed the directions to the band's house. "I know you have, Meg but don't give up. You are eighteen now and will be living in the same house. You were fifteen the last time you saw him. That makes a huge difference. I have to go. My mom said your mom has called several times. I think I can hold her off for a bit longer."

"Thank you. I know she will figure it out soon but I just want some time away from their abuse and rage. I will talk to you later, Lena. Love you."

I tossed my phone on to the passenger seat and flicked my blinker to turn into the driveway of the huge house in front of me. This was bigger than I was expecting. Apparently the band was doing better than Marcus let on. I turned the car off, opened the door and stood up. I had just shut the door when I was grabbed from behind and swung around.

"Hey, little sister! Damn you are a sight for sore eyes!" I laughed as Marcus danced me around the driveway as the band stood and watched in with smiles on their faces. He put me down and Kennedy and Dom both took turns hugging me and kissing me on the cheeks. It was wonderful to see them again. Dom grabbed my hand and spun me in a parody of the dances we used to do when we were younger. He let me go and I fell into another set of arms.

"Hey, little bit. I missed you. You look beautiful." I swallowed sharply and glanced up into the blue eyes that had haunted my dreams for more years than I cared to admit.

"Hey, Bren. I missed you too. You guys look wonderful. I have been following the band on social media as much as I can." I shivered as Bren's hands settled low on my hips and it was unlike anything I had ever felt with him before.

Marcus saw the look on my face and clapped his hands. "Let's get Meg's stuff unloaded and then we can order some dinner."

It didn't take the five of us long to get my stuff unloaded and put in the room they had set up for me. It was painted in my favorite shade of blue and the comforter set on the bed was so soft. "Thank you, Marcus."

He turned to me with a confused look on his face. "For what, sis?"

"Painting the room and comforter set. I love them both and it means a lot that you went to that kind of trouble for me."

He smirked in my direction. "That wasn't me, sweetheart. That was all Bren. He wanted to make sure that you felt like you were at home and comfortable. He knows you are going to be in the dorms this fall but he wanted you to know that this house was yours too. We have made an offer to the owner and we are buying it. We wanted a home base and Pittsburgh has been wonderful to us."

I stared at him in shock. "Bren did this? Why in the world would he paint a room in his house for me?"

Marcus looked at me like I was a special kind of stupid. "Because that man has been in love with you since we were all kids. He just knew that nothing could come from it while you were still in school. Mom and Dad never liked Bren and I think it was because they knew I would leave with him to chase after our dreams. He has asked about you after every single phone call. He wanted to risk their wrath and go to your graduation. He has always wanted you."

I sat down heavily on the bed and just stared in stunned silence at my brother. "I didn't think he saw me like that at all, Marcus. He never gave me any indication that he felt anything for me. I knew our parents didn't really like him but I never really understood that. I don't know what to do with this information, Marcus. I am not brave. I can't just walk up to him and tell him that I have loved him since I knew what love was."

A deep voice spoke up from the doorway, "Why not, when he loves you just as much? When he has dreamed of holding you in his arms and kissing those lips that he has imagined so many times?"

I sucked in a sharp breath when I realized that Bren had walked in and heard our conversation. I didn't even notice when Marcus walked out and shut the door behind him, leaving us alone in my new room.

"Why won't you be brave and take a chance on a man who is so in love with you that the sight of you completes him? I have missed you, little bit. I am sorry that you thought I didn't want you but I had to wait. Your dad pulled me aside years ago and told me that if I touched you in any way, he would make sure that my life was ruined. I couldn't risk that for either of us. I knew that you would leave home eventually and I would be able to tell you what you mean to me. I love you to the moon and back, sweetheart. I always have and I would wait a lifetime for you. I know that a lot of things are changing for you right now and I will wait for you. I just ask that you give me a chance."

I took a deep breath and realized that I would have to make the first move with this man that had been my dream for so long. I stood and walked right into his personal space. I placed my hands on his face and tugged him down to my level. I kissed him with every bit of my heart. I teased and nipped at his lips. It was just a moment before he took control of the kiss and devoured me. He conquered and I submitted. He wrapped his arms around me and with a single tug, we were falling onto my bed.

His hands on my body, set me on fire and I was gasping for breath when he slid his lips to my ear. "I love you, sweetheart. I know it seems fast but your brother has known how I felt and I can't imagine my life without you anymore. I want you to stand with and beside me for all time. Will you be mine?"

I knew what he was asking and I had only one answer. "I have loved you for so long, Bren. I don't need to wait. I was hoping you felt the same about me but I was prepared to move on. I am so glad I don't have to live with a broken heart. I want to be yours."

I shivered as he slowly removed my shirt and bra and touched me with a reverent hand. His lips slid down my throat and chest until he took a puckered nipple into his warm mouth. He nibbled, licked and bit down on both of them, causing me to thrust my chest up towards him. I felt the wet warmth between my thighs. "Please, Bren. I need you to touch me." I helped him remove his shirt and my pants. He slid his knuckles over the crotch of my panties.

"Sweetheart, you are so wet for me." He tugged my panties down until I could kick them off, then ran his fingers up my thighs and spread them wide. My eyes were huge as he pushed them further apart with his shoulders and blew a breath across my folds. He licked me slowly from the bottom of my slit to the top of my clit. He flicked the nubbin with his tongue and proceeded to devour it while I begged him for more. I whimpered as I felt the heavy pool of desire tighten in my abdomen as my climax roared to life and I fell apart with my legs around his head. My fingers were buried in his hair and I rode his face as he continued to eat me out. I slumped back as he pulled his jeans and boxers off, grabbed a condom out of his wallet and looked at me. "Are you sure, Megan? We can stop right now and I will hold you in my arms."

"I want you to make me yours, Bren. I love you and want to be with you." I took his cock in my hand and stroked it several times as he groaned with desire. I rolled the condom down his length and pushed him onto his back. I straddled his hips, grabbed his cock and brought him to my entrance. I sucked a deep breath in at the sharp bite of pain I felt as I slid down his hard shaft until I was full seated on the cock of the man that had I loved since I was a child. He gripped my hips and proceeded to help me ride him until we both fell over the edge into oblivion.

Several minutes after our hearts had slowed their wild gallop, I laid my head against his chest. I drew several shapes on his skin as I fought against the tears that I wanted to let flow.

"What's wrong, Megan?"

"Nothing, Bren. For the first time in a long time, I am happy. I am loved and I am home."

ABOUT THE AUTHOR

Brandy lives in Pittsburgh and dreams of running away and becoming a vampire. She is a diehard reader that can't breathe without adding something to her TBR list. She loves anything romance but has a special place in her heart for all things vampire related. She has a slight addiction (obsession) with coffee and it is the only thing keeping her from becoming a member of the undead.

Connect with Brandy

facebook.com/authorbrandydorsch

GLASSE AND STEELE

JEN TALTY

1

$\mathcal{V}$eronica Steele folded her arms across her chest as she stepped out of the comfort of her warm hotel and into the cold night. The frigid air clung to her skin like a wet tongue on a frozen metal pole. Her long, blond strands blew in front of her face. She flipped her head in hopes of removing the clump of hair covering her eyes. Her father had warned her that the temperatures in Pittsburgh in the middle of fall were nothing like the month of November in Dallas. She shivered as she pulled open the door to the local pub that the kid behind the hotel lobby desk had recommended.

He'd also suggested that she change her clothes.

Well, that wasn't going to happen thanks to the airline. Two more things her father had told her not to do.

First: Don't check your bag. It's not worth it when they lose it.

Second: If you must check your bag, always keep a coat with you.

Now, she was stuck with a three-quarter-sleeve Dallas Cowboys t-shirt, a jean skirt that barely came to the top of her knees, and a pair of flip-flops. At least, it wasn't snowing.

"Are you fucking kidding me?" A man at the far end of the bar tossed a napkin on the counter. "That is the worst play call ever. Does the coach not read the stats reports on the other team?"

Veronica scanned the restaurant and frowned. Only one seat left, and that was at the bar next to the napkin thrower.

"No. No. No. Goddamn it," the man at the bar said. "Why doesn't our quarterback at least *try* to scramble? Dumbass."

"Maybe if your coach played the second-string quarterback, you wouldn't get sacked so much." Veronica plopped herself onto the barstool. She should try to keep her mouth closed, but sitting in a bar during a football game next to a vocal fan of the opposing team was an opportunity she couldn't pass up. Besides, a beer, a good sandwich, and a heated conversation over the football game might make tonight salvageable. "He's faster, stronger, and has so much more potential. Not to mention, he's willing to take risks. Your number one is predictable and has lost his touch."

"But our backup is a hothead, and Coach can't control him. So, until he learns to take some direction, he's going to stay second string." The man sitting next to her gave her the once-over. He arched his brow. "You've got some balls coming in here wearing that shirt and spouting insults at the home team." He reached out his hand. "My name's Marshall. If Dallas pulls out this win, I'll help you sneak out the back."

"I'm Veronica. And, for the record, Dallas *will* win." She took the handsome stranger's hand in a firm grip. "We might be the underdog this year, but your offensive line can't shut down our defense. And your quarterback can't scramble, much less connect with a receiver. He has no confidence, and he needs to be taken out. I guarantee that if you put in the backup, it will light a fire under the rest of the players."

Marshall held up his beer mug. "I wish I could say you were wrong. Can I buy you a drink?"

"I won't say no to a free Corona." She swiveled in her chair and did her best to act as if she weren't checking out the super-sexy man wearing a white, button-down dress shirt with his tie completely undone, and his sports coat hanging on the back of his chair. A dark five o'clock shadow dotted his face. He had jet-black, slightly wavy hair that kissed the top of his collar. It looked a little unruly, but at the same time, sexy, as if he'd walked right off the pages of a men's fashion magazine. But what nearly knocked Veronica off the barstool were his dark blue eyes that held her spellbound. They were as vibrant as the Mediterranean Sea and as captivating as a car accident you couldn't look away from. "And for the record, the airline lost my luggage. Otherwise, I'd be wearing a bulky sweatshirt, which next time I'll remember take on the plane."

"That's always a good idea," Marshall said.

The bartender set a fresh beer on the counter along with a menu.

"Oh, I know what I want," she said as she shoved her lime into the glass bottle. "One of those weird sandwiches Pittsburgh is famous for. You know, the ones with French fries, coleslaw, cheese, and tomatoes."

Both the bartender and Marshall laughed.

"Sweetheart, that's the Almost Famous, and you can only get them at a Primanti Brothers restaurant," Marshall said. "There is one about three miles away, and they will have the game on."

That would require her to take a Lyft, and besides being starving, she didn't want to go out in the cold again until she had to. "I'll just take a cheeseburger with lettuce and tomatoes, a side of fries, and a side of coleslaw."

"I can do that," the bartender said with a big grin. "But it will cost extra since you're a Dallas fan."

"Just put it on my tab." Marshall clinked his beer against hers.

"No way. I'll take a drink, but not a meal. I'm not here to meet anyone. I just want to watch the game, stuff my face, and get a little buzzed." She handed the bartender her credit card.

"Understood," Marshall said. "But how about we make this interesting? If the Dallas win, I'll pick up the tab. But if the Steelers wins, it's your treat."

"Hey, Marshall, look at this." The bartender held up the piece of plastic she'd given him. "The last name is Steele, and yours is Glasse. Kind of ironic when you consider we are in the city of steel and glass."

"That's amusing," Marshall said, pointing to the television as everyone in the bar let out a collective gasp. "Your team scored."

"And we're about to go up by one since they will do a fake and go for the two-point conversion."

"This early in the game? That's unlikely." Marshall tipped his beer to his lips and stared at the screen above the bar. "Holy shit."

"I told you."

"How did you know?" He set his beer on the counter.

Discussing football typically gave her a thrill, but with him staring at her with unblinking eyes, it only made her nervous. It reminded her of what she faced in the morning and what it meant for her career. "When your coach was the offensive coordinator for the Dolphins—"

"He was fired for making rash decisions," Marshall said.

"He was traded three times as a player for taking unnecessary risks."

"You're making my point for me." Marshall waved his beer in the air. "That's the same reason he won't put in our second string. It's one thing to take a calculated risk—one that pays off more often than not. Or a Hail Mary at the end of a game. But when his decisions cause more losses than wins, well...those risks aren't worth it."

"The problem now is that your coach is gun-shy, and everyone in the league knows it. And they are going to exploit it. But if he occasionally does the unexpected and opens his eyes to his weak spots, he'll change the trajectory of the season."

"You know what? I think you might be right."

"I know I'm right." And that was exactly the attitude Veronica needed tomorrow. She sipped her beer and waited patiently for her food. Maybe, after the interview, she could find an actual Primanti sandwich. Hell, if she got the job and moved to this cold tundra, she could have one whenever she wanted.

That was if she liked the Almost Famous sandwich.

She glanced at Marshall. If the food was anything like the view, she was going to love it here.

2

*M*arshall watched the sexy lady pile French fries and a dollop of coleslaw onto her cheeseburger as she tried to build her own Primanti sandwich.

"This looks disgusting but smells amazing." Veronica lifted half the sandwich and brought it to her mouth. A large clump of coleslaw and a glob of mayo landed on the plate.

He laughed. "And it's messy."

"My taste buds just went crazy." She wiped a finger across her mouth. "Something tells me I'm not even getting this one close."

"I can tell you from experience, you can't create an original Primanti Sandwich. There is nothing like it anywhere."

"I feel that way about my grandmother's chicken-fried steak. No one makes it better than her. I've tried a hundred different places, and it's never anywhere near as good."

He pushed his empty plate to the side and wiped off his hands. "Six minutes is a lot of time at the end of a game."

"You'd have to score a touchdown and a field goal to win." Veronica dunked a lime into her beer and brought the longneck to her plump lips. She had a petite frame, at maybe five foot four, but it

282

was her spunky personality that had him re-thinking his plans for the rest of the evening.

"Many teams have come back from a more significant deficit with about the same amount of time." For the last couple of hours, Marshall had discussed the finer points of football with a woman who he couldn't stop staring at—and he'd tried, more than once. He'd come to the bar to drink, eat, and watch the game with a room full of strangers so he didn't have to be alone, but he hadn't expected to find a sassy blonde who was more entertaining than the game.

His ex-girlfriend would have a field day with that concept since one of the reasons she'd dumped his sorry ass was because he valued sports more than her. Or so she'd said. He rubbed the side of his shoulder where his electric razor had landed when she tossed it at him the day she'd kicked him out.

But sports, specifically football, was his job, and over the last couple of hours, he'd discovered what he needed to tweak in his algorithm for his report tomorrow—all thanks to Veronica. Hopefully, the organization would take his thoughts—*hers*, actually—seriously.

Everyone in the bar shouted angrily at the television when Pittsburgh fumbled the ball. Not only did Dallas recover it, they also ran it all the way in for a touchdown.

"Looks like dinner is on me." He tapped his finger on the counter. "Close me out," he said to the bartender.

"You don't have to do that," Veronica said as she rested her warm hand on his biceps.

That put his libido into overdrive.

"I insist." He nodded at the bartender. "It's snowing outside. Do you need a ride?"

She lowered her chin and raised a brow. "What kind of girl do you think I am?"

He bit back a laugh. "I didn't mean to imply anything other than it's freezing outside, and you don't have a coat or proper shoes. I just want to make sure you get home in one piece."

A sweet smile spread across her face. Her almond-colored eyes twinkled with mischief. "That's kind of you, but I'm staying at the hotel right around the corner."

"Why don't you at least let me give you my coat and walk you to the lobby."

"With the way everyone here is eyeing me, I'll take you up on that offer." She tipped her beer. "But I don't want to give you the wrong impression. I'm not inviting you up to my room. I've got a busy day tomorrow."

Boldly, he took her hand in his and pressed his lips against her soft skin. "My mother did raise me to be a gentleman. I wouldn't expect to be invited up, but I *would* like your phone number. Maybe next time you're in town, I can buy you a real Primanti Brothers sandwich."

"I'd like that. If all goes as planned, I'll be back in a couple of weeks for an extended stay."

"Now that sounds promising." He hopped off the bar stool. Snagging his sports coat, he draped it over her shoulders. "Shall we go brave the cold?" Had it not been so late, he might have offered to buy another round. He found himself enjoying the timbre of her voice, and her smile made his heart beat a little faster. He hadn't gone on a single date since his break-up. It had less to do with being heartbroken—which he wasn't—and more to do with how busy he'd been at work and the fact that it was football season.

"Do you ever get used to the cold?" Veronica tugged his suit coat tighter around her body. Wet snow melted the moment it landed on her tanned skin.

He looped his arm around her waist and guided her down the street. "I don't mind the cold or the snow, but I don't like it when it's more rain than snow."

"That doesn't answer my question." Her shoes made a smacking noise with every step she took.

"I've lived in Pittsburgh my entire life; I don't know any other climate."

The lobby doors swung open, carrying a rush of warm air. He stepped inside, wishing he were the type of man who would push for an invitation upstairs. "How long are you in town this time? I could take you for a real sandwich tomorrow evening."

"That's kind of you, but my flight leaves at seven p.m." She pulled her cell out of her back pocket and handed it to him. "Call yourself. That way, you'll have my number, and I'll have yours. If tomorrow goes the way I want it to, I'll be spending a lot more time in this snowy, wintery wonderland."

"I had a shit day at work today, but meeting you tonight made up for it in spades. You're a lot of fun."

"I had a great time, too." She turned and pressed the elevator button. "What the hell," she muttered as she curled her fingers around his biceps and yanked him into the elevator with her. "You want to come upstairs, right?"

He gripped her hips, pressing her back against the mirrored wall. He searched her face for a reason he shouldn't go to her room, but she stared at him while biting her lower lip. Talk about a sexy expression; one he found nearly impossible to turn down. "Of course, I do. But—"

She hushed him by holding onto his shoulders, lifting to her tiptoes, and slipping her tongue into his mouth, swirling it around in a dance that made him dizzy. "I don't want you to think I'm a floozy."

"I don't want you to believe I'm a player."

She laughed. "You don't have the right kind of moves."

He opened his mouth, but the elevator dinged. He followed her down the hallway, watching her hips sway back and forth as she walked. Her calf muscles flexed, and he found himself wanting to bend over and kiss them. Who was he kidding? He wanted to kiss every inch of her body. Run his tongue over every soft mound and dive into every crevice.

"I must have some moves, or I wouldn't be stepping into your hotel room."

She slammed the door shut behind them. Her fingers toyed with the hem of her shirt. A sultry smile slowly stretched from one cheek to the other.

Quickly, he yanked his tie over his head and tossed it across the room. His chest heaved. It became difficult to fill his lungs when she exposed the white, lacy bra that lifted her full breasts, pushing them together in an erotic picture that made him drunk with desire.

Thank God he'd been carrying around a condom in his wallet. He dug into his pocket and tossed it on the nightstand before removing his belt.

"I don't do things like this." Veronica kicked off her flip-flops and hooked her thumbs on the waistband of her jean skirt. "I recently broke up with my boyfriend of two years. He's the reason I'm looking for a change." She rolled the denim over her hips.

Marshall stood by the edge of the bed, staring. Her sun-kissed skin shimmered under the light of the moon that filtered in through the window. He licked his lips.

"I'm totally over him, but it's been a while." She dropped her hands to her sides. "Wow. I sound pathetic."

"Not even close. I like listening to you talk, and I want to know whatever you want to tell me." Swiftly, he unbuttoned his shirt and let it fall to his feet. "Besides, I understand. My ex and I ended our relationship months ago. But I've been so busy with work, I barely have five minutes to myself. Going out tonight was a treat."

"Looks like you get a treat *and* dessert." She did a little curtsy. Closing the gap between them, she reached behind her back and unhooked her bra.

He swallowed.

Hard.

It had been months since he'd had sex. And years since he'd had sex with anyone other than his ex. Not that he was worried he'd forgotten how. That would be absurd. But he *was* concerned for his heart because, for the first time in a long while, he found himself wanting to get to know a woman.

Yanking his pants off, he pushed all the lovey-dovey thoughts out of his mind. She didn't even live in Pittsburgh, and it would be a long time before he'd be able to work regular hours again. "You're incredibly beautiful."

"I bet you say that to all the—"

"You're the only lady that matters right now." He pulled her to his bare chest and crashed landed his mouth on hers, swirling his tongue, tasting her sweet nectar. Her hair smelled like an orchard, and her supple skin tempted his fingertips. Lifting her off the floor, he gently placed her on the bed and removed her scant panties along with the rest of his clothes.

He tangled himself with her, kissing every inch of her tight body. He did his best to keep the pace of his lovemaking tender and slow, but she had a raw animal instinct that pushed him over the edge.

With every tender stroke of her hand, his breath caught in his throat. Their bodies melded together as though they were old lovers reunited after a long separation.

The room filled with the sounds of her soft moans and his deep, throaty growls. They collided together, making intense music that shocked his system. His body beaded with perspiration as he allowed himself to be lost in their passion. He hadn't been prepared for such deep desire, and now that he'd experienced it, he wasn't sure he could ever let it go. Or Veronica.

But did he even have a choice?

Her body quivered as she called out his name, bringing his climax to the surface. Long moments passed as they caught their breath.

He collapsed on the bed, closing his eyes and pulling her close. He had no desire to leave her side, but he knew that his time with her was about to come to an abrupt end.

She patted his chest and glanced up at him with a sexy smile. "Are you ready for me to stroke your ego?"

"Sweetheart, you've already sent my ego to new heights, thank you very much."

3
_____

*V*eronica stretched out her arm and blinked open her eyes. "Where are you going?" She propped her head on her hand and watched Marshall hike his slacks over his tight ass.

"It's almost six, and I've got to be to work by seven."

She dropped her head back to the pillow. "That's when I've got to get up."

"So, why don't you go back to sleep?" He sat on the edge of the bed and pulled her into his arms. "I'm not a fan of one-night stands, and I like you, but this is my busy time of year with work."

"You don't have to explain anything to me. I understand. And things in my life are crazy right now, too."

Cupping her cheeks, he held her gaze for a long moment. "You're a special woman, Veronica, and I hope I get to be with you again soon."

"The feeling is mutual." Letting the sheet drop to her waist, she wrapped her arms around him and kissed him with her breasts shamelessly pressed against his bare chest.

He groaned. "I really have to go. I have a report due, and my boss is a pain in the ass." He slipped from the bed and finished dressing. "Good luck with your presentation today."

"Thanks." She had no idea why she hadn't told him about the job interview, other than maybe she didn't want to jinx it. This position was the opportunity of a lifetime, and if she were being honest with herself, she'd be devastated if she didn't get it. "Can you hand me my phone before you leave?"

"Sure thing." He set the cell on the pillow. "It would probably be really weird if I asked to take your picture right now."

"Weirdly flattering, but as long as I'm totally covered, and it's for your eyes only, go right ahead."

He smiled like a teenage boy who had seen a boob for the very first time. He held up his cell, and she did her best not to giggle like a schoolgirl as he took the picture.

"I'll talk to you later." He winked right before closing the door.

No way in hell would she be able to go back to sleep for half an hour, so she found the customer service number for the airline.

"Hello. This is Veronica Steele. My luggage went missing on my flight to Pittsburgh. I've got a claim number. It's 89964219."

"One moment please," a young man said.

The sound of clicking came over the line.

"Oh. Yes. We found the bag."

"Thank God. Yesterday, I was told it would be delivered to my hotel. I'm in a bit of a crunch for time because I have a job interview this morning."

"Ms. Steele. I'm so sorry, but your bag is in Tulsa. We can have it sent to Baltimore, but it won't make it to Pennsylvania until eleven."

"That doesn't do me any good. And I fly back to Dallas tonight."

"We can have it sent there," the man said. "And I'm authorized to issue you a two-hundred-dollar voucher to help cover any costs for your inconvenience. I can have that sent to your billing address."

She let out a long sigh. "Thanks. I appreciate it. Please just send the bag back to Dallas. I can pick it up at the airport when I arrive."

"It will be with customer service in baggage claim. Is there anything else I can do for you?"

"No." She tapped the screen and tossed the cell onto the mattress. How in the hell had her luggage ended up in Tulsa? Well, at least they had found it, and they were giving her money. That was something.

But that didn't help her with her interview or the fact that all she had to wear was her outfit from last night. Besides the clothing being inappropriate for any professional setting, wearing a Dallas Cowboys shirt to a potential job with the Pittsburgh Steelers would be the kiss of death.

But what choice did she have?

"What's up?" Marshall peeked his head into his boss's office.

Marshall had been working for the Steelers organization for the last five years. Last month, he'd recently been promoted to lead statistician in charge of the entire data analytics department. He had four people working under him, and currently had one open position on his team.

"Interesting report on last night's game," Tucker said.

"I ended up watching the game with a Dallas fan, and she had some excellent insight. My team will be checking the stats this afternoon. We'll have a completed report to send the coach before dinner." Hopefully, the information would help the coach see the areas where the benefits of risk-taking far outweighed doing things the so-called standard way. Using data analytics this way in sports might be a relatively new concept, but the numbers didn't lie.

"That's great, and in part why I wanted to talk with you." Tucker waved his hand in front of the empty chair next to his desk. "Sunday's game-day report is incomplete."

Marshall didn't have time to explain to his boss for the third time why they weren't finished, but he'd have to suck it up and take a seat. "My team is still looking at all the data regarding the two big upsets. We had to rewrite an algorithm because of it, and I'm taking some of the things I learned from the Dallas fan last night and applying them to past games. We've found a pattern, but I need a little more time.

I'm also double-checking everything myself, which is why I'm so glad you're spearheading all the interviews today."

Tucker shook his head. "Not only do I want you to handle the interviews, but I also want you to give all the potentials a tour and grant them access to some of the data to see what their opinions are."

Marshall stiffened his spine. "We agreed you'd do the initial interviews and narrow it down to a couple of candidates, and then I'd give those some demo data to see what they came up with. Why are we changing the process?"

"The data team wouldn't exist had you not talked me into bringing it mostly in-house, and the powers that be are impressed. However, the last person we hired turned out to be less than a good fit, and I believe that's because I did the interviews."

"No. It's because he lied about his qualifications." Marshall pinched the bridge of his nose. This was not how he wanted to spend his day.

"This team is your baby. There are five scheduled today." Tucker pushed a folder across his desk. "They are coming in a half hour apart, starting at eight thirty."

"That's crazy, and it's going to take up my entire day. My team is depending on me to finish the new algorithm."

"Can't they do that?" Tucker asked with an all-knowing, arched brow.

"I suppose." Of course, they could, but that wasn't the point. Marshall glanced at his Apple watch. He had forty-five minutes to finish the algorithm before the first interview. He should be able to do it, but he'd have to pull one of his team members off their project to work with him in case time ran out. "I better get to work." Marshall stood and tucked the folder under his arm.

"You've got the conference room for the day. I've informed the coach that your report might be delayed another twenty-four hours. He's okay with it but will take any partial data you feel comfortable giving him."

Marshall felt bewildered that Tucker hadn't led with that information, but it made no difference. "I'll make sure he gets something by lunch." With that, Marshall left his boss's office and headed to his own that he shared with his team.

It was going to be one hell of a long day.

He tapped the picture icon on his phone and smiled. At least he had the memory of last night to keep him from going crazy.

4

*V*eronica gripped the door handle and sucked in a deep breath as she stepped into the business office of the Pittsburgh Steelers.

The receptionist's jaw dropped. She quickly snapped it shut. "How may I help you?"

"I'm Veronica Steele. I have an interview today."

The receptionist blinked, her mouth still gaping open. "An interview? Here?"

"Yes. With Mr. Winston."

"Lisa," a familiar man's voice echoed from down the hall. "There has been a change of plans. I want you to send all interviewees to my office, not the conference—" Marshall stopped mid-step and mid-sentence about ten feet away. "Veronica? What are you doing here?"

She opened her mouth, but only a grunt escaped her lips. She cleared her throat. "Me? What are *you* doing here?"

"I work here," he said.

"You two know each other?" the receptionist chimed in with a grin. "Well, that's interesting, because she's your first applicant."

"You're not Tucker Winston." Veronica reached for her hair and frowned. This is why she never wore it up. Quickly, she shoved her hands into her pockets. "I was supposed to meet with Mr. Winston." This couldn't be good. Her heart hammered in her chest, and her cheeks flushed.

"Since I run the data team, my boss asked me to do all the interviews." Marshall waved his hand. "Why don't we start with a quick tour of the office?"

She nodded as if she were a bobblehead. If she hadn't had that third Corona last night, she wouldn't have thrown caution to the wind and flung herself at Marshall. Had she not slept with him, this wouldn't be so awkward.

And this position was more than her dream job.

It represented a change in her life that she should have made a year ago.

"Can I ask you a crazy question?" she whispered as they walked down an empty hallway.

"I doubt it will be crazy, but shoot."

"You didn't know I was your first interview this morning?" She clenched her fists. Being played would be worse than having to walk away from a job because of her lousy choices.

"I found out less than an hour ago that Tucker wanted me to run the interviews today. I haven't even looked at any of the candidates. I was too busy using some of the information you unwittingly gave me as we watched the game last night to tweak a new algorithm. So, trust me, I'm as shocked as you." He glanced over his shoulder. His broad smile only made her pulse increase. "Bold choice in clothing."

She narrowed her eyes.

He had the nerve to laugh. "Don't worry about it. We're pretty relaxed around here."

"Right. Because your designer suit and tie scream 'casual.'"

"Yeah, well, according to my team, I'm uptight." He rested his hand on her back and nudged her toward an open door. "You didn't tell me your business meeting was a job interview."

"I'm weird about things like that."

"It does put me in a sticky predicament."

Her stomach lurched. She glanced up at him. "Maybe I should pull my application."

"No. I don't want you to do that." He rubbed the back of his neck. "But because of last night, I don't feel as if I should be the one with the final say on who gets hired."

"I'm not comfortable having this conversation with you."

"I have an idea. Since my boss changed the hiring process on me last minute, I'm going to let my team make the final decision." He held up his hand, wiggling his fingers. "I've got five interviews today, and my boss didn't spread them out. The next one will be here in a half hour, and I've been trying to figure out how to do this. But now I know."

"Please don't put me at an unfair advantage by telling me this strategy," she said. "I need to go. This is a bad idea."

"By taking myself out of the hiring equation, it's a great idea." He curled his fingers around her biceps. "Most people would have called to reschedule because of lost luggage. But not you. Nope. You sucked up your pride and showed up wearing a Dallas Cowboys shirt of all things. That tells me you want this job, and you deserve your shot, regardless of what happened between us."

"But—and this is just a hypothetical—what if I get the job? What happens then? Because—"

"We'll cross that bridge if we get there. Now, let's jump right in and meet the team."

5

"I want to thank everyone for staying today. I know it's been the hardest on those who were here first, and I know some of you have other places you need to be this afternoon."

Veronica crossed her arms over her chest and kept her gaze on her flip-flops instead of Marshall. It took a lot to make her uncomfortable in her own skin, but sitting in a room with four other professionally dressed people applying for the same job made her skin feel as though she'd been rolling around on sandpaper.

That said, she had to admit that she'd had a lot of fun playing around with Marshall's algorithms and data analysis. Talk about impressive. Wow. The man had to be one of the smartest people she'd ever come across in this business. To work with him would be a dream come true. She wanted this job even more now. So much so, that she'd gladly give up any personal relationship, sexual or otherwise, with Marshall if it meant she would be offered the position.

"Each of you brings something unique and different to the organization, and I'm honestly impressed with all of you. This is not going to be an easy decision."

Thank God he wasn't going to announce who'd gotten the position in front of everyone. That would have sucked. Veronica sat up taller and rested her hands in her lap. She'd spent a little time problem solving with each of the other candidates, and they were all smart and qualified. Any of them could be offered the job.

"I'm hoping we will have an answer in the next hour. As we discussed, the new hire can start immediately," Marshall said. "Thank you all for coming in, and I'll be in touch."

The other four candidates jumped out of their seats and rushed toward Marshall and the rest of his team. They all stretched out their hands and offered praise and thanks, along with a dozen reasons why they were the best for the job. Veronica chose to take a more laid-back approach and waited for things to calm down before thanking each member of Marshall's team individually and then quietly making her way toward the elevators.

"Thanks for staying," Marshall said as he stepped between her and the cab doors. "I should have payroll take your information for the day. You might as well have handled half of those interviews."

She tried to hide her smile, but it proved impossible. "Sadly, I get off on running numbers."

"I'll remember that next time I'm alone with you in the bedroom," he whispered.

Heat rose from the bottom of her feet to the top of her head. "That's not how—never mind." She pressed the elevator button. "I've got a flight to catch. When will you be making the phone calls?"

"Before you board."

She had so much she wanted to say, but the other candidates stood only a couple of feet away as they too waited for the elevator. "It was a pleasure meeting you."

He leaned in a little too close. "I want to kiss you so bad right now."

Her cheeks flushed, but she ignored his statement. "I look forward to hearing from you." She slipped into the elevator, stepping into the corner as her counterparts stood in front of her. She nodded, giving Marshall an all-knowing smile. No matter what happened, he'd be a memory she'd take to her grave.

He'd be the one that got away.

The next hour went by in a haze. Veronica stood in the security line at the airport. For the most part, she'd managed to shut her mind down, keeping thoughts of a naked Marshall from her mind's eye, along with the excitement of the data team he'd put together. His concepts were truly cutting edge and would change the way all industries analyzed the data they collected.

Marshall wasn't an average numbers geek. He was pure genius, and Veronica wanted on his team...

And in his bed.

But she couldn't have either.

"Veronica," a male voice called out.

She took a step toward the TSA agent and glanced over her shoulder. She dropped her cell, her boarding pass, and her driver's license to the floor. "Marshall?"

He bent over and picked up her belongings before tugging her to the side. He lifted a large plastic bag. "I brought dinner."

"What?" She watched two people pass through security.

"Don't go back to Dallas. Have dinner with me."

The sudden ringing in her ears intensified. "I need to go home, and you have phone calls to make."

"I've made all but one." He looped his arm around her waist and tugged her away from the security line.

She dug in her heels. "I've got a plane to catch, and you're making me late."

"We need to talk about a couple of things," he said, dropping his hands to his sides—the large, plastic bag bouncing against his thigh. "I thought we could do it over dinner."

She focused on the words written across the plastic.

PRIMANTI BROS.

"Is that one of those sandwiches?" Why did he have to be the kind of guy that thought about other people? Why couldn't he have just let her get on the plane and called her tomorrow with the sad news that he'd hired someone else? Instead, he had to show up with food in hand to deliver the bad news personally.

"I thought we could celebrate."

Her heart skipped a beat and then increased to a dangerous level. "What do we have to celebrate?"

"The fact that my team voted unanimously that they want you for the job."

"Your team, or you?" God, how she wished she hadn't slept with him. If she hadn't, she might be able to believe that he had nothing to do with their decision.

"My team. I didn't even make a recommendation. But I do agree with them. You are the best person for the job. Though that's not the reason I raced down here with two sandwiches in hand."

She swallowed her breath.

"Is there anything you have to get back to Dallas for tonight?"

She nodded. "My suitcase is there."

"There is a mall a few miles from my apartment. We can stop and get you essentials for the next few nights. Then, this weekend, I'll go to Dallas with you to get whatever you need. After, we can come back here and look for a place for you to live, although I know there is a unit in my building for rent."

"Can you please slow down?" She took him by the hand and navigated the sea of people waiting to enter security. "I'm exhausted, and I'm not exactly following what you're saying." She might be tired, but she didn't miss his meaning, she just needed a moment to take it all in. "The position is mine if I want it?"

"Yes." He took her chin between his thumb and his forefinger. "And we can explore whatever this is between us."

"Don't the Pittsburgh Steelers have a no-fraternizing rule or some—?"

"Not in the department we work in." Marshall paused to give her a quick but passionate and meaningful kiss. "Are you going to take the job?"

"Yes," she said calmly, only her heart beat so fast, she thought it might burst right out of her chest.

"Are you going to come back to my place and eat these sandwiches with me?"

"Only if we can do it naked."

ABOUT THE AUTHOR

I'm a USA Today Bestseller of Romantic Suspense, Contemporary Romance, and Paranormal Romance.

I first started writing while carting my kids to one hockey rink after the other, averaging 170 games per year between 3 kids in 2 countries and 5 states. My first book, IN TWO WEEKS was originally published in 2007. In 2010 I helped form a publishing company (Cool Gus Publishing) with NY Times Bestselling Author Bob Mayer where I ran the technical side of the business through 2016.

I'm currently enjoying the next phase of my life...the empty NESTER! My husband and I spend our winters in Jupiter, Florida and our summers in Rochester, NY. We have three amazing children who have all gone off to carve out their places in the world, while I continue to craft stories that I hope will make you readers feel good and put a smile on your face.

Connect with Jen

 facebook.com/AuthorJenTalty

 twitter.com/jentalty

 instagram.com/jen_talty

Tracy Kincaid (signature)

DUGOUT
FANTASY

TRACY KINCAID

1

ABBY

"Hey, I meant to ask if you wanted to go to the ball game this Saturday? Oh, that's cute!" Patty says as I hold up a baby blue shirt. We are at our favorite gently used store in the North Hills.

Treasure House Fashions is a great shopping experience in Pittsburgh. The way they have the store set up by color and size, makes shopping too easy sometimes. Not to mention the volunteers and staff are fun to be around, with their crazy sales. They dress up as Star Wars characters for their sale in May and in November they dress as Pirates. It makes shopping a blast! And it's a non-profit that benefits women in crisis and transition so as you shop, you're doing a good deed.

"Sure, who's going?" I ask as I add the blouse to my growing pile to try on.

"Myself and Kirby, Ginny and Mike, and you." Great the fifth wheel, again. Seeing my misery, Patty adds, "You could always invite someone."

That's the joke of the century! I'm a single mom with a mediocre job, I'm a hot mess. Taking a deep breath, "I'll think about it."

"Don't think about it. You're going! Come on, it will be fun," she whines, "I'm sure Kirby can find you a date if you want."

"No, absolutely not! The last time you guys set me up on a blind date, I almost needed therapy. Where are the seats?" The last guy they set me up with needed a mom not a girlfriend. I swear it was like having another kid.

"Kirby got us into section 119 row C." Kirby works at PNC Park in the marketing department so he gets a lot of perks. The view alone in that section is amazing. "And I promise, no blind date. Just come, you need a break from being a mom, and from your job."

"Fine I'll go." I grab a pair of shoes to try on.

"Great! Let's find something to wear to the game!" Patty heads over to the counter. "Hey, Tracy, where do you have the sportswear?" We shop here so much that we know the store manager.

"Gym, or sports teams?" she asks.

"Pirate shirts."

"Hey, Abby!" she says to me, "The rounder by the dressing rooms has the sports teams. You two going to the game this weekend?"

"Yeah, are you?"

"Yup, third base side. That's the only place I'll sit, the view of the city is perfect."

I've visited several ball parks as a kid and by far Pittsburgh has the best views.

"Maybe we'll see you there!" I add.

Patty and I leave our items in the dressing rooms before scoping out their Pirate gear. I find a cute V-neck with the old pirate mascot on it. "I'm getting this one. I hate that they don't put the pirate on the shirts any more. He will be my date for the day."

"He does have that rugged look to him that you seem to like."

I laugh as we return to our dressing rooms. Of course most of what I try on fits and I love them all. Good thing Treasure House has great deals for single moms!

The rest of the week flies by relatively fast considering the hellish week at work. I work as a checker at a local grocery store. The hours work for me but I will need to find something more substantial now that Eric is getting older. With the Pittsburgh weather to be nice this weekend, barbecues will be had by a lot of locals. The running joke here when someone asks what the weather's like in Pittsburgh we say, "Give it ten minutes." It can change in a flash, so we just prepare for anything and everything.

Before I had Eric, I was in Hollywood dealing with talent. That was how I met Eric's father, Robert. We hit it off right away but it wasn't until much later that I found out he was using me for my "in's" in the industry. He stuck around long enough for me to get pregnant and then took off at the first movie gig he got. I loved my job, but the hours were all over the place and I really didn't want to raise Eric in the industry, that's why we up and left Hollywood behind soon after he was born.

We are better off without Robert in our lives. It's just easier knowing that I have to do everything by myself. After I had Eric and he was old enough we moved to Pittsburgh, the housing market is easier on the pocketbook here. Now Eric and I live comfortably in a two bedroom house in the North Hills.

Eric started kindergarten this past fall. He's the light of my life, as long as we have each other we don't need anyone else. Patty and Kirby are neighbors, they are great friends and have been there for us whenever I needed an extra hand with Eric or around the house.

2

FELIX

*W*alking out to the plate with my song of choice, *Radioactive*, playing as I take my stance. Waiting for the pitch to come my way is the most exciting thing for me. The chance of hitting a home run on my home field is the icing on the cake. The first pitch is a curve ball and I miss. Taking a few practice swings I step up to the plate, take a deep breath and wait for the next pitch. The pitcher releases the ball, a fast pitch, I dig my foot in and take the swing. The adrenaline is pumping through my blood as I watch the ball soar across the field. It's been a while since I hit a homer and the feeling is out of this world. The crowd cheers as they all stand and watch in awe as the ball flies over the heads of the outfielders. I start down the white chalk line to first base, slapping hands with the first base coach, I round second and third. I'm in the home stretch when my cleat slips and my ankle rolls. I collapse on the dirt holding my left foot two feet from home base.

"Fuck!" I scream as the team doctor comes with the coach to investigate.

Questions are flung my way as silence descends upon the stadium. I answer the best I can, the less I move my leg the less pain

I'm in. "I need to touch home." I grit through the pain after a few minutes.

"You can't walk on it Felix, we can't tell if it's broken or not." The coach says sadly.

"Then I'll crawl." I growl, I want this homer on my record.

The doctor and coach back away as I gingerly flip myself onto my front. I slowly drag my knees up and get my balance. I brace myself for the pain I know I'll be feeling as I do this, but I have to touch home base. I drag myself forward, trying not to do any more damage. The crowd gasps and claps when they see what I'm attempting to do. Once I touch the plate, the team doctor and coach help me stand and take some of the pressure off my swelling ankle as they guide me down to the medical room to be examined.

"That was a stupid move, Felix," Jim, the team doctor comments.

"I was two feet from the plate, you know I had to do it."

The doctor checks me over and rules it a sprain. I'll be on the bench for the next few weeks to heal.

*T*he only good thing about being injured is that I can walk around the stadium during a game and watch from just about anywhere. Some of the guys will sit out in the bull pen or in the dugout. I've tried that, I just feel so useless sitting there not able to play. As long as I disguise myself, I try to blend in with the crowd the best I can. It's been a few weeks since my injury and with all the exercise and physical therapy I've been doing, I should be able to play in the next game.

I'm incognito as I walk around the ballpark. People are in line at the food stands and drink vendors. I head for the *Skull Bar* on the field level because the fans are most entertaining there. The bar is filled as usual with fans watching the tv's. This never made much sense to me, why pay to go to a ball field to watch tv when it's live and in color in front of you.

I find an open seat at the bar. "The usual?" the bartender smirks when he sees me.

"Yup."

"When are they releasing you?" he asks quietly as he sets the bottle of water in front of me.

"I get checked out next game and hope to be back then."

"Good! These guys could have used the help today." He walks away leaving me to watch the people and the game. The boys are having a hard time getting out of their rut today but I have faith they will pull through in the end.

I turn away and watch the crowd, I'm surprised no one has recognized me yet. It doesn't usually take this long. I guess the week long scruff is working to my advantage, maybe I'll keep it.

I lazily people-watch, some are eating and drinking, all are talking and then I see the most beautiful woman in the ballpark sitting in the corner, by herself, drinking a water. She has long blonde hair up in a ponytail that is threaded through the back of a Pirate baseball cap and a Pirate V-neck t-shirt that shows off quite a bit of cleavage. She's stunning.

Burt, the bartender comes my way again, "Hey, who's that, do you know?"

"Bookworm is what I call her. She comes every now and then, shows up around the third inning and sits reading a book on her phone."

"Interesting!" Another person who comes to a ballpark to do things other than watch the game.

I watch as a grin spreads across her face, must be a good book. I feel the need to find out what her story is, so I walk over to her table, "Is this seat taken?" I ask with a grin.

She looks up at me, her hazel eyes sparkling in the sunlight. "I guess it is now." She returns to her phone.

"What are you reading?"

She glances up, "A vampire romance."

"Ah, you're one of those? I prefer "do it yourself" or mysteries myself."

"I'm one of those?" Raising her eyebrows, "I guess I am, and I'm proud of it. But to be honest I love almost all romance genre's. It's too bad none of that stuff happens in real life. But what better way to get away from everyday life, than in a good story?"

Bookworm seems to be a good nickname for her. "Do you come to many ball games?" I ask because I'm enjoying the normal conversation, and she apparently has no idea who I am.

"Not as many as I'd like, my friends invite me when they have extra tickets. How about you?"

"I go to all of them." I smirk.

"Ah, season ticket holder. Nice!" She glances down at her phone again clicking on a few buttons.

"Not quite a season ticket holder. My names Felix, what's yours?" I reach my hand across the table to shake, hoping that maybe some sort of recognition will register with her at my first name.

"Abby." We shake, her hand is warm and soft. I like the way it feels against my skin.

"It's nice to meet you Abby. So why aren't you watching the game?"

She sets her phone down on the table and takes a swig of her water. "I was tired of being the fifth wheel so I sit with my friends for a few innings before coming up here to read."

"Don't you like baseball?" I quiz.

"I love baseball, but to be honest, today's game is kind of dull." She shrugs.

I agree, the boys do need to step it up. Before I can ask her another question someone steps up to the table.

"There you are, Patty sent me up to find you." My friend Kirby stops at the table, but the strange thing is he's not looking at me, he's looking at Abby.

"I needed to get out of the sun for a bit," she replies. "Kirby this is..."

Kirby looks my way and recognizes me, "Felix! Damn, I barely recognized you with all the fur on your jaw. How's the ankle?" Kirby reaches a hand out.

I glance over to Abby and it's as if a light bulb goes off in her head and she finally sees me. "You're Felix Monroe, I didn't recognize you. Eric is going to freak out when he hears about this." She laughs.

I wonder who Eric is? By now some people in the area have over-heard that it's me and now a crowd has gathered. Damn, I was really enjoying my conversation with the beautiful Abby.

"Well, I guess the cats out of the bag." I shrug as the first auto-graph wanting patron steps up to me. I take my time and chat with each person as I sign whatever it is they hand me. I laugh at some of the things people ask me to sign. From ball caps to body parts to their popcorn containers. The crowd seems to grow the longer that I sit here, but if I stay much longer my hand will cramp up.

"Please excuse me, I've got to get back to the dugout." I say as I stand up.

"That didn't take long," Kirby says as he steps up beside me.

"Took longer than normal, actually. I was starting to think that people had forgotten about me."

"Nah, it's the scruff." He teases.

I glance over at my table companion, surprised that she didn't flee once the crowd grew. "Abby, I'm sorry about that."

"Occupational hazard, I'm sure." Abby smiles. God her smile lights up her face.

"Just a bit. I wish I could stay and talk more but I should get back." But I really would rather hang out and get to know her more.

"It was really nice meeting you, even if I didn't recognize you at first."

"I must say that was a first and I think I liked it." I return her smile.

"Abby, are you coming back to the seats or are you going to stay up here?" Kirby asks.

"I think I'll head back with you." Abby stands and I get to see more of her. She's as tall as I am, wearing shorts that show off some amazing tan legs that lead down to sandaled feet. I laugh at her toes that are alternating yellow and black. I love a woman who supports her team.

"What?" she asks when she sees me laugh.

"Love your toes."

She blushes as she looks down. "My son thought I should paint them for the team, for good luck."

A son? I wonder where he is. Where's the father? "Well, he has good taste." I snag the ball cap from my head and sign it. "For your son."

"You don't have to do that." Abby looks stunned.

"I want to, maybe someday I'll get to meet him." I wink.

"He would love that. Thanks again," Abby says as she turns to Kirby. "I'll meet you at the seats I need to stop at the restroom."

"Sure."

"It was nice meeting you, Abby," I say as she turns away. She looks over her shoulder and waves to us.

"What's her story?" I ask Kirby as we watch her walk away.

"She's Patty's BFF and happens to be our neighbor."

"Where's the boys father?" Kirby looks at me with a funny look on his face, "What?"

"Are you interested? Because let me tell you she only wants someone serious. That woman has had enough heartbreak in her life she doesn't need a playboy."

I hold up my hands in surrender. "Look, I only asked a question. And you know damn well, I'm not like some of the other guys. I don't mess around."

Kirby lets out a heavy sigh, "Her ex dumped her and her son before he was born. He's some actor in LA. She moved here soon after he left and started a new life for herself."

Out of nowhere I feel angry. Angry for her, "Who the hell does that?"

"Her asshole ex."

"And I bet he has nothing to do with his son."

"You got it. I don't think Eric has even met the guy. He's a good kid. Look I need to get drinks for the girls, I'll catch up with you later. Give a call if you want to hang out sometime."

"Sure." I continue my walk back to the locker room. I still have this overwhelming anger that came out of right field. I want to get to know Abby and I want to show her son that not all guys are assholes.

3

ABBY

Once I get inside the restroom I head straight for a sink. The restroom is almost deserted which is nice. I turn the cold water on and splash my face, then stare at myself in the mirror. Of all the guys to sit at my table here at the ball park, I never in a million years thought that Felix Monroe would be one of them. Eric has a poster of him hanging on his wall. Felix has always been his favorite player. I thought he was hot in the poster but in real life... And with the ruggedness...parts of me that haven't been awake in a long time, seem to be wide awake now.

I was at the game that night that he got hurt. I'm glad to see that he seems to be back to normal. But why out of all the fans here at the park did he choose to sit and talk to me? Did he take pity on me because I was sitting by myself? I have no idea.

I've met some of the ball players at events that Kirby has invited me to. None of them paid much attention to me. I always had Eric with me and for a lot of the guys, being a mother is a big turn off. But when Felix heard I had a son he didn't even blink an eye. I'm sure I'm reading too much into this. He was just being nice, and I did have an empty seat at my table.

I feel better thinking that last bit. I can't afford to get my hopes up for love. Love? See this is why I don't go out much, I get around one guy and think I'm falling for them. I need to have my head examined.

Felix is one of those hot baseball players. You know the kind, perfect arms, nice looking butt and I know what he looks like in uniform but I bet he's even better out of it. And of course he had to have the rugged look that I'm attracted to; blue eyes, squared jawline with just enough stubble and hair long enough to grab ahold of. I laugh at myself and splash more cold water on my face.

I rejoin my friends in our seats, Kirby had grabbed me a bottle of water before he came back down to the seats. He hands it to me, "Thanks."

I get settled in my seat when Patty and Ginny huddle close to me. "So what did you think of Felix?"

"Damn it, Kirby set that up, didn't he? I told you guys not to set me up with anyone. I knew it was too weird for him to come and sit with me out of the blue like that." I knew it was too good to be true. I knew he was too cool, too perfect, too hot for someone like me. And I swore after my ex that I would avoid high profile men. And as much as I hate to admit it, Felix Monroe is a high profile ballplayer.

"Hey, Kirby you didn't set that meeting up, did you?" Patty asks.

"What meeting?" Kirby and Mike are talking about the last play on the field.

"Felix meeting Abby?"

"No! I had no idea he was up here. The guy does his own thing. Why are you interested?" Kirby looks at me expectantly.

That is the real question; am I interested? If I didn't have a child at home, maybe. But I can't afford to take any chances with my son.

Because I don't answer right away, "Abby I promise I didn't set you up. Felix is a good guy, he's not like some of the others. If you're interested, I can talk to him. You think about it and let me know."

We all turn our attention to the field as everyone stands and cheers. The batter hit a home run for our team and the Jolly Roger makes its appearance, as fans pull them out to cheer our team on. It's the ninth inning and we need another run to win the game. It's been a close one all night.

The batter takes his stance and prepares to swing. The ball is pitched and everyone holds their breath as the batter swings and hits a line drive down center field. The runner on second books it down the line as the third base coach waves him to keep going home. The batter is not far behind. The centerfielder throws the ball as hard as he can toward home, but his attempt is futile because the Pirates score the winning run! Everyone in the crowd cheers as the bench clears to congratulate their teammates. This is going to be a fun season for the team and the fans alike.

The walk back to the cars is the way it always is when I'm out with my friends. Mike and Ginny are hand in hand talking to each other like newlyweds. They've been married for four years and they seem to still be in love with each other. Patty and Kirby are the same way, except they have no issue showing public displays of affection.

I just about collide with Kirby as he and Patty stop in the middle of the walkway. "Why did you stop like that?" I ask, concerned.

"Sorry, Abby, I got a text and had to stop to read it." Kirby apologizes.

"It's okay." I step around them and continue to the parking garage.

The ride home doesn't take very long and I'm happy to be home with my baby boy. He's sound asleep of course since its way past his bedtime. I pay the sitter and get myself through the shower and off to bed. That night I dream about a certain ball player.

FELIX

After the game the guys wanted to go out and celebrate the win. I said I'd go but I'm not feeling like hanging out with them. Most of the guys just want to hook up with women. I've never been one to have hook-ups like that. I didn't like the fakeness of it. I tried hook-ups early in my career but found that I preferred relationships. What's the point of sleeping around with someone you don't know and will most likely never see again?

I hit the bar with the guys but only stay for one drink. They give me a hard time but I don't care. Right now I have my mind set on one leggy blonde.

That night I dream of sitting and talking to Abby while a little boy that looks like her plays.

♥

The next morning I text Kirby asking if he wants to meet up for coffee this morning. So we meet at the local coffee house. It's early enough that a lot of people don't pay much attention to me since they are busy trying to grab a cup before work. Kirby joins me after grabbing his own cup.

"What's up with you? You look like shit." Kirby comments before taking a swig of coffee.

"Didn't get much sleep I guess." I run my hand through my hair. May be time for a haircut.

"Why not? The team won and you will be back for tonight's game. What are you thinking about?"

I'm not sure how to broach the subject so I just jump in. "I was thinking about Abby."

Kirby looks up at me and leans back in his seat. "Look, she thought that I had set that meeting up. That was all you my friend. Why were you thinking about her? Are you interested?"

"I don't know, to be honest. I thought she was beautiful when I first saw her, but when I sat and talked to her, she captured my interest. No one has sat through a crowd of people that size and waited for me to finish. Most women would have thought I was being rude and left after the second autograph. She seems different from other women I've been around."

"I'm telling you Felix you have to be careful with this one. She has a sweet kid and I feel protective of her. So does Patty."

"I just want to get to know her." I plead.

"Let me talk it over with Patty and see what we can come up with."

"Thanks man, I owe you one. There's something about her and I'd like to see what that is."

ABBY

I wake Eric up and get his breakfast ready. "Eric, honey are you ready for breakfast?"

Eric walks in the kitchen with sleepy eyes, rubbing them as he sits. "Morning, Mommy." He digs into his cereal with gusto, my hungry growing boy.

"Morning, baby boy." I kiss the top of his head. "Did you and Wendy have fun last night?" Eric loves when Wendy, another neighbor, watches him.

"Yes, she took me to the park. I wanted to play all night and I didn't want to go to bed but she said I had school."

"That's right! But you know what?" He shakes his head, "I got something for you from the game last night. You can take it to show and tell if you'd like."

"What is it?" His eyes light up and he's wide awake now.

"I met your favorite player at the game last night and he asked me to give this to you." I grab the hat and hold it behind my back. "Which hand?"

Eric jumps out of his seat and chooses my right hand. I pull the hat out from behind me and he jumps up and down in excitement. Examining the signature and noticing the number, "That's Felix's number! Mommy this is Felix's hat!"

His excitement is contagious, "It is and he was wearing that hat before he signed it and gave it to me to give to you. Isn't that cool!"

"You met him?" He looks at me with huge eyes.

"I did and he's very nice." Yes, very nice, nice eyes, nice strong arms, nice hair and jawline. Crap I need to get my head out of the clouds. "What do you think? Do you want to take it for show and tell? As long as you don't lose it."

"Yes! And I won't lose it I promise." Eric gives me a big hug as he runs to his room.

I follow close behind. "So what do you want to wear today?" I ask because he has gotten picky with what he wants to wear to school. Who knew boys could be picky about things like clothes?

He goes through his closet until he finds his Pirate jersey. Felix's jersey to be exact. I help Eric get dressed before I walk him to the bus stop. I'm lucky with the school that he goes to, the kindergarten is all day.

After I tidy up from breakfast, I put my uniform on and head for work. I figured until Eric started elementary school full time that I was stuck in jobs like these. Now that he's in school full time I can begin looking for something that pays more and is geared more to my expertise. With three major sports teams in the city I should be able to find a job with one of the teams PR departments. But so far, being a mom has been the best job ever. It just doesn't pay the bills.

4

FELIX

$\mathcal{I}$t felt good to finally get back out on the field after my injury but I'm looking forward to a day off. We've been on the road for the past several days and I'll be happy to get back to the City of Steel. Our winning streak has continued on and we hope the momentum stays strong.

Kirby called and said that he and his wife were having a barbecue at their house and invited me to attend. I arrive in the quiet little neighborhood close to North Park. Kirby's house is a small colonial style with red brick and white trim, colorful flowers line the driveway and walkway. I step onto the porch and ring the doorbell, standing for a few minutes but no one answers the door. I can hear kids playing in the backyard and figure everyone is out back.

As I make my way back a boy comes flying at me with a group of kids chasing him. The little blond boy uses me as a shield from the others who all have water guns. It doesn't take long before they take aim at us. "Don't you dare!" I laugh as the kids giggle and shoot water from their guns. The boy behind me is fine since I'm taking on the firing squad alone. I laugh along with the boys as the water contin-ues, who knew those guns held so much water, I'm soaked.

"Boys!" I hear a woman call out, "Oh my God! Eric, Billy, Xander, get your butts over here right now!"

"Oh, man!" One of the boys comments.

I follow the kids as they hang their heads on their way to the most tempting site I've seen since the last time I saw her. Abby is scolding the boys for shooting at me. "I'm so sorry. I had no idea they would go to the side yard."

"It's not a problem, Abby. We were all young once. It's just water and it's hot outside. I take it one of these is yours?"

Abby stares at me for a moment before the young blond boy steps up to me and pulls Abby's arm and says, "Mom, that's Felix Monroe!"

"You must be Eric. It's nice to finally meet you." I shake Eric's hand.

"Yes, Eric that is Felix Monroe. Boys, why don't you take the water guns to the lower yard so no adults get caught in your cross fire."

The boys take off at full speed down the steps to a lower yard. Eric yells to the others, "That's Felix Monroe! My mom knows him..." I can't hear the rest of what he says.

"Let me get you a towel." Abby spins and walks up the stairs to the deck. Her ponytail swishes, I get a hint of coconut as she moves. She is wearing a blue tank top and shorts. Everything about this woman makes me want to get to know her better. From the way she looks at me to the way she handled the boys.

I follow her up the stairs, "Hey, Felix! Have an accident?" Kirby teases when he sees me come up the stairs.

"Apparently there was a water war you didn't tell me about."

"Here, I'm really sorry," Abby says as she passes the towel to me, our hands brush against each other. You know when you read books or watch movies and they always talk about that zap of electricity? I never thought that was true until Abby and I touched.

"Thanks." I whisper, she takes my breath away.

"Hey Felix, we are so glad you could make it!" Patty says as she comes in for a hug. "I see you've met my friend Abby."

"We met at the game Patty, you know that." Abby rolls her eyes.

"Why don't you put the beer in the cooler, the one by the grill is for the adults."

"Sure." I smile as I walk over to the grill.

"So, what do you think?" Kirby asks.

"About?" I pull the box of beer open and add some to the cold cooler, taking one for myself before closing it.

"Abby."

"I still would like to get to know her, but please tell me she knew I was coming? And why didn't you mention she was going to be here?" I hate blind dates, more than I hate striking out at the plate.

"Patty says she talks about you all the time, more so now that you shared a table with her."

That piques my interest, "Really? She talked about me before I met her?" I look over to where the girls are sitting watching the boys in the lower yard.

"You're Eric's favorite player. So, needless to say, you tend to be hers as well." Kirby explains.

I smile at that news.

ABBY

When Patty called me over to have a barbecue and said that Eric and the neighborhood boys could play with water guns. I figured that it was just that. It wasn't until a few minutes before Felix got here that I found out that he was coming.

Patty and I are standing at the railing looking down to the lower yard at the boys as they play. "Why didn't you tell me when you invited me that Felix was coming?"

"Because I wanted it to be a surprise."

"You know I hate surprises."

"If it makes you feel any better, he didn't know you were going to be here either. At least I gave you a heads up before he got here."

"I wish you guys would stop trying to set me up with men. If I wanted to date I could find my own."

"I believe you can find your own but I thought since you can't stop talking about him and he asks Kirby about you every time he sees him, I figured that we could have you both over and you could get to know each other. Come on just relax and have fun okay?"

"I'll do my best."

I turn and see Felix and Kirby enjoying a beer by the barbecue. Patty and I join them.

"Would you ladies like a beer?" Felix asks.

"Sure," we both say.

"The burgers are getting close, Patty. Do you want to get things ready?"

"I can help." I stand and Patty stops me.

"I've got it. Why don't you and Felix chat!" Patty smirks as I sit back down. Kirby follows her into the house a few minutes later.

"So, was that a total set-up or what?" Felix comments after a short silence. Reaching up and rubbing the back of his neck.

"It's not the first time. I'm sorry about the kids getting you wet and the fact my friends don't know how to back off."

"I don't mind on either case. It could be worse I suppose."

"How so?" I ask as I take a drink of beer.

"Well, I could have been an old cranky guy," he says with a straight face.

I laugh, "And I could have been a nun."

"Well, I'm glad neither is the case. So tell me about Eric, he looks just like you."

I smile, this is an easy topic, "Eric turned five last April and started kindergarten this past fall and is doing amazingly well in school. I am one proud mama."

"That's wonderful! Does he do anything outside of school?"

"He started t-ball in the spring. I'm not sure he likes it too much."

"Why's that?"

"Well, he likes watching you big boys play and t-ball is so different. I keep trying to explain to him that you all had to start in t-ball.

But you know how young kids are, they think they can do everything the big kids can."

"I remember hating t-ball. One time a kid was sitting in the outfield playing with some flowers, it didn't take long for a bee to come by. The poor kid got stung and everyone started crying."

"You can remember that far back? I'm lucky if I can remember what I had for breakfast. Did you always want to play baseball?"

"My dad gave me my first glove when I was four. Ever since then I knew what I was going to be."

I find Felix so easy to talk too. It's been a long time since I've had a conversation with a man that I could be interested in. I don't think I'm ready to open my heart just yet, but I could see myself doing so with Felix. We eat and talk for several hours. He is happy to answer any questions that are thrown at him from the kids. I love the way he is with the kids. It's sweet.

We are all sitting around the campfire. The sun has gone down and Eric is sound asleep in my arms. "I should get Eric to bed."

"Put him to bed then come back out. The night is still young," Patty says as she brings out dessert and after dinner drinks.

"If he stays asleep I will."

"Can I help?" Felix pipes in as he stands.

"Oh you don't have to do that. I've been doing it for years." I chuckle.

"Let him help Abby," Patty says as she sits down.

I look over at her and she gives me a thumbs up. I roll my eyes. I try to get up but with the extra drinks I'm finding getting up with a little boy on me is a challenge.

Felix swoops in and gently lifts Eric as if he weighs nothing, then he offers me a hand as he helps me stand. Felix quietly follows me next-door to my house. Inside I lead him to Eric's bedroom where he gently lays Eric down. He's so gentle that Eric doesn't even bat an eye.

"You're a natural," I comment as I remove Eric's shoes and pull the blankets over him.

"My sister has little ones so I get to see them and help when I'm home."

"That's sweet."

Felix looks around Eric's room, it looks like a typical little boys room with light blue walls and his favorite ballplayer all over; posters, pirate gear of all shapes and sizes, even the Pirate parrot graces the room.

"Like I said he's a fan of yours." I shrug.

"Do you have a pen?"

I leave the room and grab a sharpie from the kitchen drawer handing it to him when I go back into the room. He takes it and writes a note on the poster.

It was nice hanging out with you Eric, I hope we can do it again someday!
Felix Monroe

"Since I didn't get to say a proper good-bye." He grins as he hands me back the pen.

We leave the room and I grab the baby monitor so I can hear if Eric wakes up. "Thank you for being so nice to him."

"He's a sweet kid."

We head for the door, "Abby, do you think you'd like to go out sometime? Just the two of us?"

"I'd like that, but I'm going to be honest with you Felix. I've been through hell and back and I won't do anything that will hurt my son. I know that I can live through whatever is thrown my way, but I will protect that boy at all cost, including my happiness."

"I would never think of doing anything that would upset Eric or you and I will follow your lead on everything. I like you Abby and I'd like to get to know you better." He steps up to me on the back porch and brushes a stray hair behind my ear. The gentle touch buzzes through my body and I crave more. But I must protect my heart and my son. I look up into his blue eyes and see understanding and somehow, I know that he won't hurt me.

His hand lingers on my cheek and I lean into the touch. It's been so long since I've been touched by any man that I feel dizzy. I slowly move forward keeping my eyes on his the whole time. He follows my lead and kisses me. It's one of those toe curling kisses. A kiss that promises so much more. I thread my fingers in his hair and lose myself in the kiss.

"Mommy?" I hear coming from the other side of the door.

"Oh God." I disentangle myself from Felix and spin to open the door. Eric is standing on the other side. "What's the matter baby?"

"I had a bad dream."

I turn to Felix and feel my face as it flames with embarrassment. "Would you let Patty know that he woke up and I can't go back out tonight?"

"Of course. Hey, Eric take care of your mom and it was really nice meeting you."

"Bye, Felix," Eric says but before I can close the door he flies out and hugs Felix around the waist.

My heart pounds in my chest at the sight. Felix doesn't seem to mind as he returns the hug. When Eric breaks the hug, Felix squats down to his level. "Your mom said that you are playing t-ball." Eric nods. "Work extra hard. I know it's boring now, but that's where I started."

"Okay Felix." Eric turns and grabs my hand.

"Good night, Felix."

"Can I call you?"

"Eric, go into your room and I'll be right there." Eric leaves. "Let me get something to write on."

"Here what's your number?" Felix pulls his phone from his pocket and opens the text. I give him my number and he sends a text. "Now you have my number too. You can call or text anytime. I had a good time tonight."

"So did I."

"Mommy!" Eric yells from the other room.

"I better go. Good night." I close the door and head for my son's room.

To be continued...

ABOUT THE AUTHOR

Tracy Kincaid is a native Southern Californian who transplanted to Southwestern Pennsylvania in 2013. A wife, mother of three children and a Grandma to 3, 1 dog (Buc), 1 cat (CB) and 1 Bunny (Jace). When she's not writing you can find her reading or working with a local non-profit (Treasure House Fashions). She enjoys the outdoors, whether it be working in the garden or hanging out with family and friends.

Connect with Tracy

facebook.com/tracykincaidauthor

twitter.com/tkincaidauthor

instagram.com/tracykincaid

WHERE THERE IS SMOAK

SIDONIA ROSE

1

"On behalf of the crew of flight 8687, we'd like to welcome you to Pittsburgh International Airport. Local time is 11:15 am, and the temperature is 65 degrees.

For your safety and comfort, please remain seated with your seat belt fastened until the Captain turns off the Fasten Seat Belt sign. This will indicate that we have parked at the gate and that it is safe for you to move about. At this time, you may use your cellular phones if it is within reach. Otherwise please wait until the Fasten Seat Belt sign has been turned off to access your bags."

As the flight attendant continues with instructions, I turn off the airplane mode on my phone. It takes a minute for my phone to connect to a network, then nothing. There should be a message waiting for me, except there are no new notifications.

From the seat next to me, I hear the familiar notification of a new text message. It's not a single notification. Instead, it's a series of four, make that five notifications. Before the phone chimes again my brother gives a quiet cheer like he just received good news.

Pushing his elbow into my arm, my brother, Cole, leans closer to me, "Did you see the message from Anders? He says we can watch a practice and he got us tickets to a game."

The announcement from the speaker is warning us about opening the overhead bins and encouraging us to collect our things. My phone is still not getting any messages. As if he senses my frustration, my brother says, "If your Wi-Fi is on, you won't get any messages until we're off the plane."

Scrolling back to my settings, I check the Wi-Fi setting, sure enough, it's turned on. That explains it, every time I fly, I forget to turn it off when we land.

Vibrating in my hand, I get multiple notifications of new messages on my phone. There's a certain message I'm hoping to get, but it doesn't look like she's responded to me. She's been playing it cool with me lately. I told her I'd be gone a few days, so she must not be responding again. The other option is probably that she's at work and she doesn't text while she's at work.

Looking through my other message, I see that my cousin has messaged, just like Cole said. The other bit of information is that he's waiting in baggage claim for us.

We're seated about halfway back in the plane, so it doesn't take too long before it's our turn. As we get up, the lady behind us asks, "Excuse me, could you get my bag down for me?"

Before I have a chance to turn around, Cole reaches up to get her bag. He takes a minute to talk to her before he starts carrying it to the front of the plane.

Having my brother tag along with me was a last minute decision. It was my mother's idea; she said something about a no kids weekend at home. My three sisters were all going off somewhere together for the weekend, they claimed a girls weekend, leaving Cole at home. Normally Cole is inseparable with his twin sister, Quinn. This is unusual for them to go their separate ways, but I'm willing to help out. Maybe it will get me in my father's good graces. That's something I need these days.

It doesn't take long before Cole is walking beside me. He was quiet on the plane watching a movie or something; now he's full of questions.

"Do you think Anders will let me skate with him? I know he's not been signed to a full contract, but do you think he'll stay here in Pittsburgh?"

Our cousin is an amazing hockey player, but he didn't make the draft last year. That left him with a few options; one of which was to get offered a PTO. That's a professional try out, the team here in Pittsburgh offered him one. He doesn't expect to stay with the NHL team; they have another team somewhere in Pennsylvania with the AHL, that's where he expects to play most of the season. Wherever he plays, at least he's playing hockey.

Ignoring Cole isn't easy. He's been following hockey a lot more than I have, so he's spitting out lots of statistics. He seems to think Anders has a great shot at playing in the NHL this year.

As we ride the escalator, he mentions the primary reason we're in Pittsburgh this weekend, "Do you think Dwight will let you visit him?"

That's the million dollar question. Will Dwight allow me to visit him?

It's been six years since I've visited Dwight, I don't count the few minutes I saw him last year at his grandfather's funeral.

Pittsburgh is where his father grew up; Dwight lived here when he was younger too. When his parents died, the only family he had were his grandparents living in Pittsburgh. He was sent to live with them. He seemed to be doing well until he was arrested for setting fires, which is why he was sent to a treatment center. Two years ago, he was improving so much that he was approved for outpatient care. He went back to live with his grandparents, but that only lasted a few months as his grandfather died. His grandma said she couldn't keep up with the outpatient schedule at the time before they could move him to a group home; he had a relapse.

He's better now; his doctors think he's ready to try the group home again. Last week when I talked to his grandma, she sounded positive this would work for him.

"There's nothing I can do if he doesn't want to see me." It's an obvious answer. "I talked to his grandmother last week; she said he's in a better place now. I'm going to help her find a place for him to live."

Cole walks down the last steps of the escalator before he steps off, "Let's get this party rolling."

Even amongst the crowd of people in the baggage claim area, it's easy to spot my cousin. At 6'4," he stands taller than almost everyone else around him. Although we aren't as tall as Anders, my brother and I are no slouches in the height department. From across the way, Anders sees us and waves.

Before he takes off, Cole says, "There he is!"

Dodging around people I catch up to Cole as I hear Anders giving him the rundown for the weekend, "I had to borrow my teammate's car to drive you guys around. It's not like you'd both fit on the back of my bike."

Smiling Anders gives me a one-armed hug, "It's about time you came to visit."

Nodding, I agree with him, "It's that life thing that gets in the way. You said you had to borrow a car? What happened to that fancy car you just bought?"

Grinning, he shakes his head, "It's a crazy long story."

At the same time, Cole and I both say, "That means there's a woman involved."

He holds up his hands like we're trying to rob him, "Was a woman, definitely was a woman. It's a story better told with beer."

$\mathcal{W}$e stop for sandwiches before going to Anders place. He's been telling me about these sandwiches since he got to Pittsburgh. The photos on the menu don't look that great, neither does the idea of eating a lump of shredded cabbage on a sandwich, but when the server drops a pizza pan loaded with French fries covered in cheese, all thoughts of cabbage disappears.

With a mouthful of food, Cole asks his hundredth question of Anders, "Do you think they will sign you for a full contract?"

Anders is chewing half of a sandwich as he looks sideways at Cole. Growing up, he wasn't much of a conversationalist, even less when there was food on the table. Most of Cole's questions have been answered with a single word or a few grunts. He gets a grunt this time too.

Wiping his mouth he drinks some water before saying, "It's still the preseason, I'll probably play for the AHL team this season. My agent says since I didn't make the draft, this is my best chance."

Growing up, there were more hockey teams around than there were football or soccer teams. Naturally, we all played on a hockey team at one time or another. It was Anders that excelled at the sport if he wasn't playing hockey he was watching it.

As we finish eating the conversation turns to Dwight, the reason I'm here this weekend. Anders and I are the same age; as kids, we were both friends with Dwight.

"You said something about Dwight living on his own. Is that going to be safe for him?"

The truthful answer is that I don't know. This is a decision made by a judge that has limited options to offer him. Moving from a treatment center to a group home is a step up for him.

"This is the only option he has." Taking another drink from my glass I offer my honest opinion, "I think it would be best for him to move back home with us, I think it's what he wants too. The only problem is the judge isn't going to let him leave the state just yet."

Cole doesn't miss the chance to offer his opinion, "Mom wouldn't be happy about it, but Dad already said Dwight could live in the apartment over the garage."

The apartment over the garage is where everyone wants to live. It was a storage area until my aunt needed a place to live. It took dad a few weeks to get enough guys to help make it into a two-bedroom apartment. The rooms are small, the kitchen even smaller, but the rent is always affordable to everyone that needs it. My sister Reese has been living there while she's in school.

"I talked to Dwight's grandma yesterday. She's not sure he will be willing to see me, but I have to try. I'm also going to go with her to look at a few places for Dwight." The prospect of looking at group homes for my old friend doesn't sit well with me. "This afternoon she will pick me up so we can look at a few places. She said I could borrow her car for the weekend also."

Cole perks up at the prospect of transportation. It's easy to schedule a car for quick trips; he was hoping we could do some sight-seeing that requires us to drive longer distances.

"Hey, so can we go do that hiking trail I told you about?" He pulls out his phone to show the map again, "It's still about forty minutes from here, but the views are unbelievable."

Our family has spent many hours on hiking trails over the years, unlike my brother, it's not my favorite activity. He pushes his phone across the table in an attempt to entice Anders to join him. As they start to discuss the logistics of the activity, I take the chance to step away to make a phone call, "Hey, just going to confirm with Mrs. English."

Stepping outside, I walk around to the side of the building before dialing the phone. After the second ring, Mrs. English greets me with a warm hello, "Hello, is that you Thorne?"

She never seems to trust that the name on her phone is correct, "Hi, Mrs. English, its Thorne. I wanted to see if we can still visit Dwight this afternoon."

"It's so good to hear from you, dear. How was your flight? You left early this morning?"

It takes a few minutes to make arrangements for her to pick me up. She visits Dwight at the hospital three times a week; today is her regular day to visit him. He was supposed to meet with his doctors this morning for his final release papers. After they are processed, he could be released as soon as next week.

Dwight got into some trouble when he was fifteen; he was accused of setting a fire at his high school. The story he told the police never seemed to make much sense. That worked in his favor, and his grandparents were able to find a lawyer that got an insanity plea for him. Instead of serving time in jail, he's spent most of the last nine years in a psychiatric hospital.

The group home was recommended for him as his best option. He still needs some supervision for a few months. If that's successful, he will have a full release.

"Thorne, he's changed so much, even in the last few months he's changed." There's sadness in her voice. He was barely nine when he went to live with his grandparents. The best intentions of spending summers together didn't work out as expected. Dwight had a few rough years, and this is the woman that was there to take care of him through it all.

"We'll get this figured out for Dwight; I'll make sure he has a chance to make this work."

That's a lot of ambition in a simple statement. Helping Dwight is going to be difficult. If he can't figure out how to motivate himself, there's little chance that anything I do to help him will work. The one thing I can do for him is not to give up on him.

3

*I*t's been more than an hour since we arrived to see Dwight. As we were signing in to see him, there was a note for Mrs. English to meet with his physician before our visit. She assured me this is normal, except it didn't seem normal to me.

At first, I didn't want to get distracted, so I flipped through a couple of magazines. They weren't that interesting. My phone rang a few times, the first time I got a lot of questionable looks especially from the lady at the counter. When she pointed to a sign that said to turn your phone to silent, well I did that. So luckily, when it rang again, no one could hear it.

My phone rings again; this is the third call from a girl I met more than a month ago. We talked a few times on the phone; we never went out. So it doesn't make any sense why she would be calling me today. For the third time, I hit the ignore button.

Without much to do, I open my messages from Britton. We met a few weeks ago; it took a bit to get her phone number. She tried to tell me that she doesn't use her phone except for work calls. She also doesn't have any social media. So it wasn't like I could see what she likes without directly asking her. The last message she sent me was that she was going to work. That was three days ago.

Me: Hey, pretty girl!

Usually, when I text someone, the little bubbles appear telling me that they are responding. That doesn't happen when I text Britton. When she told me that she's a bagel maker, I thought she was kidding. It wasn't something I ever considered; it makes sense that someone has to make the bagels. It turns out that person is Britton.

Me: Here in Pittsburgh, waiting to visit my friend Dwight.

She's still not responding to me. That could mean she's at work. She said she got the phone to be able to get extra shifts at work, so when she's at work, she turns the phone off. I'm going to have to convince her to keep her phone on so she can text me.

Me: call me after work

Sometimes if I ask her to call me, she will. She has never just called me, or even initiated a conversation via text messages. It's a little frustrating to me, usually, if I offer my number, the girl will at least send me messages.

Like Angie, that's now calling me for the fourth time today. Walking to the door, I answer on the third ring this time.

"Hey."

The high pitched voice coming through the phone makes me wince, "There you are! Did you get my message?"

Now outside I can talk without getting the stink eye from the receptionist.

"No, you left a message?"

There was probably a message on my phone, but I didn't look. She should have gotten the message I didn't want to talk when I didn't answer the phone the other three times she called.

She makes a noise like she's having a tantrum. That is why we never went out; I'm not interested in the drama. She must have forgotten that I told her I wasn't interested the last time we talked.

"I know it's been a while," she starts before adding a pout to her voice, "but you said you were going to be busy with school or something."

The something I told her about was finishing the fire academy and starting a new job. She seems like a high maintenance kind of girl; there's no time in my life for that right now.

"Anyway, I thought maybe you'd like to come out to the lake to relax for a few days. I have my parent's lake house for the week; there's a bunch of us that are going to hang out." She takes a breath before she continues talking even faster, "I can't stop thinking about you and the connection we had. I was nervous to call you, but now I'm glad I did. What do you say?"

Her words tell a different story than the missed calls from earlier. Maybe it's me, but from what she's saying it sounds more like her date for the week canceled on her.

"Well thanks for thinking of me..."

She interrupts me pouting again, "No, no, you can't turn me down. All you have to do is show up; everything is taken care of." That again sounds like I'm a last minute invite. Since I'm not interested and I'm about to decline that doesn't bother me. "If it helps, there's a boat, we can water ski, and did I mention me and my girlfriends never wear our swimsuits on the boat."

That's quite an offer. If I remember correctly she has some hot friends.

"Thanks, but I'm going to decline." She makes that pouty noise again as I see Mrs. English walking through the lobby searching for me. "I need to go; you should delete my number. I'm seeing someone else."

She doesn't have time to respond before I disconnect the call. Telling her, I'm seeing someone else is a bit of a stretch, but when I get home from this trip I'm going to make that happen with Britton.

Walking back into the lobby, I find Mrs. English, "Sorry, I had to step out to take a call."

She places her hand on my arm, "Oh, don't you worry about it."

"Can we see Dwight now?"

The disappointed look on her face gives me my answer, "I'm sorry, he was looking forward to seeing you, but he's having a bit of a bad day."

Nodding as if I agree, I ask, "Can I come back later?"

Shaking her head, she sadly explains, "He doesn't get any other visitors, these days it's just me. It would probably be fine for you to stop by, but he was a little agitated that you're here."

The last time I saw him was at his grandfather's funeral. He was agitated then too. We had a few minutes alone to talk, some of the things he told me I've only shared with my father. Maybe I should have told someone else, but it sounded like a lot of macho ego things that he couldn't possibly mean.

There are only two objectives for this trip. The first is to make sure that Dwight has an acceptable place to live. He will have to work to find a job after he's out.

The other more important thing for this trip is to talk to Dwight. He can't believe the things he said to me. He can't believe that our group, the Garrison Society, would turn our back on him. His parents were both active in our community when they died.

We only looked at two places after we left the hospital. The first place was the nicest, so after seeing the second place, we went back to the first. Even though Dwight is an adult because he's been treated for a mental illness, he still has his grandmother as his guardian. We checked last year; my parents would become his guardian in case of her death.

It pained Mrs. English to have to fill out the required papers. She wants him to live with her, but they tried that a few years ago, and it didn't work out. He ended up back in the hospital. This time is going to be different, though.

Cole was already at the rink when I returned. Anders got us tickets to watch the NHL and AHL teams play together. It's been a couple of years since I've seen Anders play a game in person.

Cole is explaining that this is a limited contact game to me as if I'm new to watching hockey.

"There's no point in them injuring each other, even though the AHL guys want to make it look good the coach has already warned them."

The game plays on as we watch and discuss the game. We both

stand as the puck lands in front of us, closely followed by three players all trying to get control of it. Around us, people are yelling as one player is shoved into the boards. There's a scrum as sticks poke in every direction; a few elbows are thrown with the hope of getting a player to move out of the way.

As the puck sails away the players follow, at the same time there's an announcement that there's one minute left of the period. It's the end of the game; the players are passing the puck to one another as one of them shoots. It bounces off the goalie. In front of the net Anders reaches out, taking another shot as the light goes on. Goal!

As time runs out on the clock, everyone is cheering. My phone vibrates in my pocket, making me want to check my messages. I've been waiting for Britton to respond to me since this afternoon. Every time my phone vibrates I check it, only to be disappointed.

Cole elbows me, "Hey, you think Anders will take us out with the guys?"

"If 'the guys' are going out, they will want to go to a bar. Since you're underage, it doesn't matter."

He makes some noise about letting him sneak in, as my phone vibrates again. It's probably just the second notification of my last message.

He doesn't stop talking until he says, "I swear I won't take your beer this time."

"No." It would be impossible to allow him into a bar with a bunch of hockey players. There's no way they will go unnoticed. The only way he can go out with them is if it's for food or a private party. "If and I mean if, they are going to eat somewhere..."

He cuts me off, "Like a place that serves food?"

"What other kind of place would we go to? What do you mean a place that serves food?"

With a cocky grin, he shrugs, "I'm just going for the puck bunnies, so whatever."

My phone vibrates again before I can argue with my brother. It's beyond me why he thinks a puck bunny would be interested in him I have no idea. Most of the players are off the ice, so I reason that it could be Anders sending a message to me.

Pulling out my phone, I see a message from Grady, a friend of mine.

Grady: Are you coming out to 3473 tonight?

A few minutes later, there are a few more messages from him.

Grady: Hey, man, you working tonight?

Grady: That girl from the bagel place just walked in.

Cursing to myself, I tell Cole, "I need to take care of something. I'll meet at the top of the steps."

He nods never taking his attention away from the few remaining players on the ice. Most of the people have already left, making it easier to climb the stairs. At the top of the stairs, I return his message.

Me: Britton is there?

The bubbles appear in the conversation box while I wait for his answer.

Instead of a response, he sends me a photo. It's dark, so it's difficult to see until I enlarge it. The photo looks like he's standing close to her, she's looking in his direction, and there's no mistake that it's her. Unlike when we saw her at the bagel shop she has her hair loose around her shoulders.

Going out on the weekends is our thing. If I were at home this weekend, I'd be at the 3473 club with him. Actually I'd ditch him without a second thought if she walked in the door.

Me: Are you talking to her? Who's she there with?

Grady: Hey, Thorne, it's Britton

That's great; he's handed his phone to her. So, of course, she sees my questions.

Me: Hey Britton

Grady: Sorry, my phone took a bath at work. I'll get it replaced in a few days. Hope you're having fun with your friends.

Grady: Here with friends.

Grady: Sorry, she took my phone before I saw your last message.

Grady: She walked in with a girl.

Me: Have you seen her there before?

It's hard to say if I've ever seen her there before. The first time I noticed her was a few weeks ago when she was handing out water with the Red Cross. That doesn't change that I've been to the bagel shop where she works a few times a week for years. Maybe she's been there, and I didn't notice.

Grady: Pretty sure I would have called dibs long ago.

5

Our weekend in Pittsburgh is coming to an end. The one thing I wanted to do this weekend didn't happen. I've tried to see Dwight three times. He refused to see me when I was here with his grandmother. Later the same day I came back alone to see him. She suggested he might be willing to see me on my own.

He refused again.

We were able to find a nice place for him to live. It's available now; he just needs the right people to sign his release forms.

"Thorne Smythe?"

Hearing my name, I stand ready to see my friend. The person that called my name is standing by the receptionist desk. It would be more promising for me if she were holding open a door, like when they call your name at a doctors' appointment. She's not doing that.

"Are you Thorne Smythe?"

"Yes."

She smiles at me, the same way someone would just before they give you bad news, "Would you follow me please."

She scans her badge to unlock a door; she motions for me to follow her. We only go a short distance before she enters an office, motioning for me to sit in one of the chairs, "Please have a seat."

She opens a flat folder sitting on her desk, without looking at me. She shuffles some papers, "Mr. Smythe, this is an unusual situation. It seems that we have a Thorne Smythe, a Samuel Smythe, and a Freya Smythe listed as next of kin for Dwight English."

It doesn't seem so unusual to me, but if she thinks it's unusual alright then. It seems important to tell her who we are, "I'm Thorne Smythe, Samuel and Freya are my parents. Given the problems that Dwight has experienced, we were named guardians should something happen to his grandmother."

She stops moving the papers to watch me, although she doesn't seem interested in what I have to say.

"As I was saying, this is an unusual situation. I see that Dwight English has refused to see you previously. Given that he's due to be released soon, it seems strange that he would refuse to see you."

She didn't pose a question to me, so there's nothing for me to answer. He's indeed refused to see me, I'm hoping that changes.

"This morning, I received the paperwork for Mr. English to be released in the next three to five days. His lawyer also provided the details for his living arrangements. Can you please verify this information?"

She sets a sheet of paper in front of me. It has the address of the house we visited. Strangely, I would need to verify the information given to her by a lawyer.

"Excuse me, Ms..." It occurs to me she didn't tell me her name, so I look at her jacket hoping to see a name badge. There's nothing there, so it looks like I'm just checking out her chest.

"Forester, my last name is Forester."

"Oh, sorry, Ms. Forester, that information looks correct to me. If that's the information that the lawyer sent, he wouldn't have made a mistake with the address."

She raises her eyebrows as if she's surprised by what I'm saying. It's the truth; the lawyer was to provide the information. There's no need for me to verify it.

Her head tilts to the side before she offers an insincere smile, "Of course."

Returning the pages to her folder she looks at her computer before her eyes land on me again, "It has been a difficult few days for Dwight English. He's agreed to see you, but only because any behavior problems will be submitted to the judge that signed his release papers."

This being the third time I've tried to see Dwight this weekend, I thought I was getting lucky. It turns out he can't refuse to see me, or he won't be released from this place. This isn't how I wanted to see him.

Interrupting us the phone on her desk rings. She answers it, saying her name followed with a curt thank you. After hanging up, she stands signaling it's time to go, "Let me show you where to go."

We walk from the quiet office setting through a door leading to a long hallway. She doesn't say anything else to me as we walk; she's obviously bothered by this situation.

We enter a large room; it looks like a waiting room without curtains on the windows. On the far side of the room, I can see Dwight standing with his back to us as he looks out a window. He hasn't changed since the last time I saw him at his grandfather's funeral. When we were younger, we were always about the same height, that's changed as I've grown a few more inches than him.

Turning to thank Ms. Forester, I see her leaving. Crossing the room, Dwight doesn't notice me. Even when I say his name, he doesn't respond.

"Dwight."

After calling his name a second time, he turns his head as if to acknowledge me, but still, he doesn't say anything. Instead, he turns back to look out the window.

Giving him a minute, I wait before saying to him, "Thanks for seeing me today."

After a few minutes, he finally says, "It wasn't like they gave me a choice." Without looking at me, he sits in the chair next to the sofa I'm sitting on. He shakes his head as if to release tension before he continues, "They signed my release papers."

This should be news he's celebrating, yet he seems indifferent that he will be able to leave this place.

"I talked to grandma this morning. She said she couldn't come to see me today because you have her car." He points at me when he says the word 'you.'

"I'm sorry; she didn't say anything."

He doesn't let me finish before he shrugs his shoulders, "Doesn't matter right?"

"I was here with her the other day." It doesn't make sense to remind him he refused to see me then. Instead, I try to focus on something positive for him, "We found a place for you, I think you'll like it. You'll be able to use the buses for now."

"Right, because I can't drive."

The last thing I want is to fight with him. There's no reason for him to be here still. There's nothing I want more than to take him home with me, but that's not an option.

"Dwight, I didn't mean anything by it. That was one of the criteria we had to meet." He gives me an unsettling smile; it's the same smile he would use when he was planning something when we were kids. "I just started working, so I'm not able to take much time off yet. Maybe this summer, we can arrange for you to come and stay with me?"

He leans forward in his chair like he's going to stand, "Why, because I'll be able to take time off from work?"

He's right; it doesn't make sense. Two days ago, I was prepared to see him. It might have been easier to have his grandma here as a buffer; that was my plan.

"I'm sorry, you're right." Pulling a box out of my pocket, I set it on the table in front of him. He looks at it like he's confused for a minute. Motioning to the box that contains a cell phone I say, "I wanted you to have this. They said you could have it here; I already filled out the paperwork, so the administration knows you have it."

After staring at the box, he finally looks at me, "Why are you doing this?"

Some of the tension has left his voice, but he's still angry.

"I added some contacts to the phone already. My number is one of them; I hope you will use it. It's easiest to text me most of the time because my schedule changes a lot. I'll be going home tonight; then tomorrow I'll start an eight-day stretch at the firehouse."

He lifts the box from the table and opens it to take out the phone. He turns it on as he focuses on the phone.

It doesn't mean he's not listening, so I continue, "I added a couple of apps on there you will want, a few games, a couple of other ones you might find useful too. If you go to the app store you have a credit there you can use it to get what you want."

He holds the phone close to his chest as if to protect it. He eyes me wearily, "This is from you?"

Wincing at his words, the last thing I want is for him to thank me for helping him. Nodding I tell him, "The phone is set up on an account for you. You can change anything you want, even the number. Just if you change the number, you have to give it to your lawyer and stuff."

"I'm not an idiot!"

This is harder than I thought it would be. He's ignoring me, focusing his attention on the device in his hands. He's had a phone while he was here before. His last phone broke a few months ago, and they suggested waiting until his release to get him another one.

"Dwight, I know this has been rough for you."

He looks over the top of the phone at me; I can see the anger in his eyes. Every word he says to me is dripping with venom, "You don't have any concept of rough. You with your perfect family."

Holding his phone in his left hand, he attempts to slide it into the shirt pocket over his heart; he misses twice before it finally slides home. He leans closer to me before he says, "You have no idea," he pauses to look around as if he expects someone to be listening to us. "I did all of those exercises Samuel told me to do. It wasn't working just like I said, then one time I experiment, and I end up here."

"Dwight, it takes time to learn. It took me years to be able to master the right breathing techniques."

He laughs at my words, "My, my, my, what pretty words we use."

353

He moves from the chair to sit on the sofa beside me. To anyone else, it looks like we're just sitting next to each other talking. Except we aren't just talking, this is different.

"Remember that summer we went camping; it was the last time my parents went on the retreat. My mom," his voice cracks when he mentions his mom. If he only knew how much we all miss her. "My mom, she was supposed to teach us after football practice, because we were missing the regular society classes. Later that night, she told me that you and I were so much alike. She was so proud of us; she never thought you cared I was a half-blood."

"Dwight..."

He shouts, "Don't!"

A few people across the room look at us. When they see nothing else happens, they both get up and leave. That's probably just in case.

"Thorne, I don't want to hear your excuses. You and me, we aren't that much alike. See you've been given every advantage. I, on the other hand, well I was exiled by the society. They made it look like someone wanted me, but you were all happy to see me go."

He's wrong; he's so very wrong. It's been too many years; he's had too much time to create what he thinks is the truth. There's no way to know what he's been told over the years, but I have to try to get him to understand.

"Dwight, my parents wanted you. It had nothing to do with the society, they couldn't petition for you, but my parents could, and they did. Your grandparents wanted you; they insisted you come to live with them."

"You think you know everything. You don't. My grandparents couldn't understand what I needed; they couldn't teach me how to use my power. The only advice they had was to keep me active in sports. So they did, they kept me busy with soccer and football, and baseball, and every other sport they could send me to so I wasn't at home."

As he names the sports he participated in; he gets more upset. His breathing is faster as his voice lowers, so only I can hear him talk. He's always felt a little misunderstood.

354

"The society turned its back on me for the last time. There was a time I was willing to follow what they wanted done. That time is over. They saw to it that I was here, but that hasn't stopped me from working on my skills."

Raising his fingers to his lips, he gently blows out a breath. As the air flows from his lips, I watch half intrigued, half worried as the tips of his fingers turn a shocking shade of violet as flames ignite. As fast as the flames appear, he puts them out by closing his fingers, making a fist.

He drops his fist onto my knee before he says farewell, "It's amazing the things you can learn to do when you have nothing but time on your hands. Make sure you tell them I won't be denied my birthright. I won't be denied the things I'm due. See you soon, old friend."

He gets up to leave, his phone in the pocket over his heart, the box safely in his hands. He looks around the room then quickly turns his back to the room, so only I can see him, "One last thing, don't think it was an accident."

Taking a deep breath, he exhales a flame that he catches with his hand extinguishing it before anyone notices. These are not the skills of someone that hasn't been practicing. These are skills few people ever master, even fewer can do it alone.

Dwight was a teenager when he was caught setting fires. He was sent here when he told people he could breathe fire. Luckily he wasn't able to prove it back then. If his grandparents would have allowed it, my parents asked for him to be sent to live with us. Their request was denied.

It's now up to me to go home and notify The Garrison Society that Dwight English has mastered his skills. He's not only done it alone; he's fulfilled his debt to the courts that make him a free man. It's up to me to report back that Dwight needs to be registered as a Dragon with The Garrison Society whether he wants to be part of us or not.

AFTERWORD

Thank you for reading Where There Is Smoak. Yes, smoak is the obsolete spelling of the word we use today, smoke. There's a reason I'm using that spelling, and I hope that you will read more from The Garrison Society books to learn the secret. The next book will be Flash Over featuring Thone and Britton, releasing October 15, 2019, in the Prophecy of Magic Box Set.

I'd love to hear from you! You can find me on social media, leave a review, or come out to the Authors in the Steel City Author event. When you see me at the event, tell me, "Dare to step into the flames," and I'll reward you with swag, not on the table.

ABOUT THE AUTHOR

Sidonia Rose grew up in Pennsylvania. Growing up Sidonia cultivated a love of books, both reading and writing. Over the course of her life, she has written everything from newspaper articles and short stories to full-length novels. Notorious for her book suggestions and voracious appetite for the written word; she is rarely found without a book or Kindle in her hands.

Sidonia writes compelling romance novels with the ability to capture the hearts and minds of those that read it. You can find her books at Amazon, including the Love U Series- Love Shots, Proof, and If There's a Chance.

Connect with Sidonia

 facebook.com/SidoniaRoseAuthor

twitter.com/SidoniaRoseAuth

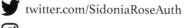 instagram.com/sidoniaroseauthor

UNFINISHED BUSINESS

AVA DANIELLE

1

The sudden aroma of literature and words of true romance tickles my nose as I enter the quaint bookstore I have found in this city of steel. The bell clatters as the door closes behind me. A sweet, but older man greets me from behind the counter. He reminds me to let him know if I need anything, meanwhile my mind is merely focused on all the wonderful books sitting on shelves, organized by genre, type, color. It's a bit chaotic, but in an organized way that makes complete sense.

Gliding my finger along the books while taking a small glance at each one individually, I'm drawn to my favorite aisle. The romance sections. You would think as an avid book reader I would have read every book known to exist, but I haven't. In fact, I had to broaden my interests to find newer and more interesting books. After the book funk I found myself in, I indulged in some indie authors, you know, those authors that sit at home and do it all by themselves. The authors that work endless nights writing stories, then editing them, formatting them, have a few beta readers and proof readers lined up, then publish it themselves, market their books, and try to find readers. Those are the authors that surprise you when you read a story.

Those are the authors that need to be read more, to be found and given a chance. Those are the books to boast about.

While looking down at the shelf, I suddenly notice a person next to me, who knows how long they've been standing there. I excuse myself while trying to lift my body up from hunching down too long. Suddenly a cramp takes over my leg and I find myself near tears pretending to still be looking at books on the bottom shelf almost holding my breath. After the pain finally subdued, I slowly make my way up and have to catch myself before bumping into his body. "Sorry," I whisper but he didn't even seem phased by my sudden abruption. "Hmm," he grunts reading the back of a book.

I make my way to the other side of the shelf but instead of looking at the books on the shelf, I look between the books and stare at him. There's mystery to him. I stare so long admiring his long hair, the way one piece of hair keeps ending up in his eyes while he's trying to read and he pushes it aside, only for it to return. He looks frustrated, but not enough to put the book down. The lines on his forehead show whatever he's reading to be of interest or confusion. There's a crook in his smile on the right side of his lips while his eyes move back and forth. He's oblivious to me.

Initially, I'm embarrassed I'm just standing here staring at him, but he also fascinates me. He rubs his scruffy beard while searching for another book. I'm peeking through while walking along the way he's walking. I've turned into a stalker. Not my proudest moment. But I don't seem to care.

He walks toward the end of the shelf when suddenly; we completely run out of shelf and are met face-to-face. I'm pretty sure at this point my face is the color of a tomato. I feel my face flush and heat and there's no doubt it radiates.

"I'm sorry," he mumbles and moves to the side smiling at me.

"No, I'm sorry," I apologize.

Continuing on, I choose to ignore his existence and do what I came for – look at books and perhaps find my next perfect read to blog about. I need something different for my blog, something that stands out, but still enjoyable and ready for the world to want to read.

Something I can review with so much passion, as if I'm part of the storyline, the character I'll be reading about. Something that will make the reader desire the story as much as I had. That's what I need to find.

With a stack of books in my hand I make my way to a nearby table to read through the synopsis and find the book I don't think I could live without. Maybe even more than one book. Caught off guard, I feel a hand on my shoulder, "you mind if I sit here as well," the man from earlier struggles with a stack of books.

I look around; this seems to be the only table in this tiny bookstore big enough to hold more than one single book.

"Of course," I scramble and stutter moving some of my books out of the way.

"It seems this bookstore is only big enough for a handful of customers to be browsing at once. And I couldn't decide just standing there which books I actually wanted to purchase," he confesses.

I nod in agreement, "same" are the only lame words I seem to utter.

After a few minutes of us sharing the table fiddling through our stack of book choices, I can't help but notice the books he's chosen.

"I see you're a profound Stephen King fan?" I can't help but acknowledge the stack of horror books.

"And I see someone can't decide on which Danielle Steel book it will be today," He remarks.

And it's true. I can't decide. There are so many books that I haven't read that she has written in the past and so many that she still publishes that I haven't had a chance to read. If I were to ever become an Author, I hope to one day be as creative as she is. It's a dream of mine, but it's farfetched, I could never create stories with so much finesse and adoration.

It feels like hours have past. We sit at the tiny table and discuss stories amongst stories and the authors that create them. It's not until the owner reminds us of the store hours and how close we are to getting kicked out. I've never connected with a stranger as I have with this man. We've gotten to know each other on a deeper level than I've ever gotten to know someone, there's just one problem, I don't know anything about him or even his name.

"I guess we better pay and leave before he calls the police on us," he jokes while choosing four of his favorites.

"You're probably right," I agree as I grab two books and beat him to the register.

"It was nice meeting you," he shouts after me as I leave the store and walk onto the dark streets of Pittsburgh.

Back at the hotel, I can't help but think about him. Think about the way we connected on a level that I wasn't expecting to connect with a stranger. Thinking about a man that caught my attention not only for his looks, but his brain. The way he smiled and brightened a room.

2

$\mathcal{W}$aking up in my Hilton Hotel room, number 200, at six in the morning, I stretch and look out the window noticing the fog filling the city. I didn't sleep much. My mind was reeling about the stranger I met at the bookstore. I've never met anyone I could talk with for hours about books. Silence never fell in our conversation. We always found something to talk about. Except, we never talked about anything personal and the chances of me ever running into this man again are slim to none. I'm not even from this city. I'm from Knoxville, Tennessee, here for passion and fangirling. I'd like to say it's for business, but that's not even true. I don't think you can consider blogging a real business, but it's a nice play for an avid reader to find a platform to boast about favorite authors, favorite books, and connect with other readers while getting to know your favorite authors. It's the best platform the Internet could've invented.

Fumbling through my suitcase, I'm searching for the perfect outfit for today's event. I've been invited to blog about an author signing from various Indie Authors around the world. It's a big popular signing that only happens once a year and showcases everyone's work so beautifully. I've been jealous the past few years and was so grateful when asked if I'd like to be part of it as a blogger. Of course, I couldn't resist and had to jump on board immediately. The drive here didn't even bother me. The cost of the hotel, the least of my worries if I got the chance to meet some of my favorite authors that I've been talking to here and there on Facebook. But Facebook isn't the same as face-to-face.

"Maybe this dress?" I spin in front of the long mirror in the bathroom, "Nah, I don't like this one." I always speak to myself out loud. "Perhaps the leggings and this shirt?" I do another twirl unsatisfied with my choices.

Sure, I brought enough to last me for a month, but that's only because you can vary every piece of clothing with the other. When it comes to fashion, I'm very anal about what I wear. The right outfit will put you in the right mood. The right outfit determines how you feel about yourself. At least that's how I feel.

Finally, after a long debate with myself, I decide on the perfect outfit. It's a flower dress, with a white collar. The flowers are mainly different shades of pink and white over a blue dress. I wear a black pair of leggings with my brown knee-high beige suede boots and matching leather coat. It's the perfect outfit for fall weather. With my bag of goodies, I make my way to the event only a few hotels over. The rooms at the Marriot were already booked up so I had to find something close by with availability.

Walking through the automatic glass doors I'm already met with a group of ladies, "Elizabeth, you made it," someone shouts while running toward me.

"Oh my god, Charlie, is that you?" I'm pulled into the arms of the organizer of the event.

"In the flesh," she smiles, "you ready to meet some of your favorites?"

"Am I ever," I admit full of glee.

We enter the massive event hall. The floor's orange, red, and blue swirly design, it captures my attention, covered by a considerable number of tables prepared for today's author signing. One minute I'm in awe and the next I'm overwhelmed. To be invited and part of such an immense event is an honor and quite the achievement for my blog. I worked my way up as a hobby to find a place to meet other readers in love with stories I mention, but it's turned into promoting my favorite authors and reading ARC's to review for them. Now I get to meet these fine humans face-to-face and I'm nervous and super excited. More excited than nervous.

Confidently I follow Charlie to the table she has set up for me in a corner by the door where most traffic will go in and out and notice me first. I set up my notebook, my pens I had customized for the event, and a big framed poster for all authors to sign. I have my camera in one hand, my phone in the other prepared to record some author interviews before the crowd shows up and starts storming the place.

I'm so focused on all the authors, there's one that abruptly catches my attention. I ignore everyone around me, while feasting my eyes on the one author I didn't expect to see here. One author I didn't even make the connection with. One author that until now I didn't even know he was an author.

Sidonia Rose is just a sweet and kind lady. I have read Love Shots and Proof and fell madly in love with the characters Kyle and her three overprotective brothers. She writes with such a familiarity and homey feeling. Reading her work is refreshing beyond doubt.

Nicole Zoltack has magical words that will transport you into another dimension. You will find yourself in a fairytale of darkness. There's so much romance within the paranormal world that will whisk you away.

Desiree Lafawn will make you fall in love with men you didn't know you wanted to fall in love with. You will want the bad boy. She will make you believe in fairytales, because that's where it's at. She has a magical aurora about herself.

Jaime Russell is one of my favorite people and being able to hug her in person has exceeded my dreams. She's a kind soul. She is loving, smart, and one hell of a writer. She definitely knows how to pull you into her stories. One of my favorite stories written by her has been featured in the Dirty Fairytales Anthology and it's a naughty story about your favorite Disney characters. Definitely worth a read.

Jen Talty has a smile that will allow you to tell her your darkest secrets knowing she'll never spill them to anyone else. But when you're down in the dumps, her smile will lift you up. Add in the fact her bestselling stories take you to Hallmark romance.

Victoria Monroe is funny, witty, sarcastic, a kind-hearted woman with so much wisdom, I would hope she never stops writing. She and I have had many private message conversations and let's just say, I plan on buying each book and she better sign each one with a catchy phrase that I can laugh about for years to come.

And Oliver Evans. Oliver Evans has written many stories, some romance, some thriller, some horror, some suspense. And I've read them all. I fell in love with his characters and storylines after reading the first page. He pulls you in with his words. You can't put his books down. And suddenly he's in front of me, but not for the first time. Oliver Evans was the man that crossed path with me yesterday at the bookstore. I never even recognized him. Could also be because until now, I never knew what Oliver Evans actually looked like.

"Elizabeth?" a voice whispers as a hand shakes me on my shoulder.

"Uh huh," I mumble never taking my eyes off Oliver Evans.

"Would you like me to sign this?" she asks.

"Uh huh," I nod handing the frame over the table to her.

"Are you okay?" I blink and come back to reality.

"That's Oliver Evans," I lean over and whisper to her and watch her giggle.

"Yes, it is," she smiles.

"I saw him yesterday in the bookstore." Why am I acting like a teen girl that is crushing for the first time in her life?

"Oh, that's cool. Well, go say hi," she grins.

I can't just go say hi. I mean, I guess I could, but I can't. Confidence, Elizabeth, confidence; find it.

Slowly, I strut toward him and already see a smile cross his face once he notices me. As I get closer, he stands up, "fancy seeing you," he grins and I feel like melting right into the floor.

"I wasn't expecting you here," I admit, "I honestly didn't even know you were an author. I should've though," I'm blunt.

"Happens to the best of us, but I didn't realize you were an author either," he looks surprised.

"That's because I'm not," I giggle. Why the fuck am I giggling?

"Oh?" The way his eyebrow raises when he's unsure of something is an extremely sexy thing.

"I'm a blogger," I admit, but I make it sound like it's not worthy of what he does.

"That's amazing," he utters.

"I wouldn't say that, I would love to be able to write stories like you do," I go straight into fangirl mode, "you're so articulate, and miraculous, and your stories are filled with so much soul. They get me hooked right from the first word. You have an opening for your story that pulls you right in," I can't seem to shut up, "I love each and every book you've ever written."

Blissfully he smiles at me. You can tell he's enjoying my adoration, or maybe it's the way I hurry through each word trying to get my point across. Or maybe because I haven't once shut up about how I adore him. Had I known who he really was in the bookstore, I wouldn't have been able to shut up then. Instead, I thought he was just another reader looking to buy some books.

Our conversation is abruptly interrupted when the announcer asks everyone to take their seats and prepare for the swarm of fangirling women and potential men interested in awesome books.

I sit at my table chit-chatting with readers, meeting the many great authors participating in the event, but never taking my eyes off Oliver for too long. Of course, his table is packed with readers and attention. He doesn't get a second to breathe, while I get too many seconds to stare.

"It's so nice to meet you."

"I love your work."

"You're such an amazing blogger, I can't wait to read what you write next."

"Have you ever thought about writing a book? You should totally write a book."

All the compliments won't distract me from what I'm really thinking about. My mind goes straight to gutter when I see him. I try not to. But I can't help wanting to kiss his luscious lips.

I've never felt this way. Ever! This is completely new territory for me.

3

*A*fter mingling with authors, readers, soon-to-be bloggers, and finding new fans, I'm exhausted. The past eight hours have been interesting with glances and smiles toward Mr. Evans. He has also taken an interest in me. How do I know? Every time I try to be sneaky looking at him, I caught him staring at me. I've been going around and around in my mind trying to find the right words to ask him out for a drink or something after the event. There's an after party he's most likely invited to, as I am, but I was hoping to get some time alone with him. Selfish of myself, I know.

Packing up all my goodies and swag into my bag, my back is turned toward him. I feel a tap on my shoulder. Excitedly I turn my head with a smile hoping deep down it is Mr. Evans.

"Thank you so much for coming," Charlie surprises me with a gift basket, while I secretly wished it was Oliver.

"Thanks, you shouldn't have, you know I love you all," I accept the gift basket and thank her for having me.

Back in my hotel room, I fall flat on my back and regret the decision of leaving without talking to Mr. Evans. Oliver. Whatever I should call him. I should've found the courage to tell him exactly what has been on my mind. On second thought, maybe that's a good thing.

After long consideration, I grab my bag and decide to go to the after party and have a little bit of a good time before driving back home. The hotel room is a little lonely now that I think about it.

Pulling the door open, checking my pockets for my phone, I manage to stumble into a person on the hallway.

"Sorry," I mumble not even taking another look.

"Wait, I know you," I hear a male voice say while looking right into his gorgeous brown eyes.

"Mr. Evans," I stutter.

"Oliver."

"Huh?"

"Oliver. You can just call me Oliver," he chuckles.

"Uh huh," I never take my eyes off him.

What is wrong with you? Get your shit together, Elizabeth. Concentrate. He's just another man. One fine booty, sexy as fuck man. Just. A. Man.

"Are you okay?" he's curious.

"You staying here?" I'm surprised.

"Yeah, this is my room," he pulls the keycard out of his pocket.

"Uh huh. Mine here." I sound like a caveman.

He laughs, "I see that. Have you had something to drink?"

I'm shocked, "Me? Oh god no. Not yet at least," I joke.

"There's a bar downstairs, want to grab a drink together? Or do you have plans?"

"I was going to go to the author after party, but I'm still not sure."

"How about you decide after a drink at the bar with me?"

Uh hello? How can I say no to that? I can't.

"You sure?" I don't want to sound overly excited.

"Of course. Or I wouldn't have asked. Hang on one second, let me drop my stuff in the room," he rolls in a suitcase and I stand there debating if I'm supposed to follow him into the room or just stand and stare at the carpet and walls that don't seem to match.

However, by the time I've figured it out, he has returned.

"Ready?" he brings me back to reality.

As we walk in silence to the bar, a million questions run through my mind what I can ask him. What it's like to be an author? Why he chose Suspense? Why didn't he write Horror if Stephen King is his idol? Why was he at an event mainly filled with female romance author? Is he married? Single? Divorced? Does he have kids? Not that it matters. Well, maybe it does.

We sit at the bar and he doesn't waste any time ordering me a drink.

"You don't even know what I like," I rebut.

"I just took a wild guess; would you like me to change it?"

"Actually no, what you ordered would've been exactly what I order," I admit.

As we both sip on whiskey on rocks, I start to get comfortable around him. We discuss our careers, "yeah, I'm actually an accountant, but that job is so boring," I mumble on and on until the alcohol suddenly hits me harder than I expected.

The conversation flows wonderfully. I find out he's a full-time writer, not only does he publish under a name with a big publishing company, he refuses to mention that name to me though, and he self-publishes under a different pseudonym. "You're a busy man," I mention. He is indeed single, but only because his work takes up all of his time. He's got such gorgeous eyes. He smells like a mix of cedar and citrus. Refreshing.

His hand suddenly touches the top of mine and I feel electricity shoot through me. I'm awestruck just staring at his hand on top of mine. I want to take my fingers and caress his hand, but that would seem odd.

He notices my eyes on our hands and quickly removes his. Maybe he thinks it's uncomfortable for me? Instead of pondering, I slide my hand back close to his and wait for a reaction. He doesn't hesitate and takes mine into his again. This time our fingers lock. I've never felt so close to someone I had just met, but there's something intriguing about Oliver.

"Would you like to go for a walk?" he asks.

"This time of night?" I'm shocked.

"Especially this time of night," he takes my hand into his hand while sliding some money across the bar for our drinks.

We walk outside the hotel premises. There's a little section in the back by the woods. It's a little creepy outside in the dark with the bright moon shining down on us. A little worried I try to come up with an excuse to go back to the hotel room when he pushes me against the hotel wall and leans into me placing one of the hottest kisses on my lips that I have ever tasted. I'm taken back by the moment. I want to push him away, but I'm enjoying every second of this kiss. There's undeniable chemistry between us.

The kiss feels like it goes on for hours. His tongue caresses mine, our lips are busy caressing each other, his teeth bite down on my bottom lip, he moans into me. He's ravishing me. I can't even take a second to take a deep breath.

"I've been wanting to do that since yesterday," he offers up against my lips, his hot breath against mine.

"Since yesterday?" I whisper as I open my eyes to look into his,

"Uh huh," he groans.

His groan suddenly turns me on so much I pull his lips close to mine with only my teeth. The tables have turned. I make him mine now. Grabbing the back of his neck, I pull him closer to me. His hands wander up my shirt and electricity shoots through my body when I feel his finger gently caress my nipple. He pulls and squeezes and I kiss him harder. We're both fondling each other against a cold stone wall when a voice interrupts us.

"Mind taking that inside?" We both look at a younger lady as she looks at us horrified.

"Um, sure," Oliver smiles as he takes my hand and walks me back inside the hotel.

Once in the elevator we both burst out in laughter. But laughter turns back to heat as we stare at each other. I'm hungry for him.

"Yours or mine?" he asks as I shrug.

I'm not the type to just go to bed with anyone. I'm not the type to have a one-night stand. I'm not the type that loves without being in a relationship. But he will break that. He will make me do things I've never done before. He will make me feel things I've always wanted to feel, that adrenaline of the unexpected.

Stumbling through his door while kissing, our clothes fly off our bodies so swiftly, he tosses me onto his bed extremely roughly, and I'm not denying him. All the shyness I have ever felt is disappearing rather quickly. I'm fully invested in him, naked and ready to be taken.

His tongue and gentle fingers give me every feeling of ecstasy I have ever wanted to feel. I close my eyes and allow him full access to every inch of my body. I allow myself to be his, even if it's just for one night.

4

The following morning, I wake next to him, my head on his shoulder as I listen to his heartbeat and rapid snoring. My eyes flutter as I reminisce the past few hours we spent together. I fear the moment we part and go back to our old lives. I'd much rather wake with him next to me every morning, especially after the magical night we just spent together.

As my thoughts flow, I feel his body shift next to me as he opens his eyes and stares right into mine. He smiles a genuine smile and leans in to kiss me.

"Ew, dragon breath," I mumble, but he doesn't seem to mind.

"Breakfast?" he asks and I nod.

"Are you alright?"

"Uh huh," I grin and watch him grin with me.

How do you act after a one-night stand? Do you go on like nothing happened? Do you put on your clothes and disappear? Did he ask me for breakfast, but secretly hoping I would say no and leave? Am I reading into this too much? Going back and forth in my mind I watch him get off the bed with no care in the world if he's wearing clothes or not. Every wrinkle in his body shows, every ripple, every flaw and imperfection show, and I'm more attracted to the imperfections than the perfections.

"After breakfast, maybe we can walk the city? Unless you just want to stay in bed," he teases my inhibitions of moving.

"Walk the city?" I'm shocked he wants to spend the day with me.

"Unless you have to leave town already? I booked until tomorrow. I had planned to do some sightseeing today, I would love if you came along," he utters as he gets dressed in some jeans and a white t-shirt.

"Um, sure. I don't have another night booked; I was planning on leaving tonight actually."

"You can always spend the night here if you don't want to drive during the night," he winks at me.

Is that an invitation? Does he want to spend another night with me? If I could be any emoji right now, it would be the one with the big eyes.

After breakfast in the hotel lobby and great conversation, we both separate to clean up for some sightseeing. Wearing a gray cami, my favorite gold-rose cardigan, jeans, and comfy boots. I'm comfy yet chic. My long hair curled with minimal makeup applied – I've never been one for excessive amounts of color in my face.

Grabbing a small purse with the essentials, I make way out of the room as I yet again run into someone.

"Fancy meeting you here," he teases.

He's wearing this bright orange polo shirt that definitely compliments his eyes and dark hair. His white jeans might not be good idea around me, but he doesn't know how bad of a klutz I am, not yet at least.

"I'm a bit of a klutz," I laugh as I make sure I've closed my room door.

"I can live with that," he winks, "You ready for an adventure?"

"Depends on the level of adventure," I admit.

"Oh, I know you can get adventurous, I'm just testing my limits," he teases with a kiss on my cheek.

I don't think it's normal to go on a date after a one-night stand, is it? I'm a little confused. But I'm thoroughly enjoying this time with him.

We're walking along Allegheny Riverfront Park enjoying the sunshine beaming down on us. We're into conversation and never run out of things to say. Admiring the city and Roberto Clemente Bridge when I realize, this is all way too perfect to have to leave. We pause conversation to kiss. We hold hands. We're like any ordinary couple you will find walking a city they both have never ventured to. We're two lovers that are lost in conversation. But we're not, because after today, it'll all end and we'll be unfinished business. He will live his life in Atlanta and I will live mine in Knoxville.

"Even with all the industrial, this city is actually pretty nice," he utters as he pulls his phone out of his pocket, "come here," he pulls me in close, "smile."

After a selfie together he pushes a few buttons on his phone and grins, "I have to show off what a beautiful city this is."

"It's our faces, there's not much city to see," I jokingly respond.

"That's the point, you're far more beautiful."

"Thanks," I blush.

Stopping by Bruster's, according to Oliver, it's the best place to get ice cream in Pittsburgh. We buy ourselves each a cone. His is covered with two scoops of one vanilla and one chocolate, meanwhile I brave outside of my comfort zone and grab some Banana and Tiramisu. I've never been to Italy, but this ice cream nearly screams gelato.

And once we each finish our ice cream, do a little more sightseeing; we already regret the words we'll be uttering in only a few hours. I have fallen in love with not only this city, but also a man I slept with after only meeting him twenty-four hours earlier.

Maybe we're not finished? Maybe we still have a chance in another time and another place. It can't be we part this way!

THE END... maybe?

ABOUT THE AUTHOR

Ava Danielle is a bibliophile who has her nose stuck in a book every moment she can. When she's not writing or reading she's either listening to old records dreaming of New York City, obsessively posting memes on Facebook, talking to her friends scattered all across the US and Europe, attending her high schoolers functions, or watching This is Us and A Million Little Things on television. Growing up as an army brat and then being an army wife, she's currently living in middle Tennessee with her husband, almost adult daughter, teen twin boys, youngest son, and three cats.

Connect with Ava

facebook.com/authoravadanielle

twitter.com/AvaDanielle1

instagram.com/authoravadanielle

THE COST OF IMAGINATION

NICOLE ZOLTACK

1

PENNSLYVANIA,
PITTSBURGH BOTANIC GARDEN
THE SIXTH OF SEPTEMBER 2019

*W*ith a contented sigh, I shut the book and lean my head against the towering oak. My eyes close, and I smile. I might be eighteen and "too old" for fairy tales, but there's something so satisfying about a dwarf proving his worth and breaking a curse by earning the love of a princess.

Yes, I still read fairy tales. Why wouldn't I? My life couldn't be anything less like a fairy tale. My parents... I don't know. I never met them, never knew them. I don't know if they're dead or alive and just gave me up, but I'm eighteen now. I outgrew the system. For the past few years, I've basically been on my own. The worst part? I have no true plans for my life yet. I have no idea what to do.

The only time I feel happiness is when I'm reading about others being happy. Yes, I, Madison Martin, am a sap, a romantic, a fool.

Well, there's one other time when I'm happy. As far back as I can remember, I've been dreaming about a man. Not just any man. A father. My father. And what's more is that, in the dreams, I have two older sisters. It's ridiculous how much I cling to those dreams, to the memories of being with them. Not that I'm truly with them, but over the years, I've grown up with them each night, and I love them as if they truly were my sisters.

And maybe that's why I never had any friends. Between the reading and the strange dreams, I don't exactly fit in.

Hmm. If I dream about them tonight, maybe I'll tell them about the fairy tale. I wonder what my sisters will think of it.

My eyes open, and I glance around. The Pittsburgh Botanic Garden is such a lovely place, but I always go off from where most of the tourists go. I ignore the Bookworm Glen, the magical fairy garden, the life-sized bird's nest, and the fairy houses. Instead, just beyond the lotus pond, bypassing the bridge in favor of the stepping stones, is my spot, under this trusty, faithful oak.

A dragonfly lands on my knee, and I giggle. I'm so happy and content right now, but it's almost five. The botanic garden closes then on Fridays, but I don't want to move. Again, my eyes close, and I drift off to sleep.

2

The moment my eyes open, I know something isn't right. I'm not dreaming, or maybe I am, but it feels so real. The slight breeze teases my long brown hair, and as I stand, the skirt of my long dress billows about.

Wait. A dress? I don't wear dresses. I was wearing jeans and a t-shirt.

Exotic flowers I've never seen before bloom at my feet. I lean down and sniff. They smell sweet.

I've never been able to experience the sense of scent in a dream before.

Unnerved, I pinch myself. Yes, I feel the sting, the pain, but I'm even more alarmed because the oak I had been sleeping under isn't there anymore. In fact, all around me is rolling grassland.

If this is real and I'm not dreaming, how did I get here? Because I'm not in the botanic garden anymore, and this dress...

My hand touches the top of my head, and my fingers touch something metal. With trembling hands, I pull the object loose and gape at it.

A crown. A simple, plain, silver crown.

I'm wearing a crown and a dress.

I must look like a princess!

Okay. Being able to smell aside, this has to be a dream. It just has to be.

In the far-off distance, I can just spy a few buildings. Having no better idea, I head in the direction. At the base of one of the small hills is a young boy. He's plucking a few berries from a bush, and when he sees me, his hand hovers in mid-air, having been about to eat one of the fruits of his labors.

"Hello," I say easily.

"P-P-Princess!" he sputters.

I blink and back up a step. "Do I know you?" I ask.

He shakes his head. "No, but you're the princess!"

"I'm not—"

"I have to go tell my friends! The princess! She talked to me!" And he runs off with several backward glances. How he doesn't trip and fall is beyond me.

Me. A princess. It's ridiculous. Everything about this place is wrong. The grass is so much greener than even in the gardens, the air purer, fresher. Nothing is as it should be.

My breathing comes fast, too fast. I can hardly catch my breath, and the bodice of the dress is far too tight for my lungs. Maybe it's from panicking, or maybe it's from shock or confusion or fright, but I do a rather princess-y thing.

I faint.

A groan slips out even before I open my eyes. As I sit up, my hand flies to my head. I'm still wearing the crown, and I'm still in the same strange place. Nothing looks any different, the sun in about the same place in the sky, so I must not have been out for long.

"How are you feeling?"

I jerk back, my hands falling to the soft grass to brace myself. A hooded woman wearing a cloak hovers over me.

"Forgive me," she continues as she lowers her hood to reveal a kind face. "I did not mean to frighten you."

"Who... Who are you?" I ask, even though I'm tempted for some reason to ask her *Who am I?*

"I am known as Mortia," the woman says. "Are you hungry?"

I nod. Mortia reaches into a small pouch tied to her belt and removes a strange purple fruit. She hands it to me, and I stare at her as I bite into it. Only after I swallow that first delicious, juicy morsel that I remember you aren't supposed to eat food from a fairy. She doesn't look like a fairy, though, not that fairies are real. Yet... she doesn't look exactly human either. I can't say quite why.

Since nothing seems to happen from my ingesting the first bite, I devour the fruit. Once I finish, she smiles. "I think you should be heading home."

"To the castle," I say slowly.

Mortia's smile only grows, and she points north more when I started earlier to the northeast.

"Go on home," she says.

Those simple words make me want to weep. I've lived in houses before but never a home. To call a castle home is utterly ridiculous, but that doesn't stop me from heading northward. After a few steps, I glance behind, but Mortia is nowhere to be seen.

3

I don't make it far before a carriage halts before me even though there's hardly a path, and I never heard the horses pull it along. The footman insists I come, and at this point, I see no reason not to comply, especially because he bowed and called me "Your Majesty" from the start.

The castle is majestic, marvelous, magnificent, but before I can take in its wonder, the front doors open and out rushes two familiar teenagers.

My sisters.

This must be a dream, but I never hugged them before. They tug on my hands, dragging me inside as if I belong here.

"Come along, Madlen," the one with the same shade of blue eyes as I have. Her locks are golden, as if kissed by the sun.

Madlen? Strange. Now that I think of it, they never called me by name in any of the dreams I had.

"Agnes," I venture.

She winks a blue eye at me.

"Do not tarry," the other says, her brown hair identical to mine. Even the same waves tumble her locks.

"Brida," I say.

"Yes," Agnes answers. "Why are you acting so strange?"

"Is it because you already heard the news?" Brida asks sadly.

They lock arms with me, trying to get me to venture inside, but I do not move my feet.

"What news?" I ask, my heart filling with dread. I don't know what to think about any of this, all of it, but it just seems so very real and decidedly un-dreamlike.

"Father," Agnes starts.

"The king," Brida supplies.

"He is missing," they say in tandem.

"Where?" I demand, my throat thick.

"In the forest, or so we've been told," Agnes answers.

A lost king wandering in the forest. That is precisely how the fairy tale I read before falling asleep started. This must be a dream!

"Do not worry," I assure them, squeezing their hands. "I will find him."

"But—" they cry.

No matter. I am already motioning to the footman, and he drives me away to the outskirts of the forest. He helps me out of the carriage, and I enter the forest, stepping with great care, critically memorizing my path.

I see no one, hear nothing, not birds, not insects, no rustling underfoot. This place is unnatural, yet I'm not worried. I'll find the king. I know I will.

With ease, I duck under branches, sidestep a massive pine tree, and stop short. A figure is bent over, petting a stag.

The king?

No. The figure stands and lowers her hood. It's Mortia.

Seeing the helpful, kind woman again has me blinking back tears. I lean heavily against the pine tree, afraid I'll collapse if I can't find a way to ground myself.

"My dear, what's wrong?" Mortia asks.

I say nothing.

"You can tell me anything, ask me anything you like," she says softly.

I hate feeling like this. I'm beside myself, so unsure and scared. Maybe it's foolish, but I trust this woman, and I hear myself ask in a timid whisper, "Is this real?"

"Oh, yes, goodness yes!" She holds out her hands, glancing around. "The world is a strange, magical place."

Magic. I want to scoff, but that would be rude.

"You, Madison Martin, were never meant for Pittsburgh."

I gasp and take a step back. I never told her my name, and whatever place this is, it most certainly isn't anywhere in Pennsylvania.

"I wish you had an easy time," Mortia continues. "I do not understand why no family would ever claim you. I understand well why you buried yourself in books. You never truly belonged there, and that was why you clung to nature so. You wanted to find your place in the world, but it was never there, could never have been there."

How does she know all of this?

"Eighteen now and out of the system, but you still need to find your place, your purpose, don't you?"

This has to be a dream. It can't be real. How else can she know all of this about me?

"Not even a boyfriend, no kiss, no true friends..." Mortia shakes her head sadly. "I will say this, though. You should be grateful the Jamison family passed you by. They were terrible fosters. They abused the children, just viewing them as a means to make some extra money."

Okay, now I'm even more frightened. Some of what she's said was generic and could have applied to a lot of people but the Jamisons? They got in trouble with the authorities a few years ago.

"Please don't be alarmed," Mortia whispers. She holds out a hand toward me but does not step nearer.

"How do you know all of this?" I ask, my words faint.

"I must confess that I am a witch."

I gape at her.

"And more so, I brought you here."

"You brought me here," I repeat. "Take me back!"

"I can," Mortia says with a slow nod. "I can return you to Pittsburgh, to 2019, but you will die in two days' time. The plane you will take to check out a college on the west coast will crash."

I haven't looked at many colleges yet, but one in California caught my eye.

I swallow hard. "I'll just drive," I offer.

Mortia nods some more. "The trip will take you three days, and on the morning of the second, you will be involved in a car crash and die."

"Fine," I spit out. "I'll avoid college and just become a... a waitress."

Mortia just eyes me kindly. "You will work at a seedy diner and be caught in the crossfire when a fight breaks out."

She has an answer for everything, but can I believe her? Her knowledge seems so vast, though, but a witch? Magic? How is this possible?

"Where is here?" I demand.

"You aren't truly Madison Martin," Mortia says. "You are a princess, Princess Madlen Martz of the kingdom Saxonia, daughter of King Riff Martz. I brought you here because you belong here, and you can find not only your true place but also happiness, a family, and even love. All you have to do is trust me."

Trust her. A witch. Most witches in fairy tales were bad, evil creatures, but Mortia didn't seem like that.

Reluctantly, I nod. "Okay, then. I'll stay."

"Because of the chance of having a family?" Mortia asks.

"All of it. My family, happiness, love...

Mortia beams and then scowls. She crosses over to me and grabs my hands. "A dwarf you will be until you claim the love of the prince three. Loyalty and obedience are what you are after. Ask him to kill for you, and you will be you and loved thereafter."

I gape at her, not realizing what she's saying until the curse gripes me. A sharp pain stabs my chest and sweeps up and down over my body. I can feel myself shrinking, and I don't have to glance in one of the many nearby puddles to know I'm a dwarf.

"You can find your true place," Mortia says as she touches me between my eyes.

A sensation of falling overwhelms me. I land on my feet, and I know immediately that I'm in another land, not Pittsburgh, but perhaps another kingdom.

Sure enough, as I head toward the nearest village, a sign states Stilo, Kingdom of Imaginium.

Imaginium. Imagination. Maybe this isn't real. Maybe I'm not a dwarf. Maybe this is all a dream.

But in my heart, I know. This is real. I'm not asleep. I really am cursed, and the only way I can get my promised happiness and love is if I can make a prince fall in love with me. Yeah, because that will be easy.

What am I going to do?

4

I linger just outside of town, staring at the sign but not truly seeing it. Somehow, I know now that I must return home, not to Pittsburgh but to Saxonia.

But only after I break the curse.

Prince three, Mortia said. The third prince. Are there three princes here in Imaginium?

My heart begins to pound but not from fear. Honestly, this is very much like a grand adventure, a fairy tale in the making. Even if on the off chance this is just a dream, well, the thought of a family and happiness and love is enough to have me play along for now.

Some travelers enter the town, and I wince, stepping back, not wishing to be seen in such a state. A dwarf. How cruel.

Unsure what else to do, I head back to the spot where Mortia sent me. Off to the south is a forest, and I plunge inside. As before, I notice where I'm walking, each and every step, and this time, I do find a man. He's braced against a tree. Sweat beads on his forehead, and the crown resting on his head suggest he's a king.

I immediately try to sink into a curtsy. "Your Highness."

As his gaze shifts to me, I self-consciously pat the top of my head. My crown is gone. Good. A crowned dwarf would be far too obvious.

The king stiffens. "Who are you?"

"Madlen," I say, much to my shock. I would've though habit would make me say Madison, but Madlen rolled off my tongue.

"Well, Madlen, you wouldn't happen to know the way out, do you? I'm hopelessly lost. I've been stuck here for days. I swear this place is cursed."

I smirk and nod. "Follow me."

Thankfully, his supposed curse does not affect me, and I do not walk in circles but rather lead him all the way out and then to the castle.

The king grips my hands in his beefy ones. "Thank you. Thank you! Please, you must come with me to the castle. I want you to meet my sons."

"Your sons," I repeat dully.

"My three sons," he says firmly.

I smile almost despite myself. Yes, Mortia cursed me, but she could have sent me to a kingdom with no princes at all. Instead, she sent me to one with three, the precise number I need to break the curse.

Maybe she wants me to succeed. I certainly know I do.

5

IMAGINIUM, A FOREST,
POSSIBLY MAGICAL,
THE SIXTH OF SEPTEMBER 1271

"*T*hank you, Your Highness," I say, curtsying deep. Clearly, he can see beyond my stature as a dwarf. Perhaps his sons will be able to as well.

"Will you come with me, then?" he asks.

I risk glancing at him, truly taking him in. His pants were a bright green color, his surcoat red, his crown gilded and encrusted with emeralds and rubies without being overdone. His hair was dark, spotted with a few gray strands, giving him a distinguished look. Despite being lost in the forest for days, he does not seem worse for wear. His large green eyes were kind, and I just know he's a good king. If his sons favor him, they all will be handsome indeed.

Of course, I need the youngest son to have a pure heart. Looks aren't most important, especially when I need him to be loyal and obey me...

Obey me. That feels so strange, and I decide right then and there that the loyalty and the obedience would be mutual. After all, isn't that what love is all about? I think. I can't know for certain. I've never been in love before.

The king eyes me curiously, awaiting my answer, but my mind

races. How can I ensure that everything will work out? I need more time.

"I appreciate your generous offer," I inform the king as sweetly as I can. "I will send for your third son in a week, if that pleases you."

The king blinks a few times. Most likely, none has been so direct with him before, but I saved him, so perhaps he will forgive me.

"Very well," the king agrees. "One day, though, you will come to the castle."

"I hope to," I say, not wanting to dream about being married there yet picturing the scene just the same in my mind.

As if by magic, two horses seem to be waiting just for us, and the king heads toward the castle whereas I just pet my horse's nose. This truly is like a fairy tale, but the idea of killing frightens me.

A dwarf you will be until you claim the love of the prince three. Loyalty and obedience are what you are after. Ask him to kill for you, and you will be you and loved thereafter.

I grin. Mortia never said it had to be a human death. Perhaps a cow would work or another animal we could then eat.

As for gaining his loyalty and obedience... Well, first I have to meet the prince and hope that he is one I would have fallen for regardless of the curse.

he horse leads me to a small villa. While the main town that houses the castle has water running throughout and most likely canals, the countryside is lush and vibrant. The villa appears abandoned but well kept, again as if waiting for me. The roof is gabled, above the door is a hood ornament, and the tall, arched windows make me feel as if I'm a princess all over again. The garden out back is beautiful, too.

But my reflection in the small pond in the middle of the garden is most certainly not beautiful. My hair has become brittle, almost like brown straw. My eyes are lifeless yet glassy, much smaller than normal. My arms are too long, my body so short, my legs stout. When

I turned into a dwarf, my clothes changed to basically something akin to a sack. I look ugly and nothing like myself. Not that I think I'm beautiful, but this is… this is a shock.

I avoid the puddle from then on and eat from the garden. Inside the villa are a few blankets I use as a bed, and I'm not shocked to stay here, in this world when I wake. Several days of bliss pass me by, and it's on the morning of the seventh day that I realize I hardly ever think of Pittsburgh. I don't exactly miss my old life.

Besides the blanket, there is a trunk in the villa. Inside, I've found some clothes, that all match my new body shape even if they aren't the most aesthetically pleasing, and a few bowls and plates. This morning, I also find a few pieces of armor, enough that I can disguise myself as a dwarf guard. The helm covers half of my face, but I do not know if that's enough that for me to pass as a male guard, but regardless, I can make do.

What a perfect way to ensure that I can try to get to know the prince before he meets me? Yes, this is perfect.

The armor, though, certainly hadn't been there before.

Thank you, Mortia.

It's strange to think the witch who cursed me is helping me, but this place has so much magic in it. To think that the magic is just helping me spontaneously isn't something I can accept.

The horse, although never tethered, has stayed this entire week, and he trots over to me the moment I leave the villa. A dozen doves fly around before landing on the roof. I wave to them, giggling, feeling hopeful but also wary. Who knows what this day may bring?

It's never been easy for me to climb onto the horse's back, but I manage, and in two hours, I arrive at the castle. I'm too nervous to even take in the sight, too focused on the guards at the door, their shining armor, the weapons on their backs… They bar the way without being threatening.

I clear my throat and try to sit tall on the horse, which is impossible given my size.

"Please, I am here on behalf of the dwarf who saved the king a week ago. I have come to escort the third prince to her as was promised."

The guards glance at each other. Has the king not informed them about the agreement?

"Just a moment," the guard on the right says.

He enters the castle, and I have to wait nearly an hour before he appears with the prince. With dark hair and finer clothes than even the king wore, the prince is handsome but what of his heart?

"Let us not keep the dwarf waiting," I say, wondering how he might respond to my giving him an order, even if only a small one.

"Yes, of course," he murmurs, his voice soft, hesitant.

Perhaps he is as nervous as I am.

A horse is brought for the prince, and we ride off. My mind races, but I can think of nothing to say. The silence bothers me so much that I blurt out, "Would you mind if we stop so we can eat a bite?"

"The tavern up ahead?" the prince suggests.

I grin. "Yes!"

The place is fairly empty, and we sit at a bench. The trencher is filled with stew. Before I can break off a piece of bread to dip in, the prince starts to inhale his food. His manners are atrocious, and he's eating like a pig, almost as if he's half-starved. I know that. I've been hungry before, and when given a chance to eat as much as I want, I took advantage.

But why should a prince be that hungry?

Just then, a crowd of five men piles into the tavern. Immediately, they cross over to us. I expect them to say, "Your Highness," and talk to the prince with respect, but they clap him on the back, calling him Zane.

I stand and cross over to the tavern owner. "What is the name of the prince?" I ask.

"Which one?" he asks without looking at me, his gaze on the group I left behind.

"The youngest."

"Ruberto. Prince Ruberto Santo."

I nod. "And Zane?"

"The cow herder?"

Ah. The prince isn't here. I do not blame him. Who would want to see a dwarf? The king never promised we would wed, but he is reluctant to see me. Honestly, I would be the same.

A week later, I again dress as the guard and go to the castle. The prince that comes out this time is as handsome as the first, but I'm wary. This time, I'm prepared to check and see if he is the prince or not. I can almost guarantee he isn't. Fairy tales have a thing for threes.

Not far into our trek, I turn to the prince. "Might we pass through the marketplace?"

"Whatever you wish to do," the prince says.

So agreeable. Too agreeable. A prince wouldn't be, and I'm proven correct. We aren't in the marketplace long at all before someone asks "Ruberto" how his geese are. Yes. He's a goose herder. The prince tried to pass himself off as a goose herder.

Perhaps the third time will be the prince because I am not willing to give up. I will not spend the rest of my life as a dwarf. I refuse.

6

IMAGINIUM, MY VILLA,
THE TWENTY-SEVENTH
OF SEPTEMBER 1271

J'm nervous, by far more nervous than even the first time I ventured to the castle. Again, I'm dressed up as the dwarf guard, and I'm so grateful no one along the way has patted an eye at a dwarf guard, whether or not I can pass as male or they recognize me as female. I have never seen the king, so the chances of anyone supposing I am truly the dwarf the prince is to me is slim.

This man, this prince, is as handsome as the others. The previous ones had either green eyes or dark hair, like the king, but this is the first to have both. He is nose also seems similarly sloped, the jawline comparable, yet I already know how I will see if he is indeed the prince.

We bypass the tavern and the marketplace and come to a small lake.

"It is so hot," I comment. "Might we stop and swim at the lake?"

"As a prince, if I am to be wed to a dwarf, I won't start matters off even worse by arriving late."

My breathing hitches. Marriage has never been spoken of, and I hate that he thinks he will be forced to wed me.

With trembling hands, I remove the helm. "Prince Ruberto..."

"Yes?" he snaps without looking at me.

"I am Madison. Madison Martin." I swallow hard. "I am the dwarf you are to meet."

He now glances at me. "You? Why would you disguise yourself?"

"Why did you send a cow herder and a goose herder in your stead? Perhaps for the same reason." I inhale deeply. "And, ah... wed?"

"That is how these matters go, do they not? And I am the third prince. You asked for me specifically because you thought the king, my father, wouldn't refuse. The first born to marry a dwarf..."

"Yes, so terrible," I mutter.

The prince blinks and raises his eyebrows. His lips quirk almost to the point of faintly smiling. "Do you mean to say you don't wish to marry a dwarf?"

"I don't wish to marry someone who feels compelled to marry me," I snap. "And as I said, truly, your father and I did not discuss marriage. I only... I just wanted to talk to you."

"Why?" He narrows his eyes suspiciously, his eyebrows lowering. "Can a dwarf have magic? Is that how you were able to lead Father out of the Foresta di Incantesimi?"

Forest of... Incantations? Enchantments?

"Why was he in the forest in the first place?" I ask.

The prince frowns. "I... I don't know. We were so worried. Search parties had gone out to find him, but none thought to look in there. The forest can make a man so lost that he ends up dying there."

I shudder. "Why not just chop the trees down?"

"Because of the enchantments. It is said that if one can spend three nights there and leave, they will have all they wish for."

"Ah. How... How long was your father there for?"

"Two nights."

"Perhaps he will still be able to have all he wishes for."

The prince smirks. "Such as marrying off his sons?"

I shrug innocently.

He wipes a bead of sweat from his forehead. "It is hot," he admits. "Go on. Have a dip in the lake if you wish."

"I..."

"I won't look," he assures me stiffly, as if offended I would think otherwise.

"I have nothing to change into, and the thought of putting this armor back on after swimming..."

"You were trying to determine if I were the prince," he accuses.

"Can you blame me?" I counter.

"Have I passed your test?"

"You certainly act haughty enough to be a prince," I retort, lifting my chin. Then, I tap a finger to my cheek. "The cow herder, the goose herder... did you tell them to do everything I asked?"

The prince says nothing.

"Because if they refused to go to the tavern or to the marketplace, you might have had me fooled," I admit.

"I doubt that very much," he says. "I never realized a dwarf could be so clever and wise."

"Tell me, Prince Ruberto," I say, deliberately not calling him "Your Highness" but unwilling to drop his title entirely, "do you know many dwarves?"

"No."

"That won't change," I murmur under my breath.

"I beg your pardon?"

"It's not far to my villa," I say, urging my horse forward. "Perhaps we can have a bite to eat and then return to the lake to swim."

And that is precisely what we do.

Several times a week from that day forward, Prince Ruberto comes out to see me, and we actually become friends. I'm not sure which of us enjoys teasing the other more.

And then, one day, after we somehow push and shove each other playfully until he winds up on top of me in the garden behind my villa, Ruberto almost kisses me.

We're friends, and we just might become something more, yet I remain a dwarf. The curse remains unbroken, and I won't be myself again unless Ruberto can prove his loyalty, his obedience, and his willingness to kill for me. As much as I care and have even grown to love him, will he do what is necessary to save me?

7

*T*wo entire months have passed since I first met Roberto, and I wake to find a raven pecking at a window. I come outside, and the raven drops a piece of parchment into my hand.

> *Madison,*
> *Won't you come to the lake this day?*
> *I await you there.*
> *Ruberto*

I smile, my cheeks growing warm. Every day, he has called me Madison Martin, and I always call him Prince Ruberto. That he has shortened our names can only prove how much our feelings have deepened.

It's cold out, and I dress warmly. There will be no swimming on this day. It hasn't snowed at all yet, too dry I suppose.

As I leave, three doves are resting on the roof. I do not know why they like my villa so much, but I enjoy their company all the same.

It does not take me long to reach the lake, and the sight before me makes me gasp. The prince has laid out a blanket with some wine poured in glasses already, some sandwiches and cheeses and pastries awaiting us.

"What... What is all this?" I ask, almost too shocked for words.

Ruberto steps around a tree and takes my hands in his. It wasn't until we became friends that I realized the first two "princes" never truly looked at the guard, but Ruberto had and has every day. He sees me, even if he only sees me as a dwarf.

His deep green eyes penetrate to my soul. "Please, Madison, marry me."

"Ruberto!"

"I know you think you and Father did not agree to that, but you did. Naïve dwarf." He chuckles. "Regardless of the promise, I wish to marry you."

My eyes flutter closed, and I refuse to cry. As much as I long to say yes, I long to be human again. I will not remain a dwarf for the rest of my life. More than my appearance, I have discovered other changes to my body. My back aches, and I do not enjoy nature as much as I did before. If anything, I find myself wishing I lived in a cave or even underground instead of my villa. I've woken a few times in the middle of the night to find myself in the garden, digging until my fingers bleed. Dwarves are perhaps not meant to live above ground. I do not know enough about dwarves to be certain.

Whenever my fingers are bloody and torn up, Ruberto says not a word but rubs certain herbs on the afflicted parts, soothing the injuries and causing me to love him all the more.

He is gentle and fun and ridiculous and charming, but is he loyal and obedient?

"I..." I open my eyes.

Ruberto chuckles and kisses my forehead, "I surprised you. I am sorry. I thought..."

"You aren't wrong," I murmur.

"But you aren't ready. Why? Is it because you think my people will begrudge me for taking a dwarf for my bride? They will not speak one word against you. I swear it."

"Ruberto..." I smile despite myself and have to pull him down, so I am tall enough while on my toes to kiss his cheek. "I just need a little time yet. That's all."

"Of course," he murmurs. "Some wine?"

We drink and wat and laugh and talk and even walk on the ice. Yes, the lake has frozen over. Oh, to be with him every day for the rest of my life!

But the curse must end first.

The night, as I am about to fell asleep, I come up with an idea. I should seek out Mortia. Now that I think Ruberto might be able to break the curse, I'm terrified. I'm so afraid that if the curse isn't lifted correctly, something might happen to the prince, and I... I love him dearly.

My eyelids shut, and I fall asleep. I have not dreamed much at all since come to Saxonia and then Imaginium, but I dream of Mortia now.

"Congratulations on your success so far," Mortia says, "but yes, if the prince does not kill and soon, disaster will rip the two of you apart, and you will have no family, no love, and no happiness."

"You truly did curse me," I say, shocked.

Mortia hangs her head, but I can see the sorrow and worry in her eyes. She wishes for me to succeed, but she's the reason for all of this in the first place. Can she honestly tell me that Ruberto and I never would have met if not for my turning into a dwarf? He is the third prince in one land and I the youngest princess in another. Surely our paths would have crossed.

Eventually. Perhaps after one or even both of us were already wed.

I wake with my mind made up, and when Ruberto arrives on his horse, I rush out to him before he can dismount.

"Madison, please, marry me," he says.

"Yes," I whisper.

"I will ask you every day until—you said yes?"

I giggle. "Yes, but... please," I beg him, "I know this will sound strange, but before the wedding, you must kill a... a..."

It's wintertime, and there are so few animals about. So far save for the doves. As much as I hate to have one killed, I wonder if Mortia has sent them here for a reason, for this very specific reason.

"You must kill a dove as a... a special sacrifice for the wedding. If you don't..."

Ruberto reaches down and cups my chin. "If you require this, so be it."

He glances around and spies the three doves on the roof. The prince dismounts and removes a small dagger from within his boot, the one he uses to cut up fruit.

Clearly magically inclined, the doves fly off the roof, straight for him, and Ruberto glances at me.

"Chop off the head of the middle one," I call desperately.

Please, Ruberto. Please obey me and be loyal.

The doves swoop. He snatches the middle one, and in one swift move, without a hint of hesitation, he chops off its head.

A stiff breeze whirls around me although the day has been quite calm, and I'm lifted into the air. I'm turned around, my body tingling, and by the time my feet are lowered to the ground once more, I am no longer the dwarf but the princess I was when I first came to this land.

"Madison?" Ruberto asks. He carefully lays the dove and its head on the ground, perhaps because I said it was intended for a sacrifice for our wedding, and then he rushes over to me, holding me at arm's length.

"I was cursed," I murmur. Tears spill down my cheeks."

"You are..." His eyes widen as he takes in the crown I feel atop my head.

"Princess Madlen Martz of Saxonia," I murmur.

"Not a dwarf."

"No." I bite my lower lip. "Are you disappointed?"

Ruberto laughs. "Dwarf or princess, I love you just the same. Now, am I wrong, or am I right, but do we not have a wedding to plan?"

*N*ot even a week later, Ruberto and I are wed. My family from Saxonia comes, and both kingdoms rejoice, and the curse has entirely lifted. I have a home now. I have a family. I have happiness and love.

I have found my place in the world after all.

8

IMAGINIUM, MY VILLA,
THE FIRST OF MAY 1288

*S*eventeen years later, I am still in Imaginium, but my husband and I visit Saxonia every month. For now, I am out in the royal gardens. I'm back to myself, loving nature, and my daughter, sixteen and beautiful, lovely, and gracious, tends the garden besides me.

Just then, the wind stirs, and I know we aren't alone without even having to turn around.

"Sophey," I say, "can you go and see if your father is prepared to eat the midday meal?"

"Certainly, Mother." She squeezes my hand, stands, fixes her skirt, and sweeps into the castle.

I wait until her soft footsteps fade before standing and turning around. "Mortia," I say warmly.

Although she attended the wedding, Mortia never approached to speak with me, and by the time I had a chance to look for her, she had gone. We have not seen each other since, and I am most happy to see that she is with child.

With child. Pregnant. My, being here for nearly two decades has certainly changed me!

"I wish to apologize for cursing you," the witch starts, but I just shake my head and laugh.

"What is meant to be will always find a way," I say firmly. "You were right. Pittsburgh wasn't my home. I was born at the wrong time. You helped me so much, and that is why my first daughter was named after you. Mortia Sophey Santo."

"You are indeed as extraordinary as I always knew you would be. I cannot say why you were born in another time and place, but here is your home."

"My heart is here, so of course it is my home." Impulsively, I embrace the witch. "I cannot ever thank you enough."

"Just be happy and enjoy your love." Mortia cups my face and then disappears.

My heart is so very full as Ruberto himself comes to fetch me for the meal. My love for him has only grown as the years have gone by. Other than thoughts of the botanical garden, my memories of my time away from this magical land are fading away, and I am perfectly fine with that. Love, loyalty, obedience, happiness, family, all this and more I have found here, and I will never ever be alone or feel as if I do not belong ever again.

The Cost of Imagination is a retelling of Hurleburlebutz by the Brothers Grimm. It is set in the same world as my Once Upon a Darkened Night series, a collection of twisted fairy tales including Cinderella, Sleeping Beauty, Beauty and the Beast and more. Enjoy the retellings where the traditional villain is now the hero or heroine.

ABOUT THE AUTHOR

Nicole Zoltack is a USA Today bestselling author who loves to write romances. Of course. She did marry her first kiss, after all!

When she's not writing about knights, superheroes, or witches, she enjoys spending time with her loving husband, three energetic young boys, and precious baby girl. She enjoys riding horses (pretending they're unicorns, of course!) and going to the PA Renaissance Faire dressed in garb. She'll also read anything she can get her hands on. Her current favorite TV shows are Game of Thrones and Stranger Things.

Connect with Nicole

 facebook.com/AuthorNicoleZoltack

twitter.com/nicolezoltack

 instagram.com/nicolezoltack

FIRE IN THE BURGH

JAIME RUSSELL

1

HARLEY

18 YEARS OLD

I feel an elbow, hitting my rib cage, and I wake up from the most amazing dream ever. "What the hell, Serena?" I bark at my best friend.

"Wake up, or you're going to miss it." She tells me with a big smile on her face. I look out the window of the plane, seeing the lights of Pittsburgh lit up. It's very bright. The stadiums, the bridge, and all the buildings. It's my favorite place in the whole world, especially at night, and I can't get rid of the smile on my face. The flight attendant tells us to put the trays up and buckle ourselves because we're going to be landing soon.

"It's the most beautiful sight I've ever seen in my life," I sigh happily.

"You're so weird," Serena laughs, as we stand up, once the flight attendant lets us know that we can leave the plane. Serena has been my best friend, since she pushed me off the swing, because she wanted it. I cried and told my mom, when she picked me up. My mom and Serena's mom met one day and forced us to have a play-date. I pushed her in the mud, and she cried. We ended up having a tea party, and since then, we've been inseparable. We're going to the same college, and I'm excited she's on this new journey with me.

"Don't you think that was the most beautiful sight that you've ever seen in the world?" I sigh, tilting my head with a smile on my face.

"You're so fucking crazy, girl," Serena laughs.

"I've been dreaming of coming to this city, since I found out that my dad lived here. I visited him a couple of times and fell in love. He told me that I could always live with him, whenever I wanted," I tell her.

"Harley," She grabs my elbow to stop me from walking, as I look for a coffee kiosk. "Are you sure this is where you want to be? I mean, you just lost your mom." Her bringing up my mom starts the tears, flowing down my face.

My mom and stepdad, Stan, were coming home from their date night, when Stan fell asleep at the wheel and crashed right into a telephone pole, going forty-five miles per hour. He died at the scene, but my mom stayed alive for three days. I like to think she hung on that long, so my dad could get there, promising her to take care of me.

It was hard graduating high school without her. Then, I couldn't stand to be alone, so I sold the house in Minnesota. Packing the house, and then making so many decisions about moving without her, almost killed me. Now, I'm just trying to make it day to day.

"My dad opened his home to me, and now I guess, it's time to get to know him. He's paying for art school. Mom and Stan's life insurance policy went into a savings account, until I'm twenty-one. Stan's family got some of the money from the house. They didn't think that I deserved it, so getting threatened to be taken to court scared me. I gave them half, and then took the rest for my travel expenses here," I state, as I start to get defensive.

"I love you, and I'm just looking out for you. Please, don't be upset. You've been through so much lately, and I don't want to see you hurt anymore."

"I know, and I love you for it," I say, hugging her tight. We both applied to the Art Institute of Pittsburgh, before my mom was killed. I want to work on my graphic design and photography, while Serena wants to study hotel management. "My dad is waiting at the bottom of the escalators near the baggage claim."

"Are you nervous? When was the last time that you were here?"

"I was ten-years-old, but you know, Dad was there for the funeral and to help with Stan's family. I have a good relationship with him, as a one weekend a month dad, so we're not close. After I came here, when I was younger, he started coming to Minnesota, because he didn't like me flying alone. My grandparents still lived there, until they died a couple of years ago, and I visited them, too. So after, it made sense for him to see me at home." We're standing in the line for Starbucks, and it's almost four a.m., but I'm hyped about being here.

"I don't remember your dad very much. My mom always called him the sperm donor," Serena says, shrugging her shoulders.

"Stan called him that, too. It's one topic that always started a fight with my mom. It's not his fault that he had to move. He needed to go where the work was, and the Pittsburgh Panthers were looking for a basketball coach. I'm proud of him, and I've never hated him for it."

"Then, I won't either. I'm glad that your dad opened his house to us for the next four years or so." She says, after we order our coffees. "I just worry about you."

"I know, and I'm kind of worried about this, too. What if I just built up this fantasy about my dad in my head, and he's actually nothing like I thought?"

"Just try to remember that he's human." We ride down the escalator to the baggage claim area, and I see my dad with his red hair and freckles. I look just like him.

Serena and I bust out laughing at the sign he's holding up that's bright yellow with glitter on it. It says, 'Glad your crabs cleared up just in time for your debut in the porn movie Harley and Serena.'

Once we're off the escalator, I run to him, and he picks me up, spinning me around. "Baby girl, I've missed you. How are you?"

"I'm okay. Thanks for the great sign," I smile.

"Hi Mr. Michaels." Serena says, holding out her hand to him.

"It's Dan."

"Thanks for the sign. It was a great welcome surprise."

"I wanted to do something funny and to make you guys feel welcomed. I also plan to take you two out to a gourmet restaurant tonight after work, so you can relax. The movers came yesterday, and everything is in your rooms." He tells us, as we grab the suitcases off the carousel.

"You didn't lift the boxes, did you?" I ask with concern.

"No, the movers and some of the basketball players did all the heavy lifting."

As we make our way out of the airport, my stomach starts to flip-flop, and the reality of it all sets it. I'm no longer in the safety of my house with my mom. She's gone, and now, I'm an adult.

I have no choice, so I better buckle up and enjoy the ride.

2

HARLEY

24 YEARS OLD

*J*pull my curly, unruly red hair into a messy bun, and then race down the stairs, after noticing the time.

"Fuck a duck." I stomp my foot, and my dad chuckles, as he puts the food on the kitchen table.

"No one likes a show-off." I stick my tongue out at him. "The restaurant is closed for lunch, so I could've slept in an extra two hours."

The year I spent in college for art, and my passion for it, is gone. I think it was tied to my mom too much, and my creativity suffered, which sent me into a deep depression. Dad and I both had to deal with a therapist, because the more I sank, the angrier I became, especially at him. I'm glad that it happened because we've grown closer through it all.

I've found a new passion, cooking. I was home for a year and wanted to help my dad out, so I cooked breakfast and dinner for us every single day. I loved it so much, so I enrolled in culinary school. Now, I work with one of the top chefs in Pittsburgh, and at the hottest restaurant, in the last three years. I'm a sous-chef to Alice Botter of Steel City Eatery. She's the one that used to push the limits, when it came to introducing food to your palette, but now, I think she's afraid to do it.

"Oh, I'm terribly sorry, your majesty," he teases me. Dad has actually become my best friend, and I'm so thankful for him. He's turning forty-two in six months, and I've been busy, planning his party. I didn't get to plan a fortieth or forty-first for him, because I was in school, and he was so busy with basketball, so this is going to throw him off his game. He'll never suspect a thing. Plus, his secretary is helping me. "What are you going to do with your morning off? I'm thinking about heading into the gym for a bit." He says, as I sit down at my spot at the table, taking a sip of my coffee.

"I'm heading to the strip to pick up some fresh herbs and wander around. Monday's are usually my favorite day down at the markets. I don't know the specials, but I'll pick up the basics."

"Callie's in town, so I won't be home for a couple of days. You and Serena are on your own." I chuckle, as we eat in silence for a little bit. Dad never brings around the women he sees, but I know that he's no monk.

"Dad, I'm twenty-four-years-old. You can bring your girlfriend around."

"I know I can, but Callie doesn't fit into our world." He sets his fork down, as he stares at me. "Don't give me that look. I'm not the only guy she's seeing. Callie is not the one for me. She's just fun and worldly. If I quit my coaching job, leave you, and follow her around, then I'll be her only guy. I like being a full-time dad and coach, so that's not an option. She's not someone I'd write home about either, so I'm just passing the time with her." He's frank about things.

My parents met in middle school, and then Mom got pregnant somewhere around their Junior prom, so they married the day after graduation. I don't fault them for not making it work, and they tried for a while. Now, Dad's forty-one, living his life how he wants to live it, and no one is going to tell him differently, but he'd still drop everything and everyone for me. I often laugh, because he doesn't know how good looking he is, and the women follow him around everywhere we go.

Serena still lives with us for now. She's been out of school for about two years, and she works at a Marriott hotel, as the manager. She's dating this Rockstar wannabe named Freddy, whose real name is Bruce. He changed it to Freddy McCartney, so he could be like Freddy Mercury and Paul McCartney. I'm hoping that it fizzles out, because she's talking about moving to L.A. with him and supporting his ass, until he makes it.

"Where's Serena? I haven't seen her all weekend."

"I think she's with Freddy." My dad rolls his eyes. He doesn't like him either and wishes that he could do something about it.

We finish our breakfast, talking about basketball and work. I take our plates, rinse them, and then put them in the dishwasher. I kiss my dad's cheek, as he's now reading the paper. "Have a good day today. See you in a couple of days. I love you."

"Be careful, and remember to always use your mace." I roll my eyes, as I walk out of the door.

Walking into the garage, which is off of the mudroom, I unlock my black 2018 Lexus. It's the only extravagant item that I bought with my mom and step dad's insurance money. I figured since my dad paid for school, and I waited until after I walked across that stage to receive my diploma, that I deserved a nice treat for myself. It felt more like a gift from them, and I know it's what they would have bought me anyway.

I travel through Squirrel Hill down to the Strip District, weaving through the rush hour traffic. I hate this time of day, and I end up swearing more than anything. I finally make it to the market and park, as I grab my xl iced coffee, and then start my wandering through to the shops.

"Good morning, Harley." I look up to see Mrs. Barnes, standing behind the counter. She has the best seafood in Pittsburgh. "Late start? You're usually here two hours ago."

"Good morning, Mrs. B. I had breakfast with Dad this morning. What specials do you have for me today?" I stand there looking at the different lobsters.

"No specials. My shipment was late, so they're bringing me a second order tomorrow. What's the special at the restaurant?"

"I don't know. I wasn't there yesterday, so I'm actually flying blind here." After a bit, we say goodbye to each other, as I continue to look around. I do know that I can never buy enough fresh herbs, since Alice is known to prefer them. I check out the meat deals and talk to a few of the owners that I've become friends with to see how they're doing. Finally, I'm done, so I go back to my car, and then head to the restaurant.

Grabbing the big bag of herbs that I bought, I head into the restaurant kitchen. I see Alice reading some papers, as she stands over the counter, lost in thought. I say good morning to her, as I set the bag of herbs down on the bench near her. She doesn't even look up, so I touch her shoulder, "Good morning, Alice. Are you okay?" She jumps, grabbing her chest.

"Jesus Fucking Christ."

"Sorry. I thought you heard me. What's going on?"

"I don't know. Reservations are down, and food critics aren't coming in anymore. What should we do?" She asks, bunching the papers together. Alice is fifty-six with gray hair, but she has the heart, soul, and attitude of a twenty-one-year-old. She parties with the best of us, but I can tell she's worried.

"Can I do anything to help?" I ask, as she scoops up the paperwork, before the other workers start to come in. We open for happy hour on Monday, instead of waiting until dinnertime.

"Just try and think of something to boost sales." I nod my head, as she hands me the list for dinner. I sigh, because it's the same specials, as last month. Chicken alfredo, steak, and shrimp scampi are the headliners. We are so damn predictable.

I start writing the particulars on the wipe off board in the kitchen for the rest of the cooking staff, before heading into the office to print off the insert for the menus. Once I'm finished, I head to the front and work on the chalkboard in the dining room with the bartender. He's making cracks about how he can set his watch to our specials. I agree with him, and also, point out how bland they've become.

I go back into the kitchen to the other cooks and waitstaff, standing around the board, "What?" I ask, as they point to the board, like they're saying again. "Guys, I'll talk to her, but let's get to work." I sigh in defeat.

Something has to change, and it has to be soon.

3

ELI

$\mathcal{T}$he alarm starts going off from my alarm clock, and I hear little laughter, coming from the covers next to me in my king size bed.

"I'm hearing noises coming from my bed that shouldn't be in my bed, but in their own room." I yawn, as they laugh louder. I fake yawn again, before swiftly moving to tickle my twin nieces, well my daughters, Lily and Jasmine. Family tree wise they are my nieces, but in the eyes of the law and the state of Pennsylvania, I'm their dad.

My sister dropped them off one day and never looked back. That was seven years ago, and they were just three days shy of their second birthday. At first, I didn't know where she went, but I finally tracked her down to sign over her rights. My ex brother-in-law was a lot easier to find, and he was more than willing to do it. So, on their fourth birthday, I adopted them.

"Stop Daddy. That tickles." They squeal, and it makes my heart melt.

The girls know who their parents are, and I've never lied about that to them. They even had a picture in their room for a little while. Lily and Jasmine know that I'm Uncle Eli, but they both asked if it would be okay, if they called me Daddy. My heart still swells, when I hear them call me that.

"Does it?" I stop for a minute. "When did you get into my bed last night?" I ask them, as I get out of bed.

"I don't know what time, but it was after your third really loud snore. We counted." Jasmine tells me. She's the spitting image of my sister with black hair, bright, blue eyes, and a smart, sassy mouth on her. Lily is more like Marv with brown hair, green eyes, and she's super shy. They're both brilliant, and I can't imagine them not being my kids.

"Oh, really now? I guess it's cold cereal for you two, while I have waffles." I state, as I walk out of my bedroom, getting hit by pillows in my back, and I can't help but to laugh. "Don't touch the toaster, until I get in there," I yell, while walking into the bathroom.

I hear my mom telling the girls to calm down and have a little bit of patience. My sister, Erin, didn't have the kids, until she was thirty-five. My parents were older, when I came around, so Erin and I are seventeen years apart. I was an oops baby, as we often joke. I had just graduated from fireman's school, starting my first job with the company, when my sister left the girls. My mom had already moved to Tampa to retire with her friends, but she moved back here to help me raise them, and I couldn't have done it without her.

I walk into the kitchen to the girls putting the waffles in the toaster and pushing down the button, while my mom supervises them closely.

"Couldn't wait five seconds?" The girls shake their heads no. "Chocolate milk or orange juice? I'll set the table."

"Chocolate milk," all three of them say unanimously, as I start getting everything ready for the four us. When the last waffle is done, the girls make their way to the table, and I hold out the chairs for each of them. My mom says grace, and we start to eat.

"When do you go to work?" Lily asks. I usually have a calendar up on the fridge, but I forgot to post my new schedule.

"Today at one. I'm going to do some grocery shopping, and then cook dinner for you three."

427

"Okay," Lily tells me. As a fireman, one of the hardest parts of it is my schedule. I work two days back to back, where I live at the station house, and then I work one weekend day a for eight hours. The girls finish eating and put their dishes in the sink. I'm still eating, but I tell them to go get ready for school. My mom stands with her back facing me.

"I want to take the girls to Tampa to live."

"Why?" I'm confused where this is coming from, because she's never mentioned anything about taking the girls to Florida to live, but I know she wants to go back.

"I'm tired, and I want to rest." She says, not looking at me.

"If you want to rest, then the girls shouldn't go with you, because you'd have them full time by yourself." She still won't turn around, and then it hits me. The secret phone calls in her bedroom, racing to get the mail every day, and buying her own laptop, so the girls can't use it. "Erin lives in your house, doesn't she? How did I not see it?" I stand up, bringing my dish to the sink, and then I turn, looking my mom in her eyes, "Lily and Jasmine are my daughters, not Erin's. I don't care what kind of life she's living now. You can go, but my kids are not leaving here. Are we clear?"

"They need their mother." She yells at my back, as I walk towards the living room, and I stop, turning around to face her.

"No, they need love and stability. They never had that with Erin or Marv, but they do with me. They're striving now, so they don't need that. I love you, but don't undermine me, because I will give you and Erin the fight of your life." I walk out of the kitchen without another word.

We live in a one-floor apartment that has two bedrooms, an office, which my mom turned into her bedroom, two bathrooms, a living room, and a kitchen. It's a good neighborhood with a good school district. I also work part-time, as the building manager to help with my rent.

"Girls! Let's go. We're going to miss the bus." They come running down the hallway, giving my mom a hug. They're chattering away, as we get into my truck. Their birthday is coming up, so we're discussing their party. I write down the food they want, who they want to come, and the theme.

The bus arrives, and I tell them goodbye, and that I'll see them in a few days. I head to the grocery story, do my shopping, and then head home. I unload the groceries from the truck, laying them on the table.

"Mom, I'm home." She comes out, and I can tell that she's not happy with me. "I'm sorry." I pull out a dozen red roses that I bought her, and she tears up, as she kisses my cheek.

"I'm sorry, too. Erin just misses the girls, and I thought it would be good for all of them to be reunited."

"What about me? What about the girls? We've never lied to them, but they know that their parents didn't want them. Erin can't pick and choose when to be in their life."

"Do you mind, if I go and visit her?" I just hope that she doesn't bring her back here.

"Can you wait, until I find a babysitter?" She nods, as she puts the food away, while I start dinner. I cook up my lasagna, because the girls asked for it, before they headed to the bus, and I can't deny them. I leave them their little notes for after school, bedtime, and when they wake up. I miss them, when I can't be with them all the time. They have a kid's tablet that has Skype on it, which allows them to call me on it, when I'm at the firehouse. I always answer it, unless I'm out working. The guys even talk to them from time to time.

"You spoil them." My mom says, looking in the fridge, because I got all of their favorites.

"Look in the freezer." I smile because I bought her favorite ice cream.

"Your wife is going to be one lucky lady." She kisses my cheek, and I tell her that I need to head out. "Call me, when you can."

I park my truck near the firehouse and head inside. "What's up, Marshmallow?" I hear my Captain yell from the top of the rig.

"Hey Cap," I say, looking up at him. "Does your daughter-in-law still babysit for firefighters?" I ask.

"Yeah, why?" He asks, coming down off the fire truck. "Your mom okay? Nothing happened to her, did it?"

"Define, okay," I sigh. "She wants to take the girls and move to Tampa," I pause, taking a deep breath, "with Erin."

"Erin, Erin? Like as in your sister?" He leans against the truck. "Damn. Well, I'll talk to her right away then." The men and women on this shift with me are my family, and they protect my girls.

"Thanks Cap. I need to go call my lawyer, so I can protect my girls. I can't lose them." I can feel myself starting to tear up.

"Yes, you do, and you have an entire firehouse behind you. Lily and Jasmine aren't going anywhere." He squeezes my shoulder for reassurance. We walk to the main lobby, so I can clock in, as he heads to his office.

I smell something burning, coming from the common kitchen area, so I head that way, before going to my locker. "Do I need a hazmat suit?" I chuckle, as I lay my gym bag on the table. "That smells like it could kill someone. Rookie, you trying to kill us?" I look at the pot of beef stew. "Move over and let me try to fix this, or you're buying us pizza for dinner." I chuckle, as I try and fix dinner, but my mind is with my girls.

4

HARLEY

♥

*T*he kitchen staff and I start the prep work, and Alice, her husband, Gus, and a couple of people that I've never seen before, are in the office in a hush-hush meeting.

The lightness in the air makes it so much easier on the staff to work right now. Alice makes everyone nervous, because even when they're doing great, she finds fault with everything, me included. Her mood lately has been harsh, and the staff always comes to me to fix it, but I don't know how.

"Is everything ready?" Alice asks, standing on the opposite side of the kitchen.

"Just about. Everything is prepped." I tell her, as she walks around each station watching them chop, mince, and dice. I told them when she does that just to concentrate on the task at hand, and not her hovering over them.

"Harley, walk with me." I follow her out of the kitchen, after washing my hands, and we walk to the dining room. "We're closing early tonight. The last reservation is at eight, so start sending people home, when things slow down."

"Are you okay?" I ask, seeing the concern in her eyes.

"Yeah. I'm just not feeling well, so I'm leaving. You're in charge, and Gus will be in the office." I turn to walk back to the kitchen with a smile on my face that she can't see. "Harley, no changing my recipes." She states, and I nod in agreement.

The shift goes by without any issues. We have fun, tell jokes, sing, and laugh a lot. The waitstaff had fun, and the customers were relaxed as well.

After the last of the customers leave, I lock up and Pat, the bartender, starts to clean up the front, while I clean the kitchen area. It takes about an hour for both, and I do a walk-through of the front to make sure the linens are off the tables for dry cleaning in the morning. Pat brings back the glasses from the front, and I help him wash them. I also double check the checklist that I made up for the closers of the kitchen staff, as I look around, seeing how great the kitchen looks.

Finally, it's time for us to go. "Gus, we're leaving. Have a good night." He waves at us, as Pat and I walk out the backdoor together, making small talk about the weather, the food that's been so over-done lately, and Alice's attitude.

His wife is late picking him up, so I stand there, leaning against my car, listening to the misadventures of Pat's money pit house that they just bought. We are laughing so hard, when she finally shows up. He tells her that he was telling me stories about the house, as they switch seats, so he can drive. Pat's wife, Marcy, hugs me, when she gets out. I went to art school with her, so we've known each other a while. I wave to them, as I unlock my car and get in. I start it and reach for my cell phone to see if Serena wants to go out for a little bit, but I can't find my purse.

"Damn it." I forgot to grab my purse, when I went to get the keys from my locker. I get out of my car and head to the front door, since the locker room is quicker to get to through there. I grab my purse and start to head out, but I hear whistling coming from the kitchen, and I smell smoke. I push open the swinging doors to fire fully engulfing the wall near the oven. I don't see anyone, so I run to the wall, where the fire extinguisher is, but it's not there.

"What the fuck?" I mutter, as I dial 9-1-1 to report the fire. I run to the sink and grab the apron, that I hung up on the dishwasher, to try and cover my mouth to keep the smoke from getting inside. I put my hand on the nozzle, and I scream out from the pain and look down, seeing the pattern of the nozzle burned into it. I start coughing, as the fire begins to spread, and the smoke gets heavier. I'm trying to remember my fire safety training from elementary school, but all I can see in my head is stop, drop, and roll.

I get down on my knees, where the smoke isn't so thick, coughing and trying to crawl, but the pain in my hand is stopping me, and the smoke that I'm swallowing is starting to make me dizzy. My chest is killing me, and I'm wheezing so much so that I get lightheaded. My eyes are fluttering to stay open, as I try to stay awake, but my last thought, before passing out, is that I hope that the firetrucks get here soon.

"Captain, I have a female here." I hear a muffled voice near me, as I feel someone touching my neck, checking for a pulse. "She's alive." The oxygen mask is put on my face. "I'm trying to get you some good air. Breathe slowly." I open my eyes to see the most beautiful blue eyes I've ever seen. "Hello there. I'm going to keep the oxygen on you, as I carry you out." I feel him pick me up, like I weigh nothing, and my body molds into him.

"Thank you," I whisper, and he winks at me. We walk through the restaurant, and I smell gasoline. I wonder why I smell gas? I don't have much time to dwell on it, as my body comes to rest on a gurney, and the man removes the mask from my face, so the paramedics can put their mask over my nose and mouth. I continue to cough, as they check my vitals. The fireman, who saved me, gets ready to leave, as I grab his arm, but yell out in pain.

"Gus," I hoarsely whisper.

"There was someone else inside?" I nod. "Captain, is there anyone else in the building? The woman is asking about a person named Gus." He asks, talking into his radio.

"The building is clear, and no one else is in here." The paramedics put me in the back of the ambulance, and we head for the hospital.

After what seems like forever, I'm finally laying in a hospital bed, and I'm starting to feel human again, despite the tightness in my chest, the pain radiating from my hands every time I touch something, and the damn coughing. I guess, I damaged both hands without even realizing that I did it, because one hurts way more than the other. The doctors decide to keep me for observation, but they're putting me in ICU, because of my breathing.

There's a knock on the door, and the curtain moves, as a detective comes in. "Excuse me, miss. Can I ask you some questions?"

"It hurts to talk and breathe, but I'll try." My voice sounds like I have smoked four packs a day for a couple of years. Plus, it's also muffled through the oxygen mask.

"The firefighter, Eli Marsh," he says, looking down at his notes, "said you were asking about a man named Gus, but you were the only one there. So, who is Gus?"

"He is the owner along with his wife, Alice. He was in the office, when Pat and I left."

"Did you start the fire, ma'am?"

"No, of course not. I walked out with Pat, the bartender, and we stood there talking, while we waited for his wife. I got into my car and realized I forgot my purse in my locker, so I went in to get it. I heard some whistling in the kitchen, so I went to see what was going on, and then I smelled the smoke." He doesn't seem to believe me, but I also explain about the missing fire extinguisher. He lays a card on the tray and tells me that, if I can think of anything else, to call him. Why would he think I'd do this to myself?

The medicine starts to make me sleepy, and I finally fall asleep. I wake up a few times, as they come in, checking my vitals. I finally wake up, after a long nap, to see my dad, sleeping in the recliner near the bed.

"Dad," I hoarsely whisper, and he smiles at me. "Water, please." I say because my throat feels like sandpaper, and it hurts so bad. "What are you doing here?"

"You were in a fire. Where else do you think I'd be?" He says with concern in his voice.

"I'm alive, I'm fine, and I'm safe. You don't have to stay." He's getting ready to argue with me, but I give him a look, letting him know that I mean business. He tells me that he'll leave, when the nurse comes in to check on me one last time.

Between the breathing treatments, antibiotics, and pain meds to help with my throat, chest, and hands, I can't stay awake. The nurses keep checking on me, and at one point, I wake up to see my dad is gone, but I see a note that says he loves me and will be by tomorrow, if I'm stuck in here again.

That's the last thing I remember, as I dose off again.

5

ELI

One of my duties with the fire department, is helping with investigations, when I'm on shift. I always try to work, when the girls are in school.

"Hey Cap?" I stand in the doorway of his office. "Do you mind if I cut out a little bit early? I need to get a statement from the victim and check out the restaurant, before the insurance adjusters and owners get to it and her first."

"Yeah, go. It's not a problem. Oh, and call my daughter-in-law. She has openings for your girls. She even has a list of babysitters for you, too, if you want to go out for a date night or need a break." I tell him thanks, as I turn and head for my truck.

As I drive through the streets of Pittsburgh, I call my mom and tell her what's going one. I explain to her that I need to do some work on the arson case that we talked about the other night, and that I'd pick up dinner on my way home.

I make it to the hospital and park. After I get out, I start walking towards the door. There's a group of nurses standing around the triage and registration, and they stop talking and watch me, as I smile at them. The guys at the firehouse always tease me because I have no game. I never know what to say or do. They also tell me that I look like some actor that plays Jay Halstead on Chicago PD, but I'm a little taller.

I get to the nurse's station and ask about the girl from the fire. They show me to her room, and her sliding door is slightly ajar, so I knock lightly, but I don't hear anything. I decide to walk in, and I can see that she's sleeping. There's a notebook on the tray, and I decide to write a note, letting her know that I was here, but when my body sits in the recliner, I relax a little, and end up falling asleep.

In the distance of my dream, I can hear my girls giggling and having a good time, but they're talking to the girl from the fire. How do they know her? I suddenly get worried, so I open my eyes.

"Oh, I think he's awake now." I hear louder giggles, as she turns my cell phone to me, and I can see my girls, staring back at me.

"Sorry for falling asleep," I yawn. "Hi girls." They both say hi.

"Your phone kept going off, and you were sleeping so sound, and I didn't have the heart to wake you. We watched *The Little Mermaid* together, and now, they want to watch *Brave*, since I look exactly like Merida." She says, smiling at me. She doesn't seem annoyed at all. My last girlfriend wouldn't even meet my girls, and I wasn't allowed to tell her friends about them either. They didn't exist in her world.

"You really do look like her. Girls, tell Grandma that I'll be home shortly, and that I'll call from the truck, when I leave. I love you." They both tell me they love me, but they don't hang up, so she turns the phone back onto her.

"Yes, I gave you my number and Skype name, but give me a couple of days to get my new phone setup." They say okay, and all three of them say goodbye. She hands me my phone, but I notice how much it pains her to hold it.

"Please tell me that you didn't hold the phone the entire time with your hands badly burned like that?" She shrinks down a little. "I'm very sorry for falling asleep, and it wasn't very professional of me at all. You were sleeping, and I was just going to leave you a note."

"My dad said that recliner has ether connected to it somewhere. He slept in it for four hours, and he said it was the best sleep he's had in a while. So, I can't fault you. I just didn't want to wake you. You looked exhausted." She smiles at me.

"I'm Eli Marsh," I start my introduction, but before I can finish, she's out of the bed and sitting in my lap.

"My name is Harley, and you're the fireman that saved me." I nod, as she hugs my neck tight. Her 5'4" frame against my 6'4" one looks funny, but it feels right. It's like she was always meant to be here, sitting on my lap. She pulls away from my neck to look at my face. She's licking her lips, and without thinking, we both move closer to each other, connecting our lips. Harley has this electricity about her, and I feel myself being pulled closer. My hands are on the back of her neck, trying to bring her closer to me. I'm pretty sure that she figures it out, as she begins to straddle me. She's now towering over me, as the recliner starts to move to a bed position slowly. I begin to part her lips with my tongue, and she moans this incredible, husky moan.

There's a sound of someone clearing their throat from behind us, so Harley and I break apart from each other, as the recliner comes to an upright position. I can't help but to stare into the green eyes of my future. I've never wanted someone as much as I do her right now. I'm going to do everything I can to get to know her. She turns around in my lap and smiles.

"Dad." She says, and my face turns as red as Harley's hair.

"Hi honey. You called and said you were being released today, but Selena couldn't pick you up, so here I am." He smiles at her, and I can tell she's his everything.

"Dad, this is Eli Marsh, the fireman who saved me." She gets off of my lap and sits down on the bed.

"Hello sir," I say, holding out my hand to him. He takes it and starts to squeeze, letting me know that he's in control here. Harley notices and gets up, as she touches our hands, wincing with the slightest touch.

"Dad, stop it now. Sorry, Eli. He gets protective of me. Why are you here?" She asks, looking at me, once our hands are separated.

"Oh, right. I forgot. I need your statement. I know you talked to the police, but I do the fire investigations as well. The police ask a different set of questions, but I also need to take pictures of your injuries and need your help with a diagram. Have the owners or their insurance company been by to talk to you, or have they mentioned anything about a settlement?"

"They sent me flowers. My purse and cell phone went up in flames in the fire. Dad just got me a new phone, so they may have called me."

"Your dad mentioned you were getting out today. Do you want me to meet you at your house tomorrow?"

"Yes, if you don't mind. I'm pretty tired, and I want to get the hell out of here." Harley gives me her address, the phone number to the house, and also, her dad's cell phone number. I start to say goodbye to them, when Harley comes rushing to me, kissing me one more time. "See you tomorrow." She blushes, and then calls the nurse to help her get dressed, so she can leave.

finally pull into my parking spot at the apartment complex, and I grab the pizzas, as I head inside.

"Honey, I'm home," I yell, as I kick the door closed with my foot.

"Daddy!" I hear two squeals, coming down the hall. They have wet hair and pajamas on. "Did someone just get a bath?"

"I don't know who got the bath, them or me." My mom laughs, as she's drying herself off. "You look tired."

"I am, but I got some sleep at the hospital," I tell her, as I set the pizza on the coffee table. I have a rule that when we have pizza the girls can have root beer. I don't like them having a lot of pop, but once in a while, is okay. They start to get their drinks, as I supervise, and I grab my glass to get my root beer as well. We all head back into the living room. "I heard we're watching *Brave* tonight." The girls nod, as I start the movie. They eat their pizza in silence, while watching the movie, before moving up to the couch with me, when they are done eating. They end up falling asleep on me, so I carry them one by one to their room. I kiss them goodnight lightly on their forehead, telling them how much I love them.

I come back into the living room to clean up the pizza boxes and glasses, and my mom is on the phone with someone. I give her some privacy, but I can see that she's visibly upset. I grab a couple more slices and a beer, as I sit down on the couch.

"I know, but I'm not going against his wishes. He is their parent now. Erin, listen to yourself. You can't pick and choose, when to play Mommy. The only side I'm taking is that of Lily and Jasmine, and Eli knows what's best for them." I can't hear what Erin is saying, but my mom is visibly shaken by what was just said. "Erin, remember where you're staying, and who is helping you out. Speak to me again like that, and that will go away. I don't deserve it." She hangs up her cell phone and cries a little. After she gets up from the recliner, I start to get off the couch, but she waves me off.

"Mom, I love you, and I'm sorry that you're in the middle of all of this with Erin, the girls, and me."

"I love you, too." She sighs, as she goes to her room.

I turn on the news to watch it for a little bit, before bed, because if I know my girls, they'll be in my bed by one in the morning.

I wouldn't trade it for anything.

6

HARLEY

$\mathcal{M}$y dad gets me situated for the night, before he leaves, since it's his last night with Callie for a couple of months. When I called Serena for a change of clothes, I asked her to get me something that I can wear to bed.

I think I overdid it, when I was on the phone with Lily and Jasmine. I stretched my hands, holding the phone, but it was fun. I enjoyed talking to the girls and watching the movie with them.

I took a pain pill, before my dad left, but it only helps for about three hours, and I can only take them every six hours. So, I lay on the couch, telling Alexa to play my relaxing song list. Finally, I drift off to sleep, but wake up screaming from a nightmare of the fire. My dad holds me, reassuring me that I'm safe.

"Tell me about the nightmare." He says, soothing me.

"I was back in the kitchen, but the fire was too strong, and I kept screaming for help, but no one could get to me. I saw you, Serena, and Eli on the other side of the fire, standing there trying to come closer, but the fire only raged higher. Finally, you all left, and I died," I cry.

"Baby girl, you're okay. It's going to take some time, but we'll get through this. Do you want me to call and make an appointment?" I nod, as I look up at him.

"Are you okay? You look like hell."

"I didn't sleep well, and no, I'm not okay. I almost lost you. When Pat called me..." He can't even finish the sentence, as he starts to cry. "I thought I lost you."

"I'm alive, and that's all that matters. I'm not leaving you anytime soon. I'm here to drive you crazy, until we're both a hundred." We laugh, as we wipe our tears away.

"Did Gus start the fire?" I shrug. "If he did, I swear to God." I don't let him finish his thought.

"Hey! No, let Eli and the courts give the arsonist their karma. I can't believe my hands are ruined. I don't know when or if I'll ever be able to work again." I sniffle.

"You don't have to work. Between your mom's insurance money and the money that I make, it's more than enough to take care of your wants and needs." I can't help but laugh, because he sounds more like a husband, wanting a wife to stay at home to take care of him. "I took this afternoon off because you need to go see the burn doctor."

"Eli's coming by, when he takes his girls to school." My dad stares at me. "He needs my statement and to document my injuries."

"Okay, I'll let him wrap them then. Do you want something to eat? You need a pain pill." I ask for some grapes because I can easily lift those without too much of an issue. My dad gets ready for work, and then he kisses my forehead, as he leaves.

"Alexa, play *Bohemian Rhapsody*, the movie."

The movie begins, as I'm getting settled into the corner of the couch, when there's a loud knock on the screen door, making me jump. "Jesus Fucking Christ."

"Sorry." Eli stands there with a smile on his face, and I tell him to come on in. "I haven't seen this movie. Is it any good?"

"I don't know. Sit down and watch it with me." He does, but he pats the cushion next to him, and I scooch over to cuddle him. I'm still wearing my black tank top with my plaid checkered boxers on, and I'm really comfortable around him. He puts his arm around me, letting it rest on my hip, as we watch the movie in silence. The film ends, and we look at each other, like we did last night in the hospital room, and I feel my need for him growing. I don't know what it is, but I've never been attracted to someone like this before. This time he kisses me, and I make myself fall back onto the couch, so he has to come with me.

"I certainly like this greeting from you." He tells me, as he kisses my neck. Eli moves my unruly curls out of the way, and my tank top strap moves down my arm, as I arch my body, pushing my breasts into his chests. My hands go for the t-shirt that he's wearing, and not thinking, I grab it, while making a fist. I scream out in pain, as I start to cry. He jumps off of me right away, trying to figure out what happened. He's standing over me, watching my hands close to my heart. He picks me up and holds me, as we sit in the recliner. "We don't need to rush anything. I should've slowed down." He tells me, and I smile.

"I'm pretty sure that I was the one that put myself on my back." He smiles at me.

"When was the last time these hands were changed?" I tell him, before I left last night. We walk into the kitchen, where my dad left my stuff on the table.

"How were the girls today?" I ask, as he smiles.

"They were good. We watched *Brave* last night, before bed, and they crashed halfway through it. I put them to bed, but it didn't last long. I had a foot in my face and a head in my side. How they sleep like that, I'll never know." He starts to talk to me about how he's not their biological dad. He explains about his sister, Erin, and his mom, as he unwraps my hands. He tells me that he has to take pictures for evidence. As he takes some pictures of the third degree burns on my palms and fingers, he writes down details that I can remember, and he works on the diagram, while I let some air get to my hands. I feel so sick looking at them.

"You okay?" I nod, as he starts to put the cream on it, adds the gauze, and then wraps it. "Now, where's that cell phone?"

"Oh, you don't have to do that," I tell him.

"Oh, I have ulterior motives. How am I going to talk to you, if you don't have a phone?" He kisses me, and I point to the counter. We start working on getting it set up and talking casually. We finish up just before my dad gets home for my doctor's appointment, and we say goodbye, and I promise to call him after it.

"Don't forget. I owe you a date." He kisses me, and I smile, as he leaves.

"You like him, don't you?" Dad asks, and I nod.

Hopefully, this is the start of something new.

The End... For now.

ABOUT THE AUTHOR

Movies, gaming, and books. Oh My!

Jaime Russell grew up in a small town in Pennsylvania, but she currently resides in a smaller town in Indiana. She lives in the country with her husband, and she is caregiver to her parents and mother in law. Jaime suffers from some autoimmune diseases, so on her good days she is active and most likely shopping. But on her bad days, she spends time curled up with her fuzzy blanket, escaping reality with her puppy Annie.

Jaime is a mom to four adults plus a couple of kids that she unofficially adopted. She is also a grandmother to a wild boy with a personality all on his own and a sassy granddaughter, and both of them have stolen her heart. She is an aunt to two crazy nephews and two nieces, as well as being the oldest child in a family of three and their spouses. Life has never been dull for Jaime, and family means everything to her.

She enjoys watching movies, shooting guns, and spending time with family and friends. She is an avid gamer when her internet permits, as she enjoys talking and goofing off with her online family.

Jaime Russell never liked reading growing up, but now she never goes anywhere without either a paperback or her Kindle because there is always a new book boyfriend to be discovered.

Connect with Jaime

 facebook.com/jaimerussellauthor
 twitter.com/mamabear824
 instagram.com/jaimelynnrussell

DOMINATING DESIRES

JM SCHALM

1

I can't say how happy the clock just made me; five more minutes, and then I'm off for three days. I do love my job -- Celeste Sullivan, Executive Assistant to Mr. Ripley. He's by far, one of Pittsburgh's leading attorneys. Going on his 38th year, he has received the most prestigious award every year. Of course, the last 10 years he has had me. We make a great team. He actually treats me like one of his kids, and I adore his family. I am invited to holiday parties quite regularly.

Stepping into his office, he looks up, "So, young lady, do you have any fun plans this evening?"

"As a matter of fact, I'm going out with my best friend Rachel to celebrate her birthday."

"Good, I'm glad you are spending time with your friends. I'm not a fan of that boyfriend of yours- what is his name again, Lennie?"

Gasping for breath, I correct him, "No sir, it's Leslie."

To say most everyone I know is not a fan of Leslie is an understatement. The sex is amazing -mind-blowing even- but he gives new meaning to the word asshole. They just don't understand why I'm with someone like him. They keep telling me that amazing sex can only last for so long and I deserve so much better.

Waving goodbye to Mr. Ripley, I grab my things from my desk and head out. Pittsburgh traffic is going to be a bitch on a Friday evening, but I'm used to it.

I need to look like a fucking knockout according to Rachel. Thank God I had a mani-pedi done a couple of days ago. I live in a cute two-bedroom apartment in the Upper Lawrence district of Pittsburgh. It's becoming very popular among young professionals. The nightlife around there is so great. We have lots of stores, coffee shops, bars, and restaurants.

Walking into my apartment my cell dings, it's a text from Rachel.

Rachel: We will be there at 7 to pick you up. Gotta stop to pick up Will on the way.

Me: Ok, I'll be ready.

I decide I'm going to soak in the tub first for a bit. I pin my hair on the top of my head while running my bath water, then grab my phone to text Leslie.

Me: Hi, Baby. I'm going out with Rachel for her birthday tonight. Love you.

As I relax in the steaming water, I go over my relationship with Leslie in my head. I mean, is it a real relationship? It feels real when we are together, but when we aren't, I barely hear from him. I feel like I'm always the one initiating contact. I love him, but distance has become our enemy lately.

Taking a deep breath, I stand and step out of the tub to dry off and get ready. I pull out a little black dress that barely covers my ass. The amount of leg I'll be showing should be illegal, but I'm going to make my legs look even more fabulous with a pair of strappy, black Louboutin 4-inch red bottom heels.

Letting my long blonde hair down, I pin some curls up to make it look sexy. Taking time with my makeup, my smokey eye is on point tonight. Now, to add some lashes. Looking in the mirror, I believe I have filled Rachel's fucking knockout request; which makes me start to wonder where we are going tonight to celebrate. After I apply lotion to my body, I pull on a lacy pair of black panties before slowly easing into my little black number. And the finishing touch, I lean down to pull on my Louboutins.

Glancing in the mirror, I release a breath. Wow! I know that I'm an attractive woman, I've never lacked confidence. I'm a size 8, very curvy, soft in all the right places.

Just then, the doorbell rings. "Game on." I laugh.

Opening the door, I'm greeted by Rachel and Will. Both of their mouths drop open when they see me.

"Oh hell yes!" Rachel yells. "She's on the prowl tonight."

Laughing, I look at Will. "It's ok, you can put your tongue back in your mouth now."

Shaking his head, he responds, "Wow, Celeste. You look great... just great. Not sure your dress can get any shorter." Smiling, I thank him for the compliment.

"So, what are we doing tonight?" I ask.

Glancing at each other, Rachel answers, "Well, since it's my birthday, I want to check out the sex club."

My face must show what I'm thinking, because Will starts laughing.

"Rachel! Are you kidding me? What the hell!"

"Come on, Celeste. It's going to be fun. Tell her, Will."

Grabbing my bag, I roll my eyes. If I don't leave with them now, I might lose my nerve to go, but I secretly have always wanted to check out one of these clubs myself. The idea of it turns me on so much.

*W*e are at one of Rachel's favorite restaurants, a local steakhouse, and I've been asking questions about the club since they picked me up. It's hard not to be curious of a place I thought only existed in erotic novels.

"What time do people usually go to the club?" I ask, just as we're finishing up dinner.

"Well, we'll get there when they open, which is kind of early, but people will already be there. It gets busier as the evening goes on." Rachel says as she waves to the waiter for our check.

Taking my third shot, I feel myself starting to loosen up. A few more of these and I'll be taking my dress off. Oh God, that's an awful thought.

Stopping at the liquor store, we buy a bottle of whisky. The nice thing about the club is that it's BYOB - Bring your own Booze. Soft drinks and snacks are on the house. I'm actually a little buzzed as we speak, but as soon as we get there, I'll be taking another shot to shake my nerves.

As we pull up in front of a warehouse looking building, I notice a few cars in the parking lot.

"Well, let's get this over with." I mutter to myself.

Stepping inside, I'm taken aback. It looks really nice, just like any other club in the downtown area - large dance floor with an amazing D.J. The bar is super nice too, not like the other clubs downtown. Oh, shit! There's porn playing on all of the TV's behind the bar, except one that has a baseball game on. I am so not a porn watching girl!

Grabbing another shot, I down it. Oh yeah, I'm feeling good now. Sitting down at a table, I start to people watch, but I quickly notice I'm the main attraction for the unattached men here tonight. I have no idea which ones are single or married.

Sitting down with me, Rachel and Will are already groping each other and locking lips.

"Ok guys, you don't have to babysit me." As soon the words leave my mouth, they are standing up and heading to a private room in the back. God, must be nice. As the night goes on, I see a tall, dark haired guy walk in and head towards the bar. He's extremely good looking. As I sit here, I'm thinking *Holy shit, Will is giving it to Rachel back there.* The chair beside me pulls out, and down sits the hottie from the bar. Turning my head to smile at him, he speaks first. "Hi, my name is Brian." Shaking my hand.

"Hello, I'm Celeste. It's nice to meet you."

There was something about him; I felt a pull instantly, his voice was so very deep and the stare he was giving me gave me chills in a good way.

"So, Celeste, what has you coming to a place like this? Do you like to watch?"

Oh, his words excited me, and the air around us was so hot. He has not looked away once. He just keeps staring at me.

"Actually, I came with friends. They seem to have disappeared to one of the rooms. I went to the restroom earlier and Will must really be pleasing her, she was screaming!"

Throwing his head back, Brian laughed. I felt myself also laughing with a huge smile on my face.

"So, Celeste, tell me what you like? Do you like role play, spankings... because a good spanking can be so stimulating."

His words had me breathless. It's like he knew my innermost secrets and desires. Pushing all the right buttons to make me want to be oh so naughty.

"Actually, a spanking can be so much fun, and as for role play, I think that's a must in a relationship."

Smiling, I have his full attention, no one else in the room exists except us. "What if I tied you up, Celeste? Does that excite you? Does it make you want to do naughty things with me? Perhaps blindfold you and let me slowly touch that gorgeous body of yours. Have you ever been so satisfied that you couldn't remember your name? The things I could do to you would have your body on fire."

My God, this man had made me wet just sitting across from him, listening to him. To say that if he leaned over and kissed me that I would be straddling him this instant is an understatement. I was totally consumed and definitely interested in what he was saying. Just then, Rachel and Will sit back down with huge smiles on their faces, and looking totally satisfied. The introductions take place and I can see Rachel looking at me like the cat that ate the canary.

Chatting among ourselves for a few minutes, Brian leans in, "So

Celeste, what is a fantasy that you have always wanted fulfilled, but have never been given the opportunity?"

I'm so drawn to him; the dominance he exudes is so exciting and scary at the same time. Thinking for a minute, I smile, "Well, I love the idea of role play. I have been naughty, so that means I'm going to need a good spanking, doesn't it?"

I watch him slowly lick his lips, watching me so intently. I'm pretty sure if he could eat me up, the dinner bells would be ringing. Sitting back in his chair, I look at his hands which look so strong.

"You know Celeste, I'm very good at giving spankings. How many do you think you deserve?"

I have to cross my legs; the tingling that's going on between them almost has me moaning out loud. I'm picturing myself sitting on his face when I see the smile spread across his. What in the world is wrong with me? I'm never like this.

All of a sudden, Will looks like he won the lottery. "Oh, someone is getting flogged in back. Let's go watch!" With that, Rachel and he are out of their chairs. Looking up at Brian, he nods and I know he wants to watch as well. As we walk over to the room, I feel a hand at the small of my back and goosebumps form on my skin. This man is a force to be reckoned with.

Stepping into the room, it's dark until my eyes adjust to the dim lighting. I turn to the corner of the room and see a woman in just her panties being swatted with what looks like a soft horse tail, but made out of leather. I'm so intrigued, the moans coming from her are so hot. Wow. Shifting on my feet, I feel someone lean into my back. Just then, in my ear, Brian speaks, "What is going on in that beautiful head of yours? Are you wondering how that would feel across that beautiful ass of yours? Thinking how wet you would get as it slides between your legs? If I had you on that, we would take breaks so I could slide a finger inside that hot pussy. I bet you would cum for me as soon as I put it in, wouldn't you, sweetheart?"

I turn to look at him. There is a fire in his eyes, and it seems I'm the cure for it. I glance around, and Rachel and Will are nowhere in sight. Go figure. We spend a few minutes more watching, and then decide to go for a walk.

They have rooms set up with beds in them, new sheets put out and rooms cleaned after anyone goes in there. Oh my! One room has a sex swing next to the bed. I have never been in one of those. Just as we pass a room, we see a couple having sex- OH MY GOD! It's Rachel and Will! Sweet lord, he's huge! No wonder she's screaming so loud. Glancing up at Brian I see his eyebrow raised like *'whoa, get it, Will.'*

I hurry past the doorway. I definitely saw more of my friends than I ever wanted to. I feel Brian grab my hand and pull me into the next open room. Behind me, I hear a male voice say, "Oh yeah, I can't wait to see her."

Brian lets go of me, slamming the door shut, and then I hear the lock turn. I'm sure my heart is beating out of my chest. Slowly, he walks towards me - like he's stalking his prey. Running my tongue along my lips, I hear him groan, then his lips are on mine. The kiss consumes me. I can feel my arms going around his neck. We are pressed completely together. Suddenly, he grabs my wrists, pulling them up above my head. I'm breathless as I look into his eyes. I know I have to speak.

"Brian, I can't do this. I'm seeing someone. Although, it's not a great relationship, it still is one." He's staring at me. It feels like my soul is bare to him. Releasing my hands, I feel him squeeze my hips as I slowly lower my arms. Taking my hand again, we leave the room. Walking back out into the bar area, there are two stools in a corner; we grab them, sitting so we could look at each other. His smile is so sexy.

Looking away, I grab my cell, anything to put some space between us. Taking it from my hands, he calls his phone with it and saves my number.

"Real smooth." I say and he laughs

"Well, Celeste, I have been known to be quite smooth. I can't wait for you to really see how smooth I can be."

Figuring I will never hear from him again, what harm can come from this? Finally, here comes the nymphos, they have to be tired-- I am from listening to them.

"Wow, you guys ready to go? Or do you want to go back for another round? Honestly, I think Big Willy is thinking about it."

Just then, Rachel shakes her head. She's in need of sleep, I can tell. Turning my attention back to Brian, I smile at him.

"Thank you for a great night. It was a lot of fun." Seeing him look me completely up and down made me very hot.

"No, Celeste. Thank you, and I can't wait to see you again."

Walking out of the club, Rachel is the first to say something. "Whoa, he is totally your type. Wow, the sparks you two were letting off... crazy hot, girl."

As I turn and laugh at her, my cell dings.

"Be safe getting home, babe." Oh my! He so sent me a text as soon as I left him! Sliding my phone into my purse, I let out the breath I have been holding. On the way home, I stare out the window. What just happened tonight? My mind is going so many different directions. I'm so tired. I can't wait to go to bed, and regroup tomorrow. Rachel pulls up in front of my apartment. I grab my purse to get out of the car and turn to wave bye. I'm more than ready to call it a night.

*I*t's been two weeks since I was at the club, and Brian still sends me random texts so I know he's thinking about me. He has me fantasizing about things I probably shouldn't be. I shouldn't feel guilty, especially since Leslie has been a piece of shit lately. I have no idea what I even mean to him; One moment he says he loves me and the next he's MIA for days. I understand he works long hours and his job is stressful, but lately I'm feeling more like his fuck buddy. Would it be asking too much to go out and have fun once in a while?

I'm still feeling numb from our conversation yesterday. He asked if I wanted his friend to come watch us have sex. He even asked if I wanted him to join in, because his friend thinks I'm hot. He didn't show one ounce of jealousy. How can you say you love someone and want to watch them have sex with another person? Leslie thinks I want this because I went to the sex club, which couldn't be farther from the truth.

I'm so drawn to a possessive man who doesn't want to share- who claims me as his own. BDSM has me so interested and turned on, picturing my hands being tied, surrendering my body and soul to a man, I can't think of anything more sexy than wanting to please him and be rewarded for my good behavior.

I'm sad thinking I have loved him knowing this wasn't the ideal relationship. I find myself backing away some and keeping my feelings in check. In the beginning he consumed me to the point it was scary. I loved him so much, but I knew deep down it was more one sided. Knowing I'm going to have to make some hard decisions very soon, makes my head throb.

I can't believe I told Rachel I would go back to the club tomorrow night. Staying away would be the right thing to do, but the need to go back is even stronger. I feel like I have an angel on one shoulder and the devil on the other. The naughty things I have thought about have my head spinning. Absolutely no one would believe the intense craving I have to be bent over and spanked. Thinking of it now has me rubbing my thighs together. Having a man want that kind of control over me, makes pleasing him the strongest urge I have had in a long time. I'm not sure how getting through the work day tomorrow is going to be possible. Just then, my phone dings. Looking at the screen, I lose my breath. This man must be psychic, because Brian always seems to send a message when I'm thinking about him.

Brian: Hello, hope your day went well. A flogger caught my eye when I walked by my closet, and it made me think of you. I want you to picture that while you get ready to slide between those sheets. Enjoy your night, beautiful.

Oh, my fucking stars! I need to run and hide from this man. He makes me want to be such a bad girl, and I mean taking that to a whole new level I've never experienced. I'll never sleep tonight wondering exactly how the flogger would feel on my ass.

*T*his Friday has to be the longest day in the history of Fridays. It may have something to do with the fact that I want to go be a creeper at the club and watch all the different people tonight. I haven't been this excited in a long time. I'm also wishing I was holding a glass of wine. I'm sure that would be frowned upon at work.

Rachel sent me a text earlier saying she was bringing a cooler bag full of alcohol. That would normally influence me as well, but I have made a promise to myself that I will be on my best behavior tonight.

Just when I'm sure this day can't go any slower, it's finally five o'clock, and I'm so ready to get out of here. I can't stop fidgeting, I'm always so cool and collected, but not today. Waving bye, I hurry down to my car. This night needs to get started!

As I pull up at home, I literally jump out of the car and quickly head inside. I grab a glass of crown and Diet Pepsi. I'm thinking this should relax me. Now, to soak in a hot bath! Hopefully this will help to get rid of all the anxiety. Just then, Drowning by The Backstreet Boys comes through the speakers. I wish I had that kind of love. I guess a girl can dream can't she?

Guess it's time to get this show started. Stepping out of the bath, I quickly dry off with a towel, then smooth lotion all over my body to make my skin is soft and silky. I pull out the little red dress I bought for just this night. This baby hugs all the right places and my back is completely exposed. Now, to clasp my strappy heels.

I step back to look in the mirror; makeup looks perfect, the outfit is amazing. I smile at my reflection before turning to walk out to the kitchen. I'm thinking I might have just a straight shot of crown. As the burn from the whiskey hits me, I think the good time has already started and I giggle. Hearing my phone ding, a text comes through to let me know that Rachel and Will are here to get me. Grabbing my bag and cooler, I head out the door thinking to myself, *'I'm going to make this night my bitch.'*

Walking into the club, I smile at a couple of people as I pass by. Oh God, the single men zone right ahead. Some look down right creepy. *Don't make eye contact* I chant to myself. Oh fuck! I just did! I'm silently praying he doesn't walk over here. The bartender hands me the drink I ordered. Yes, this is exactly what I need. My cell dings, letting me know I have a text. Brian's name shows up; taking a deep breath, I click on his name to open the message.

"Are you there yet? I'm on my way. Can't wait to see you."

I quickly texting back, "Yes, I'm here. The place is pretty busy tonight."

Sliding my phone back in my bag, I join Rachel and Will. They are chatting with another couple. Oh my, this is the couple from last time. I missed the orgy that took place between the four of them. I'm told it was a big hit with all kinds of people watching. As I sit down, I'm sure this couple thinks I'm down for whatever. Thank the stars Rachel tells them that I'm just here to watch.

Finishing our drinks, we head to the back. Will is excited and wants us to watch something. There is a room off to the side, and in the corner is a wooden cross with a brunette tied to it and straddling across it. She's moaning as the guy behind her uses a riding crop. Instantly, I'm turned on but I do my best to try to hide it. I just stare as the arousal builds within me with every thwack of the riding crop. I suddenly feel a hand at the small of my back and I glance to the right to find Brian with a knowing look on his face. He knows I'm turned on by watching.

Licking my lips I turn to him "Hi, How are you doing tonight?"

A sly grin touches his lips as he leans into my ear to whisper "Well from the look on your face I can tell that you are enjoying this. Tell me, how wet are you?"

Turning my head back to watch the couple, I see he now has his hand between her legs, and he's talking softly into her ear. I don't know what he said, but it was enough to make her orgasm, because her body is shaking and she is moaning so loud. Brian's hand grips the back of my neck and sets my body on fire. I'm barely keeping it together. I try to remember the promise I made myself, that I wasn't doing anything but flirting tonight because nothing has been settled yet with Leslie. I haven't been able to talk to him, but that's normal, which is why our relationship is completely fucked up.

Taking my hand, Brian leads me out of the room and back to the bar area, where we find a secluded corner. Staring me in the eyes, he wants to know what I was thinking; if I'm turned on to the point of going back on my promise to myself.

"So, Celeste, what's going on in that beautiful mind of yours? Are you thinking about how much she loved being controlled in there? About how he brought her to orgasm, but only when he thought it was time, because he controls her desire?"

Hearing it said that way made me instantly hot all over. "Well, I do have to admit that watching it all play out in front of me was very erotic. While I have never thought I could enjoy watching that, I must admit that I do."

He knows I'll never go into a room with him, but I don't think he will stop asking. Sitting here and having him knowing my hidden desires has me feeling so exposed, but in a good way. The soft talking and the atmosphere we are surrounded by, makes me want to be so naughty. Just as our conversation is getting good, I see Rachel motioning us over.

"Hey guys, you need to come here. There is some crazy show going on in one of the rooms. You need to see."

Glancing at Brian he motions for me to go ahead of him and I feel his hand at the small of my back again. Turning the corner we see one of the doors open and inside is a couple seriously going at it. She's on her hands and knees with him behind her. The crowd outside the door is really growing. Word must be going around out in the bar area. As I glance inside the room again the guy sits back and I feel like I just received a punch to the gut. It's Leslie and the chick is his ex girlfriend from out of town. Turning away from the room I walk down the hall and suddenly feel someone grab my hand. I look up into Brian's questioning eyes.

"That's my boyfriend in there! No wonder he hasn't text me the last few days."

I can see the concern in his face, then it turns to lust. Pulling me into the first room we see it's the office room, a fantasy I always wanted to do. Closing the door I hear the lock turn then I'm backed up against it. Brian cradles my face in his hands as he leans in to kiss me. I wrap my arms around him, the feeling of being wanted has my body on fire. Suddenly I'm face down on a desk my arms are straight in front of me gripping the other side of it. My dress is slowly slid up over my ass, as I feel my panties being pulled down my legs. Brian leans over me to whisper in my ear.

"How many spankings do you think you deserve for making me wait for this?"

Before I can answer, his hand lands across my ass. I gasp for breath he runs his hand over where it just connected, caressing it the most soothing way. When his lips replace his hand I'm thankful the desk is holding me up or I would have fallen down. Then it happens all over again, causing me to moan so loud. I want more. When he turns me around to face him I know he's just as turned on. Our eyes lock as he drops down to his knees and his mouth consumes me. This man has taken oral to a whole new level. I'm sure the entire back area can hear me, as the moans that are leaving me sound hoarse. I haven't even kept track of how many times I have cum he's that amazing. Standing he starts to walk backwards to the chaise lounge in the corner. He throws a clean sheet over it and motions for me to join him. Starting towards him I pull my dress slowly over my head reaching behind me unclasp my bra. He pulls his shirt over his head and I watch in anticipation as he lowers his jeans. Brian pulls a condom from the pocket of his jeans and rolls it on before he sits down. Reaching out his hand, I place mine in his. Straddling this man is what my body needs and wants. I close my eyes and abandon all logical thought, letting the sensation of him filling me take over. We are both moving and moaning. Feeling a kiss on my shoulder I open my eyes. This has me leaning in for a kiss. There was a time when I would have never let my body go like this, but tonight this is what I'm doing. I know we are both close. Speeding up my body starts to shake. Hearing him moan *oh fuck* deeply, sends me over the edge with him. Leaning forward I lay my head in the crook of his neck, his arms have me completely surrounded. After a few minutes I get my bearings and sit back as I glance up into his face and smile. He knows I'm completely satisfied that my body has felt worshipped tonight and my desires have been brought to life. As we get dressed I hear him come up behind me

"So Celeste was it everything you dreamed it would be?"

"Honestly, it was better than I had ever expected and for that I thank you." The grin on his face tells me he's more than proud with himself. Walking out of the room we round the corner and I stop to let some people by. When round the next corner, I nearly run into a half naked Leslie. When his eyes connect with mine, his face falls. He's knows he's been caught. I raise a knowing eyebrow at him and he knows I know. He actually looks guilty and I feel stupid for ever loving him. His voice sounds off as he just says Hi to me, but I don't speak to him. Then he sees Brian behind me and his face changes to one of jealousy. Turning away from him I walk out to the bar. Taking a seat, Brian and I decide to have a drink while I wait on Rachel and Will. I glance around the room and realize Leslie followed us out and wants to speak to me, which is the last thing I want to do. I tell Brian that I need to take care of this and he nods in understanding. Walking towards Leslie I feel nothing and I know it's completely over.

"Celeste, let me explain. I love you! This is all a mistake."

"Oh Leslie, this is not a mistake. You planned this night. I understand and I get it."

"No, you don't understand. I can't lose you."

"You already have. I hope you find happiness because I did truly love you, but that's gone now."

Walking away from him was easy. After this, it's time I need to explore the new me. Brian is watching me as I come towards him smiling.

"So I see from the look on his face he's not happy with what you said?"

"Oh no, but it was time for that chapter in my life to end. Now I'm going to experience a whole new me."

"I would like to help you in this. I know you don't want a relationship, but we can have some amazing fun together."

Knowing he's right I nod my head yes thinking of all the fun we could have together. With that I lean in and say, "How about you bring your riding crop over to my house tomorrow. I'll even make dinner."

Brian laughs, his smile widening. "That sounds like an amazing idea and I for one, cannot wait until tomorrow."

I see Rachel and Will walking towards us. They see the smile on my face so they know I'm okay. We decide that all of us have had enough of the club tonight. Making our way outside, Brian leans in and kisses the side of my temple.

"I'll see you tomorrow, beautiful. Be prepared to have a sore ass."

"I'll let you know on Sunday if I can sit or not."

With that he gives me that drop dead gorgeous smile and waves goodbye to Will and Rachel as he walks away. When I turn back to Rachel and Will, they're staring at me with curious looks on their faces, I raise my hand in response. "Don't ask!"

They laugh as we all get into the car. My mind is already focused on tomorrow and what kind of pleasure he will bring me. All of this time I never realized I had such hidden desires. Now to enjoy the new me because I sure plan to.

ABOUT THE AUTHOR

JM Schalm is a romance author and cover model.

Connect with JM

f facebook.com/julieemickschalm

SWEET FIRE

M.A. STONE

"I think there's something strangely musical about noise ... "
Trent Reznor

PROLOGUE

"Goooood morning Steel City! It's your crazy cool morning DJ Princess Rick with my own special blend to pump your adrenaline and get you movin' movin for that morning commute. I'll have Jenn with traffic but first your Morning Mosh report. Okey dokey artichokey my metal heads and social deviants. Just announced this morning, Cocaine and Abel will be launching a North American tour starting in the Steel City itself. So far, they have two venues booked, with the maiden voyage kicking off at Stage AE, where they got their first big break all those years ago. Tickets go on sale this Friday, so get your tix and send us the pics. Oh, and you know how we do . . . we'll be doing a giveaway for a VIP experience where you get to meet the front man of Cocaine and Abel! Stay tuned for details!"

1

GIGI

"*Oh* my gooooooodnesssss," I sang in my car, tapping my black painted fingernails on the steering wheel of my beat-up Jeep Wrangler. A commercial for a local open mic night played in the background as I pulled into my parking space at Battlefield, the tattoo/salon I co-owned with my brother from another mother, Judge. Grabbing my massive black purse and my travel mug of hot tea, I climbed out and practically danced up to the door. Jam, our other business partner, was furiously typing something out on his phone and then slid it angrily into the pocket of his low-slung skinny jeans.

"What's shakin' bacon?" I asked. Jam groaned and rolled his half-lidded eyes.

"Morning, Gigi. Today's a shit day," he muttered, not his usual cheerful self. I patted his shoulder and smiled at his *Bride of Franken-stein* tank that I would bet dollars to doughnuts; he'd drawn and designed himself.

"Female troubles?" I asked as he unlocked the door. He nodded.

"Yep, female troubles. ODB, if you piss on those flowers, I'm gonna whoop yer ass," he yelled at his five-year-old blue pit, who looked up and ambled as slowly as he could into the shop. I patted

473

ODB on the head and smiled when I was rewarded with a generous kiss from the gentle giant.

"Don't worry, ODB. Your Daddy is having problems with the ladies. You're still my number one guy," I told him as I set my mug down on my station and turned on the Keurig near the counter. Popping in a K Cup, I slid Jam's coffee mug with the wolf in place. The small area was soon filled with the aroma of coffee and I smiled. Grabbing the cup, I walked over to Jam, tapped him on the shoulder and thrust the mug in his direction. A wide grin stretched across his tattooed face and he grabbed me, kissing the top of my head.

"Marry me?" he asked. I giggled and wriggled away from him. Jam took a generous sip of the piping hot liquid and I shook my head.

"Maybe? Ask me again tomorrow," I told him as I grabbed some towels from the dryer and began to fold them. The door swung open and Judge walked in, yanking his jacket off and hanging it on the hook beside the door.

"Morning, Bestie. Did you hear the amazing news?" I sang to him as I handed him a mug with the words *Boss Daddy* on it. He smiled in thanks.

"Um let's see. Riordan's mom is going to stop stiffing me on child support? Or maybe she'll actually want to see her four-year-old son?" he snapped. I shook my head.

"Uh, no. Sorry, I wish I had news like that. I would love to make your day just by those words being true. You know what? It can wait. For later. Much, much later," I said as I walked to my side of the shop. Judge shrugged, grumbled something and went into his office. Jam came over to my side and sat in one of the vacant chairs.

"Tell Daddy all about it," he said as he rubbed his tattooed knee. I huffed a strand of kinky, curly hair out of my face and faced my side of the shop. Originally, the building had been two separate spaces. My side was a beauty salon while Judge's was a coffee shop. We bought the building, took down the wall separating the two business and Battlefield was born. Judge did tattoos and piercings while I and my fellow stylists, coiffed and cut the masses of Gettysburg, PA. I was one of the few people to do ethnic hair in the area and my clients loved not having to drive all the way to Baltimore. My side of the building was set up to look like an old school salon with teal and vintage pink undertones. Huge ornate mirrors decorated the four stations and there was a nice seating area with oversized stuffed pink couches. I sat down at my own personal station and sighed.

"Boy Toy blew me off again," I told him, referring to the much younger man I'd been seeing.

"Are you still seeing him? And when I say seeing him, I mean having sex with him," he asked, raising a pierced eyebrow. I nodded.

"He's 23, you're 32! You're old enough to be his teenage mama! What're you doing?" he asked, arms in the air. I sighed and rubbed at my forehead. I looked up at the mirror across from me and took myself in. Black leggings, cute dress with skull designs on it, curly black hair tied up in a crazy scarf on the top of my head; artfully applied makeup that offset my cocoa colored skin.

"I know. I tried telling him we should just be friends," I told him. Jam looked at me.

"And?"

"We ended up having sex again. Then he sends me messages telling me how 'addicted' he is to me and how he needs me," I moaned. Jam smirked.

"So, why haven't you seen him?" he asked. The question I'd been dreading.

"He still lives with his parents and they obviously don't know about me. I'm older than his big sister for chrissakes! And they are super conservative," I said as I made a face.

"Oh, honey child, what are you doing?" he asked, a weird expression on his face.

"I even offered to get a hotel room for this weekend. But guess what? He's a Civil War re-enactor and he's got that to do this weekend!" I yelled. Jam barked out a laugh.

"What does this man child do for you?" he asked. I bit my bottom lip and thought about it for a moment.

"Amazing orgasms, nice dick. Makes me feel beautiful and not like a potato. I haven't felt beautiful in *forever*," I told him. Jam smiled and walked over, pulling me into his arms. My head rested against his chest and I could hear the steady thump of his heartbeat. He smelled like chocolate and home. I sighed happily.

"Good sex isn't everything. You should *never* be anyone's second option. That's what happens when you do that stupid 'friends with benefits' crap. You end up being an option instead of the only choice. You need to sever ties and stop thinking with your lady boner," he told me with a raised eyebrow. I nodded against his chest, knowing he was one hundred percent right in what he was saying. Pulling back, I wiped my nose with the back of my hand and sighed.

"You *are* beautiful, and I can say that honestly without having ever been inside your 'sugar walls'," he teased. I groaned, rolling my eyes. Jam laughed and patted the top of my head.

"Thanks, Jam. You're the best!" I told him as I kissed his cheek and straightened my dress. We both looked over to see Judge at the counter, studying us.

"*C*ome on! You seriously want me to believe that a man could stop an airplane with his hair?" screeched Jimmy, the only barber in my shop. Applying color to my client's hair, I nodded. Jimmy crossed his tattooed arms over his chest, making his muscles in his arms bulge. He was a handsome guy, but too pretty boy for me with his gelled blonde faux hawk, tanned skin and artfully ripped skinny jeans.

"No way," he scoffed. I looked at him over my shoulder.

"Joseph Greenstein also known as *The Mighty Atom*. I watched a documentary on him last night. You know what, we need to educate ourselves. Nothin' wrong with a little culture," I told him, making him grin.

"Culture huh?" he teased. My client giggled. She was a regular and knew about my supposed battles with Jimmy.

"Jimmy, let me tell you somethin'. Cheetos and Boone's Farm is not fine dinin'. And just because you watch Japanese anime with the

476

subtitles, don't make you cultured," I told him. Jimmy put his head down and laughed, his client chucking.

"Ok fine then. How about music tastes? You listen to some sick shit, my darling," he told me. His client, a young black man who was getting braids, booed.

"Cocaine and Abel, Sweet Mercy, Molly Pumpers, Marilyn Manson and Black Veil Brides. What in the hell is wrong with that?" I asked. My older brother, Voight, came over and sat down in the empty chair beside me.

"Damn girl, what ever happened to listening to Aretha?" Jimmy's client asked me. I rolled my eyes.

"Stereotype right there. Just because I'm a Sista doesn't mean I have to Motown it up to please you," I shot back. Jimmy smirked and his client held his hands up in surrender. I looked at my brother and smiled.

"Look at you, looking like Shemar Moore," I teased him. My brother was six three, lean and muscular with a shaved head and long black lashes. He had our mama's blue eyes though, or so I'd been told. He really did look like a lighter skinned Shemar Moore, if Shemar had his septum pierced and was covered in ink.

"What are ya'll arguing about now?" he asked in his soft, rough voice. Voight rarely spoke and when he did, it was quietly and some- times only to me.

"Your baby sister has crap taste in music. All she wants to do is listen to that kitten killing music," called out Jimmy. Voight smirked and I was able to see the cute as a button dimples he had.

"As opposed to you being vetoed for life from playing music in the shop because all you wanted to play was Caravan Palace and one song from In This Moment?" I shot back. Voight pointed at Jimmy and nodded.

"Caravan Palace is the tits!" squeaked Jimmy. His client frowned.

"Yeah it is, if you're a sex trafficker or you're going to challenge someone to a dance off. Face it, Jimmy, you may think my music taste is 'kitten killing music', but yours is abysmal," I told him. Tapping my client on the shoulder, I smiled down at her.

"I'm going to let you set for a bit, honey. You want a magazine or water?" I asked her. She shook her head and I set the timer on my phone. Voight followed me over to the color bar where I rinsed out the bowl I'd just used.

"You enter the contest?" he asked. I swished water around in the sink and looked at him.

"Don't play dumb. You've loved and followed that band for *ten* years, Gigi. You know you'd give your eye teeth to actually meet one of the members," he told me. I nodded.

"I entered when I got to work. But I have the worst luck. I'll be happy just to go to the concert. You want to go?" I asked. Voight grinned and shook his head.

"Not that I would admit it to his face, but Jimmy's right, that music is *awful*," he said with a soft laugh. I stuck my tongue out at him and he patted me on the shoulder.

"Lunch?" I called after him. He nodded and walked back over to his side of the shop.

"Why do you two feel the need to remove your shoes when you eat?" complained Judge as he dipped a fry in his ranch that came with his chicken fingers. Jam and I sat under the big tree behind the shop and wiggled our toes. Sunshine glittered through the leaves and make intricate patterns on our skin.

"Studies have shown people who go barefoot are healthier. Studies have also shown that bare feet are essential to brain and nervous system development. It all deals with sending messages to the brain about body orientation," Jam stated. I nodded and sighed happily.

"It's true. I read the article on it. And no, before you ask, it wasn't some weirdo internet article. I read in in my chiropractor's office and asked him a ton of questions," I added. Jam nodded and grinned widely before biting into his burrito.

"Thank you, Voight, for driving to get us burritos," I said as I eyed the massive burrito, he'd picked up for me. It had to be at least four inches wide and six inches long; stuffed with shrimp and steak goodness.

"And you wore a dress today, so no whining about taking off your pants after you eat that monster," Judge told me. I grinned as I took a huge bite of my lunch. Swallowing, I wiped my mouth with the back of my hand.

"It was one time!" I complained. Jam shook his head.

"You were behind the counter, trying to figure out a way to work without your pants on. We all heard you," he told me. I flipped him off and took another huge bite of my burrito; moaning.

"So good," I said as I wiped my mouth with a napkin.

"Love it when you make those sounds," muttered Jam. Voight gave him a dirty look and Judge shook his head, laughing.

"You have to admit, she does moan kind of sexy," added Jam, not realizing if looks could kill, the ones my brother was sending his way would have leveled him in a millisecond.

"Thank you, Jam. Much appreciated. Maybe you could pass that on to Boy Toy who thinks running around in the dirt is sexier than I am," I replied. Jam nodded.

"I'll send him a sex picture, that'll get him motivated," he replied, finishing up his burrito.

"A sex picture?" I asked. He nodded and wadded up his burrito wrapper.

"Yeah. I'm gonna need one of your ass though, that way I can photo shop it in such a way that it looks like we're having sex," he told me, his face serious.

"Over my dead body," grumbled Voight. Judge barked out a laugh and tossed his trash out in the garbage can.

"I'm trying to help her out, Voight. You know I wouldn't use it for my own personal use," he told him. Voight tossed out this trash and stormed back into the shop.

"He needs to lighten up," muttered Jam. I nodded.

"He does. I'm not fourteen anymore and we're not living in a foster home. We're safe and he needs to understand that. Hey, I have a question," I said. He raised an eyebrow.

"Shoot," he told me.

"Want to go to the Cocaine and Abel concert with me? I'll buy your ticket," I told him. He looked thoughtful for a minute and then rubbed his shin.

"Sure. It'll be fun and I'll get to check out all the pale, black-clad ladies. I bet you there are tons of girlies with daddy issues in attendance," he said with a grin. I shoved his shoulder playfully which only widened his smile.

Fridays were usually super duper busy at the shop and I sighed in relief as I swept the floor at eight that night. Barefoot, I hummed to myself as I heard Jam singing a Billie Eilish song. Quickly, I swept up the hair and deposited it in the trashcan at the back. ODB laid on one of my pink couches, snoring. Putting away the broom, I switched on some Cocaine and Abel, playing it low as I closed everything out at my counter.

"ODB, tonight calls for some chocolate cake, the seven-inch high kind from Three Hogs. With a big old glass of Type 2 sweet tea," I told him. He chuffed out a response and yawned. Closing out my computer, I grabbed the day's receipts and bank bag; shuffling over to Judge's office to deposit it into the safe for him. He usually did the bank drop at night, saying that the neighborhood was too sketchy for me to do it by myself. I didn't argue, not when it came to Judge-logic. Grabbing my purse, my shoes and my car keys, I waved to Judge and Jam before walking out the door to the shop. Glancing down at my phone, I saw that there weren't any messages nor missed calls. Sighing, I climbed in my Jeep and started her up.

"Chocolate cake, here I come," I muttered as I pulled out of my space.

2

ABEL

*S*itting down in front of the massive mirror in the dressing room, I looked into my hazel eyes, dark rings under them from lack of sleep. I was always way too amped up to get any sort of rest the night before a tour kicked off. I could get to sleep; I could just never stay asleep. Even with the meds my doc prescribed. My skin thrummed with invisible electric energy and I licked my lips. Flexing my fingers, I shook my head from side to side; working out the kinks. I ran a hand through my long black hair, then ran a finger over my lips that were painted black. Argus McFinley, our drummer, walked behind me, shirtless and rhythmically slapping his sticks into the palm of his left hand; hair wild. Cain Berringer, my bassist was talking furiously on the phone; an angry expression on his face. Loen Gardener, my rhythm guitarist, slid into the chair next to me. His dark eyes danced, and I grinned at the Nirvana t-shirt he was wearing; it was of Hanson, with Nirvana under it. He loved ordering weird shit from Wish.

"Excited, mate?" he asked me. I shrugged.

"Abel?" he asked. I looked at my oldest friend and nodded.

"This was where it all began, Loen. I just have this weird feeling though," I admitted. Loen, with his spikey white-blonde hair and crystal blue eyes; cocked an eyebrow.

"Something's brewing. I feel it. I just don't have a good feeling," I told him. Loen looked over his shoulder a minute and then back at me.

"You and me both, brother. I couldn't sleep last night with worry. After this concert, we'll talk, yeah?"

"Yeah. Let's do this concert and then the VIP meet and greet after," I reminded him. He nodded and grinned.

"Let's rock the socks off this place," he said, hopping up and punching me lightly on the shoulder. Laughing, I stood and followed him to the corridor that would lead us to the stage.

"Thank you, Pittsburg! We'll be in you for two more shows and then it's on to Ohio! You guys fucking rock!!!!" I yelled as I pumped my fist in the air; to the roar of the crowd filled the venue. Loen nodded beside me and we handed our guitars off to the roadies.

"Stellar show, mates!" called Loen, raising his fist in the air. Argus chugged a water and dried his sweaty torso off with a towel. Cain just stalked ahead of us, not saying a word.

"What crawled up his ass?" asked Angus, pointing to Cain. Loen and I both shrugged. Cain was in a rocky relationship and had been on edge lately. He was either holed up in his room at the hotels or glued to his phone; talking in hushed whispers.

"Let's go do this VIP shit and get to the hotel," I muttered. Loen nodded. We made a beeline for the dressing room and I changed out of my sweaty tank and replaced it with a red t-shirt with a diagram of an actual heart on it. Sliding my phone into the pocket of my pants, I walked down the hall to the VIP room. Tall, skinny model-type women in barely there clothing huddled up with guys in suits and various other non-descript people littered the large room. A huge table with food on it and drinks was in the middle of the room.

Loen was already there, piling his plate with sandwiches and cookies.

"Doesn't your mother feed ya?" I teased. Loen nodded and shoved a Twizzler in his mouth.

"Aye, she does. Same old shit here, I see," he nodded toward the pretty people and the bottom feeders.

"I sometimes wish an actual fan of our music would come to one of these. It'd be refreshing," he commented before backing into someone. A feminine whimper met my ears as Loen crunched down on her foot with his heavy boots.

"Oh my god, lass. Forgive me. Wow, you're a pretty one!" he told the women standing in front of him. She wasn't a model, she had ample curves that a model would scoff at. Her long black waves were piled on her head with a red bandanna tied around it. She was wearing a simple, spaghetti-strapped red dress and flip flops. Her pretty, heart-shaped face was screwed up in pain as she stood on one leg. She looked like she would fit in more at a country music festival than one of my concerts, if not for the ink literally covering her arms and chest. She had large green eyes with impossibly long lashes and full, pouty lips.

"Do you always assault the women you think are attractive, honey? I'd hate to see what you do to the ones you think are ugly," she said in a sassy southern accent before she sank down onto a couch beside the table.

"Not usually. You're the first," he replied, sitting next to her. Shaking my head, I walked over and looked down at her foot.

"Who wears flip flops to a concert?" I asked. She looks up at me, gets a starstruck look in her eyes and then quickly recovered. She looked me up and down; sneering.

"What are you? The fashion police?" she snapped back. Loen chuckled.

"Flip flops are probably the worst footwear on the planet. They're terrible for your feet and can actually cause you to break an ankle," I retorted. She snorted and it was fucking adorable.

"Thanks, *Dad*. I'll make sure to remember that. And you two wonder why no actual fans come to these things. One of you is rude as hell and the other one stomps all over people like a bloody giant!" she laughed. Loen smirked and I had to let out a short laugh.

"Oh my goodness! Abel can smile and he even has a sense of humor! Alert the media!" she teased, like she'd known me for years. Loen elbowed me in the ribs and cackled.

"I like her!" proclaimed Loen. I crossed my arms over my chest and nodded.

"Enjoy the show?" I asked her. She nodded and grinned widely.

"It was better than the first one!" she said, her large green eyes full of light.

"First one?" I asked. She nodded enthusiastically.

"Loen? Ice, please?" she told my bandmate, who immediately hopped up to honor her request.

"Yes. I saw you guys here when you first performed. It was good but you guys have really improved over the past ten years. I'm a bit of a fan and was super stoked when I won the radio contest to get two VIP tickets," she told me. Loen came back with a bag of ice wrapped in a paper towel. He handed it to the Mystery Girl and she graced him with a kind, welcoming smile.

"Two tickets? So, you're not here by yourself then?" I asked. She shook her head and pointed to a skinny, heavily tattooed man with his hair up in a man bun and an inked-up face. He was talking to two model -types and he raised his bottle of water to us; a gleeful grin on his face.

"Boyfriend?" asked Loen. Mystery Girl shook her head.

"Nope, he's my best friend. We work together. Thank you for the ice, Loen. And thank you both for the show. It was truly great!" she said with a sincere smile.

"Name?" I asked. She looked confused.

"What's your name?" I asked. Before she could answer, the door to the VIP room burst open and reporters busted in.

"Abel, is it true that your bassist Cain Berringer was arrested tonight after the show?"

"Abel what do you have to say to the numerous allegations of child sexual assault by your bassist?"

"Are you guys cancelling the tour?"

"Did you know your bassist was sneaking underage girls back to his hotel room while you were on tour?"

"Are you guys disbanding?"

I looked at Loen and he was just . . . *gone.* I felt someone grab my arm and I looked down at Mystery Girl. She gave me a determined look and motioned with her head.

"Come on, we're getting outta here," she told me and practically dragged me away. We went out a doorway at the back of the room and I let out a breath as the door slammed shut behind us. She limped down the cinderblock lined hallway.

"Come on, Rock Star, we've only got minutes before they follow you. I know some place where they won't find you," she told me. She grabbed her bandanna, untied it and quickly tied it around my head. She grabbed sunglasses out of the pocket of her dress and slid them on my face. She yanked on the waist of my skinny jeans until they were snugly cupping the underside of my ass. She grabbed her phone and hurriedly texted. Sliding it back in the pocket of her dress, she looked at me.

"You look crazy, but you don't look like a rock star," she told me as she dragged me down the hallway. We exited onto the street and climbed into an orange Jeep that was waiting for us. Tattooed Guy was behind the wheel.

"Where to, peeps?" he asked. Mystery Girl smiled from the back seat.

"Home, Jam. They'll never think to look for him there," she said. I sighed and buckled my seatbelt.

"*A*re you kidding me? Are you fucking kidding me? I am at an utter loss for words!" I screeched as I paced around the living room of my hotel suite, the tv showing the destruction of my life on a constant loop. My black pit-bull, Sugarlips, whined from one of the couches and I walked over; rubbing the top of her head.

"Sorry, baby. Daddy's just having a nervous breakdown," I told her. She licked my hand and thumped her tail against the couch. Running my hands through my long black hair, I wanted to rip it from the roots. I could already feel a fucking migraine coming on like a freight train.

"I can see why you'd be getting a migraine, with the way you're tuggin' at your hair," said a soft voice. Sugarlips hopped off the couch and walked over to Mystery Girl, plopping at her feet.

"Your guard dog is broken," she said as she knelt and loved on my dog. Standing, I noticed she was wearing a long t-shirt that'd slid off her shoulder, exposing smooth, cocoa skin.

"That's Sugarlips. Now you know her name, pray tell, what's yours love?" I asked her. She smiled and sat down on one of the couches.

"Gigi. My name is Gigi Simone," she said with a smile. I sat on the couch opposite her and resisted the urge to grab my hair.

"Nice to meet you, love. So how did we end up here at my place? And where's your friend?" I asked. She grinned.

"Well, honey, your life pretty much fell apart last night, am I right?" she asked. I nodded.

"My plan is to take you back home with me after I have Jam check you out of the hotel. He can pose as your assistant and no one would bat an eyelash," she told me calmly and evenly.

"Are you a nutter?" I asked. She grinned, showing beautiful dimples.

"Nope. I'm as sane as a country preacher. I live in the middle of nowhere. No one would think someone like you would slum it in the backwoods while you hide out from the shit show your bandmate caused," she told me. She grabbed the remote and switched off the TV.

"You don't need to marinate in that negative stuff. From what you told me last night, the label put the tour on hold indefinitely and Cain is MIA now," she stated. I nodded, my stomach churning. I stood up and ran for the bathroom; falling to my knees and losing the contents of my stomach. After staring at the ornate floor tiles for what seemed like a millennia, I stood up, rinsed out my mouth and walked out into the living room.

"You okay?" she asked, her voice soft and full of concern. I nodded and then shook my head.

"I'm not a namby pamby little mama's boy. Not in the least. But the things they're accusing him of, I can't push that aside nor can I defend it. They have his laptop, his phone. They have factual evidence!" I yelled. Gigi nodded.

"Have you talked to any other band members?" she asked. I nodded.

"Loen is on the first flight home. His wife is pregnant and due any day. He's taking advantage of this. Told me he couldn't sleep and kicked a hole in the wall of his hotel room. Thinks he broke his foot," I replied. Gigi smirked.

"Sorry, it's not funny, but it kind of is," she laughed. I nodded.

"He's a definite nutter," I laughed, feeling a bit lighter for the first time. I sat down on the couch and sighed.

"We were supposed to have this big conversation, Loen and I. That's not happening now. Maybe going to your town or what ever it is, is a grand idea," I told her. She nodded and stood; her long legs unfolding and making my heart race a bit. What can I say? I'm a leg man.

"I'll go get dressed and we'll get our game plan together for today. You might need to call your people and make arrangements," she told me over her shoulder as she walked toward the other bedrooms. I stared after the firecracker that'd inserted herself into my life and couldn't help but chuckle.

3

GIGI

"That's your plan? Bring him back to Gettysburg?" squeaked Jam as he shrugged his t-shirt over his head. I'd showered quickly and shrugged on my dress from last night. My dress smelled like a concert; that earthy, excited smell.

"Pretty much. And besides, I don't live in Gettysburg, I just work there," I told him. Jam rolled his eyes.

"Potato, tomato," he snapped back.

"That's not the . . . you know what, never mind," I told him. Jam slid his feet into his Vans that were decorated with flamingos and ran his fingers through his messy hair; tying it up on the top of his head.

"You're going to leave a rock star alone in that wilderness you call a house?" he asked. I nodded and slung my purse over one shoulder.

"He'll get to relax, enjoy the quiet. Easy peasey, lemon squeezy," I told him. He shook his head and looked at me with his warm, soulful eyes.

"Why?"

"His whole life just imploded. Nuclear. I've been there. You know, when someone lights a fuse inside a gasoline can and your world is decimated? Yeah, I can relate to that, Jam. I saw the people around him who scattered like roaches the minute someone shined a light on

488

him and his band. He needs some people in his corner," I told him. He nodded and gave me a hug.

"You need to protect yourself too. Remember that, ok? Don't go in ass over tits and get yourself decimated again," he told me. I nodded and pushed him towards the door.

"We have to get back," I told him, not really in the mood for all the touchy-feely stuff. Jam smirked and whistled as he walked out into the living room.

"Sugarlips, stop licking him!" groaned Abel as we drove towards home. Jam laughed and patted her on the head as he turned onto the turnpike.

"She's fine, really. I have two big ol doppy pit bulls at home myself. Bonnie and Clyde. Big old lovers, the two of them," Jam told him. Abel just nodded.

"What is it that you two do, exactly?" asked Abel. I smiled.

"I co-own a business with my friend, Judge. He runs a tattoo parlor and I own a salon. Jam is a rockin' artist as well as a tattooing god," I replied. Abel nodded.

"That sounds great," he replied genuinely before yawning. His face looked pale and drawn; showing to me that he hadn't been sleeping.

"So, you live out in the woods?" he asked. I nodded and brushed a strand of hair off my forehead.

"Yep. I bought a farmette a few years ago. I wanted a big house and that's what I got," I said absently as Jam took the exit for my town. Abel was quiet, not really wanting to talk. His phone kept pinging and he ignored it. Soon, we were driving down Main Street.

"Welcome to Ardent Hills," I told him as he looked out the window. People walked slowly down the sidewalk, window shopping. Jam turned down the road that would lead to my house and looked at me out of the corner of his eye. Trees soon replaced houses and buildings. The road began to get windy and Abel's eyes widened.

"You live out here?" he asked, his eyes round. I smiled.

"Yep," I said, my stomach a ball of nerves. Jam smirked.

"You like to live where the people aren't, don't you, love?" he commented. I laughed. Jam turned down a hidden road and I smiled at the trees that lined both sides of the road; grown up to make a natural canopy of green loveliness. The sun shone through gaps in the branches and birds hopped in trees here and there.

"I love it out here," I sighed.

"It's so . . . green," whispered Abel in awe. I nodded. Jam took the sharp turn in to my lane and I waited for Abel's reaction. Soon, my sprawling, two story log cabin with massive side deck came into view. The large floor to ceiling windows on the front of the house glittered in the sunlight. My brother, Voight, was sitting on the deck, glowering.

"Uh, who's big man on the deck"? asked Abel nervously. I sighed and rolled my eyes as we came to a stop in front of my house.

"That's Voight," I muttered as I got out of the car.

"What's a Voight?" he asked; following me.

"He's my big brother. He's protective," I replied. Jam snickered and I shot him a dirty look. Sugarlips inspected the property and huffed in approval. Voight stood up, set down his coffee mug on the table and crossed his arms over his chest. He shot a murderous look at Abel and Jam laughed.

"Shut up," I hissed. Jam shook his head.

"Uh uh. He's going to kill you," he replied. I shook my head.

"You're an accomplice, you're equally in trouble," I shot back; his face paling. Abel walked right up to my brother, hand out and a confident grin on his face.

"Hey there, mate. Name's Abel," he said. Voight walked right on past Abel, grunting.

"Gigi," he said in warning. I held up a hand and sighed when his chest plowed into it.

"Voight," I said. Abel stood there, shocked.

"What did you do?" he asked, his face inches from mine. I sighed.

"His life blew up, Voight. He needed a safe haven," I whispered. Voight closed his eyes and murmured something under his breath.

"Hey purty mama boy. Come give me some sugar!" called out a mature feminine voice. Voight's eyes flew open and he groaned. I smiled. Abel turned to look at the source of the voice and choked back a laugh. I lived with our aunt, Didi. She was short, round and dressed in black leggings and a white tank top. Her skin was pale and dotted with freckles and her black hair was piled high on her head. She was talking to one of Voight's dog, Sawdust's, puppies. A little, black pit-bull puppy waddled over to her and nuzzled her bare foot.

"Is she from the South?" asked Abel. I shook my head.

"Voight got tired of her talking 'baby talk' to the puppies and their mama Sawdust. So she came up with a better idea. Talk to them in a southern accent when she felt like 'baby talk' was necessary," I explained. Abel raised an eyebrow.

"Not as annoying then?" he asked. Voight shook his head.

"About as annoying as a stranger showing up on my sister's doorstep," he said softly before brushing past us. Abel's eyebrows raised and Jam patted him on the shoulder.

"He'll warm up to you," he told him. I snickered. Aunt Didi shielded her eyes with her hand and frowned in our direction.

"Let's go meet my crazy aunt. She'll love Sugarlips," I muttered as I grabbed his elbow and dragged him up to the deck. This was not my best idea, but if it provided him with refuge, I was all for it.

Sorry for the cliffhanger, folks. Truly. Please keep your eyes peeled for the full-length version of this story in Sweet Fire- coming your way in 2020. Thanks for reading!!!

ABOUT THE AUTHOR

M.A. Stone has been writing and making up stories ever since she was a little girl and she got her Sesame Street coloring books taken away for filling them with dirty words. She was born and raised in Upstate NY(which oddly makes her sound like she is from Wisconsin)and has moved around all over the east coast.She currently lives in South Central PA with her amazingly sarcastic husband and her four incredibly entertaining children. Oh and her dog who weighs over 90 pounds, but thinks she is a Shi Tzu.

Connect with M.A.

facebook.com/Author-MAStone

JERSEY
LOVE

COURTNEY LYNN ROSE

1

SUZETTE

*W*ant to know what's worse than trying to squeeze a set of tits bigger than Double-Ds into a woman's cut football jersey? Having to watch the Playoffs and root for my team in the town of the team I'm rooting against. Men tend to find it strange when they realize how much I enjoy watching football. I'm from Baltimore though, and the Ravens are my jam. I've driven over five hours to meet my best friend Ja'Vana for the game, and nothing burns my ass more than the black and yellow Steelers shit hanging outside Carson City Saloon.

It's the price I have to pay for girl time though. Ja'Vana moved here a year ago, and while we keep in touch through text and Facebook, it's the first time we're getting to really hang out. After finding a parking spot, I get out and stash my license and bank card in my bra, lock the car and slide my keys and phone into my back pockets. Opening the bar door, a million voices assault my ears and I roll my eyes as I squeeze in, searching the room for my friend.

I spot a tall, voluptuous, ebony-skinned woman standing on the opposite side of the room. I know its Ja'Vana by the ombre black to purple hair color. Thank god she's rocking her Ravens gear still. Her jersey reads Flacco with the number seven on the back. I grin as I

497

make my way, bobbing and weaving between people. She has worn Flacco's jersey since he joined the team, and I've worn Lewis, number fifty-two.

"Thank god you ain't wearing that ugly ass black and yellow, bitch," I say coming up behind her.

She spins around with a huge smile on her face, setting her bottle on the bar to wrap her arms around my neck. Ja'Vana towers over me. She always has considering I've been five-foot-seven since we were in ninth grade. She's well over five-foot-ten, and usually wears heels of some sort. I, on the other hand, am rocking my Jordans with jeans. If this was a little less busy of a bar, I might have opted for a dress with my jersey over it, but I am trying to not have to smack a bunch of ass-grabbing mother fuckers.

"Hell no, hooker. I may live in the land of black and yellow, but you know my heart bleeds purple."

I laugh loudly as she turns and signals the bartender. A short blonde comes over to stand across from us. "What can I get ya, doll?"

"Bud Light, please," I say, moving to get my ID out.

"Put it on my tab, Cecile," a deep voice says from the other side of me.

Ja'Vana and I both turn and my jaw drops. The man standing next to me has to be at least six inches taller than me with short cropped dirty-blonde hair and eyes so fucking blue they'd make the ocean itself jealous. His biceps strain the sleeves of the Pittsburgh jersey he's wearing. It hugs his body just right down to a taut waist and thick thighs clad in dark blue jeans.

"Sue, this is Adam. We work together. Adam, this is my best friend from back home Suzette," Ja'Vana lays her hand on my shoulder and squeezes.

This guy holds his hand out, and like a robot, I take it to shake, unable to take my eyes away from his. The smirk on his face screams bad decisions, and that's one thing everyone knows about me— I'm the fucking Queen of bad decisions.

2

ADAM

♥

*J*a'Vana forgot to mention how smokin' fucking hot her friend was when she said she was coming up for the game. This woman is all short and curved, mocha skin with kinky, curly hair and the biggest doe-brown eyes I've ever seen. I'm leaning against the bar trying to hide how hard my dick is.

When the bartender comes back with her beer, I hold mine up for her to tap. She does with a smile on her face and then brings it to her lips and chugs half of it. My cock twitches and I take a sip of my beer as a distraction.

"So," I say setting my beer on the bar while keeping my hand around it. "Let's talk about that terrible choice of jersey you're wearing."

Suzette bursts out laughing and mimics my stance. "Not sure if you looked in the mirror tonight, but the only terrible choice of jersey is yours."

I look down at my Steelers jersey and then scan the crowded bar that is literally filled with black and yellow before bringing my eyes back to meet hers, a look of mock confusion on my face. "Listen, gorgeous, maybe you forgot where you are, but black and yellow is the sexiest fucking color in here."

Suzette snickers and rolls her eyes before taking a draw off her beer. It makes me smile. "Yeah, well, this whole town seems to have bad taste."

I step forward and lean my mouth down next to her ear. "Maybe in football teams, but wanting to taste you tells me I have good taste in some things."

As I straighten back up, I smirk as her cheeks redden, her mouth hanging open a little. I'm not oblivious to the way she squirms as she takes another sip of her drink or the way she just squeezed her thighs together.

I want to say more and watch her reaction, but the surround sound in the bar kicks on as the beginning of the Playoffs comes on the multiple flat screens hung throughout the space. Suzette turns toward the closest one, putting her back to me.

Taking a few steps closer to her, I gently slide my hand around her hip and press my hard-on into her ass. I know its forward, but that's just me. When I see something I want, I make a move, and I've always been good at reading women.

She doesn't move out of my embrace, and it's comfortable standing with her like this as we watch the beginning of the game. When they announce the Ravens players, she and Ja'Vana hoot and holler, and some of the bar patrons boo. Some of our co-workers take jabs at the girls, and it's hot how they both fire right back.

Just as the kick-off happens, I lean forward and kiss the side of her neck. She tilts her head to give me better access, so I run my tongue across her skin. Just as I get to her earlobe, I gasp as she discreetly puts her hand between us and rubs my cock through my jeans.

"Keep that up and we are going to miss part of this game," I whisper in her ear.

Suzette turns her head toward me just enough that I can see the smirk on her lips.

3

SUZETTE

*I*f the bulge against my hand is any real indication of what this man is working with, I'm super inclined to let him make it so I can't walk. My hand is resting against the crotch of his jeans and every time he shifts, I flex my hand to massage his dick.

As much as I want to watch the game, I want to find out how hard Adam can fuck.

His hand covers mine and gently, he moves it away from him, wrapping both our arms around the front of me as he kisses my neck again. "Let's pretend to at least watch some of the game before I make an excuse to take you back to my apartment."

I chuckle and lace my fingers with his. "Do you fuck all the women you meet the same night as learning their name?"

"Only the ones I'm feigning to taste, gorgeous."

A shiver runs down my spine just as Ja'Vana turns around. She glances down at Adam's arms wrapped around me and then back to my eyes with one of her brows raised. I shrug and she rolls her eyes with a smile. I do my absolute best to focus on the game and not Adam at my back.

That's way easier said than done though.

By halftime, he's already damn near made me cum once just

rubbing my pussy through my jeans. "You keep that up, and seriously, neither of us is going to see the end of this game."

I give him a grin as I lean forward and tell Ja'Vana I'm going outside for a smoke. I'm not the least bit surprised when Adam follows me outside, his hand cupped around my hip the entire way through the bar. As soon as we step outside, he pulls me around the corner and out of sight.

The breath is knocked out of me as he spins me around and pushes me against the brick building, his lips crashing down on mine, muffling my moan. I almost explode when he grabs me by the ass and lifts me, wrapping my legs around his waist. He bites my bottom lip and grinds his cock into me, causing me to throw my head back and groan his name.

"Let's make a deal," he says against my neck. "Steelers win, you come back to my place. Ravens win, I pay for a hotel room for you to stay the night."

I can't help but chuckle. "You realize we end up fucking in either of those scenarios?"

He grinds into me again and bites my neck harder than I anticipate. "Yep. Only difference is whether or not I get to take you in my bed."

"Mmmmm. You keep doing this and we aren't doing either, because I'm going to get real fucking grimy and bend over in this alley and let you take me." And I'm not fucking kidding. Wouldn't be the first time in my life I did some shit like that.

Adam chuckles again against my skin but stops all other movements. His breathing is as hard as mine and as he lets me back down on my foot, I can't help but reach out and palm his cock again through his jeans.

A smile spreads across my face and he closes his eyes, tilts his head back, and groans. "Fuck, woman."

4

ADAM

*W*atching Suzette leaning against the wall smoking her cigarette is sexy as shit. Not going to lie, she looks like something out of a music video. This woman has curves and cushion in literally all the right places. I know a lot of men like these stick-figure women, but I can't.

I fuck hard, and I need a chick that can take that. Bone on bone ain't never felt good. I want something I can sink into and hold. I want to grab hips and not worry about fracturing the bone from my grip. I wouldn't have those worries with Suzette. Mmmm-mmm.

"So, I'm gonna assume the answers no, but I'm gonna ask anyway," I say, taking a drag off my own smoke. "You got a man back where you live?"

Suzette snort laughs. "Do you think I'd be grabbing on your dick if I did? I ain't one of them bitches. When I'm with a man, I'm with him. That's it. When I'm single, I do what the fuck I want."

I like the fire in her voice. I want to hear that with her on her knees and my hands fisted in her hair.

"I didn't mean anything by that, Suzette. Not all chicks are faithful, ya know?"

Her beautiful brown eyes meet mine, and it's hard to miss the tinge of pain that rims the outside of them. "Yeah, well, all men ain't faithful either. You got a girl?"

"I do for tonight," I say in a low voice. Her eyes find mine and I toss my smoke before taking a few steps to close the space between us, grab her face, tangling my fingers in her hair, and crashing my lips to her.

She chuckles against my mouth. "You do tonight."

"Yo, halftime is over. Y'all can fuck later."

Suzette and I both turn toward the voice and burst out laughing. Ja'Vana is at the end of the alley, hand on her hip, with serious attitude pasted on that mug of hers.

"Alright, alright, calm down, bitch," Suzette says tossing her cigarette and sliding her hand into mine as she pulls me toward her best friend and my co-worker.

The three of us head back inside and make it back to our other co-workers just as the game picks back up. I keep Suzette close to me as we cheer, talk shit to one another, and just enjoy the game. I've never been with a chick that actually likes sports of any kind. I have a nasty habit of dating these high maintenance, prissy types, and they all end the same way.

The bitch cheating.

That's why I have stayed single for so long. I ain't got time for that shit at my age anymore. But as I listen to Suzette and Ja'Vana talk and reminisce about all the shit they have gotten into during their friendship, I can't help but feel something about this chick is different.

She's got this attitude, this spunk, that is contagious. I can tell she thinks differently than most women. This isn't a chick that's gotten where she is easy. She's hard but just enough. Not completely cut off from her emotions, but more in control of them.

And her confidence. Fuck me, that shit makes her the sexiest fucking thing in Pittsburgh as far as I'm concerned.

5

SUZETTE

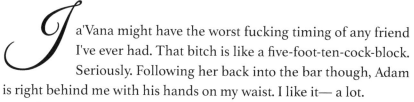

a'Vana might have the worst fucking timing of any friend I've ever had. That bitch is like a five-foot-ten-cock-block. Seriously. Following her back into the bar though, Adam is right behind me with his hands on my waist. I like it— a lot.

I don't give a shit which team wins, as long as I get to have this man in a bed at the end of the night, I will take the loss for my team. Which is funny within itself, because usually, I wouldn't put anything before a Ravens win, especially against the Steelers. But, this one time, I think the football gods will forgive me.

"You want another drink," he whispers in my ear once we get back to the bar.

The second half kick-off just happened, and Ravens have the ball. Okay, I may have thought I didn't care, but I still want my boys to win.

"Yeah," I say turning my head toward him so he can hear me over the bar noise. "But it's my last one, I have to drive."

His lips press gently against my ear. "My last one too then."

I jump and smile as his hand connects with my ass. Ain't nothing like being with a man that knows exactly how much pain to inflict on my ass and when. I hum to myself, appreciating all the delicious images running through my head.

"So," Ja'Vana says turning to face me and messing up my daydreams.

"So, what?"

"You gonna fuck my coworker?"

"If she doesn't I'm gonna be pissed at you, J," Adam says with a little attitude as he wraps his arm around me, holding two beers in front. I take one of them and take a sip.

"If this shit between you two goes sideways or gets complicated, and I get stuck in the middle, I'm gonna fuck both y'all asses up, for real."

Adam snickers and I chuckle. "Damn, 'Vana, you act like I ain't ever had a one night stand before. Go calm ya ass and let the adults do what they want."

She rolls her eyes and turns around to the television just as the Ravens score a touchdown. The groans and boos through the bar make us both laugh. I turn to Adam with a knowing smirk on my face. "Boo-yah."

He shakes his head and grabs my belt loop to yank my body to his. "Don't get cocky yet, gorgeous, game ain't over."

He kisses me before we turn around and continue to watch the game. The Steelers end up getting two more touchdowns, while the Ravens get one more. By the time the clock winds down to five minutes left in the fourth quarter, it's the Ravens ball on the forty-yard-line, and the Steelers are ahead by one fucking touchdown.

As much as I've been trying to concentrate on the game, Adam's comments have the crotch of my panties and jeans fucking soaked, and I am ready to take him out back and fuck him stupid.

"I have a very, very nice set of straps that attach to my bed. You are going to look fucking amazing tied to it," he whispers in my ear, his tongue darting out as he nips at the lobe.

A shiver runs through my body and I groan, grinding my ass back into him at the same time the Ravens incur a penalty.

Well, at least that was hidden by good timing.

6

ADAM

*T*he Steelers won.

Suzette is in my car, and we're on our way to my place. I had her lock hers up and leave it at the bar. Partly because I didn't want her driving because she ended up having another drink, and also because I don't want her trying to sneak off in the middle of the night.

I've picked up enough to know that Suzette probably doesn't do sleepovers or relationships. For whatever reason, and I fully intend to find out, she certainly is the type that will wait until a dude passes out and then leave so he wakes up alone and she doesn't risk catching feelings.

That shit doesn't fly with me. And the whole reason I wanted her at my house was so that I could have all night with her. And I fully intend to have tomorrow morning too, she just doesn't know that yet.

Pulling into my parking spot, I cut the car and hop out, moving around to get her door before she can climb out. She looks up at me like I have an extra head on my shoulders. "I'm already planning on fucking you, no need to keep up the charade of manners, Adam."

The shock hits my face and I clear it almost instantly. Puzzle pieces. That's what this is every time she opens her mouth. Just one more puzzle piece to the gorgeous, sexy as sin stranger that I am totally infatuated with tonight.

"Not a charade. Some of us were actually raised to treat a woman right. Don't get mad because I'm not your typical douche bag," I say closing her door and hitting the lock button on my key fob.

Suzette shrugs, and I take her hand, leading her up to my door. As I let go of her to unlock the door, her arms snake around my waist and she rubs my dick through my jeans. It feels so good, I stop moving and lean forward against my door.

Her lips kiss across my shoulder as she continues rubbing me, and my dick is so fucking hard it hurts.

"Fuck," I hiss as I reach down with one hand and grab hers to stop the torture. With the other hand, I finish unlocking my front door. She yelps when I yank her into my apartment, slam the door shut, and then pin her against it, my lips devouring hers.

She wriggles and moans into my mouth, and I let my hands roam over her curves. Suzette is all natural and it's sexier knowing that nothing under my hands was purchased. This is all God's gift to me tonight, and I am lucky as fuck.

She goes to grab my dick again, but I snatch her wrists up in my hand and pin them above her head against the door. "You're in my house now, love. My rules."

Her eyes widen as I give her a wicked smile. I'm going to enjoy the next several hours of my night, and wake up tomorrow, fuck her again, and then take her to breakfast. That's something I haven't done with a chick in a long time, but tomorrow, yes, that's exactly what I'm going to do.

Tonight, I want to eat something else though . . .

"Strip, woman. I want to see all that, un-obscured by the black and purple."

7

SUZETTE

$\mathcal{W}$ ithout losing my balance, I use my toes to help pull my sneakers off, bending slowly to pick them up and set them against the wall near Adam's front door. It's kind of an added bonus because when I sneak out of here later, I won't wake him trying to get them back on.

He's leaning against the wall, thumbs hooked in his belt loops, looking all types of edible. Moving slower than normal, I got to pull my Raven's jersey off and hope it comes off easier than it went on. As the cloth covers my face to come over my head, calloused hands slide up my sides and across my tits, making my nipples hard.

When I toss my shirt over onto his couch and shake my hair out so I can see his face, he's staring at me intently. I freeze for a second, my pussy already soaking since this guy has been teasing me on and off for the last several hours.

Adam leans down and kisses me slowly, his hands following the band of my bra around until his fingers hit the clasp. I gasp a little when he unhooks it and pulls it off so the cool air of his apartment hits my skin, hardening my nipples even more.

Gently, he kisses me more as he grabs my hips and moves me into the room until my ass is sitting against the edge of the couch. Before I can even wonder why, his lips trail down my neck and body until he's taking one of my nipples into his mouth. I love the way he rolls his tongue across it and then bites down hard enough to send a sharp tinge though my chest.

My legs shake a little and suddenly, I'm thankful for the couch behind me. I grip either side to hold myself up as he moves from one nipple to the other. If he continues like this, I might cum without any further prompting. I'm used to guys spending a lot of time on my tits before sex. They're huge and natural, and if I'm being honest, just fun to play with because of those two factors.

But I've never had someone make this feel the way Adam is. Like, the man has a magic tongue and I really want to have him use my thighs as earmuffs so I can get the full use out of his tongue talent.

"Adam," I groan as he bites one nipple again while pinching the other. "Bed. Now." Trying to form full sentences isn't going to happen for now.

He chuckles against my skin while kissing his way back to my mouth. "I wasn't kidding about the tie-ups. Go into the bedroom and finish stripping. Sit on the bed when you're done so I can eat."

He smacks my ass as I take a step toward the door he indicated in the middle of the hallway. I've never let a man tie me up. Like, I will do a lot of shit but I've never trusted anyone that much . . .

I want Adam to tie me up though, and that is kind of scary since I've known him all of like four hours . . .

8

ADAM

I wait until Suzette is completely in my room and the light flicks on before I turn and rest my ass against the back of the couch. Taking a couple of deep breathes, I try to calm down a bit. This woman has me all types of fucked up. I've never, ever, differentiated between fucking and making love. My whole life, as far as I'm concerned, sex is sex.

Suddenly though, I'm wondering if that isn't true. Everything in me wants to go in my room and do to Suzette what I do to every other woman. Fuck 'em hard and rough so they have trouble walking the next day. I really want to do that to her . . . but I also want to tie her up and then spend the next few hours getting to know every curve, every spot, every inch of her tan skin.

She's like a trinket and I'm the person determined to figure out what makes it tick. I've never wanted that before, and that's why she's in there and I'm out here. Because I need to figure this shit out.

After a moment, I go to the door and lean against the frame. Suzette is lying in the middle of my bed, on her stomach, with the book from my nightstand open in front of her. A woman reading a book should not be that sexy, but she is.

Quietly, I walk up to the bed and pull my shoes and pants off. My dick is hard as fuck, and I really want to just put her on her knees and slam into her. I am set on controlling all these impulses though. I am going to enjoy this woman until she passes the fuck out.

Her body jumps and tenses for a second when my lips touch the back of her knee. But as soon as I start moving up her thigh, she moans low and relaxes, her head falling forward onto the pages of the book. Kissing across her ass, I trail my fingers up her inner thigh, tapping her legs lightly so she opens them a little.

When she does, she also lifts her ass into the air. I swipe two fingers through her drenched pussy and rub her clit. Using my upper body, I hold her's down on the bed. As I move up her shoulders and kiss the side of her neck, I slowly sink two fingers into her. She pushes back against my hand, moaning louder, and I flex my fingers, moving them in and out of her in short, hard strokes.

With my other hand, I grab the book from in front of her and toss it off the bed, replacing it so she lays her head in my hand, her face turned toward me. Her eyes are closed and she's biting her bottom lip as I continue to work my fingers inside her.

Kissing just next to her lips, I fuck her a little harder with my fingers, and before long, her body is tensing and she's trying to catch her breath. The moment I know she's trying to control her orgasm, I rub her clit with my thumb, applying pressure until she's moaning my name and cumming all over my fingers.

I kiss her lips softly. "That was fucking sexy, but I'm not done with you yet, baby."

A smile graces her lips, and she sits up enough to devour me in a kiss. Before I know it, she's pushing me onto my back, and kissing down my chest

9

SUZETTE

$\mathcal{T}$hree minutes after I start sucking Adam's fat cock, he's pulling my mouth off him and rolling me back onto the bed, cursing under his breath about how damn good it was. I can't help but smile. I'm not arrogant, but my dick sucking skills are on fucking point.

"Keep grinning, love, and I'm gonna fuck that smirk off your face," he says with a grin of his own as he kneels between my legs.

As he leans over me, I'm so captivated by his body that I jump when he locks wrist restraints to my body. He chuckles and kisses my lips hungrily as he moves to lock the other wrist in. I should be nervous. A dude I hardly know has me cuffed, buck-ass-naked, to his bed. I don't have the means to get away, and my phone is somewhere in his living room.

I'm not nervous though. I'm wet as fuck and about to ask, no, beg, this man to fuck me into next week.

"Adam," I groan as he kisses between my breasts, my body arching off the bed as I pull at the restraints.

"Someone is impatient," he says against my skin.

As he comes up to hover over me, a smirk on his face, the words on my lips turn into a scream of pleasure as he slams into me, burying his cock all the way. My eyes squeeze closed at the tingling bite of pain between my legs.

"Move," I whimper, bringing my legs up and locking them around his ass, pushing against him with my heels.

"Yes, ma'am," he whispers, biting into my neck as he moves.

Adam doesn't just fuck me, he fucks me hard. For the next several hours this man pushes my body and pussy to a point of both pain and pleasure I have never hit before. I lose count of how many times he makes me cum, and by the time he's chasing his own release, I'm worried that another orgasm might actually hurt.

"One more time, gorgeous," he growls as he reaches between us and plays with my clit, never once slowing his pace.

My whole body shakes and I whimper as I cum hard again, Adam following right behind me. We're both panting, and I'm actually surprised when he hurries to unlock both my wrists. With my eyes closed, I bring my arms down and groan at the ache in them. I'm betting there are marks, however, I am too fucking happy and exhausted to give a fuck.

There's a click a second before Adam is sliding in the bed, pulling me into his arms. I can't stop the yawn that hits me as he uses one hand to rub up and down my back, while gently rubbing my wrists with the other.

He kisses the top of my head. "You better me in this bed when I wake up in the morning, woman. I mean it."

I chuckle with sleep already pulling me under. I had no plan to stay, but I kinda like being right here, right now.

One night isn't going to make a difference.

EPILOGUE

ADAM

*S*he never left.

It's been two years, and she's been in my bed every night since the first Playoffs when we met.

Never in a million years did I think I'd fall madly in love with the stranger I met at a bar and fucked crazy a few hours after meeting her.

But here we are.

Suzette is more beautiful today than she's ever been. That might have something to do with the fact she's carrying my son in her stomach. Another thing I never thought about— family.

Everyone thinks that love can't come from moments like meeting a stranger at a bar.

But it can.

The beautiful woman wearing the ugliest team colors I've ever seen, walked into my favorite sports bar, talked shit about my favorite football team, and made me fall head over heels in love with her.

Sometimes, rivals end up being the best thing to ever walk into your life.

ABOUT THE AUTHOR

Don't forget to stalk Courtney as often as you can, she won't mind!

Connect with Courtney

facebook.com/clynnrose87

twitter.com/clynnrose87

instagram.com/clynnrose87

MAGICAL MOMENTS

A POEM

JULIE MISHLER

If a moment could last forever
I would implore the stars above
To grant me just one wish
I would wish for time to stop
So this moment with you
Would never have to end

The magic of this night
Surrounded by the serenity of the water
As we sail the three rivers
Music and laughter drifting off into the distance
The ambience of the night captivating our senses
The look of adoration in your eyes
As you reach for my hand to ask
If I would give you the honor
Of sharing this and every dance
For the rest of our days
Will forever be engraved in my memory

Perfection may not exist
But if ever there was such a thing
Tonight as the radiant stars emit their magic across the sky
I know without a doubt that true love does exist

In your arms I have found
The half that makes me whole
My heart has finally found its home
Whether we are here making memories
Under the city lights of Pittsburgh
Or any other place in the world
You and I shall forever be
Two hearts joined as one
Dancing beneath the moon

JULIE MISHLER

Stealing kisses under the stars
Wishing magical moments
Never had to end

Julz

ABOUT THE AUTHOR

Julie Mishler resides in a small Pennsylvania town. She has always had a way with words, but started to write and share those words publicly in December 2011 after strong encouragement from family, friends and fellow authors. Prior to releasing her own book of poetry in 2014, Julie wrote poems/pieces for a number of other author's books, anthologies and has done personal commission pieces for display in people's homes. When Julie isn't working on a new poem, quote or spending time with family, she enjoys reading, photography, art, and music.

Connect with Julie

facebook.com/authorjuliemishler

THE
LOCKS

CJ ALLISON

1

$\mathcal{I}$f you ask me where I'm from, I will tell you Pittsburgh. I actually grew up about forty-five minutes southwest of the city, but no one would recognize the town. When it comes down to it, I'm a Pittsburgh girl, born and raised.

I was raised in the seventies during the era of the City of Champions. I still bleed black and gold. Not too many understand the loyalty we feel about our sports teams.

As a young girl, I can remember school assemblies dedicated to the championships that our teams held. We yelled and we cheered for even moments that were in the past.

The "Miraculous Reception" is currently a statue in the city airport. Live and breathe it. No one can change the mind of a child raised in those times. No matter where those kids moved to, it moved with them.

We have our own nation. It's because a lot of folks had to move away to find jobs. We are spread wide across the country, and wave our towels every Sunday during football season.

I was one of the ones that moved away, but never forsook my love for my hometown teams.

I remember the times as a teenager, heading down to the river to

527

jump off the old lock walls. The water was deep, and it sent a thrill through you when you plummeted into the darkness of the unknown.

As I head into my fifties, I think about the freedom I felt back then. The thrill of jumping into the night. I want to experience that again.

I'm not one to take unusual risks. I live my life on the straight and narrow. I need to change that. There's a pull that is calling to me.

I never thought as I head into being on this earth for a half century, I would be alone. I did the dating thing for a while but nothing seemed to work out for me. Now, I'm not looking for love. I'm happy with my life but I feel like I need companionship. It's sad really.

I vow for my milestone birthday to jump off that lock wall, no matter what the temperature might be. I would love to not do it alone. I don't know who I want to be there, though.

I set a date to head back to the 'Burgh and reach out to my friends on Facebook letting them know what I have planned. To my surprise, I get one individual who is readily onboard and says they will be there to hold my hand.

It's months away, but I find myself so excited. I'm out of shape and think that jumping into a possibly very cold river could be not a good idea at my age. At this point, I don't care. I feel like I need to do it.

2

Tara is on my mind. I don't think we would ever survive being in a relationship, but I still can't help thinking about her. There's a code. A code you don't cross. I crossed it, but she was no longer married. I think back and remember how good I felt being inside of her. How warm and welcoming she felt.

She left after that weekend and really blew me away. The usual girls I date always want more. Are in my face and texting me nonstop. Not her. She just went back to her life and acted that what we had was nothing. She's still active in my newsfeed and liking my posts, but it's not what I had expected. She threw me off my game. I don't like that. I'm not used to that.

I told her that I would be there for her to leap off the lock walls and hold her hand. I will be there. Fuck I'm scared of heights. I've been at the locks and never could do the jump, but I'll do it this time.

I'm trying to get a group together as a surprise for her. A little cookout and birthday celebration. Being Lieutenant at the City of Pittsburgh Police Department gives me a little more pull to be able to get this accomplished.

This could literally blow up in my face. I don't even think she feels anything for me, but ever since that weekend, I'm just wishing there could be something. It's like a mission. I'm surprised how strongly I feel about her. I never even thought about my ex this way, and I thought I was head over heels in love with her.

These feelings I have are something I've never experienced. I'm not sure what to make of it all. I'm a complete mess. I get distracted thinking about the plans I'm trying to make, and I'm slipping at work. I need to figure this shit out before I fuck up and get myself in trouble.

I've been trying to be sly when talking to her about her trip up here. I do know she plans to come the weekend before her birthday. It's a month out and I've already secured a spot we can set up a gathering of sorts.

Right now, she thinks it's just going to be me and her jumping off the lock wall. In reality, I've pulled together about fifty of her old classmates. I also have around twenty more of her friends that she's made over the years. I even have one coming from Mississippi that she is really close to.

I'm beyond excited and just hope I can pull it off. I don't know if this will lead to anything. After our last liaison, I got the feeling I did something wrong. Her aloofness to the whole thing made my insecurities come out. Maybe this is all it is. She hit something that made me question my manhood and performance. She wasn't taken away or wowed by what happened. Maybe my obsession isn't real and is there because I want to prove something.

I need to know. I can't move forward until I figure this out. It's become a goal of sorts to know if she's the one or not. Knowing that I've never felt like this before, I truly believe she is the one. I just hope I'm not wrong.

3

*M*ason is a mystery. I really try to play it off as not being anything more than just a one-time thing. However, I can remember having a crush on him early in my life. He didn't go to my school, but seemed to always be with the group I grew up with when we went to the locks. He never jumped. He always just cheered us on. Now, he's some kind of officer for the city's police force.

He always had a girlfriend. I remember watching him from the side. He was the life of the party and always had a way of making everyone laugh. We connected on social media during my marriage but it was just a friendship. However, when I was going through my divorce, he was one of the first to reach out. One weekend that I was home visiting my parents, he was off duty and asked if I wanted to meet up.

I was reluctant at first. I can't tell you why, only that he was a crush and I didn't really think he ever thought of me that way. After some gut retching laughs and a few drinks, I found myself back at his place rolling around naked in the sheets.

He blew me away and I got scared. There was no way this man wanted anything other than sex. I wasn't his type. At least not the type I knew he had dated. So to protect myself, I acted like it was nothing. It was far from nothing.

I don't like to play games. I'm the type that is always honest, yet I'm also very guarded. I lost a lot with my divorce. I lost half of my life and half of my family. His family, that I considered mine. All gone. I can't go through that heartbreak again.

When Mason reached out and I went out with him, I had no expectations. I didn't even think that I would end up in his bed. So of course, I played it off. When he didn't seem to pursue me, I wrote it off. I can't help but want to feel pursued— for the next man in my life to go above and beyond to be with me. He didn't. Yet he was the first to step forward to make my bucket list happen. Something I know he isn't comfortable with. He never jumped when we were kids. Now, he wants to jump off a wall with me. I'm not sure how I should feel about this.

All I know is he was the only one to reach out when I first came up with this ridiculous idea.

It took several posts. Until he shared one of mine, and then it seemed like there were a few more interested. Since then, it died off. All I know now is that I'm going. Mason is going to be there and really, I don't give a flying fuck who else shows. All I can see now is him looking at me with that amazing smile as we leap over the edge.

4

We are a week out until the surprise I have planned. I created an event to be able to keep track of what everyone was bringing and to confirm times. Tara has no clue what we have in store for her.

I made the mistake of brushing her off. Like I said, she threw me off my game and I didn't step up. I'm going to step up now. I just hope she doesn't discard me.

I've made a ton of mistakes in relationships, I won't lie. I'm an alpha male in everyday life but seem to step back when it comes to love. I let the woman run the relationship. I was walked on so many times, it's embarrassing. I realize that I need to say no. I need to pull some of that everyday Alpha in and let it out.

I thought it was the respectful thing to do. I wasn't respecting myself. Experience has taught me that. I want what everyone wants. To not die alone. I just don't want to settle.

I like my life as it is. I have a great condo and a faithful dog. I can come and go as I please, but coming home to just my pup has gotten old. I want to share things and go on vacation with someone other than my friends.

I don't want to embarrass myself though. So, I decide to text her to try to gauge her reactions.

Me: Busy?
Tara: Nope. What's up?
Me: Nothing. Just checking on you. You ready to take the leap?
Tara: Yep. Question is . . . are you? LOL.
Me: I am. Are you nervous at all?
Tara: Hell yeah. It's been a long time. I'm old and might break a hip.
Me: I'm trained in emergency situations. I got you.
Tara: My hero!
Me: LOL. Always. If you will let me of course.
Tara: Why wouldn't I? It's only you and me. I'll need someone to save me. LOL.
Me: Hmmm . . . last choice?
Tara: First choice actually. Can't imagine it being anyone else.
Me: Really? I figured you just settled since I stood up and volunteered.
Tara: Well, that. But also I was pretty excited that you did.
Me: That makes me happy. I can't wait.
Tara: Me too. I gotta go. I'll let you know when I'm leaving on Friday. Unless you want to talk again before then.
Me: I'll text you tomorrow. Good night, sweetheart.
Tara: Night, handsome.

I'm not sure how to take that last exchange. I almost stopped myself from using "sweetheart", but when she called me handsome, I found myself sitting there smiling at my phone. I definitely will be texting her tomorrow, and the rest of the week until she gets here.

5

$\mathcal{I}$'m not sure how to take that last exchange. He called me *sweetheart* and I naturally went with calling him *handsome*. It's probably nothing, but I can't wait to get there. I feel like a teenager again.

He follows through with his promise by texting me first thing in the morning. We have exchanged messages all week. Some have verged on flirting. I'm reading into things that are not really there. Right?

It's mid-May and the temperatures aren't supposed to get above sixty. Although not freezing, I can only imagine what the water is going to be. There is no way this body would be in a bathing suit anyways.

I have thermal leggings and a thermal, tight-fitting long sleeve shirt that I plan to wear for my plunge. I've talked with Mason every day. He seems really excited for my visit.

I have my bags finally packed and I'm ready to hit the road. I send of a text letting Mason know that I'm about to leave. He responds for me to travel safe.

As I'm traveling through the mountain bypass, my phone starts ringing. Mason's name flashes across my phone and car display. I hit the hands-free to answer and his voice fills my speakers.

"Hey. How far are you?" Mason opens as a greeting.

"Hey, you. I'm just getting on the road. I still have almost two hours ahead of me," I respond.

"Want company on your drive?" he asks.

"I would love company on my drive. Can you teleport?" I say laughing.

"Babe, I'm good, but not that good."

Before I knew it, I was pulling into my parent's driveway. We say our goodbyes with plans to meet first thing in the morning at our favorite breakfast place.

I can remember skipping morning classes as soon as the first of my friends got their license. We would go to the Wagon Wheel and eat a full breakfast for a couple of dollars. I can't believe the place is still standing and in operations, but they made the best breakfast. There was always a full morning crowd, and you always had a wait time.

I visit with my folks for a bit before I feel the tiredness overwhelm my body. I go into the spare room and pull out my clothes for tomorrow. It's been in the seventies, so I'm praying we have the same tomorrow. I'm also praying that the water isn't freezing. Once the sun goes down, I know there's going to be a chill.

I send off a goodnight text to Mason, receiving an immediate reply and fall asleep almost as soon as my head hits the bed.

I'm a bit disoriented when my alarm goes off. Realizing I'm in my parents' spare room, I stretch and smile. No matter what, I'm going to make sure this is a good weekend. I'm trying not to set any expectations, except for fun.

As I pull into the parking lot to the Wagon Wheel, I'm not surprised by the number of cars in the lot. Yet, when I pull open the door to the diner, I'm greeted with a room full of somewhat familiar faces.

"Surprise!" is yelled out from every corner.

There are balloons and streamers hanging from the ceiling. I notice a "Happy 50th" banner strung across the one side of the room. I cover my mouth with my hands as my emotions overtake me.

The biggest surprise is my girlfriend from Mississippi rushing towards me. "Paula? Oh my God!"

"Wouldn't miss this for the world, sis," she says giving me a huge hug. She whispers in my ear, "You have Mason to thank. He even helped with the flight and hotel."

I pull back with wide eyes, "Mason is responsible for all of this?" I say looking around.

"Yep. He put together an itinerary and everything. The man is pretty demanding too. He didn't ask, he told us to be here and when," she whispers.

"Talking about me?" Mason says coming up to my back. "Hey birthday girl. Ready for your day?"

I spin around and fold myself into his arms, "Thank you. You didn't have to do all this. I would have been happy with just a birthday waffle."

"I know you would have, but there's no fun in that. You don't turn half a century every day," he says rubbing my back.

"Don't remind me," I mutter.

"Sweetness, you do not even look close to being fifty. Me, however, looking like I have one foot in the grave," he says.

"Please. You look amazing. People are going to think I'm a cougar," I say looking up at him smiling.

"More like ask if you are taking your grandpa out for breakfast," he winks.

He walks me over to a table and pulls out my chair. The next thing I know I have "Birthday Girl" sash and a crown on my head. I can't stop giggling or wipe the smile off my face.

As I hoped, I'm served a huge waffle covered in strawberries and whipped cream. There's a single candle lit on top. The whole restaurant, filled with my friends, breaks out singing. I close my eyes and make a wish and blow out the candle.

My wish is for Mason to be mine.

Even if that doesn't happen, this has to be one of the best moments besides my son being born. I'm still giddy thinking that Mason did all of this for me.

6

The look on her face was priceless. I stood back and took pictures as she walked in the door. She was so surprised. I'm so happy I was able to pull this off. I'll remember her beautiful expression until the day I die.

I love the banter between us. I was honest, though. She's beautiful and does not look her age at all. I wish she could see how others see her. How I see her.

Once we all finish with breakfast, we jump into our cars to go to a little place that has mini race cars and other activities. I pull Tara aside and get her to agree to ride with me.

As soon as I get her into my truck, I can't help but to reach out and grab her hand. At first, she is reluctant, but eventually laces her fingers with mine. I get her shy smile as I squeeze her fingers.

"So, now that we are alone. Can I ask you something?" I ask.

"Of course, but first let me tell you that I'm amazed by everything you have planned for me today. I don't think I've ever had anyone go to this extreme for me. I can't thank you enough, Mason. I really appreciate this."

"You deserve it. I want only the best for you, Tara. Honestly. I want nothing more than for you to be happy. This may come across wrong or unreal, but since that first time we were together, I haven't been able to get you out of my head. I tried to respect your feelings and felt that you didn't feel the same as I did. However, I think we could be amazing together. I don't want to make you uncomfortable or to sabotage this event. I just need for you to know that I think you are everything I've ever dreamed of as a partner. I just hope that I haven't ruined things or our friendship," he says pulling my hand up and kissing it.

"Wow. Your honesty is everything. Mason, you are amazing. I've had a crush on you since we were young. I'm not your type and never imagined to even be close. The one time we were together, I thought that was it and have held it close to my heart ever since. I've dreamed of more but was realistic to think I would never have it and your friendship is something I never want to lose," I tuck my head and blush at how honest I'm being with him.

"Are you blushing? Babe. You are a dream come true. More honesty here. A few years ago, I would have written this off. I don't want to lose this opportunity. I'm not that stupid punk that just wants to have sex. I want something more. I want you in my life, Tara."

"This is a little too much right now. I was not expecting anything like this to happen. I'm not saying no. I'm just saying can we slow this down a little?"

"Of course, it will be at the pace you are comfortable with. Can I change my relationship status yet?" he says with a smirk. "I'm kidding...unless you say yes."

"Let's make a deal. After this weekend, if...big if...we still like each other," I say with a nervous laugh. "We can talk about it."

"Deal," he says kissing my fingers again. "I'll take what I can get."

We get to the adventure park and head inside with the rest of the crew. Mason wants to go directly to the go-carts. It's a slick track and the current group out there is slipping and sliding. It looks fun, though. I know Mason is competitive and I'm pretty much the same way.

I haven't done this is years and I've never done a slick track. I crack my knuckles and give Mason a challenging grin. "Ready, big boy?"

"Ain't no boy. Your ass is mine," he responds.

"Maybe later, but right now...you about to be pegged," I say laughing.

"Oh, dear God. Do not ever use that phrase with me. Not ever happening," he says shaking his head and laughing.

"Knowing you know what that means is enough," I say bending over and laughing.

"I mean this with the utmost respect, but fuck you," he says folding his arms and trying to give me a mean look. His lip starts turning up to a smile.

Let's just say that it was a photo finish. I think I won, he thinks he won. We decided on a tie. Even though I had them print off that photo to use as leverage in the future, because I know in my heart that I've won.

I haven't laughed this much in years. I also don't remember having this much fun. This day isn't even done and it's already the best one I've had in a long time.

7

I know she won, but I won't give in. It's my competitive nature, though. I'm having so much fun and I think she is too. At least I know that she's been smiling from ear to ear from the moment we walked in.

We are now on to the next adventure. She's in my truck and we are heading to the locks. I'm taking the long way so that everyone gets there before we do.

Once we get there, the little off-road trail to the locks we used to jump from is lined with cars. We are the last one and I'm nervous. I grab her hand and slowly make our way to the open spot in the field.

Everyone is there and there are tables set up with decorations. I'm not sure who stepped up and did this, but I'll find out and thank them later. I can smell the grill and smile when I see more than one with steaks on them. We have some amazing friends.

"Holy shit, Mason," she gasps at the sight.

"I'd like to take credit, but honestly, I put out what I wanted for you and it looks like others stepped up and made it happen. I'm pretty blown away myself."

Tara is pulled away from me and pulled into a group of excited women. I'm pulled into the group of men.

"Dude, I'm going to lose my man card because of you. Shithead. My wife already said that I need to top this for her fiftieth and I'm going into a panic. Not going to lie. Motherfucker better be there for me to plan something, because I'm lost. I can't do this same thing. You've ruined me."

"Sorry? I honestly don't know what to say. I've had help and I'll give you the names of those who have? Shit, I'm as clueless as you. But thank fuck for all the help. Do you think she likes it? I think she does, but I'm pretty clueless."

"Just look at her face. I would say by that smile, you are getting laid tonight," he says punching my shoulder.

"That's not what I want. I want her. More than just a night. Shit," I say walking away.

"Mason. Dude. Sorry. I was being a dude. You all have something special. I'm not good at this either. Don't let her go. She's special. Even an old married man can see that," he says catching up with me and touching my back. "All shit aside. Don't let your past insecurities ruin this for you. She's nothing like anyone I've seen you with and that is a good thing. You deserve the best and I honestly feel she's it."

"I know. I just don't know how to go about it. I'm rusty and I'm an asshole. I just know that I can't lose her. I'm invested. I seriously need her in my life. How messed up am I right now?"

"You, my friend, are fucked. And I'm loving it. It's about time. I've been waiting for a long time to see you get whipped as much as we are. I can tell you though, you picked a good one to be whipped by."

"I know I did. Thanks for being here for her. Seriously. This means a lot to me," I say looking around for Tara.

Our eyes meet from across the field and she give me the smile of all smiles. It's so cliché, but it's really what we all want, we all dream of, of someone looking across the room and looking at you like you are the only one there. That's how she made me feel. I've waited for over fifty years to have this moment. She's the one to give it to me.

With a little nod of my head, she excuses herself and comes to my side. "You okay?"

"I'm good. You okay?" I say.

There's still a little bit of awkwardness I find myself in around her. We walk over together to get food and grab a table to sit. I start to relax again and fall into an easy conversation.

The girls come over with a huge cake with a shit ton of candles. Tara starts laughing and yells out, "Come on. Did you need to put that many candles on the cake? I don't need a reminder of how old I am, guys! You all need to help me, I'm too old to blow out all these."

Everyone starts laughing and circles around Tara at the table. We sing her happy birthday and all of us lean in to help her blow out the candles.

"Looks like everyone gets a wish," I say as our friends laugh and call out their agreement.

The sun starts to set, and we get a bon fire going. My buddy from the precinct pulls out a guitar. We sing songs about friends in low places, and country roads.

Once the stars are fully out, I lean into Tara and whisper, "You ready to make that jump?"

She smiles nervously and looks around, "Ready as I'll ever be. I need to change though. I have some weather resistant spandex stuff I want to wear. I know this is going to be freaking cold as fuck."

I walk her back to the truck and open one of the doors to give her some privacy. In a matter of minutes, she shuts the door and I can't stop laughing.

"Well hello there, Happy Feet," as soon as I say it, I stop and start to apologize.

She bends over laughing, "I know I look ridiculous, but at least I'll be warm. Are you going to change? I mean, no expectations, but I may want you to be able to use some of your body parts later. If it goes all turtle...that may hinder our fun."

"Oh, but what fun it will be for you to bring it back to life. A little mouth to mouth may be in order," I say thrusting out my hips in a joking manner.

She makes a "oh no you didn't" face and starts hysterically laughing again. "Let's do this, before I lose my courage."

Lacing her hand with mine, we walk back and through our

friends who are cheering us on. Once we reach the side of the lock, we both look down. It looks further than I remember, although, I've never been able to actually jump.

My heart starts beating and I try to put on a brave face. "Shit."

"Don't be scared, big boy. I'm here," she chuckles.

"I'm okay. I'm okay. I'm okay," I keep repeating.

"You got this," she says squeezing my fingers.

The chanting behind us starts. I squeeze her fingers back and start swinging our arms. When the countdown hits one, I take a deep breath. We both take the leap and the air in my lungs seems to catch.

As soon as we hit the water, I lose my grip on Tara's hand. The water is dark, and I feel disoriented. I finally regain my composure and push myself to the surface. I immediately look around until I see Tara reach the top. She shakes her head and her smile beams.

"We did it!" she yells. "Whoo-hoo!"

Swimming over to me, she wraps her arms and legs around me and surprises me with a kiss. I embrace her while maintaining us above the water.

Once we make it to the ladder, we hear shouts and splashes as our friends leap over the edge to join us.

EPILOGUE

*I*t was a moment that I will never forget. Mason gave me something that no one has ever been able to give. I felt like a queen when I leaped over the edge of that lock that night.

We spent the weekend together and made magic. I didn't want to leave and go back to reality. He made sure I didn't in the end. We talked every day and eventually he retired from the police force. He had purchased land outside of the city, in the mountains and built a wonderful house. We took turns visiting each other until he finally told me that he couldn't do it anymore.

One weekend visit, he took me back to the lock wall and he proposed. I said yes.

A few short months later, we had a small ceremony with all our friends in attendance. He was in a tux and I was in a simple white gown. We held hands and kissed after saying "I do", leaping off the locks into those dark waters with cheers echoing through the night.

Every year on our anniversary, we jump off those lock walls. We will continue to do it until we can't any longer.

The End

ABOUT THE AUTHOR

Growing up in southwest PA, I always referred myself as a Pittsburgh girl. The city of champions, the Clark bar and Heinz ketchup...what else is there? Living in western Maryland for the past 27 years, I still miss home and miss those lock walls on the old Mon river.

Connect with Allison

facebook.com/CJ.allison

AFTERWORD

A NOTE FROM SALLY, FOUNDER OF TREASURE FASHION
HOUSE

Everyone has a story! A recent chapter of mine goes like this...

In 2000, I was navigating a divorce and inherited over $200,000.........worth of debt! Between the debt, legal fees and raising 3 children without child support, I was running $300-400 behind each month – a quick spiral downward! Naively, I gathered that last of my savings and purchased a small resale shop, hoping that would augment my teaching income enough to keep my head above water. At that time, "thrifting" and shopping "green" had not yet become vogue, so the women who frequented my store were those who didn't have other options; they were in my position or worse. When they chatted about their life challenges as they shopped, it sounded all too familiar and tugged at my heartstrings.

"Excuse me!" I interrupted. "You're my 5th customer today! You get a free bag of clothes!" I invented a bogus promotion, but it delighted me to see the positive reactions and flickers of hope produced in each recipient – so I kept doing it!

I continued giving away the store (literally!) for a year, and then an astute gentleman called me out on my overly generous business plan (You're not making money! You're losing money!), and he suggested that I become a nonprofit.

"Obviously you have a heart for women in difficulty!" he stated.

He walked me through the process of filing for nonprofit status and Treasure House Fashions was birthed. I dragged my sister and other like-minded women into the mission of "promoting the dignity of women, particularly women in transition or crisis. "Outward appearance is not an accurate reflection of your worth, but it can affirm the treasure that you truly are!"

Since then, we've grown...

- from 2 volunteers to 71 tenderhearted women who work the shop and extra activities
- from networking with 1 agency to collaborating with over 80 agencies serving women in the Greater Pittsburgh area – we're their "closet."
- from renting an 850 square foot storefront to purchasing an 8,000 square foot facility on McKnight Road between two bus stops, and saving $20,000 per year over our previous lease

We've received numerous awards and were featured in Woman's Day Magazine (one of the worst pictures I've ever had and one of the worst outfits I've ever worn – *nationally distributed!* UGH! ...but the story was sweet!)

Our partner agencies address various challenges: homelessness, formerly incarcerated, addiction recovery, veterans, unemployed, domestic violence, trafficking, health issues like mental health or cancer, natural disasters like floods and fires – in all these situations, women need clothing, but the underlying issue is a deeply bruised sense of self-worth. In the past 12 months, we've given away over half a million dollars' worth of clothing (calculated at our deeply discounted prices, not actual value). Clothing, however, is our means, not our mission; our heart is to affirm the worth of women on challenging journeys. We simply use the magic of "retail therapy" as a healing balm on bruised souls!

The heart of our mission is best expressed through Sponsored

Girls Night Out events. Here's an example: a local wealth management corporation underwrote gift certificates for shopping at our store and their investment clients served as "personal shoppers" for women from a partner agency. The "personal shoppers" gave their undivided attention to these women and were inspired by the strength and courage of these challenged women:

- *My gal had her spine broken by her ex and he took her 5 kids.*
- *My gal had her hand broken - one finger is still badly mangled - so she couldn't work.*
- *My gal was pregnant when she came here from Syria with her husband. When she had a daughter, he abandoned them and left the country.*

These unthinkable circumstances were experienced by women in our own backyard! This evening of shopping was an opportunity to set aside their daily challenges and be refreshed by shopping for what they wanted, as well as what they needed and having their selections affirmed with "ooohs and ahhhs" by their "personal shoppers", followed by all the ladies sharing refreshments! The agency clients left brimming with joy, encouragement and hope!

"This is the BEST day I've had in a really, really, really, really long time! Thank you so much!"

Everyone has a story ~ everyone has a journey! It's easier when we travel safely together... that's women helping women! When you need a haven to rest and to be refreshed, stop in at Treasure House Fashions! You're always welcome at our House!